# IMMORTAL

# IMMORTAL

## A Linking of Souls

## D.E. DAVIDSON

A much different version of the chapter titled NEW ORLEANS,
LOUISIANA August 15, 1990 appeared as "Changes in the Night,"
in MOSTLY MAINE, A Writer's Journal, September/October, 1994.

This book was printed in the United States of America.
**To order additional copies of this book, contact:**
Xlibris Corporation
1-888-7-XLIBRIS
www.Xlibris.com
Orders@Xlibris.com

This book is dedicated to my wife Joan. Her belief in me and her support, both emotional and financial, made this novel possible.

I also want to thank J. N. Williamson for his immensely helpful critique of the book. His insight and expertise were immeasurably helpful in bringing this book to publication.

We have made thee neither of heaven nor of earth, neither mortal nor immortal, so that with freedom of choice and with honor, as through the maker and molder of thyself, thou mayest fashion thyself in whatever shape thou shalt prefer. Thou shalt have the power to degenerate into the lower forms of life, which are brutish. Thou shalt have power, out of thy soul's judgment, to be reborn into the highest forms, which are divine.

Giovanni Pico della Mirandola
ON THE DIGNITY OF MAN [1496]

Put here by hand,

*He opened the bottomless pit, and from its furnace there arose demons in the shape of cats and scorpions, and unto them was given power over men.*

*And over them was the worm which would not die, and its name was Apep.*

# PROLOGUE

*Old Kazakhstan, 2355 A. D.*

Apep—an electrical excitement growing in his groin and spreading at once toward his head and toes—watched Conrad LuPone, an insignificant bastard, a *motherless son.* To Apep's right his guards—eight-foot tall, fur-covered men with the features of cats—paced, tails flicking, throats emitting low growls, their wide eyes lighted in golds, greens, and blues as if from some internal fire set aflame by an event which they could never understand.

Sweat beaded on Conrad's forehead. His rapid breathing became choppy and his flesh pebbled, rough as sandpaper.

Apep whiffed air sharp with ozone formed as the electrons boiled off Conrad's skin. And as the sharpness bit his nostrils he felt Dougal's soul stir deep within him, then come alive. Apep smiled. Dougal was stronger now than he had ever been. But Apep was only minimally distracted by the astral struggle of this childish soul for control of the *body they shared*. *Watch your agent, this would-be engineer of our destruction, as he dies*, Apep thought. And he felt Dougal's soul recoil from the thought as if it had been touched by hell's coals.

"Time?" Apep asked briskly.

"Twenty-nine days, twenty-three hours, fifty-five minutes, Sire," a valet offered.

Conrad's gaze darted about, pupils dilated, searching, knowing death's advance. They were the eyes of a doe under the fang.

Apep chuckled. "What do you hear, Conrad? Do you hear death's footsteps? Do you hear the crackle of the fires of hell? Do you hear the moans of anticipation of my brother demons?"

Conrad's gaze fixed on him. Apep thought he could see the aqua regia of Conrad's eyes beginning to boil beneath the surface, and Conrad's skin began to writhe as if it was formed of billions of tiny, suffering creatures.

"I saw Jeremy. He will come through the portal. He will come for you," Conrad said, his voice filled with exquisite pain, yet, controlled.

"He is nothing," Apep said. "When he comes, I will use him, then toss him on the wind as I have you." But as he said this he felt his shared-body tighten, and a knot formed in the pit of his stomach.

Conrad chuckled, his eyes filled with confident hatred. "This time he will not know you. This time *he* is young and *you* are old. This time he's fighting to save his family, not to destroy it. You will die. Or you will kill him and thereby destroy yourself. Either way, you're finished."

A chill went through Apep. *Why do I fear this mortal, Jeremy Wheeler, so?* He forced the thought from his mind. It was unworthy of him, of the worm which was his soul.

The surface of Conrad's skin began to spit off in tiny sparks, spiraling up like the stirred cinders of a campfire.

The guards were snarling now, roaring out their undirected terror, clawing at the air, striking one another.

Apep smiled. He felt a stream of warm saliva drool over lips cracked with age and down the deep furrows of his chin to be lost. His cock hardened. Conrad's body was . . . unmaking, decomposing into its basic molecules. Flying apart. Apep wanted to see every molecule burn. He wanted to watch this man's soul stripped naked. He wanted to watch it cast into the fires of hell. This was just recompense for Conrad's betrayal of him.

"Watch me well, Apep," Conrad moaned. "This is your fate."

Apep felt his smile fade, but he forced it back onto his face.

Conrad groaned. His teeth clinched. The molecules separated. Upper teeth melded with lower. His body vibrated. Billions of molecules erupted from the surface. Spinning off. Burning out. There was a pitiful pop. Conrad split apart in a flash of burning embers.

Apep though it was at once beautiful and terrifying. His flesh pebbled, yet he watched until the last molecule disappeared like a tiny sun gone nova. Then he sagged to his chair as his cock twitched one last time. He felt the warm stain spread across his lap, and he chuckled.

"I must do this again," he chortled.

# PRATTVILLE, OHIO

*August 15, 1990*

Jeremy Wheeler struggled up from sleep to the rumble of thunder, his stomach roiling. In his sleep fogged mind, he could still see the roller coaster he had been riding into oblivion—a small, blond woman and a young, red-haired boy at his side. On the coaster's front was emblazoned "Immortal."

Minutes later Jeremy stood at his bedroom window looking out on the dull, gray morning while dredging his memory for the minutia of dreams which had, for two weeks, been robbing him of sleep and then, except through strenuous effort, eluding him on waking. Sleep had come in jerks and spurts much like the jostling progress of an Amtrak commuter. He had awakened frequently because of the dreams, night terrors of a wrecked world filled with strange beings, danger and youthful people emptied of the vitality of life by an ancient vampire who sucked "spirit" instead of blood.

These particular nightmares had started at sometime in his youth, so early that they now seemed almost real, a part of his life. But until two weeks ago the dreams were a sometimes-thing. Now they were nightly, all night, robbing him of sleep, and for the first time in his life, he was beginning to feel old. And with that feeling of age (or was it with the dreams?) came a sense of urgency. It was the urgent knowledge that life was passing him by, and there was something that needed done, fixed. Something important.

Jeremy was not rich, nor successful, nor a pillar of the community. He was simply a forty-year-old man with a wife, two stepchildren, a mortgage, brown hair that used to match his eyes but which he had watched go gently gray over the past two years, and a slight paunch which seemed immune to exercise. He worked a thankless job as a psychologist for the mentally disabled, which he would have liked to think put right what the world and nature had put wrong. However, he had grown to know that his job was primarily record keeping combined with a little wishful thinking.

Jeremy went silently to where he kept his guns concealed from Cindy's teenaged girls, and manipulated the mechanisms, making sure they were in working order. In case. Just in case.

# NEW ORLEANS, LOUISIANA

*August 15, 1990*

Puffing several strands of red hair from in front of his eyes, Mark Scott applied a thin film of glue to the rear of the chrome grillwork of the model '58 Plymouth. Then he carefully slipped it into the toothless maw formed at the front of the hood and fenders. He was especially excited about this model. It was a replica of the car Stephen King wrote about in his novel, CHRISTINE.

His dad had given Mark the book, for no real reason, when the boy was twelve, and he had read it twice in the year since. He supposed Dad did a lot of things for no real reason. That was why he was here, putting CHRISTINE together alone. For a moment he imagined his dad, here, helping him with the painting and detail work. Then he shoved the thought down, and an empty feeling seemed to swell inside him, covering it over.

Mark's parents had fought Friday night. Their arguments were more frequent lately and always about the same thing. Dad just couldn't see that some things couldn't be done for just no reason, and his mom just couldn't accept that some things had to be done precisely that way.

He and his mother had slipped away to New Orleans Saturday morning. She had said it was time to start a new life, and Mark believed that whether she was right or she was wrong, it was what she needed. Nothing could change that. But the knowing only made it harder for him. He couldn't blame her for splitting up, and at the same time, he couldn't blame his dad either. They were just too different to be a family.

Mark stood, took one last look at the '58 Plymouth, nodded his approval, then walked into the kitchen. His mom was there in one of those flowery house dresses that she most often wore, her glasses, a good two inches from her blue eyes, were perched down on her nose seeming ready to fall, but he knew they wouldn't. Her dirty-blond hair was in one of her haphazard buns, and she was peeling potatoes, scraping slivers of skin from them with one of those little kitchen tools she so fondly collected. He expected she would soon have her new, N'Awlins, chef's cleaver out to behead some hapless fish.

"I want you in before dark," his mom said.

"But Ziggy said he'd take me over to Bourbon Street tonight and introduce me around. He's the only local kid I've met, and—"

Her scraping became more agitated. The potato slivers began to miss the paper bag set to collect them and scatter on the gold-flecked, yellow, linoleum floor. "I don't want you out. The French Market's all abuzz about murders in Jackson

15

Square Park." She paused for a beat, maybe two, and he waited. "Besides, Ziggy's friends aren't the type I'd like you to make here."

Mark had known his mom wouldn't approve of Ziggy. His new friend was tall, pimply, emaciated, pale, with stringy, brown hair and nervous, gray eyes, and to top off the package, he was impulsive, with a crude sense of humor. Ziggy was at once unforgettable, yet repulsive.

Mark added helpfully, "I read about the murder in the *Times Picayune*. The throat was bit out, and the blood—"

His mom frowned, and he realized he hadn't made things any easier for himself.

She looked up from the potato she was skinning. "They've found three bodies in the park this week. So until I say the word, it's home before dark. No exceptions."

"We'd stay away from the park," he tried a final time.

"I *want* you *in*."

Mark tilted his head, and gave his mother a sour look.

His mom offered him a pained smile, put down her tool, stood, and put an arm around his shoulder. "Sorry, kid. Pouting won't work. I'm not giving in on this one."

"Mom?"

"What?"

"Do you think you and Dad will ever get back together?"

She stepped back, and her blue-eyed gaze locked with his. Her eyes had become shiny, and her lips drooped at the corners. She reached up and combed an unruly, red lock of hair from his eyes, "You're so much like him."

And for an instant he thought she was going to call him her little Robert Redford. She had used the affectation since he was just a kid, and sure, he did look a little like Redford, blue eyes, red hair, square jaw—he even had the little mole on the cheek—but his dad had the same looks, and he knew that, in the end, like his dad, he would be taller and brawnier than Redford. At thirteen, he was already five foot ten, and lately, he had noticed his pecks developing through no effort of his own—a birth right he supposed.

"So tall and muscular for your age," his mother continued. You're so much like your father and yet so different in your mind. Would you really want us back together? With the fights every night? He'll never change."

Mark took his mother's hand, then let his gaze drift from her eyes. "He's trying," he said, loyally. And Mark really thought this was true. Yet, at the same time, he knew his mother was right.

His dad tried many things and failed at most.

Of all of New Orleans, Mark loved most the 90 small blocks that fit the crescent in the Mississippi River to compose the French Quarter. Restaurants of all descriptions, shops filled with oddities from Mardi Gras masks and trinkets to voodoo powders and charms, the streets clogged with tourists, and the mule-drawn carriages which carried tour guides who spouted their own unique history of the quarter, it all enthraled him.

He met Ziggy in the Quarter at the corner of Decatur and St. Peter, two boundaries of Jackson Square Park where, in spite of the murders, artists, clowns, mimes, and musicians competed with one another for the tourist's dollars. There, while watching a mime push against an invisible wall, Mark told Ziggy of his mother's demands.

With a look of deep concentration on his narrow, bug-eyed face, Ziggy rolled a package of Lucky's from his T-shirt sleeve, tapped out a smoke, then rolled the pack back into the sleeve so that it sat on his skinny biceps. He lit the cigarette, inhaling deeply, then blew the heavy, blue smoke at Mark. "Sneak out," Ziggy recommended.

Mark grimaced, then gave the tall, stringy-haired boy his one-eyed stare of disbelief. "We live in a two-bedroom walk up, not a moldy mansion," he said. "She'd know in a minute."

---

17

"Wait 'til she's asleep. Bourbon don't get hopping 'fore 'leven anyways."

Mark remembered the last time they had visited Bourbon Street. Music seemed to come from every doorway, and musicians walked the streets with a horn and a hat for tips, or sat against a wall with a guitar, it's case strategically placed open on the sidewalk. And here and there, children danced on cardboard stages to the squawks of harmonica music. It seemed that everyone and everything competed for the attention of the tourists who teemed the streets like salmon swimming upstream to a cannery, but with less direction. And then there were the stripper bars.

"I don't want to sneak out on my mom. We've always been honest with each other."

"Suppose you tol' her about Big Daddy's?" Ziggy taunted.

Mark felt the heat rise in his face. Ziggy had first scoped-him-out while Mark was hanging out in front of Big Daddy's, a strip bar. Sometimes he'd get a glimpse of a dancer if he was patient. Usually it was just a butt, but occasionally one of the dancers got careless with her breasts, and he would catch a peek. It had been his favorite activity—the one growing-up activity away from his mom since coming to New Orleans—until he met Ziggy.

"That's different," Mark blurted.

Ziggy smiled and flicked the ash from his cigarette. "Yeah? Tell you what, I'll be hanging front of Big Daddy's 'tween 'leven and midnight. Friend'll get us backstage. *Could* have us some fun. Else. . . ."

And in the cool self-assured way that was so unexpectedly Ziggy, yet so typically Ziggy, he raised an eyebrow, shrugged his thin shoulders against his shoulder-length, brown hair, turned and strolled away.

At eleven that night Mark ducked through his bedroom window into the sticky night. The humid air covered his face like a hot towel and sucked the breath from him. But that was okay, he didn't feel good about deceiving his mom, so the humidity was handy punishment. As he saw it, he and Mom were in this together, and now they depended on each other more than ever. But Ziggy was Mark's only friend so far, and New Orleans was a night town. If they didn't take advantage of New Orleans at night, what was the point of being here? Wasn't that half his mom's reason for moving here instead of going to some small town in Ohio or maybe Kansas?

It wasn't necessary to go near Jackson Square Park to get to Bourbon Street. Yet Mark wasn't surprised to find himself following the heady aroma of dung from the mule-drawn, tour carriages which stood along the park on Decatur Street.

Decatur crossed the front of the park. Street-wide walk-ways—blocked off segments of St. Peter, St. Anne and Chartres Streets—circled the other three sides. In the day, the walks were filled with mimes, artists, and street vendors, but at night only wide-eyed tourists and drunks milled in them. Mark thought this was somehow romantic, though he wasn't sure just why.

Jackson Square Park was small, well-lit, surrounded by a tall, wrought iron fence. He stared past the gates, hands gripping the bars. Except for very small areas, he could see to the fence on the other side and beyond. But he knew that, in the early morning, heavy fog—thick with the smell of the Mississippi—would roll across Decatur Street and blanket the park, making it the perfect site for murder.

"You up to no good, boy?" a deep, male voice boomed.

Mark wheeled to face one of the carriage drivers. The man was tall, muscular, black. A large, gold tooth flashed in the middle of his smile. It reminded Mark of the cannibal's tooth in "Moby Dick." The connection sent a chill through him.

"You better run on home to your mama, boy, 'fore the cannibal eats you for his snack!" The man's tooth seemed to

19

flicker with an internal light of its own, and Mark felt his muscles bunch involuntarily.

Without thinking, he turned and scurried down the fence, the man's deep laughter rolling like thunder, chasing after him.

At the west side of the park, Mark relaxed, turned onto the remnant of St. Peter, now a wide sidewalk, and continued to follow the fence. He was half way down the park when he saw something move inside the fence. He froze in his tracks, the hair on his neck standing at attention, his balls shrinking into tight little, knots the size of peanuts.

It was several seconds before he was able to force himself to continue along the fence, eyes searching, curiosity building with every stride until his whole body tingled. The movement had hooked him, but curiosity was reeling him in.

At the rear of the park stood the St. Louis Cathedral and the Cabildo Museum, two large stone and brick buildings. Two shabbily dressed men lounged in the walk between them. "Throw away men," his father called the sort they were. One, a mustached man with a dirt-smudged face, slept on a bench beneath some newspapers. A second man sat on the sidewalk with his back to the Cathedral, his feet in Pirate's Alley. As Mark watched, the man tipped a brown paper bag to his mouth. But he didn't drink. He *talked* into the bag. Mark would have sworn to it!

A fragment of a dream, which had pestered him for several weeks now, suddenly rushed to mind. He was older, older than his dad was now, and a huge tiger was lunging at him, and he was firing a machine gun. The word "Parabellum" rang in his ears almost as loud as the gun's clatter. He wondered why he had thought of that now, but no answer came, and he returned his attention to Jackson Square Park.

As he crossed in front of the Cabildo Museum Mark saw something else move inside the park. It rose up like a huge shadow, and rolled across the park, sprouting arms and legs as it came! It leapt the eight-foot fence, touching it on top with only one foot. Now a blurred figure, a fur-covered man, it seemed actually to fly across the walk that separated the Cathedral from the park. It leaped the bench and the sleeping man with ease, and ran past the man, at the corner of the Cathedral, then into Pirate's Alley. Neither man reacted!

Mark felt something inside him give a tug. Incredibly, he found himself dashing after the figure! The throw away men jumped like frightened kittens at his approach. He swung wide past them. Neither tried to stop him.

The figure turned west on Royal Street. It was a dark dot in the distance when Mark reached the street. Then it was gone.

Tears rolled down Ziggy's cheeks. He wrapped both arms around his rail thin body, and rolled into a ball among the putrid smells of the Bourbon Street sidewalk, convulsing with laughter. "You're too much, man!" he said.

Mark's face grew hot. He wasn't used to being laughed at, and laughter was especially hard to take from Ziggy whose stories often strained credibility. "Then you won't go with me?"

"Ain't personal. I know you got family troubles. But that ain't no call to make up stuff."

"I been on snipe hunts. That's all this is. I'm out to have fun, and that don't make it with me."

"Like tonight?" Mark asked. Ziggy's words had stung, and he intended to sting back.

Ziggy's friend at Big Daddy's had proved to be his cousin, one of the dancers. She had used a colorful variety of words to drive them to the streets.

They had spent the night walking the same ten-block length of Bourbon Street, repeatedly, peeking through doors, too young to get in any place except the souvenir shops.

Ziggy brushed long, stringy hair from his face, and

21

squinted his bug eyes at Mark as if measuring him. "I tol' you I'd make tonight up to you," he said, flatly. "But I ain't going on no snipe hunt. Not with the cannibal out there. That mother scares the shit out of me. Kill me if you can, but don't *eat* my ass! That's my motto."

The next day police ran over the park like ants over a day old picnic. They had found two bodies during the night.

Mark recognized the man in charge. He was one of the throw away men from the night before, the one who sat with his back to St. Louis Cathedral. Mark believed he also recognized the man from the bench, but there was no doubt about the gold-toothed, carriage driver.

He eavesdropped on their conversation. No one mentioned the fur-covered man who ran like a deer.

For the rest of the afternoon, what Mark knew—or what he thought he knew—gnawed at him. By the time the sun plunged into the Mississippi, his stomach was churning with anticipation.

At eleven that night, the walks circling the park resembled a panhandlers' convention. At least fifteen people stood or sat along the storefronts which lined the park's edge. They alternately slashed the park's shadows with their gazes and mumbled into paper bags.

Mark Scott followed Pirate's Alley to Royal Street, turned west, and walked a block.

Royal was lined with darkened storefronts and lighted in gray tones by street lamps.

Mark ducked into the shadows of a doorway, hunched into a corner on the cool concrete, and waited for the furry man. This was stupid, he knew. But something deep inside of him, something that was part of him like his dreams of bloody war—men against catmen—that screwed up his sleep, said it was right, the natural order of things, like growing up.

—

He didn't want to do that either, but it was happening. And although being here was dangerous in a totally different way, it still had to be done, just like growing up, for his souls sake. Maybe he was more like his father than his mother thought. Two hours later, he looked at his watch. His butt felt like the concrete it sat on. Again he questioned why was he here. But before he could examine his motives once more, the fur-covered man flashed past the doorway! At an easy lope, he consumed the street in large gulps. And the time for questioning was over.

Mark stumbled to his feet, and was back on the street in seconds. *This* was why he was here tonight. Yet the fur-covered man—or whatever he was—was at the end of the block and pulling away. Seeming nearly to float, he moved faster than anyone Mark had ever seen.

Nevertheless, Mark scrambled after the shrinking figure. He was sure he could at least keep it in sight, after all, he had been on the school's cross-country team, and he'd run two marathons with his dad.

But the strange man he pursued continued to pull away, and after two blocks, Mark began to slow, sure the race was lost.

Abruptly, the figure—now just a doll in the distance—stopped, turned and ran into a building in the middle of the four-hundred block. *This isn't a smart thing to do*, Mark thought, then continued on.

Seconds later Mark was standing where the furry man had disappeared. He found a three-story building covered in shiny, gray marble. The windows were dark, and it looked abandoned, forbidding. Above the walk, four, large, rusty, iron posts stood like aged, guard dogs, their milk glass globes long broken, their purpose long extinguished.

An old man in tattered clothes leaned against one of the posts. The man drank from a brown paper bag, and eyed him as he would be a stray dog.

Mark climbed the stoop's stairs, and went straight for the

door. It was massive, copper clad, the kind they put on important buildings in a time he had only read about. The door was ajar.

"Y-You ain't going in, are ya?" The old man's voice scurried up his spine on spindly legs. It was at once a grandfather's voice and at the same time that of a ghost, and Mark shivered as it crawled over him.

Mark turned to face the man. "Why not?" he asked. He wanted to sound confident, but now that he stood at the door, his knees quaked. Was it just curiosity or was it destiny or something else, something more than just a child's lark, that had dragged him this far? He didn't really know, and he was beginning to wonder if he should let that indefinable something drag him inside.

"Spooks," the old man said simply, shakily. He sketched a line with his right index finger, to a third floor window in the corner of the building.

Mark's gaze followed the line, and he felt his throat draw tight as he focused on a flickering, blue light in the window. It pulsed and vibrated, sending a chill through him. He thought it was somehow disjointed from anything he had ever seen. Anything at all.

Still looking at the light, he said, "Have you seen the spooks?"

The old man's feet shuffled on the pavement, nervously, drawing Mark's gaze from the blue light. The man's eyes shifted back and forth as if he didn't want to answer Mark's question, and was trying to avoid his own compelling honesty. "You won't tell nobody?" It was a plea more than a question. "They'd send me back to *the home* if you tole."

"I won't tell anyone," Mark said, wondering what the man meant by "the home." "Scouts' honor."

The suspicion left the ancient's eyes, and he smiled.

"Ol' John's seen the spook." He gave a knowing nod, eyes wide. "Spook's like a big catman."

And suddenly the tiger from Mark's dreams flashed behind his eyes, and his stomach grew tight, aching.

"He walks and ru-runs on two legs. He ru-runs in and out without other people seein'. Police by here all the time. Station's on the next block. None of 'em sees . . . But I see. Yeah, ol' John sees." John chuckled and squinted down at him. "You see too, don't you boy? Ol' John ain't crazy, is he?"

Mark swallowed heavily. "No, you're not crazy," he said. "Unless we both are."

Mark didn't think either one of them was crazy, yet he knew he was going into that building tonight, and maybe, just maybe, that meant he was wrong . . . about himself.

"You ever go inside?" Mark said.

John's eyes widened, and he drew back a step. "N-Not since the light come. Used to sleep just inside, rainy nights. Dry, but ain't no heat. Don't go in since the light come." His gaze cast down to the stoop.

Mark waited for more.

"Had a friend went in. Ol' Jim, he weren't afraid of nothing. Fought in Nam, ol' Jim did. We shared bottles," he said, nodding. "Then he went in and never come out."

"How long ago was that?"

John hiked his shoulders, dropped them, and shook his head. "Ol' John ain't no good at time. He blacks out."

"I'm going in," Mark said. "There's more, and I've got to see it." He knew he sounded braver than he felt . . . or more foolish. But he was sure this was either important, a destiny kind of important, or a delusion like his dad's "for no real reason" thing. And either way, it had to be done.

John's eyebrows raised, and Mark thought he saw admiration in the old man's eyes. But then John said, "You got any money for ol' John? 'Cause you won't be needing it if you go in there, and my bottle's about empty." He sounded both sad and greedy. Yet, there was no demand or threat in his voice.

---

"Ol' Jim, he were better at asking for money. We always had full bottles when Ol' Jim was around."

Mark knew he probably shouldn't feel sorry for this man, yet he searched his pockets and came up with two dollars he'd saved for beignets and coffee. He gave them to John.

John's tired eyes sparkled for a wink in time. He said, "Thank ya sir. Thank ya sir, and God bless ya." He backed away, glanced up at the flickering blue light, then turned and scurried down the street.

Mark watched until John disappeared into a doorway beneath a flickering, neon sign that offered, "Wine and Spirits, Open 24 Hours." John had never looked back.

Mark sighed softly, turned, and heaved on the handle of the copper-clad door. The hinges screamed a protest. He squeezed through the opening.

The interior of the building had the heavy smell of old dust and mildew about it. An occasional spot of light seeped through windows, dappling the darkness.

Mark remembered Dad telling him that everything leaves its mark as it passes, so he struck a match and visually checked the floor for signs of John's spook. In the dust he found animal foot prints as wide as both of his outspread hands. At the front of each print were four deep, parallel scratches. The huge prints crossed the floor to the stairwell door. Goose flesh formed on Mark's arms and made a trail up his back, but he knew what he meant to do.

He followed the tracks into the stairwell, up the stairs, past the closed, heavy, metal, second-floor door and upward.

The door on the third-floor landing was open. Thin, blue light waxed and waned into the stairwell. Mark found himself wishing he could be invisible or as small and unobtrusive as a mouse. Despite his trepidation, that *something*, down-deep-inside—

*The dreams!*

Suddenly, he was sure it was the dreams—those phantas-

mic wars, which had plagued him for as long as he could remember—that were responsible for his being here!

The stairwell opened onto a wide hallway filled with doors
and windows, all closed. That didn't matter. What he looked
for etched itself on a wall between two sets of double doors.
Blue light belched, onto the walls and floors, from a ragged
hole fully as large as one of those sets of doors. The hole
looked as if it had been blasted through the wall.

His bowels went liquid and growled at him. Inside the
hole, Mark saw from where he stood, wide expanses of grass
bowing and raising to the will of some unknown god—beck-
oning him. He felt the tow of his curiosity like some treacherous current, dragging him toward the hole. Now he could
see where the creature had come from, but . . . *where was it
now?*

Creeping forward silently, half expecting a flash of lightning to toast him like a bug at a bug light, he gazed deep into
the blue light, looking for any sign of the huge, furry creature.

*Something clutched his shoulder!*

Mark gasped, and a warm flow made a riverbed of his leg,
flooding his shoe. He tore away from the fingers, spinning on
his attacker but stumbled back.

It was his mom, flashlight in hand!

"What are you doing here?" she said.

He raised his hand to shield his eyes from the light, and
for a second he wondered why Mom was using the flashlight
when the blue light from the hole lit the hallway so harshly.
Then he looked at her eyes. They were wide open, pupils
dilated when they should be pin points in so bright a light as
flared from the blue hole.

*She isn't seeing the light! Her pupils aren't even reacting to it!*
Suddenly, he realized that for her, the blue light and the hole
in the wall didn't *exist*. To her they were standing in a deserted, dark hallway in a deserted, dark building.

———

27

Mark shuddered. His thoughts returned to the murderer. He still didn't know where the figure had disappeared. He whirled, his eyes searching, finally aware of the danger he had allowed his *destiny* to place them in.

"Mom, we have to get out of here."

"Not so fast, Mark. I'm not going anywhere. Not until I find out what's going on." Her face was strange: strained, questioning, and frightened at the same time. And still, she showed no cognizance of the hole, and the harsh blue light.

"I've been so worried about where you've been going at night. Does this have anything to do with drugs?" she said.

His knees felt like rubber for a moment. And suddenly, he realized that although he had questioned his motives many times this night, he had not considered his mother in the equation. It was his destiny, yes, but that destiny was welded firmly to that of his mother, his father, his brother and all those who cared for him for that matter. How could he think that he was alone in this decision?

"No. It's the Jackson Park murderer. I followed the murderer here," he said. He pointed toward the double doors, the blue-light-hole. "I think he went in there." The words tumbled out. "We have to get out of here before he hears us, before he finds us."

A movement in the hole of blue light caught his gaze. He focused on a figure racing through the bowing grass in that hole. Toward them! It was just as John described it: a cat and a man all rolled into one. It stood erect on two feet and was at least eight feet tall, massive through the chest and shoulders. Mark saw large, amber eyes and a narrow, furry muzzle filled with large, yellow fangs! Long claws scarred the turf in that other world within the blue light, as the creature closed ground between them. It was and wasn't a tiger, *just as in Mark's dreams.*

Mark's voice broke, squeaking from him, "Mom, he's coming! *Run!*"

Her eyes widened, and he realized that it was something in his eyes, not his words or what was swiftly approaching, that frightened her.

Nonetheless, she started to run with him. At the stairway door, he turned and glanced back to the hole. The creature was there tall, sleek, all fangs, claws, and muscle. Mark stared into its hungry eyes and felt like the mouse he had wished, for an instant, to be. He envied his mom's unknowing eyes.

They rushed into the stairwell, and he shoved the steel, fire door closed behind them. The creature hit the door before they had reached the next landing. Pieces of metal rattled down the stairwell at their heels. His mom turned the flashlight up to the door. The hinges tore loose. The door bowed and sprang inward.

Again Mark yelled, "Run!" And they did.

His mother stumbled, almost fell, as she exited the stairwell.

Praying it would delay the creature, Mark slammed the ground-floor door behind them, and started for the large copper clad door and the relative safety of the street. Behind them the door to the stairwell exploded into the room, crashed into Mark, and knocked him to the floor. Pain ripped through his head, and a fire brand burned its way up his spine. He lifted himself to his hands and knees. The room seemed to shift. He fell back to the floor.

Then the catman was bending over him. Its amber eyes shone into his. Mark prayed Mom was out of the building, safe.

Everything seemed to slow to half speed. Hot, carrion breath wafted across Mark's face. Gnarled, claw tipped digits, like fingers, reached for him. Every muscle in his body turned to stone, defying movement, but a scream burned its way up his parched throat.

A sound like a melon splitting filled his ears. Something warm splattered him. The creature shrieked. Then his mom

———

29

was above it, he saw, on the creature's back, hacking at its shoulder with her N'Awlins Chef's cleaver. She chopped the blade into the wound again. Yellow-green blood, glowing with a light of its own, splashed everywhere.

Again the creature squealed and leapt high above the marble floor, twirling and twisting. Its screams vibrated off the marble walls and danced over Mark's skin.

His mom went flying and thudded on the cold, stone floor like a bag of laundry.

Mark shook off his numbing horror. Now, he had to save his mother!

He scrambled to where she sprawled, unconscious. He glanced up for the creature just in time to see its silhouette moving toward them. A glowing patch of yellow-green covered its shoulder, chest, leg.

Then everything went black.

Mark awoke to a body filled with mind numbing pain. Every bone, every joint, every muscle hurt. He opened his eyes and found himself bathed in the blue, flickering light of the third-floor hallway. The catman's blood was everywhere.

The light shadowed. He looked into the hole. The creature was moving away into the flickering light. Its right arm dangled at its side, useless.

But Mom hung limp under its left arm!

Motionless for several seconds, Mark watched them move away. Something sagged deep inside him. Then it seemed to tear loose and gush forward with his tears. He needed a weapon—a gun. But he didn't have one. *Don't feel sorry for yourself. Make do,* his dad's words came to him.

The image of a fire ax flashed behind his eyes, and suddenly, Mark knew what he must do. He dashed to the stairway, located the fire box. There was a hose locked behind a glass door and along its side—in a separate case—was the fire ax!

The second blow of Mark's fist smashed the glass covering the potential weapon. The pain in his hand was dull; blood ran down his fingers and dripped to the floor. Then the ax was in his blood-smeared hands, but it was in his head even more. The image of the ax sinking into the creature's brain filled his imagination. He dashed down the hall, through the blue hole, toward the creature.

61-DAVI

# PRATTVILLE, OHIO

*10:00 P. M., August 15, 1990*

Rudy sniffed Chaz's hind quarters, then let out a wheeze of disgust, a dog's ultimate insult. The cat growled and slapped Rudy's jaws and the top of his head with claws out, this time, to show he meant to be left alone. But this only sent Rudy prancing around the room, nose in air, mouth opened in a big dog grin.

Chaz was weary of this game. It was Rudy's game, not his. He padded toward the door, wanting nothing more than to slip into the night, to find food, to tear at it with his claws, to taste the hot salt of its blood.

Rudy picked up a squeaky-toy, and tossed it into the air. Chaz looked away. The man who provided the food was near the door. Chaz meowed.

The man made a warm clucking noise.

---

Chaz trotted to him, rubbed against the man's leg, arched his back, and shook his tail.

Now the man made soft huffing noises, and opened the door.

*PRATT PARK*

### *10:40 P. M., August 15, 1990*

The cold rain was beginning to sink into him when Chaz spotted the human walking along the dark street and caught her familiar scent. He knew the human, but he ignored her. There was something hidden in the grass. He wanted it. He had left his dry place under the bench to catch it, but its movement had ceased with the human noises.

He watched the spot, and moved closer to the shock of grass that hid his prey, as the human moved away. Soon she disappeared behind the trees.

The grass trembled. Chaz's muscles went taut. He extended the claws of his hind feet into the wet grass. The shock of grass moved again. His haunches jogged back and forth, involuntarily.

The shock of grass sprang up in front of him. A black ball hurtled toward him, all legs and glistening fangs. Chaz froze. The hairy legs snared him.

Chaz growled, dug his hind claws into the middle of the dark thing, kicked. Blood wetted his claws. Yet, the creature's grip tightened. Chaz smelled death in the creature's fangs. Terror shot through him. He sank his own fangs into the thing's evil-smelling flesh and shook his head, rending.

Fangs stung his shoulder, filling it with the numbness of paws on an icy day. He felt his muscles grow lazy. Something fluttered inside him. His stomach rolled with sickness. He screeched, then lost his breath. The thing loosened its grip, and he dropped to the wet grass, muscles limp, unable to

---

move as he was dragged into the dark hole of the many-legged thing-of-death.

## PRATT PARK

### *10:39 P. M., August 15, 1990*

The warm rain of the mid-August evening drenched Lori Hellman's uniform as she made her way along the street bordering Pratt Park's south side. Her blond hair was flat, stinging down her cheeks, acting as a riverbed for the rain that seemed to flow in sheets from her head to her substantial work boots. Her make-up would be gone by now, she knew, revealing the faint, one-inch scar that ran from below her lip to the jaw line. Henry Rider's mark. She caught herself fingering it and brought her hand down. She didn't like for the scar to show. Not for aesthetics but for the memories it brought. She forced the memories away, crowding her head with thoughts of work.

She supposed she would be the object of many elbow pokes and smirks when the creeps she worked with saw her arrive soaked to the skin. Someone would make a crack— behind her back of course, it was always behind her back— about a wet-uniform contest, or maybe something double entendre referring to how her nipples poked out against her shirt. The men were always glancing at her breasts. Never an outright stare, nothing she could call them on. Yet as much as she hated those visual gropes, there was nothing she could do to prevent them. A C-cup on a woman five-foot two inches tall simply defied camouflage. And the men, though they were creeps, knew better than to challenge her. They knew she could handle herself. She gave a mental shrug. They might not understand women, but they understood she was the Supervising Engineer, and that was what counted here.

———

Thunder pealed, rattling the earth around her. The rain seemed to sizzle with increased vigor in response.

Hank Davison flashed in her mind's eye: his kind, gray, teddy-bear eyes staring at her from a muscular, six-foot tall, middle-aged man. For an instant Lori mentally kicked herself for not asking Hank for a ride to work. He was always there, always willing to do for her, but despite his goodness, and the unspoken understanding that they would someday be man-and-wife, she felt there was something missing in her relationship with the teddy-bear Police Chief. It was like she was waiting for someone else . . . , but who? Certainly, no one from her past.

She looked to the park. *That's where it happened. That's where Rider raped you. Made you a woman, Mama said. A hard, suspicious person, is* that *a woman?* A tremulous feeling rolled through her, and she allowed a hiss to escape. She pushed the feeling down before tears could form.

Her hands peeled a thin veil of golden hair from her face, and flipped it over her shoulder. Her blue eyes followed the slow-moving shadows of the park. She had needed to trust people since that day. She hadn't needed to trust the park.

*You're not going to let it scare you anymore.* She folded her arms across her breasts, hunched her shoulders, and quickened her pace.

A cat's shriek startled her. Chills climbed her back, and pebbled her flesh. She oriented to the cry, and backed away several, faltering steps.

Two, large, luminous, green eyes stared back from the blackness of the park.

---

35

# MARK SCOTT AND MOTHER

## THROUGH THE PORTAL

*The creature was too fast. Mark Scott saw his mother's chest explode. Her eyes went wide with terror or pain, then the light went out in them. Jared screamed, "Mother!" He ran for her, his weapon forgotten.*

*Someone yelled, "Parabellum!" Others took up the cry.*

*Mark brought the B. A. R. around in a wide sweep, trying to shoot above the heads of his militia and still lay cover for his brother. The rifle's* thump, thump, thump *drowned out the screams.*

Mark jerked himself awake. His head was pillowed on his mother's lap. The goose flesh that covered him started to retreat, then he noticed the ache in his hand. He raised it and found it wrapped tightly in a blood stained cloth.

He sat. "You should rest," his mother said.

"I'm okay."

"Still. . . ."

They were nested in tall grass that surrounded them like a wheat field run amuck. It stretched as far as he could see in all directions but one. In that direction it met blue mountains.

The hole-of-light and the hallway of the old Civil Courts building were gone. The creature they had fought there, lay face down less than three yards away. The fire ax tilted from its head, having split it wide like a stick of kindling. The creature's arm was peeled away from the shoulder, the shoulder joint cleaved through.

The copper odor of its blood wafted its way to Mark on a breeze. He leaned away into the grass and dry heaved several times. Then he turned to his mom. She had a far away look in her eyes. "Are you okay?" he asked.

"I . . . I guess so. What—Where is this place?" she said.

Mark shrugged. He staggered to his feet, and gazed about. A circular clearing, a ten-meter island in a sea of grass, was a few yards away.

"I don't know. It looks like the place in the blue light. Did you see that?" he said pointing to the circle.

"It's a camp. I got your bandages from there."

"Any signs of more of these?" He nodded to the creature.

"It was alone," she said.

Mark moved off into the camp, studying it closely as he approached. His mother followed. The campfire was recessed into the earth and walled on three sides to prevent the wind from stirring sparks. A pack had been laid at its side. Several wooden crates sat at the edge of the circle. There were eight dished-in areas in the soil along the perimeter. Fresh grass

---

was piled next to each. He thought these must be beds. The soil which would be loose in a new camp was packed to the edge of the clearing. And in the grass, where the soil was still malleable, Mark found a human footprint, large and bare, not his mother's.

"There must be others," he said. "The camp's too big for one, and from the looks of it, it's been here for a while."

"We should leave," his mother said. She had wrapped her arms around her shoulders, and was hugging herself, tightly.

Mark turned a circle, looking for . . . anything. "And go where?"

"I don't know," she said, her blue-eyed gaze darted to the west, to the horizon. "Away from here."

"I . . . I'm sorry." He tried to keep the tears from coming, but everything went bright and several broke free and rolled down his cheeks. Without thought he had involved his mother in what had begun as a child's lark, a child's destiny derived of a child's dreams, and everything had gone deadly wrong.

She put her arms around his shoulders, and hugged him to her. He remembered telling her that shows of affection like the hugging made him feel *funny*. Until now, his mother had followed his wishes, avoided the hugs. But now it felt right, and he felt weak, and more tears came to his eyes.

# PRATTVILLE, OHIO

*1:12 A. M., August 16, 1990*

*Jeremy Wheeler brought the Ruger up, but his finger froze. Dougal's bullet tore into Lori, throwing her back. She struck the floor with a sickening thud and lay still.*

*Dougal turned to him and stared for a second, a smile on his face. "I knew you couldn't kill me, father," he said. Then his gun came up. Jeremy saw the muzzle flash, felt the solid push of hot lead as it tore into his chest.*

Jeremy Wheeler wrenched himself from the grasp of his dream. He was drenched in a cold sweat and shivering uncontrollably. He sat up and stared into the dark, dumbly trying to comprehend the strange dream. What did it mean? Who was this Dougal and the woman, Lori?

To his left his wife, Cindy, moaned and rolled to her side, restlessly, in a nightmare of her own.

———

39

PRATTVILLE, OHIO

## 6:02 A. M., August 16, 1990

Hank Davison, the Prattville, Ohio Police Chief, sipped his coffee, then lifted the newspaper from his breakfast table and folded it as he had learned to do when he rode the el to classes in Chicago. The title, "Genetic Research Making New Strides," sat at the top of the resulting, book-sized rectangle.

"Car five to dispatch. Car five to dispatch. Do you copy?" A voice cracked over his police scanner, squeaking like that of a pubescent boy. Hank's thoughts were snatched from the article. The voice was Charlie Hascomb's, a recent hire for the small Prattville Police Department, and still green.

There was a short pause filled with nothing but static and blank air. Then the voice came again. "Hank, you there? Hank? God! Hank, if you hear me you'd better get down to the park. We've got big trouble!"

Hank groaned. *Charlie, you damn fool! I told you about that radio.* "This better be good!" he muttered, brushing graying hair from tired eyes. Hank leaned forward and looked at his weary, gray eyes reflected from the glass-topped, breakfast table. He was forty-five years old, and at one-hundred and eighty pounds on a six-foot frame he thought he was in good shape. However, the long nights and longer days were telling on him. He found it harder each day to crawl out of bed after four or five hours sleep.

He picked up his coffee cup, drained it, then pushed back from the table.

"Rudy, want a good breakfast?" he called.

From the second floor came the loud squeak-grunt of a dog yawn. Hank scrapped the remainder of his breakfast into a large ceramic bowl on the floor.

In Pratt Park, all six-foot four-inches of Charlie Hascomb's broad shouldered body shuddered as he replaced the radio's handset. A cold sweat covered him.

It was the dead cat that brought him into the park. Hank Davison had said, "Lost pets are a priority." *Some police department, missing pets are a priority!* And there was that cat, long dead from the looks of it, only a yellow, fur sack with eyes like raisins. Even the ants scorned it. He had found the stick to turn the carcass. *You could have picked another. One without blood all over.*

Images of blood-soaked clothing, bones, and flesh shredded to hamburger, flashed in his mind. *There weren't any large pieces!*

An old feeling crept over him like maggots over rotting meat. His nightmares would return tonight.

A lump crawled from his stomach to his throat. He lurched to a tree, and spewed up a half-digested, Egg MacMuffin, coffee.

Hank Davison arrived at Pratt Park in fewer than eight minutes following Charlie Hascomb's call. In a bug-splat town like Prattville, Ohio—too small even to be shown on state maps—everything was within eight minutes of the park.

The circus was already starting. Cars dotted the parking area for the park's small swimming pool. The street, normally deserted, was jammed with circling vehicles. A slow procession moved past the park. Taillights flared and necks craned as the cars breasted the yellow, barricade tape. Charlie Hascomb stood at the edge of the trees, outside the tape. His face was grim.

"Stay back of the tape," he said to a man who seemed to be trying to duck under. The man flinched and backed away.

Hank picked up the radio handset. "Ralph, Harvey, we're going to need both of you at the park. Traffic problem. Don't bother clocking in, just get your ass . . . your*selves* down here on the double." He tossed the handset to the car seat and walked to where Charlie stood at the barrier.

"Am I glad to see you?!" Charlie Hascomb said. "Situation's getting out of hand!" He flashed Hank a pained smile, which died in an instant.

Hank Davison narrowed his eyes at the taller officer. "Well, hell," he said, his voice low, confidential. "What did you expect? Whining over the radio like a thirteen-year-old kid who just shit his pants! Damn, Charlie, I warned you about that radio!"

"But Hank—" Charlie began.

With a flap of his hand, Hank waved him down.

"I told you when you signed up, you have to play real trouble down on the radio. Use the code, for God's sake. I think there might be two old biddies who don't know it yet."

Charlie cast his gaze at the ground.

"I mean . . . Jesus, Charlie, the whole town *listens*. And half of them can get to the scene before me. It don't look right."

Hank paused. Charlie continued to look at his feet as if he saw something interesting on his toe. Hank looked away into the crowd for several seconds, waiting for his anger to subside.

Charlie Hascomb had worked one year with the Cleveland Department, four years with the Akron Department. Yet he continued to make the same dumb mistakes. Had he made a mistake in hiring Charlie so fast?

"Why am I here?" Hank said.

Charlie's voice neared a whisper. "It's a body. Maybe two or three! I don't know."

"*Don't know!* Jesus, Charlie, can't you see?"

"It—It's all over the place! Pieces. Looks like it was blown to bits." Charlie's voice was strained. There was an almost imperceptible twitch at the outer corner of his right eye. Heavy moisture covered his upper lip.

Hank felt cool sweat forming on his brow. His stomach tightened. Charlie Hascomb's face was weathered, hard. A strong man could look at that face and be compelled to think twice about any fool notions that might be playing in his head. It was one of Charlie's best characteristics. It was *the* reason he had hired Charlie. He had needed a man whose mere presence demanded respect. But the fear Hank saw there made his own knees go rubbery. If what Charlie had seen had frightened him so, how well would he handle it?

Hank turned to the barricade, hands on hips, and watched the yellow tape wiggle to and fro in the breeze for several seconds. Then he turned back to face Charlie.

"Guess I better take a look," he said. "When, Ralph and Harvey get here, back these people up. They could be trampling evidence. Question the ones that stay. Take the names of the rest. We'll get to them later. Get those cars moving. Threaten them with tickets. Give them tickets if you have to, but get 'em moving. Barricade the entrance to the parking lot. There are a couple of horses in my trunk.

"Anyone here when you arrived?"

"No."

Hank noted Charlie's color was coming back.

"Then get to it. I've got a feeling it's going to be a long day. And . . . , Charlie?" Hands on his hips, his head bowed, Hank turned his eyes up to meet Charlie's gaze.

"Yeah?" Charlie said.

"Get a hold on yourself. People are going to be frightened enough about all this without seeing that *we* are. Understand?"

Charlie nodded, and delivered Hank a wan smile.

Inside the cordoned off area, the first things to draw Hank's attention were familiar strands of fine, blond hair half concealed beneath shreds of gore-soaked, blue cloth.

His heart paused. The hair shone like Lori Hellman's, and the blue cloth . . . , it was like the power plant's uniform, the uniform he had so often seen her don.

He touched the hair with trembling fingers. His breath came hard, ragged. His vision blurred. His knees went weak, and he sat down with bone-jarring suddenness, in the grass, in the blood-wet grass.

# PRATTVILLE, OHIO

*11:45 P. M., September 2, 1990*

J udith LuPone's slim thighs circled the stranger's waist. She released a purring growl. His muscular buttocks contracted, and she felt the thrust of his turgid flesh into her. The muscles of her groin grasped him. She bucked against him. He writhed with her. The bed squeaked in cadence. She smelled their mingled scents, went on thrusting back at him.

A tingling started at her center and radiated outward. Her toes curled. Muscles tensed, contracted. She moaned. "Fuck me! Harder! Oh yes! F . . . Ah . . . Fuck meee harrrderrr!"

Her nails dug into the stranger's back and became tight as slivers of his skin bunched beneath. He grunted. His body bucked. Her legs locked her in place. Sparks exploded behind her eyes.

Later, she wept.

—

61-DAVI

# PRATTVILLE, OHIO

*4:00 A. M., September 3, 1990*

Eighteen days had passed since the first murder victim was found in Pratt Park. Jeremy Wheeler was taking his sleep in bite-sized chunks, waking time and again to stare at the red glow of the bedside clock's numerals. The little sleep not wrecked by his own nightmares was prodded away by the moans, tossing, and turning of his wife, Cindy. At four A. M. he decided he couldn't lay still anymore.

He got up and stood at his bedroom window, gazing out. The sky was black. Ragged, cotton candy clouds, which hung to the tops of the power poles, lit with a flash of lightning. The thunder's flat boom sounded in the distance. Rain hissed against the red brick street below. Sewers overflowed. Torrents of corrupted water churned and gurgled in a froth along the curbs. The sights and sounds were at once relaxing and frustrating.

This was the third day the odd clouds had emptied their bladders on Prattville. Jeremy had not been able to make his morning walk for any of those days. His muscles were beginning to cramp from disuse. There was a dull ache in his thighs, knees, back, and ass.

*I can walk in rain gear.* He didn't like the thought. He would feel like a sausage in plastic wrap before he made a mile in that getup. Yet the alternative was wet clothing, a wet gun.

From the dark, "You going to walk?"

"Uh-huh."

"I wish you wouldn't."

"I'll be okay," Jeremy said.

"Still—"

"I'll be okay," he repeated, emphatically.

Moving through the dark room by instinct, he dodged the cherry bed posts and unseen floor clutter. He found his ragged, blue, terry robe in its familiar place on the floor, and put it on before opening the bedroom door.

He dressed in the bathroom, pausing only to stare into the mirror briefly at the silver hairs, which daily, seemed to grow more prominent among the brown, and at his brown eyes, which despite his lack of sleep—*the dreams, always the dreams*—were bright and alert. No wrinkles. No crow's feet. He didn't feel old and he supposed, at forty, he wasn't, technically. He watched his weight, ate right, exercised, and he still looked good. However, there was an extra ten pounds on his six-foot-one-inch frame, and he knew he was pushing the limits. He turned from his image and sighed.

Jeremy descended the stairs to his study on the first floor. There, he removed a brown Alessi holster and a Detonics Pocket 9 handgun from his desk drawer.

---

Less than six-inches long, the stainless steel Detonics was his favorite handgun. Jeremy smiled. Holding a gun made him feel safe and warm. It reminded him of lazy, Alabama summers, his father, and the manhood rituals so often neglected in today's world of computer games, amplified guitars, and rap music.

Lifting the tail of his T-shirt, he thrust the holster into the back of his pants, and attached it to his belt with the straps and snaps.

He checked the status of the Detonics. The safety was on, the magazine full, the chamber loaded. The familiar blue tip of a Glazer Safety Slug peaked from one magazine, the copper tip of a Blitz Action Trauma cartridge from the second. The Glazer Safety Slug contained a frangible bullet that reduced ricochet risks and produced a wound like a contact shotgun blast. The Blitz Action Trauma cartridge would sink deep, open wide, and stay inside its target, reducing the risk of the bullet passing through and hitting someone it wasn't meant for. One magazine went into his jeans-pocket, the other into the pistol.

Cindy, dressed in her ratty, pink, chenille bathrobe, was in the living room when he exited the study.

Jeremy crossed the distance between them, and took her in his arms. "Up already?" he said.

She snuggled against him, her head against his chest, and he felt something primal stir inside him. Her petite, girlish figure still did things to him, though they had been together more than five years now.

"Have to be to work soon," Cindy said, brushing her short, brown hair back from her beautiful hazel eyes.

Jeremy grunted. "The lot of a nurse."

She giggled. "We can't all be big important psychologists," she teased. "Besides, I couldn't sleep."

"I know."

Cindy looked up, a question mark in her eyes.

---

"You were making noises," he said, uneasily. "I shook you. Dreaming about the catman again?"

"Yes. It's all these murders. Did I keep you awake?"

"No," he lied, then smiled. "Well, a little. I was having nightmares of my own. Must have been bad, but I can't seem to remember them now."

"I dreamed there was a noise in the driveway," Cindy said. There was a puzzled expression on her face. "I went to the window to look out. The catman was there. He was dressed in a black robe, and a monk's caul covered his head, but I knew it was the creature just the same. His hands were wrinkled and bony like an old man's. He had long nails that were more like an animal's claws than a person's nails. His eyes were a cat's eyes, amber with a black slit-like pupil." She shuddered, wrapped her arms around her shoulders and rubbed as if chasing away a chill. "He was trying to pull me out the window, but he wanted *you.*"

Something she had said had given him a finger hold on a fragment of his own nightmare, a petite, large-breasted, blond woman with drowning-pool blue eyes and an insignificant scar on her chin. It was gone now.

"Me?" he demanded.

She nodded, then picked up a cup of coffee he hadn't notice before and sipped.

"What kinds of noises?" Cindy asked.

"What?"

"You said I made noises, and you shook me. What kinds of noises?"

He frowned. "I don't know how to describe them. Just disturbed noises. You know, moans and such."

"I'm glad you woke me. The dream was . . . I don't know how to explain it, but when I dream about the catman, it feels real. Even now, I feel like it happened or . . . *will* happen."

"Don't start," he said. "You promised to leave it alone."

"There have been seven murders in the past three weeks. Three in the past week alone. How can you expect me to leave it alone?"

"By doing it," he said.

"I'm afraid something will happen to you." She caught his forearm. "Stay home one more day."

"I can't," he said. It was the truth. Something inside him was pushing him out the door today. He had to walk, although he didn't understand why.

# PRATTVILLE, OHIO

*4:00 A. M., September 3, 1990*

Judith LuPone, the town librarian, awoke at four A. M. Tuesday morning. For several minutes she lay listening to the rhythmic breathing of the man

*(Ralph or Rick or Randy? What was it he'd said?)*

beside her. Then she exited her bed with well-practiced stealth.

In the bathroom, she stared into the mirror for short minutes, thinking of the dreams which had plagued her recently—the birth of a son (Conrad, she had called him) and the visitation of a strange little man with colorless or . . . no, the eyes were yellow—then raised the brush to her hair. Strain showed on the face in the mirror. Crow's feet marked the corners of her eyes. Her skin looked sallow under the harsh lights.

*What am I doing to myself?* No answer came. Judith shook

---

51

her head and drew the brush through short, light-brown hair. *Well, at least I'm rid of Mama and her plans: no cottage, no picket fence, no kid . . . Named Conrad?* The woman in the mirror seemed puzzled at the thought.

Judith dressed in a pink and blue Adidas sweat suit and slipped into her walking shoes. Because of the rain she hadn't walked for the past three days. Today would be different. Even if she had to get wet, she wouldn't be here when another man with no name woke.

*Ray?*

At the door she glanced back at the living room, appraising. A half empty Gilby's gin bottle and two glasses stood on the cocktail table.

*A half-empty, gin bottle, an empty life, and a man with no name in my bed. Maybe Mama is right.* Judith frowned, stepped through the door, closed it.

On the sidewalk she turned right, down Mineral Springs Street, toward the town power plant and Pratt Park.

The park had drawn her like sweets draw flies since the police had discovered the first body there. She wondered if the *Courier Crescent* would have an article about the murders today. It seemed as if the media had lost interest. She missed the articles. Since the first day, she had absorbed everything printed about the ghoulish events with a fevered tension that both mystified and frightened her. Today she would see the park, in dawn's light, for herself.

To her right the tall, smoke stacks from the city's electric substation belched heavy smoke into the low, roiling, black underbelly of the clouds. In the switching yard, transformers hummed, switches clicked, bells rang.

Over the sidewalk in front of her, multiple power poles carried the coiled lines that rode from the power plant on an elevated platform of rollers.

Near the power poles a spot of light on the sidewalk

caught her attention. It was just a flickering, blue spot, but it seemed to have no source.

She slowed her pace as she approached, and swung wide to circle the spot.

A strange *thrumming* sound started. Judith's gaze darted about, seeking the source.

Two, large, green eyes materialized three feet above and to her left. Her heart skipped a beat. Inexplicable pain spiked through every nerve. The air whined from her lungs in a crushed doll's cry. The gutter came up and hit her. Light exploded like fireworks in her head.

Her head cleared. She was on the ground. Had she fallen?

She clutched at the curb and dragged herself forward one inch, two, trying to get her arm under her, lift herself up. Then a spasm shook her hand, and it ignored her commands. Blood coursed onto the asphalt. Her sweat-suit top was torn open in four places across her chest and abdomen. Visceral gore spilled from her body through rent flesh. Liquid copper filled her mouth and spilled down her chin.

Her left eye wouldn't focus. And she realized that it was dangling wetly against her cheek. She imagined the gray cord of optic nerve holding it in place.

*I'll be scarred!* she though, realized the thought was irrational, and didn't care, because she knew that very soon she would be dead.

The vision of a small boy—one leg shorter than the other, almost colorless, yellow eyes, and smaller than the other boys in size, yes, but *not* in heart—flashed in her mind, and she knew it was the son she would never have. *Conrad . . . She would have called him Conrad . . . Conrad LuPone.*

She felt cold and everything was beginning to go gray. She gazed back to the flickering, blue spot of light with her right eye. Two, large, glowing, green eyes shone back at her. The thrumming, purr increased.

---

53

# PRATTVILLE, OHIO

*4:45 A. M., September 3, 1990*

The cool, odorless, morning air chilled Jeremy Wheeler's skin as his legs propelled him over uneven, cracked sidewalks.

In the beginning, his muscles protested, grunting and pulling as they warmed and lengthened, but by the end of the first mile the tightness had left. Still, he felt an uncommon tenseness he couldn't attribute to three days without exercise. He watched the slow-moving shadows with the disturbing belief that today was different from any other.

*"You can't shoot what you can't see, gunman."*

The crackling voice knifed into Jeremy. Loose muscles went tight, and he spun to face the voice, missed a step, tripped, stumbled back, almost fell.

Jeremy crouched. His right hand went to the small of his

———

back. It swept up the tail of his sweatshirt. Tense fingers slid across his gun's slotted stocks. His thumb touched the safety. His eyes skimmed the morning shadows. His heart skipped a beat, churned, then pounded with slow, jarring thuds, threatening to explode.

His darting gaze had found nothing, not at first. Then, in the slow-moving shadows of a Weeping Willow tree, a grizzled, squat figure of a man seemed to assemble in the morning fog.

He was wizened, weathered, and perhaps no more than four feet in height. A white beard, matted and stained with green, covered most of the man's face. Long, white hair swirled around his head on the morning breezes. He dressed in ragged, dirty clothing. Frayed, shirt sleeves were rolled above his elbows to withered biceps. The ragged cuffs of his faded jeans were rolled above well worn shoes. The right shoe was built-up on the bottom, Jeremy saw, indicating a deformity. And covering all his clothes were widely spaced, small, white, plastic plates arranged as if to form a suit of ill-designed armor.

*A total fruitcake.*

The man didn't appear to be a threat. Nevertheless, still crouching, Jeremy continued to scan the shadows for several seconds before straightening. His heartbeat was quick now, but without the sickening, faltering lub it made only seconds earlier.

The voice had come from nowhere, catching him flat-footed. He didn't like the vulnerable feeling that left. He felt anger and embarrassment rising in him and fought to submerge the feelings. It wasn't this strange, little man's fault that he'd been caught daydreaming.

"I'm on my morning walk, old man. I don't carry money when I go for a walk, if that's what you want."

"Conrad LuPone don't want your money," the old man cackled. He limped from the shadows into the illumination of a street lamp. "Nope, Conrad LuPone don't want your money at all." He emphasized the last two words, making them sound *"a-tall."*

The voice was phlegmy, and he cleared his throat, spitting a thick, greenish fluid onto the sidewalk. Approaching, he squinted up at Jeremy.

Green fluid clung to wide-spaced, chipped and rotting teeth. A thin line of the viscous mucous ran down his beard, seeking a home.

Using quick, haphazard strokes, he wiped his mouth with his sleeve. Then with his head canted to one side, eyes narrowed, he looked Jeremy up and down, unhurriedly.

He smelled of urine, and his breath was so thick Jeremy was sure toadstools must flourish under his tongue and in the shade of his moldering teeth. He noted the old man's blank, almost colorless, eyes appraising him over broad, high, cheek bones.

*Cataracts?*

"Conrad just wants your time," the old man said.

"I'm not interested." In spite of the man's protest, Jeremy was sure there was a dollar mark somewhere in what he had to say. He didn't feel like talking nonsense to a grubby panhandler while his morning slipped away. *Fourteen years as a psychologist's assistant has made you hard. You've lost all of your charity,* his inner voice scolded.

"Don't kill the messenger," Conrad said.

"Sorry," Jeremy said, but releasing the word was just a reflex, he wasn't sorry.

"Just here to deliver a message. Very important message. Not here to get yelled at. I'm old. Going to die soon, anyway. *He's* seen to that. Made me a *motherless* child, now that I've betrayed him. Don't make me no never mind . . ." The old man's eyes began to shift aimlessly as he appeared to lost his train of thought, and his voice trailed off to inaudibility.

"Well?" Jeremy said.

"Well, what?" Conrad returned.

"Well, what's the damn—What's your message?"

"Oh . . . yes." He smiled. "I came a far distance. Another world, gunman! Another *world!*" His eyes grew wide as he put emphasis on the words. He cackled as if he had made a point, and spat more green mucous on the sidewalk. Again he rubbed at his chin with his sleeve in a failed attempt to remove the fresh fluid.

For a moment Jeremy wondered how this man knew he had a gun. His shirt covered it. He was sure the bulge was not visible.

"Our worlds, they're connected somehow. End to end or side to side. They're connected by evil *and* magic. There's great danger in that! And *you* hold the blame of it."

"*Me?!*"

"It's Apep."

"A what?"

"Apep, Apophis, Apollyon. It goes by many names. It is the serpent of darkness, the spirit of the pit, a worm that will not die. 'And they had a king over them which is the angel of the bottomless pit, whose name in the Hebrew tongue is A-bad'-don, but in the Greek tongue hath his name A-pol'-ly-on.' *Revelation 9:11.*"

Jeremy caught himself shifting from foot to foot. *Mad as a hatter,* he thought, impatiently.

"You got to keep the worlds from spilling together. Apep will kill your world, sure as he's killing mine. Then both will die. You got to stop the process *you* started. You've got to . . ." The old man's voice faded again, but his lips continued to move as he seemed to, once more, dissolve mentally into some inner world.

When sound returned to his lips, Conrad said, "I don't know but the half of it and don't understand half of that. . . . But Apep means to bring our worlds together. But for Parabellum, he's drained my world of its spunk, its will to live, to resist him. He needs the power and the youth of yours. At the time of the new moon, thirty days from now, he'll have the power he needs. Our worlds will *die.*"

"Why would he destroy his world? Then *he* would die!" The words tumbled out before Jeremy could stop them. He didn't want to encourage the madness of this man. It *had to be* madness, didn't it?

"This world's death . . . ," he raised a finger and wagged it at Jeremy, "or yours, gunman, . . . *or yours,* would free him from his mortal prison." The old man's dead eyes burned into him. "But he would rather have *you* alive, I think. He'd rather a mortal prison than judgement day."

Again, Jeremy shifted back and forth on the balls of his feet. He wanted to believe that this man was mad, spinning a tale born of a sick mind, but something in Conrad's voice and in those strange, pale, yellow eyes, wouldn't let Jeremy dismiss him so easily.

Conrad clutched at his sleeve. His gaze turned up to meet Jeremy's, his eyes pleading.

"Apep is shadows, sorcery, and evil-spirit all in one. He rules as god. Some say he is a god. Our worlds are destined to collide 'less he's destroyed, *believe me.* Dougal sent me for you. He says only you can defeat Apep. It's a linking of souls, he says."

"Linking of souls?" Jeremy said, trying to make sense of the old man's story. "Who is this Dougal?" Once more Jeremy regretted the question before all the words escaped him.

"You couldn't believe me if I told you. But he knows you, and well. And he knows Apep even better," Conrad LuPone said, with an emphatic nod.

"I don't even know why I'm hearing you out," Jeremy muttered as he crossed his arms over his chest, confident the gun could now be forgotten.

"Even now Apep spills our worlds together through his sorcery. Doorways, blue-light-holes. Dougal works against him. From the inside, don't you know." Conrad LuPone smiled as if he had made a joke, then continued. "Because of Dougal, the links are weak. Sometimes they wax, sometimes wane in their power. But Dougal can't resist Apep much longer. You can destroy the evil before . . ."

"Before what?" Jeremy said. He found himself caught up in the old man's words, mesmerized by his voice.

"Before he uses you and your world to free himself. Those who pass the holes from my world to yours are, in many cases, *indistinct.* They pass unseen, except by the dull and the insane. The sane see what they expected to see. With their minds locked onto the beings and objects of your world, they'll be easy prey. And the death of the child negates the life of his son, and his son's son, and my world."

Jeremy didn't understand, but he willed himself to remain silent.

"If Apep lives, he'll steal the power he needs from your world and use it to make our two worlds one. All manner of evil and insanity will result. All will die, but not before there is infinite pain," Conrad said, shaking his head, sadly.

"Why me, old man?" Jeremy asked.

Conrad LuPone raised his right hand, and with an extended index finger, poked Jeremy's chest in cadence with his words. "You're the cause of it. You've been to my world before." Then lowering his hand and shaking his head he continued, ". . . just not yet. You can go there again if you care, *if you believe.* It's a linking of souls," he said once more. "You're the link breaker, the one soul who has felt Apep's power and *resisted* it! You linked him to a mortal soul, made *him* mortal. And now he must change things or face the fate of all mortals . . . death, *judgement.*"

This man's story was fantastic. Yet, Jeremy Wheeler didn't feel like laughing. Conrad LuPone was delusional, and psychosis was not laughable. Or. . . .

Jeremy blinked.

59

He realized, suddenly, that he was fighting something deep inside him that believed this tiny man, accepted what he was saying.

He stared deeply into Conrad's eyes. There was a desperate look in those faded eyes. He could feel its warm, clutching presence. It cleaved to Jeremy much stronger than the old man's hand clung to his sleeve. What Jeremy saw there frightened him.

"You've got the wrong man," Jeremy blurted the words out. And somewhere deep inside, he realized he was frightened of this little man, of his words. "You need a priest, an exorcist—or some Haldol. I don't *believe* what you're saying." It was a lie. He felt the truth in the old man's voice as it shivered its way deep inside him like some soul-rotting worm. And his belief in the old man's words was more terrifying to him than the confused story this Conrad LuPone told.

Jeremy grabbed the old man by the wrist, and forced Conrad's hand from his sleeve.

*This is insane. I can't believe this.*

"If I did believe, I wouldn't know how to help you," Jeremy said at last. This was the truth.

Conrad's face sagged. His blank eyes moved up to lock gazes with Jeremy, again. "There have been murders here?" Conrad asked, his voice low, even. "Unsolved murders? Gruesome murders?"

"Yes."

Conrad LuPone's eyes widened. "Apep's minions be the cause of it!" he said. "They're taking the power Apep needs and searching for you . . ." Again, shaking his head, he continued, "and for the other. But she's with me and safe for now."

The little man smiled, his eyes filled with an almost evil pleasure. "And you've had memories . . . dreams of strange times, strange places, strange beings?"

His nightmare world with its creatures flashed in Jeremy's

mind, but before he could answer, Conrad LuPone said, "There will be more. There's a whole lifetime of memories coming . . . memories you've yet to earn. . . . You'll come. You won't have no choice! It's a linking of souls. You'll come to save *your* family, to cleanse *your* guilt."

"*My* guilt?"

"You linked him. Then you grew soft and left my world to suffer from him. You didn't do the *necessary*." Conrad squirmed a bit closer. "If I ain't dead yet, I'll be there to guide you when you come. But to save our worlds you must cross the portal soon. Apep will come for you *and* Lori if you don't cross soon. You must send him into the *pit* before the new moon, else we will all suffer the consequences."

The old man appeared to have made his point. He backed away, reluctantly, his gaze still locked with Jeremy's, and dissolved into the slow-rolling shadows and mist.

At six A. M. a rustling of feathers drew Jeremy Wheeler's attention. He was approaching the corner at Mineral Springs and Main streets. Overhead a crow twisted and turned in the thick, morning air. As Jeremy watched, it made a landing on the top of a power pole, then cawed, as if cheering his successful stunt. A long gray object, with an eye-sized, white nodule on its end, dangled from the crow's beak. The bird grasped the nodule with sharp talons, held it to the pole's top, and tore at it with his knife, sharp beak.

Jeremy turned the corner onto Mineral Springs Street and increased his pace. The morning chill pebbled his skin.

Since talking with Conrad LuPone, Jeremy had been feeling paranoid. Intellectually, he laughed at the old man's story. Emotionally, he wasn't so sure.

*You should have listened to Cindy, stayed home today.*

The street was damp. The shiny asphalt gleamed under the street lights. He saw a green cyclone fence and the power poles that carried the large lines from the power plant to the world outside.

A deep rattling sound—like the purr of a mountain lion—startled Jeremy. Then his gaze fell on a flickering light on the sidewalk, which seemed to arise from no source, and the dusty smell of death filled his nostrils, throat. He choked it off as the stink tried to make its way down his throat. His gaze ricocheted down the street.

Sweat, unaccountably, broke the surface on his back, chest, forehead. Moisture swamped his upper lip. The muscles of his groin tightened like piano wire, and his testicles began to ache.

With his gaze still seeking, he walked to the far side of the street. Away from the plant. Away from the light. Away from the malevolent rattle. *What is that sound? Where's the light coming from?*

He strained to feel the Detonics against his back.

The odd noise reverberated from the nearby buildings and crawled over his skin like small bugs. Still, Jeremy saw nothing.

*Find it or . . .*

Inexplicably, the words of the old man came to him, "Those who pass the holes from my world to yours are, in many cases, *indistinct.*"

*The old man was 'indistinct.'* He had seemed to materialize, assemble from the early morning fog.

Jeremy found no target. But he knew that there was something there. Something dangerous. And suddenly, he knew, just knew his time to act had passed. He had waited too long to find his target. Now he had no time. *SOMETHING'S THERE!*

His right hand darted for the grips of the Detonics. His gaze flitted everywhere at once. *You can't shoot what you can't see, gunman.*

His palm touched the pistol. Shining cat eyes met his. A

crushing blow struck Jeremy across the chest. The breath honked from his lungs. There was the sensation of flying. Everything went red, then black. His vision cleared. He found himself laying in the parking lot of the Napa store, across the street from the power plant.

He tried to sit. Pain gouged his ribs like a knife. A star exploded behind his eyes.

The rumbling-purr moved toward him. Gasping for breath, he rolled away from the approaching noise.

Incredibly, a roar reverberated nearby, followed by scratching sounds like a lion scrambling for meat on polished linoleum. He drew the Detonics, flopped to his stomach, fired blind.

A scream drilled sharply into his head. The thrumming stopped, but who—or what—had he hit?

Eight feet above the asphalt—above Jeremy—large, yellow eyes appeared. They circled, moving toward him.

*Why just the eyes?* A part of Jeremy's mind asked.

He brought the Detonics up. His trigger finger twitched smoothly, twice pulling the trigger through the mere millimeters needed. Two explosions split the air. Another yowl rang in his ears. The eyes disappeared.

Then they were *back!* Three feet away. To his far left. Too far left for him to aim.

Again, he rolled, struggling for position. A blow from nowhere flipped him over twice. Agony tore through his back to his chest. His wind was gone. His heart stopped, then shuddered to life once more.

Ignoring the pain, he somehow scrambled to his feet. He spun around, searching for the eyes. His head throbbed, his vision blurred. Everything seemed to crawl upward, into nothingness. He stumbled backwards, and flopped on his ass. The air sizzled above his head.

Jeremy let out a grunt and fell back. Again, the air above him was whipped by an unseen blow.

———

Helplessness bubbled up in what was almost a hysterical laugh. It died a sour death in Jeremy's throat as yellow eyes floated into view, again. They were within striking distance.

*Close enough to kill me if—*

Everything slowed to half speed for Jeremy. The Detonics came up, without conscious effort, as if it had a life of its own. Three bullets exploded into the darkness below the eyes. There was a grunt. He fired the last cartridge. The slide locked back. The eyes vanished.

The world seemed to switch gears, and suddenly, it was flying along at top speed, carrying him with it. Jeremy groped for his spare magazine. His thumb hit the eject-button, and the spent magazine clacked on the asphalt.

He slapped the spare magazine into place, pulled the slide back, released it. The much-practiced movements took two seconds. It felt like hours.

Jeremy's ribs ached. His head throbbed. His breath rasped in and out, uncontrolled. His heart threatened to explode.

Gouts of a viscous, iridescent, yellow liquid covered his left pant leg. It trailed over the asphalt toward the power plant.

Whatever had attacked him was hurt. Hurt bad.

Jeremy struggled to his feet, and staggered forward. His vision dulled, cleared with an act of will.

He searched the light for the eyes. *The creature must be there. It has to be!*

A blue light split the air like the mouth of a cave. He watched an enormous creature gain substance and color in that cave. It was all fangs, claws, and huge, yellow eyes.

The eyes glared back with human puzzlement as if asking how this could happen. How could a mere insect of a creature hurt it? It moved back into the gaping hole of light, a creature slinking into its lair.

The light dimmed.

---

# PRATTVILLE, OHIO

*6:38 A. M., September 3, 1990*

Half an hour after the attack, Jeremy was home, dazed and confused but excited. In his study he examined his sweatshirt. It hung in tatters. Four slashes crossed the front. It gaped in four more places across the back. The multiple layers of his Kevlar bullet-proof vest were parted almost to the skin. He remembered thinking, as he dressed that morning, that wearing the vest was the ultimate act of paranoia, but he had donned it for Cindy's peace of mind.

*Thank God for paranoia, Cindy . . . and Kevlar!*

Jeremy Wheeler hid his jeans, sweatshirt, and bullet-proof vest under the flooring in the attic, and slipped into the bathroom to examine his wounds. There were angry red and purple marks across his chest and back where the creature's claws

---

65

had struck. For several seconds he imagined the slashes as they would have been without the Kevlar vest: deep, ugly gashes spilling his guts onto the asphalt. He shuddered, and his knees began to vibrate. He sat on their old claw-foot-tub's edge.

All at once he felt incredibly tired. He wanted to crawl into bed and sleep forever. Cindy's nightmares, his own disturbing dreams, and the old man's crazy story of parallel worlds, had all come to life in one horrible jumble. And he was frightened, more frightened than he had been in his life.

*If I go to the police, they'll think I'm crazy. That is, if they don't arrest* me *for the murders. They'll think I'm trying to build a case for an insanity plea. But I've got to do something. I have no choice.*

Cindy's daughters, Linda and Sam Morgan, were scurrying about their rooms when Jeremy exited the bathroom. Dueling stereos and female smells greeted him. Through the girls' bedroom doors he saw a litter of clothing, books, paper, compact disks. He couldn't see the carpet. He said nothing.

For a beat, maybe two, his mind tried to rationalize that considerations of a messy room were ludicrous considering the events of his morning. Then he overcame the weakness that made him want to shift blame from himself. He would have said nothing in any event. It was his failing. His stepdaughters didn't like him. He was an adult living in their home, not part of their family so far as they were concerned, and they ignored or took offense at virtually everything he said.

*Would I have been a better father if the girls were mine?* Jeremy shook his head slowly, released a low sigh. He didn't know. And now, with his world suddenly, terribly out of level, it didn't matter.

He went to the living room and waited for the girls to leave. There would be enough time to pack after they were gone.

From the kitchen radio, a newscaster's voice boomed.

"Prattville Police Chief Hank Davison said that there are no suspects in the multiple murders that have plagued the town for three weeks. To date, three men and four women have been found murdered in Pratt Park. All the bodies were mutilated. Forensic methods have failed to identify the victims. Police have barred the public from Pratt Park until further notice."

Samantha Morgan's high pitched screech covered the radio reporter's voice, "Linda, that's *my* blouse. You didn't ask. I'm telling Mom."

"Tell her. I don't care. You took my shoes and stretched them out. You owe me."

"Oh, no! I took your shoes because you didn't pay the ten dollars you owe me!"

Sounds of scuffling on the stairs drowned out the broadcast.

*Damn, not now!*

He picked up the book—GENETIC RESEARCH IN THE '90's—he had been reading the previous evening, from the coffee table, and opened it. The girls entered. He glanced up from the book, sought a smile.

The girls were near duplicates of their mother. Both had light-brown hair, hazel eyes, perky, upturned noses, and thin lips that dimpled, like their mother's, at the corners when they smiled. Although she was younger by two years, Sam was the taller by an inch, and though rail thin, she was still five-pounds heaver than her sister. He figured neither girl would ever make it past five-four, and Sam was there now, but at that, she was two inches taller than her mother.

From the sofa, his book still in hand, Jeremy called, "Do you girls have rides today?"

Each girl gave a sidelong glance to the other. Neither replied.

"Linda, do you have a ride to and from school today?"

"Yes, but I have band after school."

"Remember the murders. The high school is a short block from Pratt Park. Don't think you're safe because you're not in the Park. Be with people when you're out. Stay away from Pratt Park. And stay away from Pratt Municipal Power."

Again there was no reply.

*Yeah, that's cool, Jeremy. I'll do that.*

"Sam, do you have rides to and from school?"

"Yeah," she said.

Then both girls were through the door.

*You're good at this. You should have had kids of your own,* Jeremy's mind taunted him.

It wasn't an easy decision to step into the blue doorway of light. Jeremy Wheeler loved Cindy. And despite their rejection of him, he loved her daughters. And he knew that stepping into the portal of light—either through his success or failure in that other world—could separate him from them forever. Yet, he was confident that the alternative to that sacrifice was the death of all he knew and loved. Conrad LuPone was very definite on that.

He thought of calling his parents to say his good-byes. He thought of telling Cindy what had happened, what he had to do. However, he rejected both ideas. What could he say that would make this easier for them? They would have to conclude he was psychotic. And then, when he disappeared . . . wouldn't that be harder on everyone? Who could believe what had happened, what was to happen?

Conrad LuPone's words came to him, "They pass unseen, except by the dull and the insane." The hair stood on his neck, and his stomach tightened. He shook the feeling off.

In the basement he found a leather backpack. He stuffed it with a change of clothing, sewing kit, first-aid kit, beef jerky, two cans of beans, a blanket, matches, a buck knife, two handguns, ammo.

A quarter-hour search of the attic turned up a length of rope leftover from Linda's mountain climbing field trip and a large canteen that Samantha had bought for a camping trip.

An hour after Samantha and Linda had walked through the front door, Jeremy was on Mineral Springs Street. Twenty yards from the Power Plant and the light, he stopped to strap on a western-style, leather, gun belt and holster. He stuffed a stainless steel Ruger Redhawk—a monster sized .44 magnum—into the holster. His hands were wet, and his fingers slipped on the rosewood grips. His stomach felt like it was grating over his spine.

The portal was a dim, swimming blue. It was somehow different, he thought. Dimmer perhaps. Or was it less transparent? He wasn't sure. His concentration had been on the Catman earlier, and although the cave of light had been fascinating, it had taken second place in his attention. But he was sure the cave, the hole, was different from when he first saw it.

He stood staring into the light for several minutes, wondering if there would be a sensation—perhaps an electrical shock—as he passed the light years, eons or whatever one passes between parallel worlds.

His hand dropped to the Ruger's grips, seeking the reassurance he always felt there. This time he found none.

He peered intently into the light for anything conspicuously strange, bizarre. The objects he glimpsed in the light moved slowly away, as if the hole on that other world was moving, changing position. The things he saw there also appeared less distinct than he remembered them appearing when the catman stood in that portal. But was that all? And was there a significance to this?

He tested the opening with an irresolute push of his left hand. It gave way with a spongy resistance, but there was no pain. He shivered.

He expected his hand to pass into the passage and to

experience a tingling, sting, burn, shock,—something—but he hadn't expected the passage to resist him! He tried again. This time he pressed harder. The passage resisted like cold gelatin, then gave way. His hand and forearm sank into it, seemed to stick there.

Would that other world be like this? Jeremy didn't know. Would he even be able to breathe there, or would there be no need to breathe? He didn't know that either, and there was only one way to find out. He withdrew his hand, and the hole he had made closed with a wet *slurp*.

He checked the straps to his pack and the security of his guns in their holsters. Then he attached his buck knife to his belt, feeling vaguely he might have to carve his way back to his world.

He straightened once more, and stared into the light. His bowels gurgled, and for an instant he thought he might have a movement. *Some hero I'd be, diving into the breach with a load in my pants!*

Taking a deep breath, he drew himself up and backed several yards away from the portal. He stared into it for a handful of seconds, then swallowed his fear and strode firmly toward the light. His stride turned to a dash. He *was* going through!

He struck the strong, gelatinous surface at a full run, sinking into it. It pressed firmly around him and closed his nose, mouth and ears. Every muscle in his body strained. The surface beneath him turned to jelly. He kicked against it. There was no progress forward.

His hands groped sluggishly through the goo. He couldn't breathe. There was no sound. He had the queer sensation of traveling backward very swiftly. Everything began to spin. His arm and leg muscles thrashed, useless in the ooze. There was no sense of touch. There was no up or down, no in or out. His tendons and muscles shuddered, convulsed. Everything went gray and started to fade.

———

And suddenly, he felt panic swelling withing him. *I'm dying!* Then he was in *air!* Hot pokers of pain burned through his lungs and every nerve. Air swooshed past his ears and color (black, green, blue, red) flashed past him in a blur. There was a thudding sound. Something crashed into him making his teeth chatter. Then his vision cleared, and he realized he was on his back in the Napa parking lot, across the street from the power plant and the eerie, blue light.

The passage had simply spat him out, like a wave tossing a rotting fish on the beach!

# PEACH CREEK, OHIO

*6:00 A. M., September 4, 1990*

Early the next morning, Jeremy sat at his desk at Peach Orchard Developmental Center absorbed in thoughts of parallel worlds, portals, and someone or something evil called Apep.

The door behind him opened. He startled and reached for the Detonics, but brought his reflexes under control before his hand found the gun.

His office companion, Michelle Green, stood in the doorway, her aqua eyes peered out at him from behind oversized glasses that sat on the upturned nose of a classically, pretty face. Five-foot-eight with long, raven-black hair, she was dressed in baggy jeans to cover long, bird, thin legs. She rarely revealed her legs. A voluminous blouse obscured her breasts just enough to draw attention to them.

---

Her face screwed into a look of question as she struggled with the door and her typically, too-large stack of files.

"What are you doing in here so early?" She flashed a knowing smile, and he felt a surge of anger.

"Feeling guilty about calling off sick yesterday?" Her voice was high pitched, almost grating. Sometimes he thought it presaged her true nature, and this was one of those times, though she had not shown that side of herself to him, yet.

"It's not so early. I thought I'd finish some paperwork before our first meeting. Looks like meetings all day again. No time for the real work."

It was a lie, but not a big one. There were meetings all day, but he wasn't here to work. He was here because there was a teacher's, in-service, training class today. The girls were off school, and he needed a place away from them to think, to decide what he should do next.

She stacked the files she had been carrying on the corner of her desk, and still standing, started to thumb through them. "If you want to give the State some free time, that's up to you." Accusation floated on the surface of her voice. "You're the one who's always saying, 'people don't appreciate free sweat.'"

"Yeah, but sometimes there's no choice," Jeremy said.

"Did anyone tell you that we've had another death?" Her voice was matter-of-fact, without inflection, cold. "That makes six in three weeks." She found the file she wanted and sat, spinning the chair to face him she slid her butt forward onto the edge of the chair, leaned back, and began thumbing through the file.

"Who?"

"John Heck. His family has political connections. Maybe we'll get some action now."

Jeremy swiveled his chair to face her. "Was he like the others?"

"Yeah, and the Medical Director still says he thinks the

puncture wounds and the dehydration are incidental, not the cause."

"What does that mean?" Jeremy asked.

"The puncture wounds weren't actually puncture wounds. They were incidental to the extreme dehydration. The skin ruptured, he says." She looked up from her file and rolled her eyes.

"IN THE BATHROOM. IT'S IN THE BATHROOM." A mournful cry broke through the perpetual din of human voices coming from outside their office door.

Michelle shuddered, and a sheaf of papers spilled from her file folder to the grimy floor. "Jesus, who's that!" she said.

"Carl Peters," Jeremy said.

He grunted from the pain in his chest and back as he moved to help retrieve the papers. Michelle didn't seem to notice his discomfort. He hadn't expected she would. Michelle was too self-absorbed to really observe others, he thought. However, he would have to be more cautious around Cindy.

"He's been screaming the same, meaningless words for almost a week now. We don't understand why, and since he only parrots words, he can't tell us. He does it most of the time when he's here, at home. He stops when he's at the Retirement Center.

"What does the doctor say caused the dehydration and tissue loss?" Jeremy asked.

Michelle looked up from the papers she was rearranging, blinked, and stared at him blankly for several seconds, as if waiting for mental circuits to reset. She said, "Some kind of industrial chemical. He says the chemical is caustic and melts away the tissue."

Her brow furrowed in question. "That's not possible, is it? I mean, with the tissue missing from under the skin, and with the skin more or less intact?" She didn't wait for an answer.

"Mr. and Mrs. Heck demanded an autopsy. I'm glad. Nobody'll do anything if the parents don't push. Maybe with an autopsy we'll find out something. I'm frightened. My God, what if this is something *we're* exposed to?"

He grinned, nodding. "Like the pesticides?" he said.

He had shared the little hole in the wall they laughingly called an office with Michelle for more than five years. He spent more time with her than he did with Cindy. He knew her suspicions would fall on the weekly pesticide spraying.

She laid the file to the side and looked him in the eye. "Yeah, that's what I mean!"

"I think there's more to this than pesticides," he said.

At noon a call came into the office. It was for Michelle. Jeremy sat, twirling his pencil end over end as he watched her take the call. He noted her uncharacteristic reserve during the call, no questioning, no accusation, no comment. When she replaced the receiver, she looked pale, shook.

"What is it?" he asked.

She sat staring at him, eyes vacant, for what felt like minutes. He was beginning to wonder whether she intended, or was capable of, an answer before she spoke.

"The autopsy results are in."

He stopped toying with the pencil.

"John died from massive amounts of a toxin."

"Toxin?"

"They say it's a spider's venom. Someone injected it into his leg."

She made eye contact. "Murder!"

He dropped the pencil, and it rolled under his desk.

He looked up from the lost toy, and nodded to show he'd heard.

"The toxin was caustic. It dissolved the tissue. The tissue was . . . sucked out of those puncture wounds!" She paused, looking as if she were going to lose her lunch. Her color went

—

gray. She swallowed heavily. Small drops of perspiration appeared on her forehead.

His stomach did a slow roll. He had seen the puncture wounds on another resident of the facility, Anthony Bertoni. They were three inches apart and an eight of an inch in diameter. If the holes were from a needle, it would have to be a cardiac needle. Not a likely murder weapon. No known spider had made those wounds. His thoughts went to Conrad LuPone's story of parallel worlds and invisible visitors, and he forced the thought from his mind. He didn't like this explanation, the only explanation that fit.

"It's murder," she insisted. "That's all it could be. Maybe it's the killer from Prattville."

He said nothing.

She finally moved: sat up straight and reached for a file. "They've canceled the meetings," she said, making eye contact. "State Police will be here all day. They want to question everyone. Maybe they'll catch him."

Jeremy nodded, but he didn't really think they would. He didn't really think there was a *him* to catch.

The State Police questioned everyone as a group, then one by one they were taken into an office and interrogated some more. The process took all day, and then a second shift of officers arrived to question the second shift staff. Jeremy guessed there would be follow-up questions the next day. He also believed that the police would come up empty handed.

That night, Jeremy tossed and turned, sleepless. Should he tell Cindy about his experience at the hands and claws of their nightmares? He wasn't sure. *She might believe me. But I'm still not sure I believe myself, am I? Psychotics don't think they're delusional, do they?*

# PRATTVILLE, OHIO

*4:00 P. M., September 5, 1990*

The following afternoon, Police Chief Hank Davison sat in his office, staring at his hands. The room was gloomy. The only light came from the window overlooking an alley where off duty police cars parked. Yet he didn't mind the gloom. It seemed to fit this office just now.

He had eight, active, murder investigations in process as of this morning and not the slightest idea of where to go from here.

"Everyone in town is *spooked*," as Charlie put it. Almost everyone was staying at home between sunset and sunrise. Some had left town on sudden vacations. Others had become hermits.

Hank had heard gunshots near the power plant while on dawn patrol two days earlier, but couldn't find the source. In

---

the end, he had decided the shots came from one of the more venturesome souls who still walked the street before sunrise, someone who had become spooked, fired at nothing and, hopefully, hit the same.

Then today, Art Fuller had discovered Judith LuPone, one of the town's librarians, hanging twenty feet above the ground, across the limb of a maple tree.

Art had nothing to do with the murders. Hank knew that. Art was well known, a gentle man, a bartender at Gary's, a small sports bar on Market Street. No one in their right mind would accuse Art of murder, even if he hadn't been five-foot-six and seventy-five pounds over weight. Nevertheless, people were spooked. So, Hank had hauled Art in for questioning. It was all for nothing.

Art spent two hours repeating his story four times over. He was on his walk to work when he happened to look up at a cawing crow. The bird was perched atop Judith's head, picking at the milky flesh of her remaining eye as it dangled from its socket on a gray cord of putrefying nerve.

"I couldn't believe it," Art said. "My mind said it was a mannequin, just some kid's joke, up that tree. But then I knew." His eyes went strange, and tears formed in the corners. Art looked away. "So, I ran to the Napa Auto Parts' store, and they called you."

Later that day, Hank questioned the Napa Auto Parts' employees. Art's story checked out. Everyone had the same story. Art had rushed in at 9:30 that morning with dilated pupils, face red and sweaty, out of breath, and smelling of vomit. At first he wasn't rational, and some of the employees thought he might have had a stroke. It took ten minutes to calm him down enough so they could understand what he was trying to tell them. By then, the Rescue Squad had arrived.

"No, Art had nothing to do with the murders," Hank thought. And that left him with nothing.

There was a light rap on his door. "Hank?" The diffident voice of Charlie Hascomb penetrated the translucent glass.

Hank sat up straight, and self-consciously placed the hands he had been studying for the past half hour, flat on the desk.

"Come on in, Charlie." Hank was happy to have his thoughts interrupted. They were tangles of worms, squirming in upon one another, leading nowhere.

Charlie seemed to creep into the office, hat in hand. He closed the door, releasing the latch without a snap, as if he feared waking someone.

"What you got, Charlie?"

Charlie gripped his hat by the brim and turned it clockwise. "Well, Chief . . ."

Hank stiffened. His officers seldom call him Chief. When they did, he knew they were leading up to something he didn't want to hear. Bad news and no news had filled the past three weeks. Hank's nerves were raw, stretched taut. He was beginning to think no news was preferable.

The hat stopped turning. "I checked out the scene where Art found the librarian, like you told me. It isn't good."

"Go on."

"The items found on the ground all belonged to the victim." He grimaced. "Body parts."

Hank's mouth went sour. He nodded, then reached for the Styrofoam cup, which had sat waiting his attention while he stared at his hands, and took a swallow of cold, bitter coffee.

Charlie Hascomb's hard face lightened. "But on the tree we found deep scratches. It looks like someone climbed the tree with some sort of metal claws attached to their hands and feet. Maybe something like those novelty stores sell. I think they call them ninja claws."

Hank moved forward in his chair. He felt a smile crease the corners of his mouth. The sensation made him realize he had not smiled since he had found Lori Hellman's body. "Well, at least we have *something*. I thought you were going to bring me more of the nothing we had before. What else you got?"

---

79

There was a shy glint in Charlie's steel-blue eyes. "You're not going to like this Chief."

Hank felt his face tighten, ironing the creases, which were just beginning to feel right, from the corners of his mouth. "Just say it."

Charlie flinched, rolled his hat for another clockwise turn, then nodded. "Judging from the marks on the tree, the guy we're looking for has to be eight or maybe nine feet tall!"

Hank stared at Charlie, and fell silent for what seemed to him a very long time. Heat rose to his face. His head throbbed. He could feel tears of frustration and anger well in his eyes as he strained to rein in his anger. He rose from his chair and spoke in measured tones. "I want you to get back over to Mineral Springs Street. I want you to measure everything as if you've never been there before. Take photos. Make a moulage of the scrapes on the tree. When you come back— if you *want* to come back—you'd better have some better ideas. I don't want to hear more talk about a *fucking* nine-foot-ninja. Do you understand?"

Charlie nodded. "I understand." Then, "Hank?"

From between clenched teeth, "Yes?"

"We all know how hard you've been working, what with covering the park in your off hours and the rest of the town during the day. And we appreciate it. But you haven't slept in days. You need to lean on us more. You need rest. Night will be here soon."

Hank felt something sag inside him. He imagined himself as Charlie must see him, a tired, half-crazed man. He sat, started to stare at his hands again, caught himself and looked at Charlie Hascomb instead.

"I'm sorry," Hank said. "It's this damn case, Charlie. The City Council keeps hounding me. The bodies keep piling up, and I don't have anything, not a fiber, not a print. This is the only victim we've been able to positively identify. The rest... they're ... " His right eye twitched. He looked down at his hands then back to Charlie, feeling like he might cry.

Charlie nodded, his hands were turning his hat in slow circles again. His face was grim.

"I report to the City Council. They're just ordinary church going, band boosting, high school football sort of folks. They sponsor walkathons and walk in them. They lift a beer or two on a Friday night, at the Moose Lodge, Gary's or the VFW. And their biggest concern is the safety of their families, not the futility of our investigation. This isn't Saturday afternoon TV. I *can't* tell these people that we're looking for a nine-foot, cannibalistic ninja!"

Again Charlie Hascomb nodded. "I'll get right out there. Maybe we missed something."

"Thanks, Charlie. I'll see you tonight. Maybe we'll get lucky." Hank attempted a smile, but it felt more like a grimace.

An hour later, Hank Davison received a call. The voice on the other end of the line was female, older, wavering.

"I—I'm Emma Peller. I live on Mineral Springs Street, next to the power plant. It's near where you found that poor, librarian girl?"

"Yes?" Hank picked up a stub of pencil, and without much consideration, started sketching a cat's eye.

"Well, what with all the murders going on, I've been a mite more watchful of late. You know, noticing who's around more? Strange cars and such?"

"Yes, ma'am," he said. He did know. He had received more than fifty calls this week from citizens who were "a mite more watchful."

His hand started to sketch a second eye on the paper. *Out of perspective*, he noted, but that was why it was called doodling and not art.

The voice drew his attention again. "Well, I've noticed

—

81

this car. It's a little, blue, sports car. It, uh, it sits in the Napa parking area in the afternoons and evenings. It's been there for hours on end the past couple of days or so."

Hank was familiar with the car. Harvey Jacobs and Charlie Hascomb had both noted its regular presence at the Napa store. Charlie had run the plates through the B. M. V. The driver was local.

"Yes. We've noticed that car, Ms. Peller."

"You have?"

"Yes."

"But he sits there hours on end. The Napa store is closed after five of the afternoon and . . . Well, I just thought you might want to check it out!"

The woman with the wavering voice sounded irritated. *She thinks I'm patronizing her.*

"Yes, ma'am. I understand your concern. I appreciate your call. If the car is there now, I'll send someone out to speak with the driver."

Hank looked down at his hand again. The two cat's eyes were now separated by a nose—*too human, not catlike at all*—on the end of a furry, all-too-feral muzzle.

"Well, I should hope so! There's no call for him to be there all hours. It's suspicious, if you ask me."

"Is he there now, ma'am?"

"I've been watching him for close on to an hour. He just sits, staring at the power plant. Nothing else, just staring at the power plant. That's where the first victim, that poor little Lori Hellman, worked. If you ask me, it's spooky!"

Bloody cloth, bits of flesh and bone flashed in Hank's mind. The scalp with the blond hair had convinced him that the remains, which looked more like dog food than human, were Lori's. All the coroner could tell him was that the bones were from a "female, Caucasian, early twenties, blood type 'O' positive."

He had felt lighter since he and Lori first met. He had

thought he was falling in love. Now, all he felt was a vast emptiness, an emptiness that weighed him down until every movement was an effort. He wanted to catch the monster who had dug this empty hole in his heart. He wanted to find him and tear him apart like that sick creature had torn Lori apart!

"Yes, ma'am" His voice caught in his throat and he cleared it. "Yes. I know. I'll check him out myself."

"I'll be here at my home—the blue one on Mineral Springs with the roses around the porch? I'm afraid there isn't a number on the house," she said. "But I'll be here just in case you want to ask any more questions."

"Yes, ma'am. I would very much appreciate talking with you. That is, after I speak with the driver of that car. I may have to take him in for further questioning, you understand? I'll drop by later to take your statement, if that's all right with you?"

"It is. Goodbye."

Fatigue returned as soon as the handset touched the receiver. If he knew the Emma Peller type, and he did, she would be at the window timing his arrival.

He lifted the remainder of a cold cup of coffee from his desk and drank it in one, long swallow. He had been living on little more than caffeine for four days. It caused his nerves to tingle and buzz, and yet, it did nothing to clear his dull mind. He tossed the Styrofoam cup at a nearby trash can. It missed by a foot. He watched it roll a little circle on the floor and shook his head. *Need some sleep bad.*

"But first this call." He flinched at the somehow unexpected sound of his voice.

He started to rise, then looked down at his sketch pad one last time. The doodle was complete now. A feral jumble of cat and man stared back at him with hungry eyes. Hank felt a little shiver slide down his back and disappear into his boots. He picked up the doodle pad from his desk and then the Styrofoam cup from the floor, and dropped both in the wastebasket.

When the police cruiser pulled into the Napa parking lot, Jeremy Wheeler slid his handgun, a Ruger Redhawk .44 magnum, between the center console and the passenger seat, and slipped from the car to the asphalt. He locked the car, leaving the keys in the ignition.

Hank stopped his cruiser several yards from Jeremy's car, paused for a second to gather his thoughts, then picked up a clip board and referred to the name the B. M. V. had given him. Then he eased from the car to the asphalt.

The man matched the B. M. V. description, six-foot one with graying, brown hair and brown eyes. He was in his early forties, around two hundred pounds.

As Hank Davison approached, he assessed Jeremy Wheeler. He was well groomed. His eyes were alert, but not squirrelly, and although he didn't have a hard appearance, he didn't look like a pushover either.

Hank waited until he was within three feet of Jeremy, crowding him, before he spoke. It was bad technique, Hank knew—technique that could get him killed under the wrong circumstances. But he wanted to rattle this man, make him make a mistake now if he was going to make one.

With one hand holding his clipboard and the other resting on his belt, near his Smith and Wesson, Hank said, "Let me see your driver's license."

Jeremy's gaze met his. "What's the problem, Officer?"

Hank thought Jeremy looked relaxed, sure of himself. He was leaning back on the blue Toyota, his arms crossed. "This is a private parking area, and it's after store hours."

"What's your point?"

"My point is, I could arrest you for trespassing." Hank

made his voice husky, flat, professional. He didn't like this man.

Jeremy's eyes went flinty. There was no flinch, no withdrawal. Instead, a small smile formed at the corners of his mouth. He eased forward off the car, and his arms lowered to his sides. Hank decided, pushing Jeremy Wheeler's buttons was going to be harder than he had hoped.

Jeremy fished a black nylon wallet from his jeans-pocket and removed his license. With the smile still at the corners of his mouth, he handed the license to Hank.

"I'm not trespassing. I have the owner's permission to be here."

"You know the owner, Mr. Bricker, then?" This was a ruse. The owner's name was not Bricker, it was Craddock, Paul Craddock. Hank remembered meeting the man at a church function several months back. He was a jolly man who laughed at his own jokes and eyed the women like he was a starving man looking at a good meal.

Jeremy chuckled. "I don't know this Bricker. The owner's name is Paul Craddock. A heavyset, red-haired guy, with male pattern baldness setting in. Laughs at his own jokes."

Hank believed he succeeded in maintaining a poker face. So this Wheeler knew the owner, what did that prove? Still, he could feel himself retreating, losing his edge. Once again he noted Jeremy's smile. It was as if this man could read the retreat in his eyes, and that thought made Hank feel even more off balance.

"Can I ask what you're doing here?"

"Of course, Officer, uh—" Jeremy paused and squinted at Hank's plastic name pin. "Officer Davison."

Jeremy's ease sent a chill through Hank. Everyone else was nervous when a strange policeman approached, even another policeman. Yet this man was stone steady. Hank felt himself take another mental step backward. Jeremy smiled as if he could read his thoughts. *He knows I'm off balance, dammit.*

"I'm just looking." Jeremy said. "I thought I might see something that could help you with your investigation. With all the murders going on, and with the Prattville Police Department so understaffed, I thought I would keep an eye open when I had a chance. Lend a hand. We're all in this together, you know?"

Hank looked at the driver's license and clipped it to his board. Then he returned his gaze to Jeremy. "Maybe. Maybe not. You could be the murderer for all I know. In any event, your presence here has disturbed people in the neighborhood. I'm going to have to ask you to move along."

Jeremy rocked back against the Toyota, and crossed his arms, again. "I'm sorry if I've disturbed anyone, but there isn't an actual law that would keep me from just sitting here, is there?"

Hank felt his blood rise in anger and worked against it. Jeremy confused him. *This guy is okay,* he told himself. *He knows people. He's connected. Don't open a can of worms!* "No, but—"

"Fine, then," Jeremy said. "I'll let you know if I see anything, and you can assure others that the last thing I want to do is to disturb them. I'm a civic-minded person.

"You know, Officer Davison, a neighborhood watch might help your department cope."

Hank knew there was something wrong with this whole interaction! Now the man was telling him how to handle his job. He believed this wouldn't be happening if he was rested, mentally alert. Still, he couldn't understand just how things had gone wrong. He felt as if he was moving in slow motion while everything else was speeding along at normal speed. *End it. Get back to your office. No! Go home. . . SLEEP!* his mind screamed.

He removed Jeremy's driver's license from his clipboard

and handed it back to the man who seemed to have roiled his thoughts.

"Is there anything else, Officer Davison?"

Hank heard the question as if it came from far away. He ignored it, turned, and walked back to his car. He was exiting the parking lot before he thought, *I should see Emma Peller.* Then the fatigue covered him like a lead blanket, and something deep in the back of his mind said, *Emma Peller, get fucked!*

Minutes later Hank Davison was entering his home. Rudy whined, and jumped-up on him, his tail fanning the air.

"I know," Hank said, bending to stroke the dog's head. "I've neglected you dreadfully." In the past three weeks, he had been home only to shower, change clothes, nap and feed the pooch. Rudy had received no play, petting, warmth.

Hank checked the house for signs of Chaz's return. He found none. There were no furry, little presents on the back step, and no food was missing from his bowl. This was the longest the cat had ever stayed away, and Hank began to realize he would not return.

He sagged onto his sofa. Rudy jumped up next to Hank, and he stroked the pup until it fell asleep.

He thought of the visit from the State Police the previous day. Prattville wasn't the only place with a serial killer loose. Peach Orchard Developmental Center was having similar problems.

*Poisoning with a toxin! Well, that is novel. Still, when it comes to gore and technique, Prattville's serial killer has Peach Orchard's beat all to hell and back.*

He sighed. He had discussed the two cases with a Sergeant Smith. They had decided they had no reason to believe that the murders were connected. At the time he had been glad they weren't looking for the same person. He wanted Lori's murderer all to himself. Now, he wished the

—

murders were connected. He would like some help. *Hell, I'd like to dump this whole mess in someone else's lap.*

He gazed down at the sleeping pup and smiled. The pup's feet twitched, and his cheeks pulled back to bare teeth, then dropped and pulled back again. He emitted a short, comical growl. Hank smiled. "Hope it's a good dream pup," he whispered.

# MARK SCOTT AND MOTHER:

*In the Grasslands*

Mark Scott and his mother searched the camp. While Mom examined the contents of the pack near the fire, Mark pried loose the lid of a crate. Inside he found plastic vacuum bags stuffed with human body parts. Someone had labeled each with blood type, sex, hair color, and a name. The one on top was marked "Jeremy W." It was filled with gory parts. He could identify a hand and an eye. The one beneath was gore red inside but otherwise empty. The label read "Lori H." He closed the crate. He could think of no reason to tell his mother of these horrors he had found.

The pack Mom had searched contained a small amount of food, a canteen of water, and a flint and steel for fire.

———

"Not much," he said.

She smiled, bravely. "We're strong. We've roughed it be-fore. We'll make do."

"Toward the mountains?" he asked, nodding in that direction.

"That's where we'll find water," she said.

Mark thought that the mountains would also be where the owners of this camp would look for them, but he said nothing. Without water they would die.

# PRATTVILLE, OHIO

*September 6, 1990*

*H*ank Davison *looked up at tall, white clouds drifting on a blue sea of sky. The sun was warm on his skin, and the ocean breezes ruffled his hair.*

*Rudy romped at the edge of the waves, in the ocean's spray. He chased each wave as it receded, and then leaped into the air and dashed up the beach retreating as each new wave rolled in, chasing him.*

*A girl giggled. Hank looked down to her flawless face. Sea-blue eyes gazed back, smiling. He dug a toe into the sand, feeling young, fresh. He smiled back.* I love you.

*He took her hand, and they walked up the beach.*

Pulunk.

*A gust of wind from the beach tugged at his shirt, hair, and shoved against him. He turned toward the water, and watched as*

---

91

*angry thunderheads rolled across the churning water. The beach seemed a blank, featureless wasteland. Rudy was gone.*

*Hank's muscles tensed. He felt, unexpectedly, alone, vulnerable.*

Pulunk.

*The repeat of the strange noise sent a shock wave through everything, drowning all other sounds.*

*Hank's gaze darted about, seeking the source of the sound, seeking Rudy.*

*The giggle came again. He turned to it. A face of bone, teeth, blood, turned up to him. Black pits stared back. His muscles turned to rubber.*

*You said you loved me, but you weren't there when It made this of me.*

*Blood rolled from the empty, eye sockets. Cheek bones flooded red. Blood depended from teeth in shiny strands, forming sticky, red webs. Blood drooled over the stark, white chin and dripped into a pool of dark crimson.*

Pulunk.

Hank Davison came awake in a galvanic lurch. Breath, meant for a (mental?) scream, caught in his lungs and tore at them like a stone. Electrified nerve endings seemed to crawl inside his skin, making it goose flesh. Sweat swamped him. His muscles vibrated.

He found himself sprawled across the foot of his bed. A half-finished can of beer sat on his stomach, anchored upright by his hand. He pulled to a sitting position in tiny tugs and looked around.

Rudy lay sleeping at the head of the bed. His front feet were in the air, and his hind legs were splayed out below. His head lay on Hank's pillow. "You rascal." Hank chuckled.

He couldn't remember returning home. His head felt stuffed with cotton. His mind whirled.

For a flash, he thought he could still feel the sea breeze

and hear the hiss of the breakers. Then he realized it was his fan's breeze and hiss.

*Pulunk.* The sound from the dream came again. The bloody face of bone flashed hot in his mind. He startled, and his skin crawled.

*Did she say, "It made this of me?"*

# PRATTVILLE, OHIO

*September 6, 1990*

Warm breezes sailed tall clouds across the fading evening sky. Jeremy Wheeler sat in his car, in the Napa parking lot. He had been there for hours this time, staring at the swimming light that spilled from the portal.

Was the portal changing, or was this just his overloaded mind nagging him over nothing even meant to resemble reality?

If worlds were to collide, the portals would have to increase in number, would have to become larger. The old man had said as much. Yet there was something more subtle happening. Yes, the portal was changing. Jeremy was sure of that now. Still, it wasn't becoming larger, and there weren't baby doorways trailing down the block. Instead, there was something he had not expected, but he supposed he should have.

---

He had anticipated a *widening* of this joining of two worlds. What he was seeing was a metamorphosis, instead. It had to do with the quality of the light and the atmosphere within that light rather than the size or number of portals. The portal was becoming less obstructed; it appeared more direct. The other world was moving closer. And did the size of the portal make any difference? Could one or the other of these worlds-at-risk squeeze through the portal? Could more creatures from that other world come here now? Could *he* go *there?* Jeremy didn't know. So he sat in his car thinking of the portal's original rejection of him, trying to understand.

Time was growing short. The old man had given him until the new moon to cross the portal and stop Apep. Most of four days of that time had passed, and he hadn't even started.

*What don't I know?* Jeremy asked himself, watching with even greater intentness.

That night, Cindy's moans awakened Jeremy. Her nightmares were becoming more frequent, violent.

She flung her arms wide, connecting with a fist to his face. Stars of light exploded in his head. He rolled away, fending off his wife's unknowing blows. She sat up.

"Are you all right?" he asked.

Cindy sat staring into the shadows at the foot of the bed. She didn't answer.

"Cindy?"

"They're waiting for you." Her voice was deep, flat, dead.

A lump rose to his throat. His muscles turned to jelly.

He scooted closer to her, tried to see her eyes, couldn't. "Who's waiting?"

"Conrad, Apep, Dougal, others."

*The names! How did she know the names?*

"What do they want?"

"They want your power. They want to use you, again. They want you to *die*, again."

"Again?"

"Apep wants to rip you to atoms, to rebuild you, to make a home for his soul. Conrad wants to imprison you, or to sacrifice you. He doesn't care which. He follows the orders of the other face: Dougal."

She sat for several seconds more, then lay down and was asleep.

He didn't sleep.

The next morning, Jeremy picked at breakfast as he waited for Cindy to finish in the kitchen. He wasn't hungry. His stomach was filled with anticipation.

Questions assaulted his confused mind. Questions without answers.

Cindy entered the dining room carrying her usual cup-of-coffee-breakfast.

Jeremy pushed a chunk of scrambled egg across his plate with the tines of his fork, but didn't spear it. He gazed up at Cindy. "How do you feel this morning?" He detected an unplanned edge in his voice.

Cindy looked around at him sharply. "Fine. Why?"

"You had nightmares again last night. They seem to be . . . getting worse."

She sighed. "I've been meaning to talk to you about the nightmares and . . . other things." She was looking into her coffee, avoiding his eyes.

He thought he detected a tremble in her voice when she said "nightmares," but he couldn't be sure. He started to stand, move to her, but she waved him back into his chair.

"No, Jeremy! After we talk, you can hold and soothe me. I do want you to hold me. But not now. I couldn't say it all if you held me." She sat, placed the coffee on the table, and wrapped her arms around herself.

He sat back and looked at her, although he wanted to

turn away. He felt helpless, the way he always felt when Cindy was hurt and he couldn't take away the pain.

"Things are wrong. I want to know what's going on," she began. "Why have you been acting so strangely? Why are you away from home so much in the evening? Why do you come to bed only after the lights are out? Why have you been so . . . distant?"

He sat forward. "Distant?"

"No sex. None. Not even the loving touches."

He sat back, and felt all expression drain from his face.

"If there's something wrong, something physical, you should tell me. And if there's something else, *someone* else—"

A queasiness shot through Jeremy. "Are you serious?" He realized for the first time, he had allowed his preoccupation with the portal to hurt her, and tried to think how to put it right. "No, this is all tied in with your nightmares. We have to talk about the nightmares," he said.

Cindy's eyes narrowed, her face hardened and for a moment her lips formed into a tight, line. "My dreams? Jeremy, we have a serious problem between us, and you want to talk about dreams!"

Jeremy had never seen Cindy so mad. For an instant he thought this conversation was over. Then inexplicably her face softened, and he said, "It . . . It's important, Cindy. I need to know everything about your dreams. Just trust me."

She stared at him long and hard, as if measuring him. Then nodding, she said, "Okay, I'll tell you about my dreams. After that, you tell me what's going on with you, with us. Deal?"

A smile started to form on his lips, then died. "Deal." He hoped he could tell her what was going on with him. He hoped what she could tell him would make everything make sense.

Cindy sat back in her chair and wrinkled her brow as if she was trying to visualize something far away. Then she took a deep breath and started. "All the dreams are similar.

—

Some have more characters, creatures and scenes, but the themes are the same."

"Tell me about the characters and the creatures. Please, describe some!" He moved to the edge of his chair, feeling more a child in the grip of his favorite story than an adult in search of life and death facts.

Her brow went smooth. "No kibitzing from the peanut gallery," she said. "There'll be time for questions after I finish. Now I have to concentrate. Let me tell the story as it comes to me. Okay?"

He frowned to show his disappointment, then nodded agreement.

Once again, her brow furrowed, and the far-away look settled into her eyes.

"The dreams are hard to explain. The characters are in different places but together somehow. There is a deformed, grimy, old man named Conrad LuPone who spits green mucous and wipes it on his sleeve."

Jeremy had been staring into Cindy's eyes, concentrating on her story, he sucked an involuntary breath at the mention of Conrad LuPone's name. *She remembers the names!*

Cindy's far-away stare dissolved. "Are you all right?" she asked. "Did I say something?"

For an instant he considered telling her about his meeting with Conrad LuPone, but this startling development would mean little if he planted information in her head. He had to wait, to see if she knew more of what she *could not know.* "No. Nothing's wrong. I just had a thought, that's all. Tell me more."

Cindy stared, questioningly, into his eyes for several more seconds then continued. "The old man has long, white hair. The hair floats around his head as if there's a breeze where he is. But it's all the time. He's in a desert most of the time. When there are houses, the houses are crude or rundown, and their people are strange. Their eyes are dull, empty.

"Then there's Apep." Cindy shuddered.

The mention of Apep, Conrad's *sorcerer and evil-spirit all in one*, sent a surge of enthusiasm through Jeremy, sliding him forward in his chair, once more. "Why do you call him Apep?"

Her gaze slashed him, and suddenly, he felt like a boy whose hand had wandered far enough to gain him a slap on his very first date. His enthusiasm nose-dived.

"I *call* him Apep because he *said* that was his name. Now, hush.

"Apep dresses in a cloak like the Grim Reaper. In one dream, I looked under his cowl. He didn't have a face! There was nothing but stars and blackness under his cowl. His face of stars drew me into it, spinning and helpless. Everything was weird, unreal. I was surrounded by gelatin, and I couldn't use my hands and legs." She looked at him, her eyes frightened and questioning, then her gaze locked hard with his. He felt its grip.

"He's *you!* And he isn't you. He's a man, and he isn't a man. He's distilled evil! And he wants you—to tear you to atoms, yet, at the same time he wants to protect you from the others. He wants you alive, but alive with him is worse than the death the others would have for you." She raised a hand, palm to him, in a "halt" gesture. "I can't explain so don't ask. It's just the way it is."

Jeremy reached out and gently took Cindy's hand. "It sounds terrible. No wonder you've been so upset by these dreams," he said.

Gently, but firmly, she retrieved her hand, and he realized her hurt ran deeper than just dreams.

She nodded in answer to his statement, took a deep breath, then continued. "He's always in a modern place. Everything is sterile, stainless steel around him. When I remember that place, it reminds me of a huge Autoclave. You know, the machine we use to sterilize bandages and instruments? Noth-

ing could live there, but he does. And there's so much *power!*"
There was an awed tone to her voice when she used the
word *power.*

Jeremy started to speak, but he remembered the sting of
her gaze, and the memory froze him.

"There is so much power there that *sparks* dance on my
skin. The stars ripple, like flower petals on a pond, in hom-
age to that power!" Cindy's eyes went glassy, and for an instant, she looked as if her mind was very far away.

"The power is leached from the collective soul of man-
kind. It's being burned away like weeds on a hillside. I can't
explain that. I just know it's so."

"The other characters are at the command of Apep. He
can see through their eyes, and he moves them like chess
pieces.

"It storms in the dream. Multicolored lightning fills the
sky in the night, but there isn't any rain. *You* walk on the sea.
Danger is everywhere.

"There's another figure in the dreams. His name's Dougal.
He's faded, weak. He's good, but, like Apep, he wants to kill
you and to save you too. It's like he's two different people.
And the old man, Conrad LuPone, he wants to destroy Apep,
but he also wants to *save* him!"

For the second time Jeremy noted the name of the strange
little man whom he had met on the street. But this time he
managed to restrain his reaction. *How did Cindy know this same
name and the names of Apep and Dougal?* His own dreams hadn't
had a quarter of this detail. Mostly, his dreams were just battles
with strange creatures and of course, there was the blond
woman with the drowning-pool, blue eyes and the small scar.
The one who seemed to be Cindy, but wasn't.

"I know this doesn't make sense, but dreams don't have
to make sense, you know?" Cindy said.

Jeremy thought the dreams probably did make sense. He
didn't understand them, but he still didn't have all the pieces.

---

"The dreams all end the same," Cindy added. Now she reached out for him, touching his arm, lightly before drawing her hand back. "The characters stand in front of a split of flickering, blue light. They motion for you, and they call your name. But they're not speaking, they're *thinking* your name and smiling their macabre smiles." She hugged herself and shuddered. "Then, I wake up."

Her eyes met his, and they stared at each other for a very long time.

# PEACH ORCHARD,
# OHIO

*September 8, 1990*

The next day started much like any other at Peach Orchard Developmental Center. Jeremy Wheeler arrived to find pandemonium. Residents were screaming, throwing, spilling, breaking things, removing their clothing, and tripping over each other in the process. Some staff stood around doing nothing; others had tears in their eyes and strain in their voices. Still others growled and barked orders like drill sergeants. He thought residents of facilities like Peach Orchard often lost part of their human identity as the price of admission. In times of stress, like this morning rush, they appeared to lose all of it.

Carl Peters, a withered little man whose whole left side

---

seemed to gyrate to its own drummer—especially when he wanted it to do something else—sat in his wheelchair next to Jeremy's office door. His face was red, drawn, filled with terror. As Carl's left arm wandered through undirected gymnastic contortions, he waved his right fist in the air and screamed, "IN THE BATHROOM! IN THE BATHROOM!" at Jeremy's approached.

Jeremy shook his head. It was becoming too familiar, Carl in his chair screaming about the bathroom, an irritated, frightened staff, bodies appearing every few days. He slid the key into his office lock—

—and the last piece of this small puzzle seemed to fall into place with it.

For several weeks people had been dying at an amazingly high rate in this building. For that same period, Carl had been screaming these strange phrases. It was so *simple*. Jeremy couldn't imagine why he hadn't seen it before.

Carl, with his withered body and his poor damaged brain had been trying to tell them all along! Everyone killed had used the toilet *independently*. They were attacked in the bathroom! It was the only place of privacy in these people's lives. That was why no one saw the attacks!

Jeremy dashed across the living room and down a narrow hall to the men's rest room.

He knocked, then eased the door open and scanned the room. It was empty. He slipped inside.

*I can see this creature*, he told himself.

The bathroom was twenty-feet long. Metal stalls covered the wall to his right. A line of lavatories and stainless steel mirrors lined the wall to his left. There were no windows.

Jeremy kneeled on his right knee, and raised his left pant leg to reveal the Detonics secured in an ankle holster. He drew the gun and rose to his feet. He continued to scan the room as he pointed the gun at the ceiling, and released the safety.

Nothing in the room seemed out of place. He moved into the room, his gaze bouncing from the line of lavatories to the stalls and back again. He watched for any movement, any shape.

Nothing.

At the far end of the room he paused. He would check the recesses beneath the sinks first, then the stalls.

He knelt and placed his left hand on the floor. A shadow did a slow roll on the floor beneath the last stall door, and thousands of ants raced up Jeremy's spine. His left hand returned to the gun.

*Don't shoot at shadows!* he cautioned himself.

He gave the lavatories a cursory glance to assure nothing would be behind him, and turned to the stalls.

He stared at the gap between the door and the front panel of the stall for what seemed like minutes. The shadows didn't move. His hands began to cramp from his tension. His legs began to go stiff.

The sound of footsteps passed in the hall. *I'd better do something before someone comes in here,* he thought. "God, I hate spiders," he whispered.

He rose to his feet, feeling as if jacked to his full height in thousands of tiny tugs. He kept his back to the wall and in short, stiff, sidling steps, moved to within two-feet of the stall door.

Sweat formed on his forehead and trickled down the bridge of his nose. He lowered his left hand and wiped it dry on a pant leg, then returned it to the gun.

He flexed his trigger finger. It felt stiff.

Swallowing hard, he stepped to the door and kicked. He brought the gun down in a smooth chopping motion.

A blur of black hurtled the door and smashed into the

Detonics with a muffled thud. Jeremy bobbled the gun, then regained his grip.

Strong legs clamped onto his arm. Venom drooled down fangs Jeremy only glimpsed. The fangs scissored on the Detonics and clicked against its dull metal surface. Jeremy shrieked. He smashed his arms against the stall wall. The leggy mass ripped free, taking patches of skin with it. Raw nerve endings screamed at him.

The creature struck the floor and rebounded like a tennis ball. Jeremy lurched backwards, falling away from the cat-sized flurry of legs.

It sailed over his head to the wall above the stalls. Jeremy fired the Detonics as he fell. The bullet smashed into the creature below its head. Yellow blood sprayed the room.

Jeremy plopped to the floor on the flat of his back, and his head tapped the floor with a crisp pop. His breath whooshed from his lungs. For a beat, maybe two, sparks sprayed across the black backdrop of his mind, then he rolled to his stomach, and fired the gun dry. The creature's head vaporized into a yellow mist, and bits of tile, plaster, and mutant spider showered Jeremy.

Wheezing, Jeremy struggled to his feet. He hit the magazine release with his thumb. The magazine dropped from the Detonics, and clattered on the tile floor. He slapped the spare into place, and released the slide. The slide snapped forward, shoving a cartridge from the magazine into the chamber. The knot in his throat throbbed in unison with his madly pounding heart.

In a rush, he moved down the row of stalls, kicking the doors open, his gun held ready. Each stall was empty.

Jeremy turned back to the spider-thing, shuddered and then sighed.

In its death pose, with legs folded across the body, it formed a ball about a foot in diameter. Nothing remained of its head but shreds of black tissue covered with glowing, yellow blood. Some of his skin still clung to the hard bristles covering the spider's legs. Each leg was more than an inch thick. Curled, as they were, he couldn't estimate their length, and he couldn't, *just couldn't*, bring himself to touch the legs again.

"That wasn't so hard," he said. Then a shudder rattled his teeth, and his knees swiveled.

Jeremy Wheeler was face to barrel with Sergeant Larry Smith's Ruger .357 magnum when he stepped into the hall. In half a second, another gun barrel found a home at his right ear.

# PRATTVILLE, OHIO

*September 8, 1990*

At four o'clock, Monday afternoon, Hank Davison was answering one of an endless succession of calls coming into his office. The body-count in Prattville stood at eight. To his knowledge there hadn't been a murder since that of Judith LuPone, six days earlier. Yet the calls had increased.

Rather than feeling relief at the lull in, or maybe the cessation of, the murders, many helpful citizens appeared provoked to continue the stimulation of terror.

Domestic problems, which had stalled in the shadow of the murders, now flooded Hank's office. He thought of this reaction as a collective sigh, a return to business as usual. But no matter what the cause, it hindered his investigations.

He had returned Harvey and Ralph to first and second shifts to protect the local fast food restaurants from the

---

51-DAVI

throngs of juveniles released after weeks of home imprisonment. That left him to cover Pratt Park at night.

Hank lifted the telephone's handset and announced himself.

From the other end of the line came the voice of Larry Smith, a jowly State Trooper. Several days earlier Larry and Hank had spent an hour comparing notes about the murders at Prattville and Peach Orchard Developmental Center before deciding the crimes were unrelated.

"What can I do for you, Larry?"

"You know we're having trouble with murders out at Peach Orchard. We've had the place under surveillance since the day I talked with you."

"Yeah?" He slipped forward to the edge of his chair.

"One of your citizens went berserk out here today. He shot up one of the bathrooms."

Hank eased back in his chair. "Shot up a bathroom! Was anyone hurt?"

"No." Larry chuckled. "No damage a little spackle and some new paint won't fix."

"So, how can I help you? And who is this guy?" Hank remembered Larry as a man who loved to hear his own voice, and he didn't want to spend a lot of time in this conversation, going nowhere.

"This guy has an interesting story. Said he shot a *giant spider*. And, get this, we can't see this spider—because it's from another world! So you can see why I called you."

Hank shifted the phone to his left ear, picked up a pencil and started to doodle a long black cigar on his desk blotter. "No, Larry. I can't. Sounds to me like you need the rubber sheet squad. This guy sounds like he needs detox or long term care. Am I to take it that you want to put him in our jail?"

"Yes and no. You see, we don't want this guy. He tested

negative for drugs and alcohol, and he doesn't have a record. He's just a nut case.

"Like you, my first thought was to take him down to the State nut bin for observation."

"Yeah, and . . . ?" Hank's hand, seeming to work on its own now, drew a second segment to the cigar shape and began to add legs.

"My next thought was to call you to see if you had any ideas. If we lock him up at the funny farm there'll be all the fuss of the court commitment. Of course, that would mean a lot of bad publicity for Peach Orchard. The Director wants to get the guy out of here with as little fuss as possible.

The sketch had become a large, black beetle. Hank's hand sketched wicked mandibles onto the smaller head segment. Then it added two antennas above the mandibles before it stopped doodling and started tapping his stub of a pencil, like a drum stick, against the edge of his desk as he listened to Larry.

"Anyway, I can see how someone who isn't quite stable could fly off the handle. I mean, with murders where he lives and murders at work too, he must be under a lot of strain. I feel sorry for the guy."

Hank didn't think that Larry felt sorry for this man. What he thought Larry felt was a duty to please Peach Orchard's Director, and in turn, please his boss at the State Capital. Still, he could identify with Larry's feelings. After all, he often had to please the Prattville Citizen's Committee.

"You say this guy's a nut case, and that's the kind of perp we're looking for, Larry. Why do you think he's clean?"

"He just doesn't fit. For one thing this guy used a gun. Serial killers seldom change their M. O. Something drives them to repeat the same sick methods. Not one of the victims, here or there, was killed with a gun. For another thing this guy was afraid of the perp. That's why he had the gun. To his way of thinking, since the murders here were with

spiders' venom, the murderer must be a giant spider. He shot
the damn thing! Neatest pattern you ever saw. Seven shots,
rapid fire, inside of two-inches, at fifteen feet. And if there
was such a spider this guy would be a hero. But there isn't, so
he's a nut."

"But—"

"And there's another reason. I've checked this guy's story.
He has alibis for the times of most of the murders here. I
have a feeling that if you checked him out for the days of
your murders, you'd find the same thing," Larry said.

"You never did tell me this guy's name," Hank said.

"Jeremy Wheeler. He's a—"

Hank's heart lugged, pounded hard once, then settled into
shallow, rapid thumps. "I know the name!" he said. "I questioned him here."

"You questioned him?! Why?"

"He was hanging around the area where we found one of
the bodies. Said he was trying to be a helpful citizen. Was
doing his own neighborhood watch. Seemed okay. Didn't
sound like someone headed for *fantasyland*. In fact, he was
so solid it was almost spooky."

Larry chuckled. Hank could hear him drum a quick rat-a-
tat on his desk top. Larry said, "You'd be surprised by how
easy a solid citizen can go section eight. I knew a guy in
Nam, steeliest guy you could want to meet—"

Hank stopped doodling, and tossed his pencil stub at his
wastebasket. It tipped the rim, bounced, and skidded across
the tile floor. He could feel a long diatribe coming from friend
Larry, and he had other squirrels to skin. He broke in, "Larry,
on second thought, why don't you bring this guy out here? I
can book him on concealed carry, and we can have a court
psychiatrist from Wooster look him over. Give him the fifty-
thousand-mile checkup, so to speak. If this is a reaction to
stress, then we can drop the charges. The judge can send
him to Western Reserve Psychiatric if it's something more

serious, or have him see a psychiatrist as an outpatient, if he's safe. In either event, we can keep any mention of Peach Orchard out of the news."

"That sounds great! You're a life saver!"

"And Larry, if you bring him out yourself, we can have dinner. It'll be my treat. We have a pretty good, little, Chinese restaurant about a block from here. We could finish our discussion while we eat."

Hank was curious about the investigation at Peach Orchard. Although he and Larry had decided Peach Orchard's and Prattville's murders were unrelated, there was still something nagging him. He thought dinner with the garrulous sergeant might put his mind at ease or put his finger on what it was that made him think these cases had more in common than was apparent.

"You've got yourself a deal! I'll have him over there before you can whistle WORKIN' ON A GROOVY THING."

Hank could almost hear a smile crease the corpulent Sergeant's face.

"I'll be expecting you."

He replaced the phone's handset, and sat thinking of the conversation. It was hard to believe the man he had talked to in the Napa parking lot could be so unstable as to shoot at imaginary giant spiders.

He picked up another stub of pencil and began to doodle a large, hairy spider as questions to use in Jeremy's interrogation crowded his mind. If Jeremy was the murderer, he would find out. And he promised himself that if this man murdered Lori, *he* would handle it. Jeremy Wheeler would not slip away on an insanity plea.

Cindy Wheeler arrived at Peach Orchard Developmental Center's Campus Security at 4:25 P. M., just in time to see Sergeant Larry Smith's patrol car disappear into the evergreens lining the campus drive. Talk of Jeremy's arrest had spread across the campus in minutes.

She wondered if this had anything to do with her dreams and Jeremy's belief that he had been summoned to a parallel world by the grubby, little man who continually appeared in those dreams.

She had slept little since he had told her his fantastic story. To him the bruises on his chest and back and the tattered clothing and vest were conclusive proof of something fantastic. She couldn't believe that. The whole thing was too bizarre.

The marks on Jeremy's chest and back were large, fading, yellow and dark purple spots by the time she saw them. She had no doubt that the marks were the result of serious injuries. Nevertheless, the injuries could've occurred in any number of ways.

She had pleaded with him to see a doctor, psychiatrist or psychologist. Jeremy had refused. Despite his work or maybe because of it, he had little faith in medical doctors or psychology. He often said, "Doctors set bones and sew you up, psychiatrists drug you, and psychologists socialize with you." Nothing she said could convince him otherwise, despite the good she had seen done by his psychological magic.

Since he had told her his story, she had found herself measuring his every action. This morning she had decided, although she could not explain his belief in this parallel world, Jeremy was not crazy. However, the shooting changed things, made it harder to continue believing in him. Now she wondered if he was mad.

At 4: 30 P. M. Jeremy sat in silence in the back of Sergeant Smith's patrol car. The car sped along State Route 30 toward Prattville. He had not envisioned this possibility. His head had been so full of parallel worlds, catmen, and giant spiders, he had not considered what it might do to his credibility if he shot one of the creatures where someone might see the act but not the creature. He supposed, now that he did think, firing a gun at a creature no one else could see was a very stupid move. However, he'd believed he had no choice. He couldn't leave the spider here with defenseless people while he chased after Apep, a wizard with a dual personality who wanted him both dead and alive.

Considering the concealed weapon Sergeant Smith discovered on patting him down, Jeremy counted himself lucky it had been Smith on the other end of that Ruger .357. Most men in the position of the sergeant would have been less generous. *Hell, the sergeant even let me finish my story about the giant invisible spider. He didn't laugh once. Although, there was a glint in his eye. . . .*

The patrol car turned onto State Route 57, on its last leg of the short trip.

*How am I going to get out of this mess?*

# PRATTVILLE, OHIO

*10:42 P. M., August 15, 1990*

Lori Hellman could feel the large, glowing, green eyes following her as she ran, heart pounding, wet cuffs slapping at her ankles, rain and air tearing past her ears. She ran down Mineral Springs Street, past East Primary School, past Prattville High, toward the town power plant.

Twenty yards from the plant's cyclone fence she could hear the turbines' hum. It sounded different, too high pitched. She glanced over her shoulder toward the park. Her toe struck something. The asphalt came up. Sparks exploded in her head, and her breath belched from her in a goose-like honk. Then someone was pulling at her, tugging her to her feet. Everything drifted in her vision. The world seemed slanted. She smelled something stale, nauseating.

"Come. There's no time." It was a man's voice.

---

"I . . . Who . . . ?"

"There's danger. Hurry!" he said.

She moved her feet, aimless, sluggish movements. The man supported her, urging her toward a mountain of blue light that sprang up at the fence. It hummed and flashed like some form of harmonic lightning. The hum sank into her. It was, strangely, a feeling like good sex! Then everything dimmed, went black.

*PRATTVILLE, OHIO, 1992*

*The tall man stood in front of her, his hands folded at his waist. "My name's Jeremy Wheeler," he said.*

*"Hank mentioned you often," Lori Hellman Davison said, robotically. She didn't know how many more condolences she could carry before collapsing under their weight. Since Hank had been found near his cruiser, in a pool of blood, it seemed that everyone in town wanted to lend her some strength but left with some of her reserve instead.*

*Jeremy Wheeler was toying with his wedding band, turned it in slow clockwise circles on his ring finger as he spoke. "Hank lent me a lot of emotional support when Cindy and the girls. . . ." He paused. "When I needed it most. If there is anything I can do. If you need someone to talk to."*

*"I'll call," she said. She knew she wouldn't.*

*"The night's are worse. I'm a good listener," Jeremy said.*

*Their eyes met. Hurt sat on the soft brown surface of Jeremy's eyes. She remembered Hank saying he believed Jeremy's loss of his family had put him on the edge of insanity. But in Jeremy's eyes she saw compassion, strength and . . . danger. His eyes flashed, and something in them frightened her.*

*LORI HELLMAN:*

## *Through the Portal*

Lori lurched and was awake. The dream and the tall man with the nervously turning, wedding band, settled somewhere in the back of her mind.

A drop of water tickled its way across her temple to her hairline. She reached up and touched a damp cloth covering her eyes. She removed it and tried to sit. The world rolled.

"You ain't ready yet." A grimy elf-of-a-man sat on a boulder several feet to her left. He hopped to the ground and limped to her side. He wore a built-up shoe. His eyes were a pale yellow, almost faded blank. He was gray and shriveled, and he emanated an odor that stole her breath.

She looked past him, and to her left and right. Two, hobbled horses grazed in a small clearing surrounded by trees. There was nothing else, just trees, rocks, grass.

She laid the cloth aside. "Where am I?"

"In the mountains. I hid us." The odd, little man smiled, showing rotted, uneven teeth.

"Hid us?" she said. Her head was pounding now, and she reached up to feel a large, tender lump on her forehead.

"From Apep. Dougal sent me," the little man said, simply.

She tried to sit again and again found she hadn't enough strength. She slumped back to the ground. "I—I don't understand. Who are you?"

"Name's Conrad LuPone. One of Apep's creatures was at you. I brought you through the portal."

*Portal? Creatures?* Nothing seemed to make any sense.

Images of large, green eyes and a blue, flickering mountain of light flashed through her mind. Her stomach tightened, and a small shiver of fear rocked through her. "I want to go home." Again she tried to sit, but Conrad waved her back down with a pass of his hand.

"Don't go gettin' upset. You took a nasty bump. You're too rocky to move just yet."

He was right, and she knew it. But this place and this gnome of a man frightened her. Why the strange eyes? Why the mountain of light? Why this awful little man?

Two hours later she was sitting up, supported by a bedroll. Conrad was still explaining this new world and how she had come to it. The catmen, Conrad said, were created by a brilliant man, a geneticist named Dougal, who was possessed by something evil called Apep. Apep wanted to spill this world and her world together. Conrad said that this would kill everyone in both their times and wheres. But to do the spilling, Apep needed more power. The portal they had traveled through was a small crack, a billionth part of the opening Apep wanted to create.

"Here the portals sometimes move and sometimes split when someone comes through from the other side. Stays in place on your world, but wanders here. Don't know why. Don't think Apep does neither. He's spread his Guard thin trying to cover all the openings."

"How will I get back?"

Conrad shrugged. "We can follow the portal. Got about a three-hour head start on us. But we can catch up, with the horses."

"I can go back when we catch it?"

"Not 'till it settles. It'll spit you out if you try to go through before it settles."

"Will we have to go far?"

"Maybe hours. Maybe days. We'll have to leave soon. Apep's slave caravans follow the portals. One'll be here soon, looking for the slaves the catmen should've brought through. When they don't find 'em, they'll be following us."

---

117

"We've got the horses," she said, hopefully, sweeping a hand in their direction.

Conrad shook his head, sadly. "They'll send runners. The horses will die or give out in a couple of days. The runners will catch us in four or five, unless we find the portal first."

Conrad LuPone's prediction was right. One of the horses went lame on the stony ground while Conrad and Lori were still in the mountains. The second collapsed from heat a day into the desert. They were afoot in two days.

They came upon the portal a day later. It came to a stop deep in the desert, about a hundred yards from an established camp of Apep's guard. Conrad and Lori drew to within a quarter mile of the camp and settled.

"The creatures have good noses. But they're nearsighted, and we're down wind," Conrad said.

"I'll never get back," Lori said, tossing her pack to the ground and brushing her long, blond hair back from her face.

"Not this time." Conrad said, shaking his head slowly. Then he raised a hand and wagged his index finger at her, "But don't you give up."

Lori turned to stare across the wasteland to the small, blue light for several minutes. When she turned to face Conrad again, she found he had covered his ragged clothing with a netting of flexible white plates. A belt around his waist held two small boxes covered with switches and buttons. "What's that?"

Conrad looked up, a prideful light filling his eyes. He tapped one of the flexible, white plates with one, gnarled finger. "A trick from my world. But I only have one."

"Looks like badly designed body armor," she said.

"I've got to see a man about my past and his future. I'll have to leave you alone."

Lori felt the blood drain from her face. She reached for and clutched Conrad's sleeve. "You can't do that."

—

"Trust me."

"Do I have a choice?" she asked, releasing her grasp.

"The man is important. Without him, Apep will own us all, I think. But you're important, too. I'll stay, if I don't have no choice."

Lori Hellman watched as Conrad hobbled off toward the encampment of creatures and their captives. Color drained out of him with each step. *He's becoming transparent!* she realized.

Soon she could see the camp fire through him. Two steps further and he was gone.

Lori didn't doubt that Conrad would have remained with her if she had asked. But he seemed convinced he needed to bring back someone from her world. And although everything Conrad had told her was fantastic, how could she doubt her eyes? There were creatures around a fire less than a quarter mile away. And the multicolored lights that crawled in the sky at night told her this was not her world. And if this was not her world, then Conrad had to be telling the truth. She knew she must trust the diminutive man's judgement.

She waited for his return for two hours, then curled up, and went to sleep.

### *PRATTVILLE, OHIO, 1992 PART II*

*Jeremy Wheeler was staring into her eyes, and she into his. "Are you sorry you said yes?" he asked.*

*"Are you sorry you asked?" Lori Hellman said.*

*"You're not getting off that easy. You were remembering something. What?"*

*"I was thinking about Hank Davison," she said.*

*Jeremy's face sagged.*

*"I loved him, Jeremy. Not the way I love you, but I miss him,*

*and I wish he wasn't dead. And don't tell me you haven't thought of Cindy today. I expect you to think of her on this day of all days."*

"I love you," he said.

"I know," Lori said. "Now, let's get married."

LORI HELLMAN:

## Through the Portal II

Conrad LuPone woke Lori Hellman before dawn. He was alone. Disappointment covered him like a shroud. It showed in the way he walked, talked and breathed.

Minutes later one of the large catmen stumbled out of the light, glowing, yellow blood spouting from several bullet wounds across its chest, and fell dead.

Conrad's eyes seemed to light. "The gunman! He'll come by damn. It's for his family. He won't have no choice," he said.

Lori didn't understand. Yet she thought it wasn't important she did.

In the Guard's camp the portal went dim and started to move. One of the creatures roared, and struck out at a chained man. The man fell dead without a sound. A second creature sprang at the first, and they tumbled through the campfire to the screams of the tethered humans.

"Better leave," Conrad said. "The Guard, what's following, will be here soon, and after the fighting's finished, these'll follow the portal. We don't want to be between 'em."

Lori grabbed Conrad by the sleeve as he moved away, and he turned back to her. "Can we outrun them?" she asked.

"'Til the next settling place?" He nodded, then shook his head. "Maybe. If'n we can, you can go back to your world there."

"What about you?" she asked.

---

"I have to follow the portal 'til Jeremy comes through. I said I'd be there when he does."

The name of the man from her dreams struck her hard and burned its way into her mind. Could Conrad's Jeremy be the same man?! No that was too fantastic, she decided. Yet she asked, "Who's this Jeremy?"

Conrad shook his head. "If it were meant you should know, you'd know without the telling I think."

Conrad and Lori had walked for hours. Lori was exhausted, concentrating on her feet so she wouldn't trip over them. She didn't see the runners until Conrad spoke.

"Don't show your fear. Seein' fear puts the hot blood in 'em," he said.

About three-hundred yards to their rear, one catman was circling to their left, a second circled to the right, and two were coming up the middle at them.

"What do I do?"

"Cross your arms. Scowl at 'em. I'll do the talking. They don't speak human, but they understand."

Conrad LuPone crossed his arms, and turned to stare at the two runners who approached up the center. Lori Hellman copied his stance.

---

# PRATTVILLE, OHIO

*September 8, 1990*

Jeremy Wheeler sat on the cot of a cell, in the basement of the Prattville Court House. Two hours had passed since Hank Davison had taken his fingerprints and mug shots and locked him in the small cell. He felt nervous, tense. He had twenty-four days left to enter the portal and do what was needed to close it forever. This cell would eat up untold amounts of that time.

The jingle of keys startled him into awareness just before Hank appeared in the hallway.

For several seconds they stared past the bars into each other's eyes. Neither spoke.

*Here it comes. He's going to accuse me of the murders.*

A combination of puzzlement and revulsion seeped into the features of Hank's weathered face.

---

Hank Davison started to insert a key in the cell lock then drew back. "I have some questions for you."

Jeremy Wheeler stood, and grasped the bars of his cell door. "If it'll get me out of here, I'll tell you my life story."

Hank Davison shook his head. "You're going to be in here longer than you suspect. You're in deep shit."

Jeremy frowned as he considered this, then realized the frown might be considered as some form of admission and forced a smile. "Even murder suspects get out on bail."

Hank paused, fished a cigarette from the pack in his shirt pocket, and lit it with a match struck on the cell bars. He took a deep drag and expelled a cloud of blue smoke in Jeremy's direction, then gazed at Jeremy for several seconds without speaking.

"Sergeant Smith believes you're a psycho. He believes you saw a giant spider."

Jeremy tried to read Hank's eyes. Couldn't. "What do you believe?"

Hank smiled. "Oh, I believe you're crazy all right. But a smart kind of crazy. I don't believe you shot up that bathroom because you hallucinated a giant spider. I believe you shot up that bathroom, because you want people to think you're a psycho, that you're not responsible."

Hank paused, and Jeremy knew, from the look in Hank's eyes, that the man was waiting for a reply. He remained silent.

"In a few minutes we're going to go upstairs, and I'm going to read you your rights. I'm going to ask you for a statement concerning the murders. I'll want to know your whereabouts when each occurred. You can continue this insane act, if you want. Whether you do or don't, I'm going to nail you if you murdered those people. I'm going to nail you for the people you murdered and for the lives you ruined. I'm going to nail you for all the blood, sweat, and tears my men and I put into catching you. But most of all, I'm going to nail you for Lori Hellman. She was the best thing that ever happened to me, and if you murdered her, then, God have mercy on you. I won't.

"You may think you're playing with a bunch of small town hicks, but you may just find the hicks aren't as dumb as you think."

Jeremy continued eye contact with Hank. The man's eyes told Jeremy there would be no reasoning with him. "So you're going to frame me to clear your books. Is that it?"

Hank's face went stony. His eyes, dull-gray orbs, locked with Jeremy's. He unlocked the door and slid it open, and for an instant, Jeremy expected the man to strike out at him.

"Come with me," Hank Davison said.

That night, Hank Davison sat stroking Rudy and thinking of his interrogation of Jeremy Wheeler. Jeremy should have requested a lawyer. He hadn't and the questioning had not gone well for him. His details were sketchy. He had a lot of trouble with his dates, and there seemed to be a low heat in him throughout the questioning. In all, Jeremy appeared to be holding things back. Innocent men didn't hold back.

Jeremy was either an insane murderer or a clever murderer. It didn't much matter which. An insanity plea was just another way of saying, "I'm guilty, and I'm going to get away with it." Hank felt no sympathy for the murderer either way.

He would not allow the sick creature who had turned Lori into dog scraps to escape punishment. Today he had questioned Jeremy. Tomorrow he would question Jeremy Wheeler's wife and stepdaughters. If tomorrow went like today, if the evidence proved Jeremy guilty, then, Hank had decided, he would take care of matters. The courts were too risky, too sympathetic to the wrong people.

When Cindy Wheeler arrived at the Prattville jail that afternoon, Hank Davison refused to allow her to talk with

Jeremy. He told her that visiting hours were over. She believed there was more to it than that, but she didn't know what.

Jeremy hadn't seen a judge yet. Bail was not set. So she called her lawyer and went home to wait, think, worry.

Sleep was hard to find. What little sleep she could find rebuked her with nightmares. Apep played a prominent role in these dreams, as he had before. However, this time there were two new additions to the cast, a young boy in search of his mother and a small, blond-haired woman with a faint scar on her chin.

# PRATTVILLE, OHIO

*9:25 A. M., September 9, 1990*

Frank Dinsio or Francis, as his closest friends called him, tilted his head to the left burying the phone handset between head and shoulder as he poured himself a second cup of cappuccino. Then he half lumbered, half minced his way to the breakfast nook next to the kitchen door and parked his five-foot two-inch, three-hundred pound body onto a wrought-iron chair.

Three years earlier, Francis had been slim and slick, an older man looking for love. He was a catcher even then, but that hadn't bothered him so much as the knowledge that he was on the downhill slide, the hunter, not the hunted. Since then he had slicked the slide with food—a coward's suicide—to ease the loneliness. "Twinkies never say never," some-

---

one had once told him, and whomever that someone was—he couldn't remember just now—was right.

"Frank, your life is no different from the next whore down the block," Donna Bealer said from the other end of the phone line. Francis smiled. He liked Donna. Her advice could burn at times, but it never needed interpretation. She had become his heterosexual mentor over the past three years. In their free time they whiled away the hours talking in depth of their hopes, doubts, fears, and sexual relationships. In some ways, the distance their sexual orientations placed between them made self revelation less threatening. There was no competition or sexual attraction to counter, yet, there was a similarity in their lives.

"Sounds like the kettle calling—"

The double click of call-waiting sounded over the line.

"Whoops! Going to have to put you on hold," Donna said.

Francis frowned. "Yeah, and if it's *Gary*, you'll never come back again," he replied in his gravel rough, grandmother's voice. "I'll just sit here *rotting away* with my ear glued to this damn phone,"

"Well, you know what they say," Donna said, "all's fair in love 'n war."

"Bitch!" Francis drawled, producing his finest stereotyped affectation of the gay male voice, as the click sounded on the other end of the line.

Francis sipped his cappuccino, held the phone for two minutes, took another sip of the fast cooling liquid, then frowned as his stomach grumbled.

For a second he believed he heard the rustle of cellophane wrappers from beneath the floor. His thoughts turned to the basement, its thick stone walls, cool dirt floor, and its storage shelves, filled with chocolate marshmallow cookies and all other forms of goodies. Again came the whispered rustle of cellophane, and this time, imagined or not, it was too much.

Laying the handset on the glass-topped table, Francis grunted to a stand and waddled to the basement door. There would be enough time, he believed, to go to the basement and perhaps to even fix a snack before Donna remembered him and came back on line. *If not, then she can go on hold for a while.* He smiled at the thought, then drawled, "Bitch!" Yet, the lascivious tidbits of conversation which he hoped to extract from Donna once she did come back on the line spurred his descent of the worn, wooden stairs to the twilight shrouded landing. There he threw the light switch. The basement light flashed brilliantly, then everything went dim again.

"Damn! One more thing to put on my *to-do* list," he said to himself.

He hated the murky world the basement presented without its single light. For a twinkle in time, he considered returning to the kitchen for a flashlight, but decided to forgo that crutch.

"Buck up dear, and be a man," he chortled to himself. "No big bad men down here ... Too bad, too! Oh, hurt me big boy!"

As he descended, he found the basement quiet, save his foot falls and the protesting squeak of the wooden stairs. Once he reached the loose earth of the basement floor, even the sound of his foot falls were muffled.

At the foot of the stairs the storage shelves on the opposite side of the room were dimly visible in the light from the single basement window.

Half way across the room Francis noticed a draft. He squinted, his concentrated gaze searching the gloom in the direction from which the breeze came. Then his jaw came unhinged as he realized the basement window had not only been smashed, but torn from its station. Frame and glass littered the dirt floor.

"Damn vandals!" He grumbled to himself. He looked to the shelves veiled by the twilight of the basement. *I hope they weren't after my goodies.* "Looks like it's time to call the glass block people. Wonder how much *that* will cost? My day is fast turning to shit."

Grunting and panting, he stood the window frame on-edge and examined it. The glass was gone, the frame splintered. A ball formed in his stomach, and his hunger left him as the recent murders in his town came to mind. *Anyone could have entered the house through the window.*

His eyes scanned the room. In the darker recesses a large shadow seemed to turn languidly in his direction.

Francis took a step back. The hair stood on his neck. Then his mind said, *No, I didn't see that. It was just a trick of the dark.* But just as his muscles started to loosen, the shadow's movement gained strength. Suddenly, it rushed him, consuming the ground between them in large bites. It was broad, black and low to the ground.

Eyes wide, mouth agape, Francis watched as a cigar-shaped creature rolled up to him. Two, thin, black rods flipped out to touch his hand. A loud crunch filled his ears. Barbs of liquid fire climbed his arm. The window frame clattered to the floor, loose earth billowing from beneath it.

Francis raised his arm, and stared at it in disbelief. His hand was gone. Blood drooled down the stump.

"Oh, my God!" he screamed. He spun a little circle, unable to tear his eyes from the stump. "Oh, my God!"

His mind reeled, comprehending nothing but the black horror of his mutilation. Blood pounded in his temples, filling his ears with the rasping bump-bump of his heart.

Francis spun the little circle twice, then tumbled to the floor. His right foot and part of his calf were gone. "Oh, my God! Oh, my God!" he repeated. It was all he could think to say.

In terror, he dug at the loose earth, dragging himself over

———

129

the floor toward the stairs. Away from the creature. Away from the crunching sounds. His hand heaped dirt into small piles. It flung it in plumes at the creature, which now stalked him at a leisurely pace.

Francis dragged his bulbous body toward the stairwell. Six, four, two feet away. Then the shadow returned for his other leg. Pain knifed through him. His leg was gone from the knee down.

"No! No! No!"

Tears wet his face. Spittle slicked his chin. He rolled to his back and threw fistfuls of dirt, spitting and screaming. Stay away! Stay away!" His hand and seeping stumps flailed the air.

But the creature ignored his protests. The ever seeking rods flipped to and fro, moving up his body, tasting, smelling, seeking his remaining hand. Again there was the sickening crunch.

When the creature retreated, Francis found himself on his back, defenseless, in the basement, where the earth grew sticky with blood.

Whimpering, Francis Dinsio listened to the munching . . . and waited.

# PRATTVILLE, OHIO

*9:57 A. M., September 9, 1990*

Cindy Wheeler was surprised to hear Hank Davison's voice when she answered the phone. She had expected Jon Johansson, their lawyer, or perhaps Jeremy, but she had not considered the possibility that Police Chief Hank Davison would call. "Has something happened to Jeremy?" she asked, clutching the phone so tight that her knuckles went white.

"No. No, nothing like that," the voice from the other end of the line said. I'm calling because I need to question you and your daughters."

Cindy eased onto a dinette chair, and forced her grip on the phone to loosen. "Question us? Why in the world would you want to question us?"

"It has to do with the murders. I questioned your husband yesterday. I need to question you and your daughters to clear up a few points."

Cindy's stomach tightened. "The murders! You're not suggesting that Jeremy—"

"He's not charged with *that* yet, only the gun charges are pending now. The murder charges will depend on your answers."

"That's the craziest suggestion I've ever heard! I—" She realized her hand was once again gripping the phone tightly and was at once happy for this involuntary action, because suddenly, she realized she wanted to throw it as far as she could.

"I understand your feelings. But Jeremy had opportunity. He was carrying a concealed gun when he was arrested yesterday. That gives him a means."

"Most anyone could have means and opportunity. What about motive? Why would Jeremy do such a thing?"

"Insanity," he said. "I'm not looking for a normal man, Ms. Wheeler. The man I'm looking for, makes dog food of people."

His words rolled over her. She had questioned Jeremy's sanity, but not in this way. Jeremy couldn't do such a thing.

"You're wrong," Cindy said, flatly.

"We'll see. The story your husband told me, yesterday, left no doubt in my mind that he has some serious problems. Whether those problems are serious enough to have caused him to murder eight people will take a psychiatrist to determine. I just—"

"What story?"

"We can talk about that when you're here. It's ten o'clock now. Can we meet at eleven this morning?"

"I think. . . . Yes, I can be there."

"Fine. Then you can meet me in my office at eleven this morning. I'll see you then. Good-bye."

When Hank Davison hung up, Cindy did throw the handset. It tore loose from the base and struck the wall before skidding along the floor to be lost under the sofa, in the living room.

For the next half hour, Cindy sat puzzling and fuming over the brief conversation with Hank Davison. She wished she knew what she would be walking into at eleven. It was obvious to her that Chief Davison was playing his cards close to the chest. That made her nervous.

What was he planning?

# MARK SCOTT AND HIS MOTHER

*In the Grasslands; Day 1*

That first day, Mark Scott and his mother walked in the chest high grass until Mark found he could no longer put one foot in front of the other. And when he tried, despite his body's protest, to make that next step his leg shook from beneath him, and he dropped wearily to the ground.

His mother stooped beside him. "You rest," she said. "I'll pull some grass for a bed. We can sleep here."

Mark looked at his mother with amazement, half realizing that his mouth was agape and too tired to care. During that day his opinion of his mother, and of women in general, had grown. She was older, and he was in, what he thought, was very good condition, the equivalent of a man. Yet, on

---

134

this long trek, his mother had not complained or faltered once, and now that he had collapsed in exhaustion, his mother was *taking care of him!*

"We'll wallow it down," Mark said.

His mother raised an eyebrow, and tilted her head to gaze at him quizzically.

"Like deer wallow in for the night. We've left a trail, but that couldn't be helped, and any animal could have made that trail. But if we pull grass—"

"It would give us away," she finished for him. She smiled and eased to a sitting position. "You must have learned that from your father."

Mark nodded. "On one of the hunting trips," he said. He turned his gaze from his mother's blue eyes across the wide expanse of grass, following the small dark trail they had made through it. In the distance, about half way to the horizon, he thought he could see a widening and a branching of that trail.

"I think we should only rest here for a short time," he said.

135

# PRATTVILLE, OHIO

*10:02 A. M., September 9, 1990*

Hank Davison was finishing his good-byes in the call to Cindy Wheeler when a second light lit on his phone. While Cindy's voice had been apprehensive and cautious, the new voice was agitated, concerned.

"I need help. I was talking to a friend on the phone, and he went away and didn't come back. I didn't know who else to call."

It sounded like another domestic call. Hank picked up a pen, and started to doodle small bugs along the edge of his desk pad. "What's your name?" Hank asked.

"Donna Bealer."

Hank scrawled the name above one of his doodled bugs. "When did this happen?"

---

"I just hung up the phone, but I waited on the line for half an hour."

"This person, is he an adult?"

"Yes, but what's that got to—"

Hank began to flip the pen end to end. "Were you arguing? Has he done anything like this before?"

"We're good friends. He'd never just go away and leave his phone off the hook. I've known him for three years. He's never done anything like this.

"Why all the questions? I just need someone to go over to his house."

"We've been getting a lot of domestic calls lately. Look, Ms. Bealer, we're short staffed, and . . . well, you've heard of the murders. . . . I don't want to send an officer out just to find that your boyfriend doesn't want to talk to you. If that's the problem—"

"It's not." Now Donna Bealer's voice was urgent in its insistency.

"You're sure?"

"It's *not!*"

Hank sighed. "I'll have an officer check out your friend. If you'll give me your number, we'll get back to you."

Hank knew he had upset the woman on the other end of the line, but she would have to live with it. Cindy Wheeler was due in his office at eleven. He needed to prepare his questions. He also needed to find a volunteer to man the phones and radio while he did the questioning. His dispatcher, Doris Ricker, was still on vacation. Her replacement had been one of the early victims. Finding even a temporary replacement in the short time remaining would not be easy.

When Charlie Hascomb received the "missing person" call, he was sitting in his cruiser in an abandoned drive-through bank, on State 57 at the edge of town. He was waiting for some unwary motorist to help fill his moving violation quota for the month. He always felt a little less clean after a week of making quotas, and was pleased to be interrupted.

"Car five, check the residence at 100 Mineral Springs Street for a Francis Dinsio. He is reported to have gone missing during a phone conversation. Possible illness, injury or foul play is suspected. Be on your toes." The voice on the radio was Hank's.

Charlie lifted the handset, depressed the lever and spoke, "This is car five, I'm on my way. By the way, Hank, how is the questioning going with that Wheeler guy?"

"Charlie, are you sure you graduated from the police academy? How many times do I have to tell you about these damn . . . these radios?"

"Sorry Chief," Charlie said, feeling the heat rise in his cheeks. He didn't try to say more.

*Why did I say that? Am I stupid?* It wasn't the first time the question had occurred to him in the past weeks, and because the thought came to him so often, it worried him. He shook his head in reply to the thought. *The academy doesn't graduate stupid people. I finished last, but I'm not stupid. I'm just not as quick to catch on, that's all.*

Five minutes later, Charlie parked his cruiser in front of a rose colored, two-story, Victorian home that dripped with hot pink gingerbread. The colors made his eyes hurt. He had seen the house often on his rounds, and had wondered what kind of person would live here and if pink/rose color blindness was possible.

*If he's alive, it's because his neighbors haven't gotten to him.*

A steep slate roof overhung an L-shaped porch that half circled the house. There were two large windows on the front, at ground level. Sheer curtains covered one. A large potted tree, one of many on the porch, stood in front of the other window.

Charlie's gaze slid quickly over the house, examining it

for anything out of the ordinary. Seeing nothing odd, he exited the cruiser carrying his clip board and hat. He placed the hat on his head as he continued to scan the house. A van stood in the garage.

He picked up the handset. "This is car five. I'm investigating the missing person at 100 Mineral Springs." He tossed the handset to the seat, not wanting to talk to Hank Davison again, and approached the house.

The door bell was hand cranked. He cranked the key, listening to the tinny brattle of the bell rise and die, rise and die. No one answered.

The windows, off the porch, looked in on the dining and living rooms. Through the windows he could see neat, feminine rooms. Considering the garish parody of femininity in the house's color, he thought the tasteful interior odd.

Charlie circled the house, checking each window in turn. At the rear of the house, he found a broken basement window near the small back porch. The opening was behind a crushed, flowering bush.

He knelt in the mulch beside the window and peered into the dark basement. A strange odor, much like a mixture of dry and cheap, canned, dog foods, wafted up from the cool darkness. His stomach churned and gnawed at the odor, and his throat grew tight trying to block further ingress.

He shined his flashlight into the darkness. From his position, he could see a broken window frame on the floor. About the center of the basement, a large circle of the dirt floor appeared muddied.

Standing, he removed the portable radio from his belt and pressed the call button. "This is car five. I'm investigating a possible breaking and entering at my destination." The radio squawked with the release of the button. He paused for half a minute. There was no reply. "Damn! Hank where are you?" he said. He pressed the button again. "Hank, do you copy?" Again, there was no reply.

A strange feeling washed over him. There was something different about this call. It was as if there was no one on the other end. He had not felt that way before. Whether Hank had answered or not, Charlie had always "felt" him on the other end of his calls. It was a secure feeling, one of anticipation. That feeling deserted him now.

He considered calling for backup and simply waiting until it arrived. It would be the prudent thing to do. It also would bring out the rubberneckers, and he still stung from the reprimand Hank had given him at the Park, in mid-August. He shook his head. He could handle this.

He climbed the three stairs to the small back porch, propped his clipboard against the porch wall, and drew his revolver. He positioned himself with his back against the wall and tried the door. The latch clicked. The door swung into the kitchen and clacked against a table. Charlie looked past the door to the adjoining room, then focused on the reflection in the upper glass panel of the door. He saw nothing except a very neat and very feminine room. He eased around the doorjamb, into the room.

A single, pink rose in a cut crystal, bud vase served as a centerpiece for the small, glass-topped, breakfast table against which the door had knocked. The phone handset lay on the table. A half-filled cup of coffee sat in a saucer next to it. One chair sat back from the table, as if someone intended to return to it soon.

Charlie tested the coffee with his finger. It was cool. He surveyed the room. Other than the coffee cup and the one chair pushed back from the table, the room looked like the set of a television commercial. Nothing else was out of place. No dirty dishes, no food sitting out. There wasn't even a wrinkled dish towel on the counter.

The hair stood on his neck. No one as neat as the owner of this house would leave their phone off the hook and a dirty coffee cup on the table. And there was the matter of the van in the garage.

He examined the room once more. The basement door was ajar. He noted the unpleasant odor he had smelled at the window. However, here a strong, lilac fragrance cut its pungency. In some way, the lilac overlay made the stink more vile. It reminded him of someone trying to hide the smell of an unwashed body with cologne. The resulting stench was more noticeable, more out of place.

He removed the radio from his belt, and pressed the call button. "Car five to base. Hank, do you copy?" The radio squawked as he released the button. There was still no answer.

He tiptoed to the basement door, and peered down the stairwell into the darkness. The light switch for the basement was in the "on" position.

*Well, that's just fucking wonderful. No lights and no radio contact.*

A sound, a sort of muffled, slithering thump, came from the basement. Charlie froze. His grip tightened on the revolver. He listened for the sound to repeat for one minute, two. Then, as he was deciding the sound had meant nothing, it came again. This time, he decided, it was more a grinding crunch. It rode over him like finger nails on a chalkboard. He didn't recognize the sound, but he knew it signaled danger.

The worn, wooden stairs marked Charlie Hascomb's descent with squeaks and groans. At the landing, he shined the beam of a large, black flashlight down the stair, across the dirt floor, to the wall on the opposite side of the basement. Nothing was out of place, but a queasiness oozed through him.

On the right side of the stairwell, the wall ended five steps from the basement floor. He would have cover until he

141

passed that step. But there would be nowhere to run if some-one stepped to the end of the stairwell and started shooting.

He rolled the flashlight's spot over the earthen floor one more time, then started his descent.

The noisome odor grew as the darkness of the basement swallowed him. The uneasy feeling in the pit of his stomach increased.

Charlie took a deep breath. He ran his tongue across his lips. Then he stepped to the fifth step, and shined his light into the gloom. The muzzle of his handgun followed the beam.

Shelves lined two walls from ceiling to floor. Thousands of items lined the upper five shelves. Signs lettered in a bold, neat script, marked the items. The three lowest shelves were spilled onto the floor. The packages were either smashed, torn or crushed.

From his right came a click, a thump. He wheeled on the sound, and swung the flashlight's beam down the wall.

"Hold it right there," his voice boomed. His finger tight-ened on the trigger. The hammer came to half-cock. He squinted, anticipating the flash of the gun. The beam of the flashlight settled on a white cabinet style freezer. It emitted a low grinding sound followed by a hum.

"Jesus!" A cold sweat broke on his upper lip. His breath came hard, rasping. Then his legs went out from under him, and he crashed to the dirt floor.

Cindy Wheeler was steamed. Hank Davison's question-ing of her had gone on for what seemed a long time, and this rigid man who faced her, continued to demand the impos-sible.

Looking at his clipboard, shaking his head slowly, Hank Davison said, "Neither you nor your daughters have been very successful in establishing Mr. Wheeler's whereabouts during the murders. You're his alibi. If you can't give me more detailed information than you have, I'll have to turn Mr. Wheeler over to the District Attorney."

Cindy Wheeler slapped the table between them with the palm of her hand. The smack resounded much louder than she had expected, and she flinched. "I can't remember what we did every night. That's ridiculous. Can you remember what you were doing on August seventeenth?"

Face grim, Hank Davison shook his head. "No, but I'm not under investigation for murder, either."

Her hand rolled into a fist, and she forced it to release. "It's innocent until proven guilty, Chief Davison, not the other way around," she reminded him.

He did not respond. Cindy Wheeler gritted her teeth. She was mad, and oddly, once she had subdued her fist, instead of wanting to strike out at him, she wanted to spit on this man. She didn't. It would gain her nothing, and might hurt Jeremy.

"We spend evenings watching television, reading, doing small projects. Jeremy walks most evenings, but he doesn't walk in the rain, unless it rains a lot, and he has no choice. It rained a lot the last half of August. He walked some days, and he didn't others, but he was never gone more than two hours at a time."

Hank Davison scooted forward in his seat and his gaze locked with hers. "How do you know that?"

"Because he walks either five or ten miles, and it takes him one hour to walk five miles. His routine didn't change. I would have noticed. I've been worried about his safety since the murders started."

Hank Davison looked at his clipboard, flipped back and forth between the two pages there. Then his gaze came back to her. "Were there times when his routine did change?"

She sighed, and leaned back in her chair. "This past week. He's been acting strange. He's been out more than usual. I've tried to get him to stop walking because of the murders.

———

143

He wasn't frightened. He wouldn't stop. He said he had to go. But there weren't any murders then."

Hank Davison's eyes lit, and now, *his* hand hammered the table. "We had one. We had the librarian, Judith LuPone. The one murder that didn't fit the pattern. We had that one, and based on Jeremy's statements, he was fighting a big, invisible catman exactly where we found the body."

# THROUGH THE PORTAL:

*Conrad and Lori Captured*

In seconds the approaching catmen closed the three-hun dred yards of desert which separated them from their stoic, stone-faced prey: Conrad LuPone and Lori Hellman.

Lori waited, ready to follow Conrad's lead. He knew these creatures, this land, and in spite of his size, he had, thus far, shown himself to be formidable, fearless.

When the lead catman was within two yards, within strik- ing distance, it stopped, and Conrad, rag shrouded arms crossed, stained, white beard blowing in the breeze, raised his cold, yellow eyes to meet the creature's gaze.

---

Conrad said, "Apep sent. . . ." The words seemed to freeze in Conrad LuPone's throat so suddenly that Lori turned to stare at first at his face, frozen in wide eyed terror, mouth agape, and then, following his gaze, at the catman.

Initially she saw only the obvious: a huge, furry beast, fearfully muscled and horribly armed with two-inch fangs and tiger-clawed fingers. Then she saw his eyes, and felt her strength drain down her legs to be lost in the dry, desert sand. The creature's eyes swirled with billions of points of light, two portals, yes, yet she sensed these portals were not to the heavens, but to hell. Then the creature smiled, and she was sure she had been right about the portals in those eyes.

# PRATTVILLE, OHIO

*11:50 A. M., September 9, 1990*

A knock at the door of the examining room broke Hank Davison's concentration. His muscles tightened, teeth gritted. He wheeled on the door, and jerked it open, his mind blank with anger at the interruption, which may have cost him any advantage he had gained over this stubborn woman, Cindy Wheeler.

"What the. . . ." The words died in his throat. At the door stood a wide-eyed, teenaged girl, Samantha Morgan, Cindy's daughter. Her face was ashen.

Samantha took a step back at his truncated growl. "I—I think you better come," she said.

"What's wrong?" he said.

"Honey?" Cindy said, hurrying to the door.

Tears were in the girl's eyes now. "Someone's in trouble.

---

147

Charlie. He's been calling for help on the radio. No one answers." She waved her hands, palms up with fingers held wide, rigid, in cadence with her words.

Hank stiffened. He had failed to have someone cover the radio. *If Charlie's in trouble, it's my fault.*

He dashed down the hall to the dispatch office, his sense of urgency building.

He flicked the call switch on the dispatcher's radio.

"Charlie, this is dispatch, do you copy?" He waited for a count of five and repeated the call. There was nothing but dead air, static.

He turned to Samantha Morgan. "Can you tell me what Charlie said?"

Again she wagged her hands at him. "I don't remem—"

"This is important." There was bite in his voice. He paused then started again. "Just take your time, and tell me as much as you can remember. It doesn't have to be word-for-word."

Sam's brow furrowed. She didn't say anything for several seconds, clearly trying to remember.

"He said he was in the basement on Mineral Springs Street. He needed backup. Oficer down. He said a name. Francis Din . . . Dinsio, I think."

Hank turned to the file cabinet and pulled open the top drawer. He removed a gun belt from the drawer and strapped it around his waist.

"I think the house number was one-hundred?" A tear rolled down Sam's cheek. "He called three times. I thought someone would . . . would answer him."

Cindy put an arm around Sam's shoulder and looked into her eyes. "It's not your fault," she said.

"Of course not," Hank said. "It's mine. Only mine."

Hank rushed Cindy and her daughters out of the office. He left them standing in the hall, and ran for his car.

—

Charlie Hascomb's patrol car was on the street in front the house Hank Davison had often thought of as a French Quarter bordello.

Hank pulled his cruiser in behind it, and tried to raise Charlie on the radio again. Charlie didn't answer.

Hank removed his riot gun from the cruiser's rack, and stepped to the street. Muscles tense, hunched low, ready to dive for cover, he crossed the small yard, and clambered onto the porch. In seconds his back was to the house-wall with the front door inches to his right.

The door rattled in its frame as he pounded it with the side of his fist.

"Police! Open up."

He waited to the count of ten, then repeated the demand. No one answered. At the end of his second count of ten, he heaved a sigh.

Hank stepped in front of the door and kicked. The old latch shattered from the doorjamb. It rattled across the floor. The door thudded against the wall. He leveled the shotgun on an empty room.

". . . in the basement. I'm in the basement!" Charlie Hascomb bellowed.

A sigh of relief shuddered its way up Hank's innards and out into the still air. Charlie was alive.

"Be careful. *It's* down here. It'll *get* you, too!"

*IT?* So Charlie wasn't okay. But *it?* That didn't make sense.

Trying to be a shadow, Hank slid around the doorjamb of the first door to his right. He gave the room a scan, then moved to the next, looking for the basement door and danger at the same time.

The search was taking too long. Charlie screamed again. Hank's muscles bunched, everything trying to move two directions at the same time and freezing in the process. He wished he could scream back, ask Charlie what "it" was, or tell him to shut up. But, he didn't want to give away his position. He didn't want anyone behind him when he went into the basement.

In the kitchen he found the basement door standing open. He leveled the shotgun on the stairwell and stepped onto it. The air was heavy with the metallic smell of blood, death. His stomach hitched.

His boot thumped on the bare wood of the first stair, sounding like the fall of a woodsman's ax. The step squealed like a pig. He felt a bead of sweat break loose from his temple and roll down his cheek. There would be no slipping into this basement.

Sucking in a deep breath, he steeled himself, and clamored down the stairs until the wall, separating the stairs from the rest, ended. He stared into the dark basement at the end of the stair, and found there was more light on the stairs than anywhere else. He would be on stage, in the spotlight when he took those last five steps.

"For God's sake, be careful. *It* will get you!" Charlie screamed, again. His voice was high pitched. He sounded hysterical. Maybe crazy.

Charlie screamed, "*I'll* get *you!* I'll knock your God damned *head* off!"

Hank heard something pound against the other side of the wall in a quick whap-whap-whap. He crouched on the stair, bringing the shotgun to bear on the foot of the stairwell. When no one appeared, he moved to the partition and peeked around it, into the basement.

Charlie was on top and hanging over the edge of storage shelves which stood against the opposite wall. Light from the basement window lit his face. His eyes were wild. He had his belt off, and was using it to tourniquet his left leg. Nothing remained of the leg from mid-shin down. He held the belt with one hand and flung can goods across the room, under the stairs, with the other.

Hank turned and started down the stairs.

———

"Stop! *It*'ll get you through the stairs."

Hank stopped and shined his flashlight down the stairs. On the second step Charlie's boot sat upright in a puddle of blood. Charlie Hascomb's lower leg stuck out of it. Hank's gorge rose to his throat. He swallowed hard, forcing it back down. It looked like someone had gone after Charlie with a chain saw. And whoever maimed Charlie was waiting under the stairs. He backed up a step, and trained the shotgun on the stair in front of him.

"This is Police Chief Hank Davison. The house is sur-rounded. Move into the room with your hands up, or I'll shoot through the stairs." He waited to a count of ten. There was no answer.

Hank was standing on step five. He touched the riot gun's barrel to the center of the next step down, and pulled the trigger. The gun recoiled, kicking him hard on the inner thigh with the stock. The barrel flash lit the room like a camera's strobe. A high-pitched hiss filled the room. Boards cracked and popped like fireworks. Nails screamed their way from wooden graves, years old. The stairway rocked, and as Hank felt himself loose balance, it dropped from beneath him.

Hank dropped his flashlight and riot gun to grab for the railing. He missed. He fell. The edges of the stairs cut into his back, legs, head. Sparks sprayed across an ebony back-drop in his brain.

His vision cleared. He shook off the fuzz. To his left the flashlight's beam cut an eerie tunnel through the dust stirred by the stair's collapse. Hank drew his revolver, and grabbed the flashlight from the floor.

From his right came the *plonk, plonk, plonk* of Charlie's canned-good missiles. Hank rolled the flashlight's beam to-ward the sound. The beam stopped on the large, black crea-ture Charlie called "IT." IT was two-feet high and more than five-feet long. IT's cigar-shaped body was a lustrous black and segmented. The front segment was a head with large pinch-

151

ers that scissored like animated, hedge clippers. Two, long, black antennas flipped about, feeling the air. And all of IT was headed for Hank!

Hank's jaw dropped. Jeremy Wheeler's story of the giant spider flashed through his mind. It was still crazy. *This can't be happening.*

In spite of the thought, his gun came up, and he fired three quick rounds. IT continued to come, its hedge-clipper jaws scissoring in and out. Hank scrambled for the shelves. He was on top in seconds.

IT was inches behind him, climbing. The shelves rocked with the creature's impact. Charlie was screaming. Hank couldn't concentrate. Canned missiles whizzed past him. They plonked off IT's chitinous covering. IT's beak moved toward Hank. The large pinchers scissored in and out, seeking his flesh. Hank felt like his head was going to explode. He turned, stuck his revolver in IT's beak and pulled the trigger three times.

There was a wet, sucking feeling on his hand. He pulled back. The gun was gone. Half of his hand, all but his thumb and trigger finger, was gone!

Hank gazed at his ruined hand in disbelief. Crazily, there was no pain yet. Tears welled up in his eyes. A scream bubbled up, and stuck in his throat.

Charlie was screaming something. Hank could hear the noise, not the words. Then pain ripped through his shin and tore his thoughts from his hand. A can of corn spun on its rim, and dropped from the shelf.

"IT's down. Get the riot gun," Charlie yelled.

Hank looked down. IT was on its back. All of the creature's legs waved at the ceiling. The flashlight's beam framed IT in an atmosphere roiled with dust, a child's nightmare, all murky and crawling. Even the air seemed to crawl. Hank shuddered. Then he swallowed his fear, and tore himself from the shelves.

—

He was on top of the flashlight before he looked back. The creature was still waving most of its legs in the air, but two legs were hooked onto the shelves. IT's obscene, pinchers scissored in and out. Two wings hung on the creature's back, useless, broken at their juncture where the riot gun's slug had struck. Yet IT was pulling itself over, trying to right itself!

Hank stood staring at IT, his mind blanked. Sharp pain erupted in his ribs. A can of peas dropped at his foot.

"Find the fuckin' gun!" Charlie Hascomb demanded.

Hank felt himself come to life once more. He swung the light around, rolling the beam over the stairs and up and down on the dirt floor, searching.

Charlie was yelling again. Hank shined the light back to see the creature on its side, balanced against the shelves. The legs on the side against the floor were shoveling the dirt back, digging into the floor. The legs on the top clung to the shelves.

Hank wouldn't have much time. He hesitated for blink in time, thinking he should run before the creature could right itself. Then light reflected off the stock of the riot gun. It was sticking up from between the stairs and the wall.

"IT's coming!" Charlie screamed.

Hank looked around just in time to see IT flop to its stomach. Dust mushroomed. IT spun around and without hesitation headed for him.

Hank's eyes locked on the creature's beak. It scissored in and out. *I want your leg*, the beak seemed to say.

Hank dropped the flashlight, and grabbed the gun's stock. He prayed the dirt hadn't jammed the action, that he had enough time. He leveled the shotgun and jacked the pump. IT was on him. IT's beak was at his leg.

Hank pulled the trigger. The beak disappeared. Pain shot up Hank's arm. The room rolled inside his head, came back in focus.

—

153

IT ran a circle, and started for him again. The hedge clipper jaws were gone, but IT was still deadly.

Hank jacked the pump.

# CONRAD AND LORI
# CAPTURED II

Lori Hellman fought the creature's compelling eyes, portals to hell. Yet with all her will focused on that task, she still felt herself drawn to them. The creature's smile grew huge, dangerous.

Then with a voice echoing as if from some cavern, the creature said, "Conrad LuPone, did you think you could do anything in my world without my knowledge?"

Lori Hellman forced her gaze from the creature's eyes to the face of Conrad LuPone. It appeared to sag, muscles going slack in resignation, surrender. Then something amazing happened: The old man's yellow eyes actually appeared to twinkle, and he smiled at the creature. "You're too late Apep. You've caught me, yes, that's true enough. But I've done my job, and whether I be dead or alive will make no difference to *your* end."

Reluctantly, afraid to see the creature's eyes again, but

---

155

also afraid to not do so, Lori turned her gaze, once more, to the creature's face. It appeared to have actually been stunned by Conrad's words. Then the creature replied, "Since you've finished your work here, *motherless-son*, all that remains is to see how well you die."

*Motherless-son?* Lori's mind questioned. *What can that mean?*

The creature turned to the other three who had now encircled Lori and Conrad. "Bring them to me," he growled. And as those last words were spoken, Lori saw the swirling lights flash once, and then they were gone from the creature's eyes.

The creature, whose eyes were now the slitted, yellow eyes of a cat, growled something unintelligible to the other three.

"What did he mean by motherless—"

"Follow the one what spoke," Conrad said, gesturing with his left hand to the creature they faced.

Once more Lori settled her gaze on the little man. The sparkle had left his eyes, and now, he just appeared tired.

"He won't speak again. Can't, now that Apep left him. These creatures are to bring us to Apep at his palace, and bring us they will. But keep your eyes open. When we get into the mountains, there will be opportunity to slip away. If one comes, use it."

Lori felt a wave of hopelessness wash over her. In her world she felt confident she could handle any situation, but this world and its ways were new to her. She had never had the need or the opportunity to *rough it, go rustic* or whatever people called living in the wild. Now there was no time to learn. And from what she had seen of this world thus far, there was nothing else. "But where would I go? What would I do?" she asked.

Conrad stared at her through narrowed eyes, then cocked his left eyebrow at her. "Find the city of Parabellum," he said. "They could use such as you, and they protect their own." He nodded firmly. "Don't you fear. You ain't been this far in before, but you've been here . . . with *your* Jeremy . . . "

The name flowed over her like warm honey, closing off her breath. This little man knew the Jeremy from her dreams. But how could that be? What could it mean? And what did Conrad mean when he said ". . . you've been here?" *She* had *not* been *here* before. But even as her mind denied his statement, she knew he was right.

"And you both acquitted yourselves well and gave all you had to give," Conrad LuPone finished.

They slept during the day and traveled at a trot, sometimes at a hard run, for two nights. Through it all, Conrad LuPone had held up well for a diminutive, old man with one leg shorter than the other, and Lori Hellman had been surprised at her own stamina throughout this ordeal.

It was early on the third night that they came across a caravan driven by more of the catmen. These new creatures drove twenty-five humans—chained, whipped, dressed in tatters—but, to Lori's surprise, she could still see the spark of defiance in every eye.

Breathing easily despite the miles they had run this night, Lori watched Conrad as he scanned the ragged humans who were daisy-chained ankle to ankle and wrist to wrist in a long line. "They're from your world," he said. "Brought for the vats. Brought to feed Apep's need for power."

"I don't understand," Lori replied.

Conrad shook his head, sadly. "Apep stole all the spunk from this world. Sucked the human essence, the spirit from those what had it and fed his needs, his life, and the lives of those what support him. That's why he's alive after all these centuries. He can take what he needs out of bodies like these and feed on it."

Conrad's words, icy needles in a December wind, blew through her, and Lori shuddered. The thought—unlimited life for this Apep and his followers, sucked from the rightful owner to feed that need—was disgusting to her. Hesitantly, knowing she didn't really want to hear the answer, she asked, "What happens to the people?"

Conrad's brow furrowed, and like a mongrel dog, he showed teeth in his incredible scowl. "You'll see the leavin's. It ain't a pretty sight. Piles 'um up like cordwood, along the road to his palace. Ain't respectful . . . ain't civilized."

Not wanting to think more on this now, Lori turned her attention to the leader of the creatures which had brought them here. She couldn't understand the creatures' growled exchange. However, she understood the leader of their group had entered into what appeared to be a heated discussion with the leader of this caravan over the use of horses, which were now used to pull two carts ladened with food and water.

"Apep wants us to his palace before my time's used up," Conrad said. A sly smile crossed the little man's lips. "What he don't know, is his time is about all gone too." Now, incredibly he laughed, and turned his gaze to her so she could see him wink. "You'll have a horse. When we reach the mountains, you slip away when I give you opportunity."

By evening of the next day Conrad LuPone, Lori Hellman and the creatures were in the mountains. But long before then, Lori could tell that something more than saddle sores, aching muscles, and their precarious situation was picking away at Conrad's insides. Conrad had been silent since they had mounted the horses in the grasslands, and her attempts to spark conversation had failed.

Since noon Lori had noted the signs—mounds of human skeletal remains piled high along the trail every hundred yards or so—that they were drawing near to Apep's Palace. This, Conrad's silence, and the fact that no avenue of escape had presented itself was setting Lori's nerves on end. She was beginning to wonder if Conrad had given up on his plan to give her chance to slip away, when the little man turned in his saddle, winked at her, nodded to the left of the trail, then spurred his horse into a gallop into the trees to their right.

Apep's guards were taken totally by surprise. Roaring in anger the leader of the group attacked the catman which had been closest to Conrad's horse. They rolled off the trail as the remaining catmen charged through the heavy overgrowth after Conrad.

Lori, totally forgotten, turned her horse off the left side of the trail, and spurred him into a trot down the mountain, toward the forest which they had exited only an hour earlier. Conrad had said she should find a place called Parabellum, and that she would do. She hoped Conrad would also escape and perhaps meet her there, but Lori Hellman would never see Conrad LuPone again.

---

# PRATTVILLE
# COURTHOUSE

*1:12 P. M., September 9, 1990*

"**G**et up! You're leaving."

The abrupt order jarred Jeremy Wheeler from a restless sleep. He opened his eyes to find a shaken Hank Davison, his uniform torn and dirty, his right hand wrapped in a blood-soaked bandage, his face covered in dirt, and streaked from tears. He looked down at Jeremy from wild eyes.

"What the hell happened to you?" Jeremy said, sitting up, quickly.

"I've got an officer in the hospital. He may not pull through. If he does, he'll be crippled. I've got a hand that has three less fingers than it did this morning. And I've got an insane belief in invisible spiders," Hank said.

---

His right hand fumbled with the keys on his belt as he spoke. In its new form the hand could not release the key ring. "Get these damn keys, will you?"

Jeremy stood, reached through the bars, released the keys, and handed them to Hank.

"It'll come with time," he said.

A look of consternation melted into Hank Davison's eyes. Then his face grew calm, but Jeremy knew he was still fighting for control.

He shifted the keys to his good hand. "It sure as hell better! I'm going with you." Hank unlocked the cell door, and swung it wide open.

Jeremy narrowed his eyes at Hank. "Going where? I thought—"

"To that other world. And we're going today. Now!"

Suddenly, the calm deserted Hank's eyes, and they filled with a blaze, banked only by thin corneas. Jeremy recognized that look. He had seen it on other men. Men pushed too many times. Men on the edge. He thought Hank might be very dangerous now. He was teetering between the here-and-now, and a black abyss of helpless terror called insanity.

He didn't want to give the teetering man the nudge that would dump him over the edge. Hank needed to talk out his terror before it consumed him.

"Look, Hank, I have no problem with your going through the portal with me." It was a lie. He didn't think it would be a brilliant move to take someone in Hank's condition any-where. But Hank held the keys to the cellblock and a gun. And an unbalanced man who holds all the aces should be handled with caution. "But first I think you should tell me what changed your mind about me, about my story. You owe me that much."

Hank stood at the cell door, shoulders squared, jaw jut-ting. He was big, hard, weathered. He looked frail all the same.

———

161

"Okay, maybe I do owe you that," he said. His shoulders rounded.

Jeremy felt some of the tension go out of his muscles. He gestured to the bunk. "You're welcome to sit, if you want." Hank waved his bandaged hand at him. "No. I can't sit yet." Jeremy sat back on the bunk, and gave Hank Davison an expectant look. He said nothing. Hank returned his look with one of concentration as the events of the morning coagulated somewhere in his wounded mind.

Fifteen minutes later, now deep into his story, Hank Davison feinted to the left, slid right, then raised an imaginary riot gun. "My second shot blew away the head," he said.

Hank had calmed by the finish of his story, and now he was simply relating it as a part of his history. "I used my radio to call the emergency squad. Charlie and I crawled out the basement window before they got to the house.

"Charlie wasn't bleeding much. Neither was I. At the hospital, the doctors said the lack of blood was the result of how his leg was pinched off. They said some kind of fluid sealed the crushed veins and arteries. I guess it was the creature's spittle. Anyway, the doctor said Charlie could have lived for a long time, even without the tourniquet he made.

Hank shook his head. "Longer than he would have wanted to, I suspect, if IT could have reached him."

Jeremy felt his stomach tighten at the thought of IT crawling over Charlie Hascomb, eating the choicest parts first. He said nothing, because there was nothing to say. He simply nodded.

"I cordoned off the area before the squad got there, and I swore Charlie to secrecy. I don't want the town to know about this."

Jeremy raised his brows at this revelation. "Oh? Why?"

"Because, it doesn't matter," Hank Davison was looking at

his feet, scuffing the toe of one boot against something on the floor.

"Doesn't matter! I'd think—" Jeremy started.

"It doesn't matter, because when they go to look, IT won't be there. There was an old friend there today: A hard man, about my age, built like a six-foot bulldog with a buzz cut. I saw him just before the emergency squad arrived. I knew him when I was in the Marines. He was always a strange sort, but you couldn't question his loyalty. He never questioned an order. We became friends, and wrote back and forth for a few years.

"From the Corps, he went into the CIA. His letters never mentioned his work, but from things he said, I'm sure he handled the dirty stuff . . . assassinations and such."

Jeremy sighed. He didn't like to think his government could do such things, but he wasn't naive. Governments were made up of people, had all the faults of those people. Sometimes they had even more faults because of the presumed shield of anonymity the people running them felt.

"My old friend was at the house before the squad arrived. I'm sure he was there all along, even before I went inside. And he was at the hospital when the doctors stitched us." Hank held his bandaged hand up, and stared at it for several seconds.

"Have you ever been in an ER where the doctor didn't ask how you got hurt? Of course not. Doctors and nurses are as curious as cats.

"But this time the doctors didn't ask how we got hurt. They just sewed us up."

He wagged the remaining finger on his right hand at Jeremy. "I always wondered why the FBI or the State people didn't get involved in these murders. The FBI has its nose in everything. Every murder is a potential Civil Rights violation. The State Police are supposed to oversee murder investigations, but they were too busy this time. Thought I should handle it myself. Nobody wanted part of this mess."

Jeremy shrugged. "I don't understand. Why—"

"I think this is happening in other places. I think the Government knows about it, State *and* Federal. I don't know why they're keeping it covered up, but I'm sure they are.

"Murders like these always make the national news. Have you seen anything on television about Prattville's murders?"

Jeremy considered this for several seconds then shook his head. "No. Only on local radio and in the *Courier Crescent*," he said.

"Right." Hank saluted, bowed, turned and walked the length of the cell and then back. "After those first two victims, the news media didn't even come around asking questions. I was so balled up in trying to solve the murders and keep the town covered, that I didn't notice until now." There was a pause. Hank was looking down again, once more fussing with something with the toe of his boot. "I talked to that old friend of mine. Do you want to know what he had to say?!"

It was obviously a rhetorical question. Jeremy simply waiting for the answer to come.

"He said to stay out of it! He says, 'Your government has a stake in this, and it doesn't want you messing around, spoiling things.'

"The government's got a stake in it!" he said, giving the thing he had been toeing a kick. "Hell, I've got a stake in it! I've already put up one girlfriend and three fingers. Charlie tossed in a foot, and seven of the people I was supposed to be protecting, tossed in their lives for good measure. Stay out of it? Hell, I'm not even in it *good* yet!"

"What about the doctors you saw at the hospital? How'll the CIA keep them quiet?"

Hank gave a little chuckle at this. "People who knew

about J. F. K.'s murder kept quiet," he said. "And they died quick deaths to make sure they would continue to keep quiet."

Hank gestured to the window. "They have someone watching me now. He followed me from the hospital. That's why I said you're getting out of here now. We need to leave, to get through the portal before they figure out what we're up to and stop us."

Jeremy stood and stared deep into Hank Davison's eyes. They were strong now, unflinching. "If we go through the portal, there isn't much chance we'll come back. You realize that don't you?"

Hank nodded, then turned a circle, elbow bent to hold his good hand palm up at shoulder level, showing his world. "To tell you the truth, I don't have a lot to come back to. Maybe you should be thinking about that more than I. I'd say you've got more reason to stay here than I do."

"Yes," Jeremy's gaze again met Hank's. "But that also means I've got the best reason to go."

When Jeremy Wheeler arrived home that afternoon, he had a new pack stuffed with all the necessities of a two-week camping trip for two.

He was still not certain that he wanted Hank Davison to be with him in that other world, but he wasn't sure he didn't either. The way things stood, it was take Hank or go it alone. Jeremy didn't like the thought of being alone. It was a selfish motive, but he thought he could live with it. He hoped Hank could.

They had talked for an hour. It was sufficient time to prepare, considering they knew absolutely nothing about what it was they were preparing to do. They discussed their minimum needs considering that lack of knowledge. In addition to the items in Jeremy's original pack, the pack he brought home this afternoon contained a second canteen, a lantern,

lantern fuel, a small tent, thermal blankets, freeze-dried food, a first-aid kit with antibiotics and pain killers for Hank's hand.

He laid the pack aside and stared at it for several minutes. The imminence of the trip was almost suffocating in its reality.

It was near six o'clock before Cindy Wheeler arrived home. She lugged several bags of groceries. One of the bags bore the imprint of a car key and a martini glass, circled and slash-marked in red. She handed that bag to him. "For your trip."

He looked at the bag in wonder and then into her eyes. She was always so beautiful to him, a petite Dimi Moore with brown hair and hazel eyes. "How did you know?"

"I . . . I don't know how I know. I just know."

"Do you want to talk about it?"

She looked down at her hands, avoiding his eyes. "No, Jeremy, I don't think I can. Let's just have dinner and spend the rest of the night like nothing has happened in these past weeks or will happen in the weeks to come. There'll be time to think about what remains and what's lost, tomorrow."

Their gazes met, and tears were in her eyes and rolling down her cheeks. Then his vision blurred. They kissed, and he tasted the saltiness of their pain mixed into one bitter reality.

# MARK SCOTT AND HIS MOTHER

*In the Grasslands, Day 2*

When they had settled down to sleep that first day, Mark Scott had hoped that the branching of their trail in the distance, which he had seen or thought he had seen, had been the product of his overactive imagination. But by noon of the second day the figures in the trail behind them were clearly visible, and those figures, six, tall, fur-covered creatures, were closing on them at an incredible speed.

"They're trying to encircle us," his mother said. She pointed to one end of the advancing line of creatures and then the other. "See, the ones on the outside are moving up faster to block us, to keep us from moving north or south."

Mark believed what his mother said was true enough, but

——

167

it didn't matter. He had seen a catman run in a New Orleans street, and he knew that, on his best day, he couldn't match the creature's speed. If his mother could, and considering her amazing stamina over the past day-and-a-half, he believed this may be possible, he knew she would not leave him.

Through courage and good fortune—mostly good fortune, he believed—they had killed one of the creatures in New Orleans, yet if these creatures were here to kill, there was no doubt in his mind how the current situation would end.

"Let's go south," his mother said, her voice had an edge to it now, and it drew Mark's gaze. "If we can get past the creature there . . . "

Mark knew the pit into which his mother's thoughts had fallen. By veering south they would put the majority of the creatures further behind than they were now. But to what end? In the process they would close on the creature to the southeast. They would still have that one to contend with, and without weapons this time. Even if, by some miracle, they could kill that creature, the remaining five would run them down before dusk.

Mark turned his gaze to the creature approaching from the southeast, then to the other five to the east and northeast and finally to his mother's eyes. There was more fear in those eyes than he had ever seen there before, and he knew that fear was not for herself . . . it was for him.

He turned, hiding from her eyes. "Let's go south," he said.

# JEREMY AND CINDY'S HOME

T hat last morning in Prattville, Jeremy Wheeler lay, head propped up on one hand, looking at Cindy's face in the morning shadows. He wanted to memorize her, to burn the image of her into his mind so he could carry her with him always. They had made love, and for the first time in weeks, she had slept without the moans, tossing, turning.

He wished this peaceful feeling could continue forever. Yet, he sensed the time to step through the portal was short.

He kissed her, and she emitted a soft, not quite awake, sigh. He slipped from the bed, and went about his bath.

Cindy had a large breakfast ready for him when he came

———

downstairs. They were both more composed than they had been the night before, but neither spoke of the inevitable.

They ate together, and talked as if this morning was no different from any other. Yet it *was* different. It was artificial. Cindy had never eaten breakfast with him before. This morning, she gorged herself on eggs, ham, and biscuits with jam. He followed her lead, using the food as a buffer, trying to stretch their remaining time together through the ritual of eating. But their plates were empty all too soon, and they sat staring at them, knowing looking at one another would end their charade.

"I can cook some more," she said, her gaze searching his eyes. "If you're still hungry, I could cook some more."

"I'll still have to go, sooner or later," he said, taking her hand.

"Then let it be later," she said, standing.

The sky was dark with the same gauze-bellied clouds that had covered it the day Jeremy Wheeler had discovered the portal. Occasional heat lighting dissipated the flat morning light for a wink in time. A misty rain fell.

Hank Davison and his dog, Rudy, were sitting in his cruiser in the Napa Parts' parking lot when Jeremy Wheeler walked out of a small copse of trees opposite the store. He was carrying two packs. A broad-brimmed Stetson covered his head against the weather.

Jeremy noted two things, Hank Davison's cruiser and a black sedan parked about a quarter of a block up Mineral Springs Street. The sedan was opposite the garish, Victorian house that Hank and Charlie had crawled out of the day before. There was one occupant of the car. It was the man Hank, after finishing his story of the horror which had taken place in the basement of the house on Mineral Springs, had pointed out as a CIA agent.

The man in the black sedan stared fixedly in Jeremy's

direction. Jeremy exited the cover of the trees and walked to the police cruiser. Hank rolled the Cruiser's window down, and Jeremy leaned in.

"Did you get everything?" Hank's voice overflowed with anticipation.

"I've got everything," Jeremy said. He rolled his eyes toward the black sedan. "I see you have company."

Hank glanced in the direction of the car, reached to pat the large, shaggy, white pup sitting next to him, then opened the cruiser's door and stepped to the asphalt." Yeah, he's a tagalong. I haven't been able to ditch him."

Jeremy chuckled. "He's about to see a disappearing act like he never saw before."

Jeremy turned to gaze at the portal. "Can you see it?" he asked turning back to Hank.

Hank's brow furrowed. His gaze moved to the portal. "I've been watching the light storm going on over there for over half an hour. I guess, losing three fingers opened my mind to new worlds."

"Have you seen Charlie Hascomb today?"

"I talked with him. The doctors told him he'd be fine. He lost very little blood, considering.

"The CIA's been at him. I'm sure they bugged his phone. He talked funny, like he knew someone was listening."

Peering over Hank's shoulder, Jeremy watched the man in the black sedan as they talked. The man was using binoculars to watch them now. "It appears we have your friend's interest aroused. Maybe we should finish our conversation on the other side, before he decides to call some buddies and lock us up in that fine establishment of yours."

"You may be right," Hank said, glancing in the agent's direction.

"Better grab the riot gun and some shells. We may need 'em."

Hank nodded. "I'm way ahead of you. Open one of those

packs and take it around to the trunk." Hank walked to the trunk, keyed the latch, and stepped away.

In the trunk Jeremy found ten boxes of twelve-gauge shotgun shells. Half were rifled slugs, and the rest were triple-ought buckshot.

"Looks like you came loaded for bear." He put the boxes into the lighter pack, and stuffed two, small packages in beside them.

"Never hurts to be prepared."

Jeremy cinched the pack, and handed it to Hank.

Flipping it over his head in one smooth motion, Hank hung it on his shoulders with the straps. He slung the riot gun over his right shoulder.

"When we close this trunk, my friend over there is going to get suspicious," Hank said. "He may come to see what we're up to. He may start shooting." Their gazes locked, and Hank raised an eyebrow in question.

Jeremy opened the leather pack, and pulled out the western holster with the big Ruger. "I hope we don't have to do any shooting."

Hank nodded, and Jeremy knew that he understood, if there was shooting, there would be no quarter.

"How do we do this portal thing?" Hank asked.

"Walk into the portal. I ran into it, and it spat me out. It was storming the day the catman went through, and it's storming today. That may have something to do with the energy needed to get through." Jeremy paused. "The only other thing you have to do is believe."

"Believe?"

"Believe. We're not working with something mechanical here. The old man said Apep was a wizard. He said something about a linking of souls."

Hank's eyes became wide ovals, and his facial muscles went lax. "You're saying we're dealing with the occult?"

"I'm saying, I had to believe to see the catman and the

---

giant spider. And *you* had to believe to see the portal. Beyond that, I'm not sure."

Hank smiled. "You're sure of that?" he asked.

"I'm sure, and you had better be sure too, or you're going to have a lot of explaining to do to the CIA.

"But Charlie and I didn't have to believe to see the beetle."

"I've been thinking about the beetle. Charlie lost part of his leg. That made a believer out of him. And seeing the belief in Charlie and what IT did to him, made a believer out of you. You were lucky, that's all."

"Maybe," Hank said, looking at his ruined hand. "But I don't feel all that lucky."

Jeremy rested his hand on the Ruger's grips, and gave it a squeeze. He felt something flow up his arm releasing the tension in his muscles. He released his grip, and lowered the hand to his side.

"You ready?" Hank said.

"I'm ready. You taking the dog?" The large, white pup was sniffing Jeremy's cuffs.

"I thought he might tag along."

Their gazes met. Jeremy sensed that the dog was probably the only living thing Hank was close to in this world. He nodded.

"Let's get going, then." He flipped the leather pack onto his shoulders, and slammed the trunk of the cruiser with a thump.

They started to walk toward the power plant's switching yard. Rudy stood beside the car, and whiffed the breeze for several seconds. Then he trailed along after Hank, nose to the ground, tail curled above, fanning the air.

Jeremy's gaze moved to the black car as the distance to the portal decreased to ten yards, then nine, then eight. The man was out of the car and watching them closely now. He made no effort to move closer.

———

"He isn't following us!" Jeremy said.

Hank chuckled. "He doesn't know about the portal. All he sees is two guys with packs, walking toward a green, twelve-foot, cyclone fence."

The two men stopped at the opening in the fence. They looked at each other and laughed.

"Well, time's a-wasting. See you over there," Hank said. He looked at Rudy, "Come on pup." He turned and stepped into the flickering, blue light. Rudy followed.

Jeremy looked over his shoulder at the man from the black sedan. The man shook his head then craned his neck as if all he would need was a different perspective to make Hank Davison and dog reappear.

Jeremy smiled, turned, and stepped into the light.

# THROUGH THE PORTAL

*Chief Hank Davison*

On the inside, the portal was like a porcelain tube. Light bounced from the sides in frenetic detonations of blue and green. The light blinded Hank Davison until he stepped free of the portal and collapsed onto gnarled roots, rocky soil, rotted and rotting leaves. *The image of a driver's license, the glint of morning sun off metal, an explosion, muzzle flash, blood, pain erupted in his mind. Darkness swirled up at him.*

A throaty growl snatched Hank Davison back to awareness. He found himself standing. Rudy stood to his right, eyes fixed, muscles tense, tail tucked. Shakily, Hank brought the shotgun down from his shoulder, and traced the pup's gaze with his own.

A wooded area of old growth oak, maple and hickory surrounded them. The floor of the forest was a patchwork of sunlight and shadow. He saw nothing else. Rudy's growl deepened, and he bared his fangs.

Hank jacked the shotgun's slide. He thought of the bullet-proof vests wrapped in brown paper and stuffed into the top of his pack. He had planned to show them to Jeremy on this side of the portal. A surprise and a gift for a new friend.

*Where is Jeremy?* He looked back to the portal. A phantom's ax, it moved away from him slicing through trees, yet leaving them standing. His stomach knotted. He was alone and lost. There was no old man to lead the way, and no Jeremy. He turned back to the pup.

Rudy had inched forward. The dog was ten feet from him now, still growling.

From the forest a voice growled, "It's not Jeremy."

Hank tightened his grip on the shotgun.

The forest erupted in throaty gargles. Rudy began to bark and back toward Hank. A creature of fur, muscles, and fangs stepped from behind a tree. Galaxies of stars spun in its obsidian eyes.

Hank felt its gaze slide over him like millions of inchworms. His stomach lurched. His throat burned.

"Bring them to the palace," the creature said.

Hank leveled the shotgun. The galaxies went out of the creatures eyes, and the eyes glowed a shiny blue for the half second before the shotgun blast tore its face off.

Hank jacked the shotgun's slide again. The forest came alive.

Often times, to win us to our harm,
The instruments of darkness tell us truths;
Win us with honest trifles, to betray's
In deepest consequence.
                    —William Shakespeare, MACBETH

# IN THE PORTAL

*Jeremy Wheeler*

Jeremy Wheeler felt his mind expanding, filling, overflowing. Stars: brilliant, white dots against a flat, black backdrop, surrounded him like a cocoon. There was the sensation of movement. It was slight at first, like a bus just moving out of a terminal, filled with jiggles and bumps. But as the speed continued to build, all smoothed, and then as it doubled, tripled, quadrupled, the light seemed to bend, the stars stretch, blur.

The cocoon grayed. Then all light rushed away from him as if in fear. Still, the sensation of consummate speed filled him.

———

177

Before him, a single dot of infinite blackness, darker than the coal black of his cocoon, grew. It fanned out like a black moth then coiled into a worm, a larva, feeding on the surrounding blackness. A quiver shot through Jeremy, and he shook violently with its force.

He felt the clawing anticipation of horror deep in his bowels. *Light! I need light.*

*Would you leave me so soon?* Jeremy startled. The thought had slipped into him like a knife. Yet it was cloying with good nature and friendship.

In the larva's place floated a cloaked figure of measureless blackness. The coal black of the sky glowed white around it.

Jeremy felt his intestines knot. *Wh-Who? What are you?*

*I am he who is, alpha and omega.* The thought surged into his brain, roiling his consciousness until his mind felt like pudding. Alpha and Omega, it was something he had heard in church. Was this blackness God? He rejected the thought.

*Can you reject me so easily? Were you here when the gases of the universe seethed from a bit of matter so small that it would sit on the point of a pin? Did you ride on high in the firmament when the lands belched forth from the seas? Did you behold the magnificence of the garden?*

*No.*

*How, then, are you so sure, that I am not he who is?*

*I will know my God when he allows me to look upon his face.* (*Was that a bluff? His thought or this creature's?*)

*Do you want to look on my face, Jeremy? The thought tittered through his brain. Do you have such heart, such strength?*

*I'm not afraid.*

*Oh, yes you are. Oh, yes you are!* Their peal rocking his mind, the words flowed into his brain and became solid. *You cringe at the thought of what might be under my cowl, and your heart falters at my words. Yet you needn't hold such consummate fear. We can come to terms, you and I. LOOK, Jeremy. LOOK!*

---

The black figure's bulky sleeves moved to its cowl. Withered and gnarled fingers, finished with long, yellowed claws, crawled from the sleeves, and drew back the cowl. Beneath, galaxies whirled. An irresistible force clutched him and dragged him into the swirling vortex.

"*LOOK, Jeremy. LOOK!*" His brain throbbed. *See and understand!*

The force of something ancient and powerful propelled his consciousness through the gases and dust of space. A glassy planet infused in ice whirled by. An icy volcano spewed its contents into the sky. It floated back frosty white. An enormous planet of seething gases, marked by one grand, whirling, blue spot, spun at him and was gone.

In the distance he saw a boiling, yellow sun, and felt its warmth sink into his cold bones. Then, a red planet, desolate, crisscrossed with canyons, and circled by two moons, zipped past. Yet, he moved on, toward the light and its warmth. A blue planet with a swirling, white overlay, expanded in the distance, and Jeremy's mind screamed. *Enough!*

*All that you have seen and more can be yours, Jeremy. A galaxy of your own, all the power of a god can be yours.*

Jeremy struggled for an answer. Tremendous weights lugged and tugged against his thoughts pulling them away. *At what price?*

*Little price to you. All you have to do is pledge yourself to me.*

Again Jeremy struggled for an answer, searching for his own thoughts among those of this ancient thing-of-blackness. Yet, his thoughts squirmed away, lost like worms in spaghetti.

*What profiteth a man—*

*Oh, come now Jeremy. All I ask is for your pledge, not your soul. Can your little mind not fathom the glory I offer you?*

*You will have a galaxy to rule as a god. Power over night and day, life and death, that's what I offer you. All you have to do is pledge yourself to me. Is that too much to ask for making you a god?* The siren songs of this ancient evil invaded Jeremy's befuddled mind despite his attempts to shut them out.

---

*What profiteth—*

*Oh! Now, you're behaving like a child! Would you give up being a god for the lives of those you knew on your wretched little planet? Either way, you'll never see them again. Would you give up being a god to save your soul? Gods keep score with souls. They're tally marks! Nothing more. Would you give up this?*

Images swirled on the black backdrop of his mind. Primitive people sacrificed animals to him. Maidens walked smiling into volcanos for him. Whole worlds bowed at his feet. Whole societies fought to the death in his name. The foreign thoughts wouldn't separate from his. He felt his will crumbling.

*No more! No more!*

*Say yes, and all will be right with you.*

*What prof—*

*Be gone then!*

Jeremy felt consciousness slip away, and darkness consumed him.

### THROUGH THE PORTAL

## Jeremy Wheeler, Day 1

Jeremy felt a sickening loss as he spiraled up from the black abyss of unnatural sleep. When he opened his eyes, it was to the blinding brilliance of the noonday sun.

He found himself lying crumpled in a ball, like a discarded tissue. A thin mixture of sand and fine, yellow-green dust covered him. He lay on hot, cracked hardpan. Every muscle, every bone, every joint ached. His mind shrank from consciousness, wanting to escape the pain, to sink back into a bottomless well of soothing black. But something in the middle of him pushed him to the surface, into full consciousness.

He rolled to his back, and stared into a cloudless, gray-blue sky. A dry, hot breeze moved over him from left to right. A small drift of yellow-green powder and sand had piled against his sleeping body, outlining his fetal image on the desert floor.

He sat up, and squinted through the harsh sun to the wasteland encircling him. It was blinding, white, flat, blank, stretching from horizon to horizon. Save for a blue haze sketched low on the horizon to his right, it was all the same.

He struggled to his feet. Every fiber of his body protested every centimeter of the movement.

The desert seemed to rock beneath his feet. He tried to swallow, but he had no spit, and his tongue was swelling to fill his mouth. He took up his canteen and drank. The water, hot from the desert sun, burned its way into him.

He thought he must have lain here for a long time. He couldn't remember breaching the portal, his entrance into this world, or the coming of night. All he remembered was a horrible nightmare of jumbled thoughts. He had a feeling something was wrong, but he wasn't sure what. Then he remembered Hank Davison and the dog. *They should be here with me.*

He scanned the bleak wasteland again. All that he saw was miles and miles of flat sand and dust, dotted with sparse outcrops of desert grass. His heart sank.

*Maybe, they didn't come through.*

He scanned the area a third time. A low monument stood on the flat plain a few yards away. He shambled toward the structure, and sank to his knees at its base.

The small shelter was about eight-feet long and two-feet high. Bricks cut from the hardpan of the desert floor formed eight support posts. Desert grass, woven into a mat, formed a roof. Building this small shelter had cost someone dearly in time and strength.

He looked inside. It was cool, dim, enticing. He crawled inside, curled up, closed his eyes, slept, dreamed.

---

181

*OF ALL POSSIBILITIES*

## *Prattville, Ohio, December 16, 1990*

*"Jeremy?" Cindy said.*

*He looked up, half aware this wasn't the first time she had called his name. "Huh?"*

*"I said, Linda, Sam and I are going shopping. Do you want to go?"*

*It was the second week of December. It was morning, and the weather was unseasonably warm. Save for the gray sky, it was more like spring than winter. A light snow, which had fallen on Thursday and Friday of the first week, had melted away over the weekend, and it had rained the night before. It was the type of weather that made him lethargic, but Linda and Sam had been scurrying about all morning.*

*"No. I'd spoil your fun. I'm in a reading mood today."*

*Cindy smiled. "If you're sure. Leftovers are in the fridge when you get hungry. We'll have lunch in Canton."*

*They kissed a lingering kiss, and Jeremy felt a strange sense of loss, an emptiness as their lips parted. For an instant , he wanted to drag her back, forbid her to go.*


*THROUGH THE PORTAL*

## *Day 1*

Jeremy was not sure how long he had been staring at it without comprehending. He was not even sure how long he had been awake. When he opened his eyes, the hardpan support post was there, with its scratches. He guessed he had lain unseeing for minutes before the name, obscured by dust, seemed to jump from the post into his consciousness. He reached a tentative hand to the post and brushed at the dust

---

coating. Other indentations appeared, spurring him to increased efforts.

The scratches read:

*Apep is all powerful! He made all men. Time cannot defeat him. Men cannot challenge him. He controls the seas, skies, and earth beneath. All must serve him, so the lights will serve the people.*

Jeremy read the message twice then vowed, "Time may not defeat him, but *I* sure as hell will.

The white-hot sun cycled to a brilliant orange then a dark violet, before relinquishing its mastery, over the tortured land. A black sky filled with stars canopied the sands of the desert. In the eastern sky hung swirling, multicolored lights.

Jeremy Wheeler flipped the leather pack to his back, and set off toward the lights.

The hardpan of the wasteland floor was covered by as little as none and as much as four inches of fine sand and dust. The sand flowed from beneath each foot fall, causing each step to be irregular, uphill. The straps from the leather pack cut into his flesh, pulled him back, caused his neck and shoulders to ache.

Ten hours later he paused, sat, sipped some water. Dawn was coming on and a night of constant, strenuous hiking had added no noticeable definition to the blue haze on the horizon. He shook his head, sighed, fished jerky from his pack, and chewed it as he looked out over the wasteland.

His lips, dried and cracked from the constant wind, drew back from the burn of the salty meat. For the first time he noticed the strain in his muscles and the sting in his face where the sand from the desert's dust devils had pelted him through the night. For several seconds he studied the horizon, and wondered if he would reach that distant goal before the wasteland claimed him. And then he stared into the sky, imagining he could see his sun, and that Cindy on her world was looking up at him.

—

For an hour he collected desert grass. It had a heavy, waxy exterior and when broke, exuded a fine, green oil onto his hands. The oil dripped from his fingers and soaked into his jeans and shirt. It smelled like unwashed laundry, days old.

Finally, he used the leather pack to scoop the desert sands from the hardpan. He formed long, two-foot-high mounds, and anchored some of the grass between them to make a roof. The rest he bundled into a log. It burned with a slow, red flame giving off heavy, black smoke that wafted low across the desert.

He wasn't prepared for this trek. His experience with deserts to this point had been an occasional "Animals of the Desert" series seen on educational television. This wasteland was not as he would have expected. It was flat. And the wind blew, with unnatural constancy, in the direction of the blue haze on the horizon. It was as if someone had punched a small hole in this world's atmosphere, causing the air to seep out along the desert floor.

As he puzzled over the desert, the sky came alive in hews of orange and purple, and the sun broke the horizon. He watched it climb, crowding out the crawling lights and the stars, once again asserting its mastery over the land. Then he crept into the shelter and waited for night.

The next three days went very much as the first. Jeremy walked for ten hours each night. He nursed the water well beyond its ability to give moisture to his drying husk, and ate the jerky that burned his lips more as each day passed. He took two hours each morning to build his shelter and watch the sun rise. Then he cleaned the dust and sand from the Ruger, and oiled the mechanism.

The haze on the horizon grew each day until mountains peeked above the shoulder of his new world, and he discerned a green finger of lush forest at its base.

On the third day, Jeremy drank the last of his water while

he studied the snowcapped mountains. He had too much of the wasteland to cover before he would stand in the green at the base of the blue mountains. It was hopeless, and he was sure this wasteland would soon suck the life from him.

The sound was a sharp, chattering hiss. Jeremy startled, turned to it, tripped. His teeth rattled against the sand-covered hardpan. The desert floor filled his mouth, gritted over his teeth, and burned his lips and tongue with its saltiness.

Again, the cicada chirr trilled out a warning. Jeremy's hand found the stocks of the Ruger. The gun shifted in the holster. His head turned, following the sound. Three feet away a dog-sized crustacean posed with claws extended. Its tail was raised high above its back. It hissed and chattered at him like a cornered crawfish.

*Scorpion?!*

The creature's tail cocked, poison drooled to the stinger's tip, then the air tore with its strike. The tail whipped at him, blurring.

The revolver cleared the holster with a crisp rasping sound. The handgun roared, and crashed back in Jeremy's hand. Ropes of flame belched from the barrel. The barrel kicked skyward. The creature's head exploded. Glowing, yellow blood sprayed the desert floor. The tail pounded into the sand at his shoulder. The gun roared again, and the poisonous tip disappeared from the tail.

Jeremy's breath came fast, rasping.

Something large and sharp skittered over his ribs. Flames of pain shot through him.

His mind screamed. He rolled away from the hurt. Keen claws clamped down on his arm, stalling his retreat. Then a weight followed him over, riding his arm. White-hot barbs of pain battered his ribs.

His horrified eyes stared back at him from an obsidian eye dotted with a coal of red. He screamed, and slammed the

185

butt of the Ruger into his image. The eye exploded, spattering him with its glittery goo.

The claws released. The creature's tail thrashed at the desert floor. Jeremy slid back over the sand on the seat of his jeans, away from the death dealing tail. The gun came up. The creature's head exploded.

Burned gunpowder stung Jeremy's nostrils. His ears rang from the crash of the gun. He drew himself to his knees and spun a circle looking and listening. Save for the creatures' tails which did a dead dance, writhing and drumming against the desert floor, the night was still.

Jeremy reloaded and holstered the handgun. Then he looked to his injuries.

Below his left arm, his shirt hung in blood soaked shreds. The wounds were not deep, but the ripped flesh was swelling, turning an angry red, pulsating with fever. He could feel the heat racing through his body, and he knew he was in *deep doo-doo,* as his father liked to say.

Settling to the sand, he let the pack slide from his shoulders. Brass cartridges whispered a protest to their rough treatment. He unfastened the pack's flap, and dug into the contents for the first aid kit and the bottles Cindy had provided.

Seconds later he touched the wounds with a gin soaked gauze, grimaced with the pain. Then he scrubbed. Soon the wounds numbed from the poison, gin, and rough treatment. He flooded them with gin, covered them with gauze, and sat back against his pack.

He felt a loginess rolling over him, and realized it was only a matter of time before the poison would overtake him. The numbness in his side was spreading.

He started to build his shelter. He didn't know if his body could fight off the toxins, but he knew, if he didn't finish the shelter before the fever, chills, delirium came, the sun of the next day would finish him.

He arranged the desert grass, pinning its ends to the

mounds with sand. The desert was beginning to waver before him. The grass squirmed in its place like snakes, its ends striking at his hands.

The scorpions rose and rattled toward him. He drew the Ruger, fired and only then realized the trick of his mind.

Less than an hour passed before he finished the shelter. But the world was weaving and slithering around him as he studied the structure and grunted his approval. He wanted it to be right. He knew this might be his tomb.

He took up his pack, crawled inside the structure, curled up, slept, dreamed.

## OF ALL POSSIBILITIES

### *Prattville, Ohio, December 27, 1990*

*Everyone but Hank Davison had left. Jeremy Wheeler had shaken hands, accepted hugs and kisses, and listened patiently to well-intentioned condolences all morning. None of it seemed real. The ceremony had been closed-casket. How did Jeremy know they were really in those boxes? If Cindy, Linda, and Sam were really dead, there should be a knife-in-the-gut feeling that said this was real. There was nothing, no feelings at all, just a hollowness that caused every thought and every word to echo through him.*

*The funeral director's people waited for an hour, then lowered the canopy, removed the fake grass, folded the brown, card-table chairs. This was the third ring of the circus, and the roustabouts had to move it along to the next town, for the next show.*

*"Find him," Jeremy said. He flinched at the loudness of his voice. Somehow it made all of this real.*

*"We will," Hank Davison said.*

—

*THROUGH THE PORTAL*

## *Day 5*

*Serial killer. Escaped. No suspects.* When he awoke, the words still rolled around in the back of his sleep shocked mind, smacking together like billiard balls. He stared through the opening of his sandy grave. A man approached. Tall and gaunt, he glided over the sand with broad strides, crunching the desert underfoot, consuming it with ease. The man was dressed in a white caftan, his head covered against the desert sun with a white hood.

He stopped short of kicking sand in Jeremy's face, and knelt before him.

The hooded head moved closer, and the hood slid back to reveal a swirling vortex of stars. A scorpion struck at him from the stars. His mind screamed. Blackness took him.

Eons later, the sound of cascading water filled Jeremy's ears, and he struggled to clear his mind of the heat-filled tangle of darkness. A frigid cold enfolded him and the darkness buried his thoughts.

### *DAY 6*

*The hissing trill challenged him from out of the dark. It stood before him, eyes aglow. Its tail curled above its back, drooling death. Universes swirled in its obsidian eyes. The armored tail crashed down. His hand went for the Ruger.*

Jeremy Wheeler awoke in a cold sweat to the ghost of a hissing chatter. He was on his knees, groping for the handgun. The world spun around him. There was no gun, no sand, no creature.

He knelt on a thin, lumpy mattress suspended in a low,

wooden frame and hung on ropes formed of the desert grass. He was in a room lit a gloomy, red by an oil-fed lantern that hung from a peg in the center of the ceiling. The room was small, the furnishings, sparse. The walls and floor were of rough-hewn hardpan. A small stand, with a bowl of water and cloths, stood by the bed.

Jeremy sank back onto the meager mattress. It smelled of his fever and the desert grass. An angry rumbling erupted from his stomach, and he realized he was hungry, but he was too weak to sit up again. Then the room seemed to waver before him and grow gray. He sank back to the black depths from which he had surfaced.

### DAY 7

Gray-toned shadows of semiconsciousness swam in and out. His world rocked. A pin point of light floated in front of him. He stretched for it as if for a brass ring, and it fanned out.

"Eat," came the command. Jeremy felt a sinewy arm cradle his upper body. A rough hand pried his mouth open, and warm liquid poured over the slime set interior to his throat. His throat absorbed the moisture like a sponge.

He opened wide one, burning eye. The second would only slit. He found himself staring up the nostrils of a Grecian nose pinned to a leathery, brown, wrinkled face. Two, sparkling, blue eyes hung above the nose, staring back at him. Again the voice commanded, "Eat." More of the warm liquid etched its way through the muck fixing his mouth and down his throat.

His stomach grasped the warmth and cramped as it squeezed it. The pain was exquisite.

"Eat," the voice said. He clamped his mouth, and turned his head against the liquid, feeling like a baby avoiding a dreaded strained vegetable.

"Eat and you live. Don't and you die," the voice said.

---

189

The voice was matter of fact, the face was unmoved. Jeremy opened his mouth, and more of the liquid joined the rest in his writhing stomach.

He ate. His cramping stomach relaxed. The man talked.

"You was stung by the beast. The men of this sea don't die of it anymore. But you ain't of this sea. Anyun' could see that."

*Sea?* He tried to speak. A squawk, a low, flat, guttural croak, like the mating call of a frog, escaped his mouth.

"No need trying to talk. The poison steals the voice for a bit."

Jeremy let his muscles go limp.

"Luck shipped with you. I remember the magic of my father and his before him. Not all do. I come from a long line of men of this sea. It was the old magic what saved you.

"Med Cin they called it."

The man looked old. Jeremy couldn't guess just how old. He had a hard, weather-beaten face. He slicked his thin, gray hair back like a gangster in an old Humphry Bogart movie. He was perhaps six-foot three-inches tall, and although thin, his bare arms knotted impressively with muscle.

The man dipped into the bowl, and spooned a juicy piece of meat into Jeremy's mouth. Jeremy found his stomach had relaxed, and he chewed the morsel, like a dog with a stolen treat, and sent it to mingle with the warm juices. The meat had a sweet taste like lobster or crayfish, but it stewed in a unappetizing, brine broth.

"If Apep wills it, my son will follow the line. My son found you set adrift. You killt two of the beast. It will anger Apep's tax collectors that you fished of the sea without permission." He gave a knowing nod, his face, solemn. Then it brightened. "Still, this sea is at the edge of Apep's kingdom, and his taxers stay mostly ashore." The man laughed, showing missing, chipped and discolored teeth. "And we'll have the meat et soon." He gestured to a kettle in the corner of the room.

Jeremy followed the gesture with his gaze, looking to the kettle. His mouth went sour. The stewing lump of meat in his stomach seemed to swell and crawl along the interior, seeking exit. He forced it back down. He had eaten worse, he supposed. Though, just now, he couldn't remember when.

When he returned his attention to the man, he realized the man's quick, blue eyes had caught his reaction and misinterpreted.

"You sleep now. You need to gain strength for the voyage. This anchor will fish out soon." He paused. "My son will be here when you wake. He would like someun' to talk to other'n me. Your voice may return by then."

The man removed the soup. His tall, gaunt frame unfolded from the chair, and with many small awkward bows, he backed to the doorway. There, he pulled a small, black cap from his rear pocket, and smoothed it onto his head. Then he disappeared behind the desert grass mat that served as a door.

Jeremy pondered the words of this man-of-the-sea. It appeared the wizard he had come for was more like a god or a king. He was a leader of men, and more. Much more. Jeremy wondered how much he could learn from the man and his son, and as sleep took him, he wondered how safe he was here.

## OF ALL POSSIBILITIES

### Prattville, Ohio, 1993

*"Doctor Lee says it's a boy," Lori Hellman Wheeler said.*

*Jeremy frowned.*

*Lori wrinkled her brow in question. "That's okay, isn't it?"*

*"Of course, it's okay. It's just that—I guess I'm old-fashioned,*

191

*but I always imagined I would be sitting in a waiting room all nervous and jittery, and a nurse would come in—"*

Lori extended a hand and placed two fingers on his lips, stopping his brattle. *"You'll be a good father."*

*"I hope I will."*

*He remembered the first day he was sure he was a father. He had known immediately, before the doctor had seen her, before Lori, before he had rolled off her to lay panting in their bed. He had experienced a calm, a feeling of evil leaving him and goodness entering. He felt clean inside, something he had not felt since he had taken his revenge on Cindy's murderer, Marion Brand, since he had seen the coal-black worm swim to the surface of Marion's eye, and launch itself at him.*

## DAY 8

Jeremy awoke. His thoughts came slow, gradually soaking through the cotton in his head. He rose to a sitting position. The room rocked, then righted itself. His head ached, and he felt off balance, and weak. But the fever had lifted.

Briefly he remembered the dream, the woman, the baby, and wondered what it all meant. Then he shook off the thought. *It was just a dream, something to fill my loneliness, loss.*

Clutching the bed to steady himself, he swung his feet to the floor. The rough hardpan felt cool, and gouged at his tender feet. He took a deep breath. His clothing reeked of desert grass, fever.

Using the bed for support, he stood. His vision doubled, and his legs swivelled. He locked his knees. The room settled to a single, fixed image. For a moment he stood as stiff as a mannequin, afraid to test his strength. Then he released the bed and waddled to the door, grunting and hissing, on electric feet.

The door opened onto a narrow hallway about three yards in length. To his right a second door opened onto a small bedroom. A grass mat covered a third opening at the end of the hall. A thin, red light glowed beyond the mat.

He waddled down the hall, hissing and groaning, and peeked through the loose weave of the mat-door to the adjoining room.

Two lanterns hung from the hardpan ceiling, and filled the small room with the same flat, red light as filled the bedroom. This room, like the bedroom, also had little furniture. A small fireplace, with a tiny, black kettle hanging in it, dominated the opposite wall. A crudely built, wooden table and two chairs stood in the middle of the room. A pipe and tobacco lay on the table. A thin line of blue smoke stretched from the pipe to the ceiling, loading the air with the pungent smell of tobacco.

Jeremy moved the mat aside and entered.

He found his gun belt on a peg to the right of the fireplace. His pack and shoes lay on the floor.

He slipped on the shoes, then lifted the gun belt from the peg, strapped the holster to his waist, and tied it low on his leg with the leather thong. The rig's weight was oppressive. He drew the gun and checked its condition. It was clean, loaded. Someone knew about guns here!

His eyes searched the room.

Save the door he had entered, the walls bore no openings. The only possible exit was a crude ladder that entered a circular hole in the ceiling and disappeared into darkness. It had to be a way out.

Jeremy wondered if he had the strength to make the climb. It could be a matter of feet. It could be stories. And if it was stories, there was the added problem of his fear of heights.

He stepped onto the first rung. The ladder squeaked, but it was steady. He grunted his approval, and started to climb. The hole was a tight fit, built for someone tall and thin like the seaman. It wasn't deep. Five rungs into the black hole Jeremy's head struck an obstruction. The obstacle moved.

―――

There was a flash of white light, then darkness as the object, a trapdoor he believed, fell back into place. Dust, jarred loose by the collision, sifted past him into the dull, red light below.

*Light, I saw light up there!*

The light made him stronger, and he moved upward as if on a column of air, bowing his head, placing his shoulders against the impediment. The ladder groaned, and his knees wavered. The blockage moved, sliding back, letting in the light.

He poked his head up and found himself staring over the barren wasteland to the multicolored lights of the desert night. He breathed in the cool odorless air, and it filled him with the strength stolen by the poison. He was shaky, but he was on his feet again. He climbed out onto the desert floor and stood.

Ten minutes later, he found the seaman about one hundred yards from the opening. Before Jeremy could reach him, the old man stood, shambled forward, then fell back to the sand-covered hardpan, twice.

Dark purple and red circled the seaman's eyes. Bruises colored his jaw. Dried blood caked beneath his nose and at the corners of his mouth, and a thin line of it ran from his right ear down his neck. Jeremy fought his eyes to keep them from turning away.

The seaman looked up at him through one swollen eye. The other was closed. "You're on your feet early, ain't you, mate?"

"Thought you might need the bed for a while."

The old man chuckled, then groaned. "I'll be all right, when the deck stops rollin'."

*DAY 11*

It had taken Jeremy a week to figure a way through the portal to this world. He had lost track of time in the desert, but he was certain he couldn't have wandered for much more than five days—eight at the outside. The creature's sting had cost him three more days. That was eleven here, eighteen total. Now he was spending more of his precious time caring for the old seaman, who had saved his bacon. Yet this was a debt he did not mind repaying. This man was hardworking, honest, giving. He reminded Jeremy of his father, and the memory was good when he was so hopeless, so far from home.

The old man's strength surprised him. He was able to sit up in bed on the second day. They talked for hours.

"Name's Aral," he said, nodding solemnly. "I've seen seventy summers, and like my father, and his father, and his father before, I fish the inland sea."

Jeremy frowned. In describing her dream Cindy had said, *"You* walk on the sea." And perhaps because of that, or perhaps for some reason hidden to him, Aral's continued reference to this desert as a sea grated on him somewhere deep inside.

Aral nodded, and there was a glint in his eyes as if he had read Jeremy's mind. "Not much of a sea you might say. But was a time when the sea was deep water; fed millions." Aral sighed, then, flinching in pain, he picked up his pipe and a match from the bedside table, and began to tamp the tobacco in the bowl with his thumb. "Now, the water's gone. Has been, near on to three-hundred years."

Jeremy considered this: *Why would people continue to fish a dead, dry sea?* But that was, perhaps, the wrong question. "What happened?" he asked.

"They leached its source. Two rivers. All the water went to the fields. The land was poor. Salts from the water finished the soil; crops failed."

Aral struck the match with a flick of his thumb nail, and held it to the tobacco in the pipe's bowl while he puffed on the stem. Several large, blue clouds of fragrant smoke rose toward the ceiling before he continued. "Then they tried to farm the sea bed. Tortured it, they did. Made it flat. But they couldn't farm it. Nothing but sea grass grows now. And the sea's dry." He sighed, shook his head sadly, then puffed slowly on the pipe for several seconds before adding, "Many fish the sea even now."

Jeremy narrowed his eyes at Aral. Perhaps, now it was time for that question. "Fish? For what?"

Aral's eyes opened wide, and his forehead wrinkled in an expression of surprise. "For the beast, boy. We fish for the beast. We net, like my father and his father. We sell some live. We salt down the rest. That's how my son found you. He was running the beast when it stung ya."

"Ah, your son." Jeremy realized he had forgotten about the son, the reason for his being here, being alive. "What happened to your son?"

Aral drew back at the question, and his eyes shifted like those of an often kicked dog. "Apep. His Guard caught us."

"Apep's Guard?"

"Ayuh. They shanghaied Aryan. They beat me and left me for dead. I was too old for their purposes."

"What are their purposes?"

Aral hung his head, and gave it a slow, side-to-side shake. "Apep's slave work. They often shanghai young men, women too, if they have enough pluck, enough spirit." Aral's eyes were sad. "Aryan always had too much pluck."

Jeremy thought worriedly of Hank Davison. He had pluck. "What kind of work does Apep have for these slaves?"

"No one knows," Aral said. He shrugged his muscular shoulders, raised the pipe for a gentle puff, then lowered it to his lap and said, softly, "When Apep's Guard takes slaves over the mountain, the night-lights glow brighter. Some say he feeds the slaves to the lights." Aral shuddered. "Only the one-what-come-back could say for sure."

"Is that where Apep lives? Over the mountain?"

"He comes from there when he comes."

Jeremy moved to the edge of his seat, had the urge to grasp Aral's arm, resisted it. "Is that often?"

"He sends his Guard, mostly. Some say Apep sees through the eyes of his Guard. They're gruesome creatures! All fangs, claws and muscle. They can tear a man apart. They could've killt me. Instead, they just pained me a little. Played with me, they did, like a ferret with a rat."

"Catmen!" Jeremy said.

Aral shook his head slowly. "Whatever they may be, it is said they come of the island. They say the beast come of the island too."

Jeremy's brow rose, involuntarily, and his gaze zeroed on the old man's eyes. "What island?"

The old man heaved his shoulders, and shook his head. "Many islands of this sea. Don't know how to tell just the right one. The tales say Apep performed his sorcery on the island before the sea dried. Gen Etics they called it, after the Genie. When the sea dried, his magic walked the seabed. Only Apep can control the creatures and the beasts. He uses the ones you call catmen for his Guard. They're the taxers, and they collect the young people.

"Apep led the Guard himself in the time of my great, great grandpa."

Jeremy's brow wrinkled, questioningly. He wondered who was fooling whom here?

Aral's gaze met his then moved away. The old man paused to stir the pipe's tobacco with a match stem and tamp it with his thumb before striking a second match to light it again.

Jeremy waited patiently as the old man puffed out several more clouds of the fragrant smoke.

Finally, Aral said, "Question if you want. I think as how I would. Still, Grandpa and me saw Apep before I could cut bait. Grandpa said, when he was as young, him and his grandpa saw Apep. His grandpa said Apep was the same as when he was a child. Grandpa told me the same."

"When was the last time you saw this Apep?"

Aral's brow wrinkled with thought. "Must have been a

---

year or more. He had changed little since I was a child."

*Only a year? Then he does live!* Jeremy wasn't sure why he should question this wizard's existence this late in the game, but he had. "How can I find Apep?"

Aral's eyes went as hard as blue agate. "It's not something you should wish to do." He paused for a second, then he hiked his shoulders and allowed them to drop in a sign of resignation. The agate in his eyes turned to ice and ultimately, melted. "It's said the-one-what-come-back knows the way."

Jeremy's throat tightened with anticipation. "The-one-what-come-back? How do I find this person?" If he could find a guide, he could regain some of his lost time. Maybe he still had a chance.

"She came from the mountains. She journeyed with a man to the desert. Apep's Guard took both, there. She escaped somewhere on the mountain. They say Apep killed the man." He paused. His face was unmoved. "Scuttlebutt has it, the people of Parabellum keep this woman safe."

*Si vis pacem, para bellum,* Jeremy thought. *If you wish for peace, prepare for war.* His friend, Al Farris, had taught him that bit of Latin when they had competed in an IPPSC combat shoot in Pittsburgh two years ago. He wondered if the meaning was the same on this world. If it was, the people of Parabellum might be people he would like to know.

"If you go to the wood at the mountain's base, someone will direct you. The wood's people hate Apep. They defy him and his Guard. He lets them live. No one knows why."

"Will you guide me?"

"Oh, my! No, mate." Aral's face dissolved into a haggard look of doom. "I would slow you. Ain't been off this sea for fifty years. Wouldn't know what to do on land." He flashed a shy smile. "Besides, fishing at this anchor is poor. Time that I move further out to sea."

Jeremy looked into the Aral's eyes, and felt the old man's

fright bridge the space between them. Apep had fished the pluck from Aral's sea.

### DAY 12

The following day Aral was on his feet, fending for himself. And as the evening lights swarmed over the sky, Jeremy prepared to leave in search of Apep.

"Can't offer you much for your journey, just some meat of the beast, water, and advice," Aral said. Aral handed Jeremy a large portion of salted meat and a long, sausage shaped, water skin tied as a sling. Then Aral's gaze locked with Jeremy's. The night-lights swam over the steel blue surface of his eyes. Each reminded Jeremy of the last planet he had seen in his dream on arriving on this world.

"This is the advice," Aral said. His eyes went as hard as flint. Jeremy wanted to move back from them. He didn't. "Stay away from Apep's town! Stay away from Aralsk! Everyone bows to Apep there. He's their god. Of their own will, they bring their children to be his slaves. Stay away from Aralsk!" Aral's eyes went soft, human again, and he raised a hard, calloused hand and patted Jeremy's shoulder with the gentle touch of a grandfather.

Jeremy released his breath. It came in a hiss, and he felt his muscles give up tension he had not realized was there. "Thanks for the advice." He paused, continuing to peer into Aral's eyes. "And thanks for my life."

"Use it well," Aral said.

———

# HANK DAVISON IN CAPTIVITY

*Day 5*

Hank Davison's body lurched to the left, then was snatched back to the right with the same suddenness, sending a sharp pain through his left chest, down his legs and dragging a gasp from deep within him. Sluggishly, he opened his eyes to see a large, brown, horse's ass above and above that the canopy of leaves—now thinning visibly—which had shielded him and his fellow travelers from the sky for the past two days. The travois, on which he was strapped, bucked again as it rode over something he couldn't see. To his right a catman growled and another, further ahead of them (perhaps the one leading the horse, from where he lay Hank couldn't see) growled back.

———

They had been traveling this way for most of three days now. Occasionally, Hank would see Rudy following, but most of the time, the pup remained hidden even from his eyes. Twice, the lead catman—the one whose eyes periodically went wild with a vortex of spinning stars—had sent out one of their number, Hank assumed, to catch or kill the dog, but each had returned without their prize.

The catman to his right leaned in to gaze into Hank's eyes, then the vortex of stars spun into those cat eyes, and the creature spoke. "Ahh. Awake I see."

Hank thought he could discern an almost human smile form on the creature's face. Then over the cat's shoulder Hank saw a ripple of color cross the leafy background, much like the image distortion seen when one tosses a pebble into a reflection on a calm pond. Then again, from the corner of his eye, something small, a blur of light much like heat rising off hot asphalt.

Suddenly, the whole forest came alive with movement. A human voice bellowed "Parabellum," and the sharp crack of automatic gunfire tore the forest's calm. The catman to Hank's left erupted into geysers of blood.

As shouts of "Parabellum" rained down on them from the forest, the swirling stars blinked out of the catman's eyes. He spun on his heals, leaped astride the horse pulling the travois, and spurred it into a gallop. The travois crashed wildly through the forest, bucking its way over, and bashing its way past obstacles. Hank saw Rudy's head pop up from the brush, and then he lost sight of the pup as the horse, catman, travois, and Hank exited the forest, and started into the mountains toward Apep's palace and almost certain death.

———

# JEREMY WHEELER

*Day 13*

Jeremy estimated that the trip to the edge of Aral's sea would take two days. In the green pastures at the edge he'd rest, and seek information from the agrarian people who Aral said lived there. By his guess, twenty-two of his thirty days would be gone then, fifteen used up in this world, seven in his. Unless he found a guide, he would lose his race to stop Apep before that monster dumped their two worlds together, destroying both.

His injury had cost him his stamina, strength. His muscles were stiff, weak, and the muscles withered from the beast's poison caused him to limp. The limp became more pronounced as that first night grew old. Aral's sea seemed all the more dominant, all the more insurmountable. Still, he pressed on, testing the limits of his altered body, walking until his

—

muscles screamed and trembled. Then he scooped sand and pulled the desert grass.

When the morning sun peeked above the horizon to chase the evening lights from the sky, he sat cleaning the Ruger, thinking.

He thought about Aral's warning. He worried about Hank Davison. But, most of all, he tried to remember his wife, Cindy. His memories of her were growing dim, as if years, rather than days, had passed since they had said their goodbys. He wondered if he would ever see her again, and if he would remember her when he did.

Later, in the heat of the day, pocketed in his shelter of sand and desert grass, he dreamed of the woman he loved. This time, she had blond hair, blue eyes, and an insignificant scar on her chin, and her name was Lori.

## DAY 14

Jeremy had been walking in grassy plains for two hours before the sun burned away the mountain's lights. The sand-covered hardpan of the sea had given way to soil covered in a dense growth of chest high grass similar to sea oats. The grass had a thin stem and was top heavy. The breezes tossed it in waves, and bent it low to writhe against the ground.

The uninterrupted expanse of grass spread on for miles until it met the green finger of woodlands sketched against the base of the mountains. He did not see signs of life.

The sun was above the horizon this day before he began to limp, and thirst and hunger forced him to stop for sustenance. He had expected to find some evidence of civilization by now. Instead, he found another sea, a sea as formidable, in its own way, as Aral's desert sea.

He sat to rest, and as he stared across the waves of grass, the image of Lori, the woman who was and was not his wife, crept into his mind. And from her arms a child stared at him, eyes ravenous, dangerous.

The squeak and rattle of board upon board and the shriek and jingle of metal on metal jarred him from his daydream. The sounds were almost on top of him before he could react.

The gun belt released a soft groan as he rose to a crouched position, his head just above the writhing grasses.

Dragged by a large square-rigged sail that billowed in the wind, an odd conveyance squawked and clattered its way across the grassy waves. It rode six feet above the ground on wooden-spoke wheels, three on either side. Wooden crates and barrels stood in deep stacks on its rough, weathered decking.

A large, well-muscled man steered the vessel using a massive ship's wheel. He had a swarthy complexion and dressed in baggy, white pants and a voluminous shirt that tied at the waist and flapped in the wind. Jeremy thought the man looked like he had been cast for the role of Blue Beard in an Errol Flynn movie.

Two other men moved to the orders of the first. Both men were smaller, younger than the man at the wheel. They padded around the deck on calloused yet nimble feet, their bare backs baked black by the sun, their long, dark beards and hair tangled by the wind.

One of the men pointed to Jeremy and called to the man at the wheel. All heads turned his way.

The man at the wheel fixed his gaze on Jeremy for half a minute, then raised a cone-shaped device to his lips. "Ahoy, mate. We're three days out of Muynak; destined for Aralsk. Care to come aboard?" The man lowered the cone. His coal black eyes sparked with sunlight, and his teeth shined unnaturally white against his dark skin.

"How far to Aralsk?" Jeremy didn't know if he could trust these men, but he did need information and supplies. And despite its odd appearance, the vessel seemed to consume large expanses of the plain in ease. Its speed would gain him a day, maybe two, and it would be good to ride, to rest. He would need his strength when he found Apep.

In Aralsk he planned to get supplies and directions to Parabellum. The people of Aralsk didn't need to know his intentions. That was his business.

"One day. Maybe less if the wind holds." The man maintained his smile. Yet the expression on his face told Jeremy he was being measured.

"What price?"

The man's brow wrinkled with puzzlement.

The lumbering mass of timber, steel, and sailing cloth continued to close ground. It was almost on top of him before the man replied.

"The wind is free, a gift of Apep. The deck space does not cost me. I'll not charge you."

The words seemed guileless. Still, Jeremy sensed danger here, yet, this was a peril he'd have to face. His goal was untold days away, and time was growing short.

Without further discussion, he began to trot alongside the clattering transport. The tall grass beat at him, pelting him with its broad flat seed pods. His eyes searched for a landing on the flatbed. His hands fumbled for purchase. For an instant, he saw himself falling, going down beneath the wheels, his upraised hands waiving in vain, the broad, steel band of a twelve-foot wheel bearing down on him. In his mind's ear he heard the crunch of bone. Then his hand found one of several belaying pins along the edge of the craft. Grunting, he swung himself onto the deck.

Jeremy found the captain and crew of the vessel to be simple, hard-working men, thirsty for conversation. They appeared anxious to hear his story and equally as eager to tell their own.

Syr, a forty-five-year-old man with a hard face and dull eyes, captained the ship. When he was not at sea, he lived

—

with his wife and two sons in Aralsk. His main function in life was to ferry cargo from Muynak, a small port on the south coast of Aral's sea, to Aralsk in the northeast.

The cargo consisted of food items, metals, and gems sent to pay taxes owed Apep by people of the lower provinces. Syr said Apep's Guard would receive the cargo in Aralsk. From there, the Guard would act as guides for the caravans that carried the cargo over the mountains.

"No human has returned from that trip," Syr said. He frowned, and Jeremy thought the younger men looked surprised at his expression.

Syr smiled when he spoke of his wife and children, but his face went blank when he talked of his work, and Jeremy supposed that Syr's devotion to Apep was not passionate. Jeremy liked this man.

The two deck hands, Amu and Darya, were another matter altogether. They were from Muynak. They were young men, both less than twenty, Jeremy judged, and they had signed on with Syr as an adventure. Both planed to continue, with the cargo, across the mountains to the fabled palace of Apep. Their goal was to become members of Apep's court. They spoke of their hopes with the innocence and passions of youth.

When it came Jeremy's time to talk, he spun a tale calculated to hold to the facts of his quest as much as possible. It left less to trip him up should the men ask questions. He told the men, the people of his province had fallen prey to indestructible beasts. He and Hank Davison had set out for Apep's palace to seek his help and counsel. They had wandered apart while searching for food. So he had gone on alone, hoping to find Hank later.

The three men appeared to take his story at face value, although each declared they had never heard of the province of Prattville.

"A strange name, that," Syr said. The others agreed.

The vessel moved on through the day, jarring its way across the grassy plain. But as the night-lights rose in the sky, Syr dropped the sail.

"Daren't navigate by the night-lights. This sea is treacherous!" Syr said. "We'll sail at first light. We shall port in New Aralsk at noon."

Jeremy was reclining on his pack. He sat up. "New Aralsk? I thought you were bound for Aralsk."

Syr's brow furrowed then smoothed. "I assumed you knew, although there is no reason you should. The people abandoned Aralsk thirty years ago. It was the decree of Apep. New Aralsk is in a valley some fifty miles closer to the wood."

Again, Jeremy leaned back on his pack as the implication of Syr's words played on his mind. The people of Aralsk had moved from the place on the sea where they and their ancestors had lived for hundreds of years. And they had done this not because the sea was dry, it had been dry for three-hundred years, but because Apep had decreed it. How much would these people sacrifice, how much more would they do for Apep?

Jeremy Wheeler found it was much cooler in the writhing grasses than on the sands and hardpan. The men gathered around a crude iron stove for warmth during the evening. Jeremy sat with his back to the mountains as he cleaned the Ruger. The three men faced him across the stove, sitting cross-legged on the hard, wooden decking. Their conversation was animated at first, but it gradually faded, leaving only the chirr of insects and the whisper of the wind through the grass.

When he finally looked up from the Ruger, Jeremy found the gaze of all three men fixed on the multicolored lights above the mountain. Their faces were blissful. Their eyes held a dreamy stare. Queasiness, slick and greasy, slid through Jeremy's core.

"We can't see the lights from my province," Jeremy said, hoping to reanimate the mannequin like figures who stared his way. His eyes flicked from face to face.

No one spoke. Jeremy watched the night-lights dance and strike like multicolored lightning in their flat eyes. His muscles tensed. His stomach hitched up until his balls hurt. He began slipping cartridges from his belt and sliding them into the Ruger's cylinders.

He was tempted to look around at the night-lights, questioned if they could perform the same hypnotism on him, decided not to risk it. Instead, he offered another question.

"Syr, have the lights always been in the night sky?"

Syr's words came slow, dropping from his lips in a lazy drool. "The lights have been there for a hundred years, and more. Apep gave the lights to the people and the people have been happy since. The lights serve the people. The people serve Apep."

Jeremy didn't like the dreamy sound of Syr's voice. He slid the last cartridge into the large, Ruger handgun, and closed the cylinders.

"How long have the people served Apep?"

"Always," Syr said.

"Has anyone ever defied . . . ever challenged Apep?"

Distantly, Jeremy heard a buzzing like a million mad bees. As if in response to this, Syr's voice grew deeper, more mechanical. His pupils dwindled to the size of grains of sand. "The people of Parabellum challenge Apep."

Jeremy noticed the hand gripping the Ruger was beginning to sweat.

"The people of Parabellum do not serve. They do not know the way. The lights do not serve the people of Parabellum."

"Does Apep have a weakness?"

"Apep is all powerful!" the three men replied at once, and the questioning session turned into a chant. "He made all men. Time cannot defeat him. Men cannot challenge him. He controls the seas, skies, and earth beneath. All must serve him, so the lights will serve the people."

Jeremy cocked and leveled the Ruger at the men.

*He is not God.*

The night-lights flowed across the surface of the men's eyes, growing brighter and changing color at a frenzied pace. Syr started to vibrate, his ass bouncing on the rough, sun bleached decking. An eerie, almost imperceptible sound started low in Syr's throat. The sound increased in pitch and volume like the air horns of a train approaching from many miles away. The more the sound increased, the more Syr vibrated.

*What the hell?* Jeremy's mind questioned. He brought the Ruger up, and aimed it at Syr's breast bone. His finger was tight on the trigger. The winds began to rise around the vessel whipping at him. The night-lights flashed like a stroboscope. Jeremy wanted to look behind him, but he didn't dare move his gaze from Syr.

The *thump-thump-thump* of Syr's body against the weathered, deck boards filled Jeremy's ears. The ship began to rock. Syr's eyes filled with stars, and he lifted from the deck! A protective bubble of multicolored light surrounded him as his body rose high into the swirling, night air.

The sound in Syr continued to wind up and up, until it broke from his throat splitting the winds with fog horn intensity. "You cannot challenge me. Give up your foolish chase. Bow down to me. Look into the lights, and the lights will serve you and make you happy."

Jeremy's muscles turned to stone at the sound of the voice. He wasn't ready. He hadn't expected a challenge from Apep here, now.

A rock-like lump rose in his throat. He swallowed, and felt it tear at him. "If I'm no threat to you, then why do you

---

waste your time with me? Why don't you kill me and have done with it?"

"I'm a generous god. I don't want you to waste your life when you can be in my service."

"You are not *my* God!" Jeremy said.

His mind raced. Would someone who could destroy whole worlds hesitate to kill him if he could? Were Apep's powers stretched to their limits? Then he remembered Cindy's words, "He wants you alive, but alive with him is worse than the death the others would have for you."

Jeremy said, "I've heard you can see through the eyes of your Guard. I wasn't aware you were so powerful you could reach out and do what you've done here. You impress me," he lied. Apep frightened him, scared the shit out of him, to be truthful. But Apep didn't impress him. He revolted him.

"I am all powerful. Join me. Give your body to me, and the light will serve you."

"I wonder just how powerful you are? Tell me, when you inhabit a body do you become that body, or do you do a little ventriloquism act?" Jeremy did not wait for an answer. "The reason I ask is that I was wondering what would happen if I pulled this trigger and put some lead in the head of your host."

"You would kill this innocent man? Are you so different than I remember you?"

The child's face, that of the child Lori—Hellman? Wheeler?—held in his dreams, flashed in his mind's eye. Jeremy shifted the sights of the Ruger and squeezed the trigger.

The handgun's boom filled the night. Syr screamed. The stars went out of his eyes.

The night-lights dimmed. The wind died to a gentle breeze. Syr's body crashed to the bare deck-boards. A broad line of red marked his cheek, neck. His earlobe was gone.

"So you're invincible, are you?" Jeremy yelled. "Then why did *you* scream in fear?"

A hollow laugh bubbled up. Jeremy's mouth soured from it.

---

Later, Jeremy unpacked bandages from the first aid kit, and using gin as antiseptic, he tended Syr's ear. Syr didn't respond. He was still in a trance.

Jeremy regretted injuring this man, but he had needed to know what he was up against. He had needed to know if Apep had soft spots, limitations. And as much as he regretted injuring Syr, he regretted even more not placing the bullet between Syr's eyes while the stars spun in them. And that thought shocked him. This was the first time he had allowed himself to think of his purpose here.

And now, he realized his purpose was to kill.

### *APEP'S PALACE*

In a cool, dark, sterile room several days journey from Syr's odd sailing vessel, a dark figure stood holding his right ear. Blood streamed through his fingers and down his cheek. His eyes flamed, but an odd, hungry smile showed on his face.

"You're *exactly* as I remember you, old man," Apep said.

### *DAY 14*

The three sailors remained in a trance through the night. Yet when the sun supplanted the night-sky's churning lights, the three men came to life and went about preparing the vessel for the day.

The men greased the wheels, and examined the sail for wear and small tears. Talk was spare, related to the work. No one mentioned, nor for that matter seemed to note, Syr's injury.

Wind billowed the sail within thirty minutes of dawn. In two hours Aralsk was in sight to the north, and the vessel was turning to the east, toward the mountains. Another ninety minutes and the vessel breasted a gentle hill, and Jeremy saw a small town nestled in the valley below.

———

Jeremy was sitting out of sight of the three sailors, at the bow of the vessel. He was considering what he should do next. The spareness of the talk through the day had made him more suspicious of the men. He wasn't sure how much they might remember about Apep's visit and the damage to Syr's ear. But, he knew these men were at Apep's command, as would be the town's people. When the town came into sight, he decided it was time to part company.

The ship's wheels slipped into the ruts of a crude road which worked its way down the valley's wall. And as the vessel started its decent to the town, Jeremy dropped over the bow, between the wheels. Hugging the ground, he remained hidden in the tall grasses until the vessel was well away. Then he moved parallel and away from the vessel until he was about a mile up the valley. There he settled into a niche on the ridge where he could watch the ship enter town.

The town consisted of a very broad, main street with several, narrow, secondary streets which ended at either side of the valley. Twelve, large, one-and two-story, buildings were bunched together at the north end of the main street, six on either side. Children played where smaller buildings lined the secondary streets.

The ship wound down the side of the valley, following a wide looping road that entered the town from the south, became the main street, and ended north of the town in what appeared to be the town dump. A small stream, dotted here and there with trees and bushes, meandered down the east side of the valley.

As Jeremy watched, Syr's ship made its turn at the south end of the valley and started north. Dust plumed behind the wheels as they rolled over the worn, rutted roadbed.

The ship's arrival brought the town to life. Heads poked from windows, and people appeared in doorways as it passed. The town's people followed.

Syr's ship lumbered to the middle of town. When it

stopped the town's people circled, standing well back for several minutes. Then to Jeremy's surprise, the people set upon the ship, attacking with clubs, sticks, stones.

The people didn't touch Syr. However, they mobbed the two strangers from Muynak, clubbing them unconscious before Syr could push his way into their midst to stop the senseless bludgeoning. Jeremy watched a frantic search followed by a heated discussion.

Someone struck Syr several blows, driving him to his knees. Then all heads turned toward the hillside, searching.

An hour later, Jeremy squatted like a hunted fox hidden in his niche. He was vaguely aware of a knotting pain climbing his calves, spreading into his thighs. He ignored it. From the village, more than a hundred people approached. They walked shoulder to shoulder, stretched in a line, swinging across the hillside like a maniacal thresher of flesh and bone. Their feet crushed and ground the chest high grasses into dust. Their eyes scanned the hillside.

As they neared, Jeremy released the belts cinching his pack, and removed the Detonics, its holster, a box of cartridges, and five magazines. He began sliding cartridges into the magazines.

Fifteen minutes passed. The Detonics sat ready, loaded, in its holster at the small of his back. Five magazines bulged his left jeans-pocket. He drew the revolver from the holster on his hip. His thumb poised to sweep back the hammer. Droplets of sweat covered his face. His muscles were tight, tense, ready.

The town's people carried clubs, knives. He had the guns. Yet, there were more than a hundred of them and only one of him. And he was weak from the desert and the beast's poison. He had no illusion about the ultimate outcome if he was discovered.

They were twenty paces from him now. The crunch of

———

213

their foot falls sounded like a great beast, a dinosaur devouring the grass, coming to devour him.

His index finger moved to hook over the Ruger's trigger. His thumb eased back on the hammer. He heard the double snap as the hammer slid through half-to full-cock. They were only seconds away now. He started to rise. Suddenly, his leg muscles knotted, cramped, refused to lift him, dragged him to the ground.

Slipping back on his butt, Jeremy eased his legs out flat and massaged the screaming muscles, his eyes went wet with tears. The muscles would not give. He pounded his leg with his fist, and writhed in pain as the last seconds passed. It was no good, the muscles would not give, so his hand returned to the Ruger, and he swung it toward the crowd. He would die then, but not easy, not cowering.

Then, without signal or discussion, the mob stopped. People looked around as if they had awakened from a deep sleep. They milled into small groups, and turned toward the town.

In the back of Jeremy's mind he heard a familiar, unpleasant laugh, and the face of the dream-child flashed behind his eyes, on a field of stars. *Why this again?*

The sudden withdrawal of the town's people left Jeremy feeling all the more weak, small, incapable. He was aware that his life had been given to him by luck or fate or perhaps by the one he had come to destroy. And although this last explanation seemed the least plausible, he was sure it was the truth. Cindy had said that of the three (Dougal, Conrad, Apep) Apep was the one who wanted most to save him, although death would be better. So Jeremy was left to question whether he owed his life to Apep—or to chance?

He pressed back into his niche, and allowed his mind to wander while he waited for sleep. He had lost at least twenty pounds since he had entered the portal. His clothing hung off him in heavy, limp folds and smelled of sweat and the desert grass. The brim of his hat drooped lazily over his eyes and ears. Shrunken from the poison, his arm and the muscles of his left chest were weak. His diet of jerky, salted beast, and water had left him with small sores in his mouth. His cheeks and eyes felt sunken, his lips were cracked and his skin leathery and insensate from constant pelting from the desert sand. He had survived the desert, but it had left him a shell. He needed food, a bath, clean clothing and most of all, rest. Save the rest, the town in the valley held everything he needed, and he knew he had to go there.

At sunset the night-lights appeared, starting with brilliant detonations that made short distinct shadows. Minutes later, a chant rose from the town in monotonic waves that washed in on him with ever increasing volume as each new voice joined the chorus.

"Apep is all powerful! He made all men. Time cannot defeat him. Men cannot challenge him. He controls the seas, skies, and earth beneath. All must serve him, so the lights will serve the people."

Jeremy Wheeler entered the town from the north. He passed through the town dump, and strolled down the center of the main street. He felt like the lead turkey in the Thanksgiving parade, and he gave a silent prayer that the trance of the night-lights would blind the town's people to his arrival.

The tension in his groin increased, gnawing at him.

He didn't feel easy about this entrance into town. Nevertheless, he had considered his options, and there was no other choice. If he tried to enter with the town's people normal and aware, he would be killed or captured. And in his weakened condition, without the supplies which the town offered, he would not survive his search for Apep.

The town's people lined the west side of the main street.

Their praying voices filled the night as the gassy lights formed ideograms in the night sky for their glassy eyes. The chant seemed more frenetic, more prolonged than it had been with the men on the ship the previous night.

Jeremy scanned the street. Each building had a sign announcing its function. Other than the signs, all the buildings were the same: square, unornamented, built of the desert-sea's hardpan bricks. Each building had a single entrance and two, square-cut windows facing the street, and each abutted the next. On both sides of the street, a covered, wooden walk fronted the buildings. Apep's "Tax Warehouse" was the third building on the east side of town.

New Aralsk's population sat along the wooden walk on the west side of town. They faced the night-lights and the warehouse. Jeremy watched their glazed, fixed eyes. All were in the hypnotic trance of the lights. If they saw him, they did not react as he approached the warehouse.

As he expected, the warehouse was neither barred nor locked. No one would steal from Apep. Large, grass mats covered the entrance and windows. He stepped to the entrance and pushed the mat aside. It was dark inside. A thin light filtered in from the street. Jeremy took matches from his pack, struck one, and entered. An oil lantern hung from a wooden peg just inside the entrance. He lit the wick. It burned with the same slow, red flame as Aral's lamps.

Crates lined the walls and formed several neat rows running from the front to the back of the building. A pyramid of fuel oil barrels, stacked on their sides and held in place with large ropes and wooden chocks, ran the length of the room, in line with the entrance.

Jeremy found a hammer and chisel, and began to pry open crates. There were clothing, boots, canned goods, gold coins, precious metals, jewels and all sorts of devices and materials Jeremy didn't recognize.

He filled his pack with dried meats, jars of fruits and vegetables, and a few gold pieces. The gold, he believed, might come in handy in the event he should need to loosen tongues.

His search was running into its third hour before he found a crate filled with a suitable pant. The cut was similar to Levi Button Fly Jeans, but the pant was in a khaki, not the familiar blue. The container also contained shirts of the same khaki, made from a heavy broadcloth. It appeared to be a uniform, but he didn't care. It was serviceable. He took two outfits. One he wore; the other he rolled into a tight bundle in a green, animal-hair blanket and tied to the back of the pack. He finished his outfits with a pair of square toed, brown, leather boots and a hand-tooled, leather hat. He thought he must look like a military style cowboy in his new outfit, and for a mental beat, he wished he had a mirror. Then he thought of what the desert must have made of him, and he grimaced. He wouldn't like to see himself now.

When Jeremy stepped from the warehouse into the cool night air, the silence closed on his throat like a hand. His muscles tightened. He scanned the people who sat facing him across the broad street. They still stared fixedly. No one moved. Yet something had changed. Then Hundreds of glassy eyes shifted to fix him in a single unblinking stare! His mind froze for a second, but his hand touched the Ruger's stocks. His throat worked, reflexively, in an aborted swallow, and he realized he had no spit.

*It's a trap!*

In a slow, almost casual manner, men, women, children came to their feet. At each end of the town, people strolled across the wide street forming barriers, making retreat or escape impossible. Then they started to move toward him. Each wall of bodies picked up troops from the west walk as it closed distance.

His hand drew the revolver, and his arm swung up to form a straight line with his shoulder. The blade of the front sight

———

slid into the notch at the rear. It lined up on the forehead of a large man in the center of the line at the south end of town. Jeremy squeezed the trigger. The gun roared. Flame spat from the barrel. The gun kicked upward, and forced his hand in a clockwise turn.

A black hole appeared in the large man's forehead. The back of his skull exploded outward. Brains and bone fragments sprayed the people behind him. The man folded in on himself, swallowed by his clothing. A woman stepped over him and filled the hole he left. The people continued to move forward, stepping off the distance like a clockwork mechanism. No one screamed. No one ran. No one broke the line.

Jeremy swallowed heavily, and wet his lips with a flick of his tongue. These people weren't human. They were parts of a larger machine bent on his destruction. He raised the gun again, and squeezed the trigger. A bullet exploded the heart of a man with gray hair and a long scar on his left cheek. He sighed and dropped his sledgehammer on the toe of the man to his right. The man with the smashed toe grimaced. Then a bullet exploded his Adam's apple. He dropped to his knees, and pitched forward on his face. Dust plumed around him. The bullet had passed through his throat and into the face of a woman. She collapsed in a tangle of petticoats. In seconds, three more men dropped into the dust. The ranks that followed, trampled their lifeless bodies. Still, the line held and continued to close on him.

Stones and sticks pelted him from all directions. Jeremy opened the Ruger's cylinders, ejected the brass and backed into the warehouse as he fed cartridges to the empty cylinders.

Inside, Jeremy's gaze darted about, searching the room for an avenue of escape. There was none. The walls were thick, made of square, hardpan bricks stacked one upon another.

He was reminded of a riddle: Does mortar hold bricks

together or apart? The point of the riddle was lost here. The walls used no mortar. He looked along the pyramid of barrels to the entrance and then to the back wall, and an idea formed.

He scrambled to the rear of the warehouse, filled his pocket with matches, and tossed his pack against the wall. Then he grabbed a sledge hammer and a lantern. He ran to the pyramid of barrels, and with the hammer, drove the wooden chock from beneath the bottom barrel. The barrels sagged against the ropes. He lit the lantern, and placed it on top of the last barrel.

Three men came through the front door as he reached the street side of the pyramid. Jeremy drew the Detonics and shot the closest man through the heart. He sank to the floor, deflating like a punctured pool toy.

Jeremy swung the hammer at the front chock. The chock moved but held. He turned back to the door and fired on the other two men who were now upon him. A blade in a dead hand, slit his shirt and raked his ribs. A pain like liquid fire told him the blade had done significant damage. He fired the gun dry. Men and women fell as they breached the door.

He dropped the hammer and groped for a second magazine. The first clattered to the floor. He slapped the second into place, and pointed the gun at the body-clogged doorway. It roared. Blood splattered. Red ran across the floor. It dripped from the doorsill onto the wooden planking of the sidewalk. Still, they came. Skating on the gore slicked boards, they came. Tripping in tangles of dead arms and legs, *they came.*

Jeremy dropped the spent magazine, and groped for another. A knife flew through the air, and stuck deep in his thigh. It gave a dull, hot pain. He slid the new magazine into place, and put a bullet in the knife thrower's chest. Her lips formed an "O," and she slumped to the floor.

He pulled the knife free of his thigh. The pain burned bright, then dulled. Blood ran into his boot. The boot squeaked and sucked at his foot. He hurled the knife at the struggling, surging mass at the door. The haft hit a man on the forehead. He fell into the bloody heap of bodies.

Jeremy found the hammer, and swung it at the chock. The large, wooden brace skittered across the floor. The barrels sagged against the ropes. He swung the hammer at the plug in the first barrel. It gave way. Viscous, red oil spilled across the floor.

Sticks and stones rained down on him from the doorway and window. A stone stuck him high on the forehead. Light exploded behind his eyes. Blood blinded him. He staggered back, giving ground, wiping blood from his eyes. Then he brought the Detonics up and emptied it.

A shot went wild. The next five rounds found their marks. A bald man climbed over the bodies at the door. Jeremy shot him in the chest. He fell on his face. His teeth broke on the floor.

A knife raked Jeremy's shoulder blade. He swung the hammer at his attacker, a boy of about fifteen. The hammer struck him in the temple. His eyes rolled up. Spittle drooled from the corner of his mouth in a long string. He sank to the floor.

Jeremy looked at the boy. He wasn't any older than Linda or Sam. Why did he have to die? What was his part in this? Then he turned back to the barrels.

Swinging the hammer, Jeremy smashed the ends of the first four barrels. Oil ran in thick runnels over the floor, soaking dry planking, wetting the mob's feet. Jeremy retreated. He dropped the hammer, holstered the Detonics, and drew his buck knife. The mob moved in, filling the front of the warehouse, wading in the oil and blood.

When he reached the last barrel, Jeremy lifted the lantern, and hurled it over the heads of the mob to the front of the warehouse. It smashed on the barrels. Flames sucked up the oil, and raced over the floor.

The mob halted. People looked around in confusion. The

flames nibbled at them, then bit. Fire climbed their legs. Clothing flamed. Hair sizzled.

Jeremy turned back to the barrels, and began to saw at the rope with the buck knife. The rough rope curled away from the razor sharp edge. The pyramid collapsed. Barrels careened to the rear and front of the building, breaking open, spilling their contents. The flames lapped up the oil, and roared for more. Men, women, children screamed.

The hiss and crackle of burning flesh filled Jeremy's ears. He cringed back from the noisome odor. His eyes stung. The smoke choked him.

People spun and danced like marionettes. They beat at the flames with their hands until one limb and then another crumbled like charred kindling. The flames crawled over them, gluttonous, greedy.

Jeremy watched a woman's ears and nose dissolved like fat in a skillet. Her face became a torch. His stomach rolled. He turned away, and shambled to the rear wall of the warehouse.

Several barrels lounged against the wall, drooling their contents into pools on the floor. The collision had knocked several bricks askew.

He climbed over the barrels, and heaved against the loose bricks. In seconds a hole formed.

He lifted his pack, and looked back to the room for the last time. It was engulfed in flame and smoke. No one stood. No one screamed.

He slid through the hole, and left the dead town to burn.

Jeremy Wheeler walked, stumbled, and crawled his way to the edge of the stream at the valley's eastern side. He bathed in the stream, and sterilized his wounds with Jack Daniels, grinding his teeth against the pain. It was a damn bad waste of good whiskey. He bound the wounds with strips torn from his wrecked khaki shirt.

—

When he was finished, he watched the buildings of New Aralsk burn with tall, brilliant flames, which danced over the roof tops and along the wooden sidewalks, engulfing the whole town and belching black smoke into the night sky. The smoke and flame banked Apep's hypnotic night-lights. It didn't matter. The lights would no longer speak to the people of New Aralsk.

He celebrated being alive, and saluted the dead with a sip of the bourbon. Then he cleaned and loaded the guns and watched the flames eat until sleep took him. He had killed, but he did not hate the people he had fought. In all ways, that made the memory of it worse.

### *DAY 15*

*The stream cut a meandering way through the soil and tall grasses of the valley. Cool water rushed, churned and bubbled as it surmounted small and large stones hindering its progress. Jeremy Wheeler watched small fishes dart beneath its cool surface, and for the first time in this distant, malevolent world, he heard a bird's song. The song made a ripple in his soul, and a shudder of shame and loneliness fetched up.*

*The village called New Aralsk had given itself totally to the flames. Charred piles of debris lined the dead streets, vestiges of the wooden sidewalks with their covers against this world's sun. Blackened hardpan walls stood without roofs, testifying that this had once been an active port where people congregated, worked, lived, loved, died. The air hung heavy with the acrid odor of burned wood, oil, cloth, all mingled with the cloying sweet smell of cooked flesh.*

*Somewhere in the dense grass something approached. Jeremy could hear its slow irregular shuffle, which bent and broke the lush, green grasses at the stream's edge. Yet his searching eyes detected nothing. He knew he should feel threatened, but a bland curiosity was all the emotion he could rouse. He stood tossing small pebbles into the stream and listening as the sounds drew near.*

*Several seconds later the squat figure of a man broke through the tall grass two yards from him and stopped. He stared at Jeremy with pale, yellow eyes. His wizened face was hard, accusing.*

*Jeremy's heart quickened.* "It's Conrad LuPone!" he thought.

*Canting his head to the side, and looking Jeremy up and down with slitted eyes, he approached, mouth agape.*

*"Don't you know me?" Jeremy said. "You called me here. Or didn't you expect me to get this far?"*

*"I know who I summoned and why. Now I'm trying to see what you are—human or machine. You're here to* save *lives,* not *to destroy them."*

*Conrad gestured to New Aralsk. "Do you value life less than Apep?" He spat viscous phlegm into the dust at Jeremy's feet, punctuating his question. His eyes burned with suspicion and hate.*

*Jeremy felt something inside him sag, opening a void. Then anger swelled to overflow that emptiness. "You accuse easily old man. Where were* you *when* I *needed help?* You *said I was the only one who could defeat Apep.* You *said I was the only one who could close the portals." Jeremy staggered to his feet. "I'm risking my life and with it the lives of my* family, *my* people, *my* world. I *will not lie down and die to spare the blood of* your *people!"*

*The violent resentment in Conrad's eyes turned to hurt. That hurt hung in them like tears. He shook his head sadly. "It was* pointless! Apep can't allow you to die. That's *your* power over *him! That's why Dougal sent for you. You are here for Dougal, not to war with my people!" He turned and hobbled toward the town.*

*Jeremy stood by the stream for several seconds, feeling weak and alone now that he had spent his anger. Then he shambled after the little man. "You said you'd be here for me. I lost a friend coming through the portal. Name's Hank Davison. He'll* help. We *need to find him."*

*Conrad continued toward the ruined town. "Two-hundred*

---

223

*dead, and you want your friend! Forget him. We'll lose both worlds if you don't attend to business!"*

*Jeremy set his jaw. He would like to squash this little man who had made his life a shambles and now taunted him. "I need help, damn it. I can't go it alone."*

*"You underestimate yourself. You killed a town for a bit of food and a change of clothes. You can go on."*

*"You don't understand. I need someone to make it real. I think I'm going crazy. Everything's so removed from what I know. Like a dream. I have these dreams, these real memories—"*

*Conrad LuPone stopped, turned, and hands on hips, he narrowed his eyes at Jeremy. "Find the woman," he said.*

*"What?"*

*"Find the woman what returned from Apep's palace. She has what you need."*

*Jeremy shook his head violently. "First Hank."*

*Conrad scowled. "Hank can be no help to you. Thoughts of him . . . he will drag you down."*

*"I thought that at first. But he's stronger. I'm sure of it."*

*Conrad shook a finger at Jeremy. "Your friend has joined Apep."*

*Conrad paused, as if allowing time for the information to sink into Jeremy's instantly rejecting mind. "And so have I," Conrad said. Then the little man blinked and the lights of infinite galaxies filled his eyes.*

The galactic eyes jolted Jeremy Wheeler from sleep, wet with sweat. His breath came ragged, rapid. He was alone. Scrap images from the dream continued to flash in his mind, muddling his thoughts.

He sat up and gazed across the valley to the ruins of New Aralsk. It was the same as in the dream: burned out sidewalks, collapsed roofs and blackened walls. Yet, in the light of day and without the insolation of the dream, it was somehow worse. There was no pain, no shame in the dream. There was much of both in consciousness.

For several minutes he thought about the dream. Some of it made sense, considering his guilt and fears, and he felt more alone now than ever before.

He continued to gaze at the burned town, and thought about what he had done, what he had been *required* to do. He had to believe that. Yet, more than one-hundred people were dead. A small, unknown civilization was gone, and he was the cause of it.

He caught himself wondering how Syr and his family had died, then buried the thought. He could not allow himself the luxury of self pity. It would tear him down and make him weak when he needed to be strong. Here, he could not be absolved of his guilt, and he had seen too many people driven mad trying to free themselves of guilt by dwelling on it. Rational mathematics could not reason a hundred lives for one. But hundreds here for the billions he had left behind, maybe that worked, and if it didn't, still, he had a mission that must be completed. He could not pass it to another. If others judged him, he would have to accept that judgement, but he wouldn't do that job himself.

Jeremy stood, and brilliant, white sparks danced before his eyes. The earth moved beneath his feet, he grasped a nearby tree, and his vision dimmed into darkness. A high-pitched ringing cycled up masking the babbling brook and the bird's song. Seconds later the ringing faded, and a pin point of light opened, revealing the valley again. *I'm in great shape.*

In spite of the care he had taken in bandaging his wounds the previous night, his leg was swollen with fever. Itching frames of swollen, red tissue surrounded the wounds on his chest and leg. And although the laceration that had blinded him with gore was now closed, his head still throbbed from the stone's concussion.

---

He realized he was in no condition to travel, but he also realized he didn't have time to rest and heal. The town's pyre had burned through the night and part of the day, making a signal that could be seen for miles.

Apep's Guard would come to see what had happened to New Aralsk. Then they would follow. And if he wasn't far from here when they came, they'd annihilate him.

### DAY 17

Two days out of New Aralsk, Jeremy Wheeler found a half-obliterated camp fire as he crossed a trail smashed through the forest by large animals. The fire maker had scattered the charred wood and ashes, but the job was either hurried or sloppy. Some of the larger logs were still warm. The builder of the camp could not be far.

Jeremy searched the camp, but found only one set of human tracks. He or she, the tracks were small, was following the animals' trail eastward. The thought of another person, another voice sent a pleasant tingle through Jeremy. He followed.

In the evening, he found the makings of a second campfire. The trampled brush was cleared from a circle twelve-foot in diameter. Furrows scarred the earth to the ends of two, small logs which had been dragged to the center of the clearing and lain crosswise. Kindling was piled at the juncture of the logs.

He scanned the surrounding forest for signs of the camp builder. He saw none. But near the campfire he found a small leather packet filled with flint, steel, and dried meat.

The owner would miss the kit, and would come for it during the night. It was a tantalizing thought.

An hour later, in the slow-moving shadows of the forest, Jeremy spotted a plump rabbit. His hand drew the Ruger and fired, like an automaton. The rabbit rolled over and lay still. He looked at the rabbit, then at his hand. As in New Aralsk, the hand had made the decision to shoot, to kill. He wondered if this was a good thing or a bad thing. He couldn't decide.

Jeremy Wheeler skinned and gutted his kill. He carried the carcass back to camp. As the fat, pumpkin-orange sun sat above the horizon, he struck a match to the kindling, and spitted the rabbit near the yellow flame. Then he settled down to clean the Ruger.

Every few minutes he rotated the spit. The meat turned from a pinkish white to a rich, mahogany red as he watched. Air, redolent with the scent of roasting rabbit, wafted into the surrounding forest. Still, there was no sign of the kit's owner.

When the rabbit was cooked, he moved it away from the flames, and built the fire higher. Then he moved closer to the flame, and tried to appear concentrated on the task of tending the fire, while watching the forest from the corners of his eyes. He listened for sounds of the kit's owner creeping toward the camp, and for more. Just what he wasn't certain.

The night-lights had dimmed since New Aralsk. He didn't know whether cutting Apep's supply line and killing his worshipers had caused this effect or if it came from another source. Nevertheless, he was glad for it. For now, the sky was more as it should be.

However, the previous night he had noticed, in the muted shadows of early evening, the forest went silent, and the tree's branches seemed to move without the assistance of the westerly breeze. Then, he had believed it was just his imagination, that he had been talking to himself too much. Still, the silence of the night, in stark contrast to the hubbub of animal gossip in light of day, left him chilled. He did not like this world and its beasts.

———

The crickets ceased their chittering serenade as the sun slipped behind the shoulder of the horizon, and the sky went black. Throughout the forest several, high-pitched squeals died a sudden death. Then the night was silent.

Minutes later a rustle came from the forest. It was followed by a human shriek. Jeremy stood and stared into the shadows. A boy bounded from the forest at a full run toward the fire. A tree branch seemed to lunge at the boy's head. It tangled in his hair. The boy screamed again, pulled free. Then he was in the open and closing ground at an incredible pace. His eyes were wide with the terror of youth, and he continued his shriek until he slid into the cleared circle like a professional baseball player taking home plate. Nothing followed him.

Jeremy watched the boy drink in great gulps of air and fight back sobs. Several seconds passed before he made eye contact, then he managed between gasps, "You took my camp and my kit. I want them back." The boy's right hand rested on the haft of a large knife still sheathed on his side. His left hand combed a lock of red hair back from his blue eyes. The boy's eyes burned holes in him.

Jeremy assessed the boy's determined, tear-streaked face, and felt a smile struggling to surface. It was good to see a human face, especially one so young, especially after New Aralsk. He fought the smile. The boy wouldn't understand.

He picked up the kit, and tossed it to the boy.

"The packet's yours. We'll share the fire."

The boy's gaze darted to the spitted meat and back to Jeremy. "And the rabbit?"

Now Jeremy did smile. "And the rabbit," he said.

The boy's grip on the knife's haft relaxed, but his hand continued to rest there. Jeremy tore the rabbit free of the spit, halved it, and passed half to the boy. As he ate, the boy's hand forgot the knife. It joined the other in stripping the carcass of its meat and stuffing fingers full between greedy lips. Still, his cautious eyes flitted back-and-forth between the rabbit and Jeremy, leaving no doubt as to his continued suspicion, caution, even in the face of hunger.

Jeremy watched in silence as the meat disappeared. The boy gnawed over each bone, and sucked his fingers dry of the grease. He wiped the grease from his lips onto his shirt sleeve.

He judged the boy to be between twelve and fifteen years old. His hair was fiery red, his eyes blue. His body was well muscled and bronzed from the sun. However, his face betrayed his innocence. Unlike the children of New Aralsk, it was more weather abused than weather toughened.

Jeremy fetched one of three remaining glass containers from his pack.

The boy's hand went back to the knife's haft.

"I have some fruit," Jeremy said. "It's very good. It tastes. . . sweet."

The boy's eyes cut a trace up and down him and then focused on the container.

"You first." He nodded to the container.

The boy's caution spoke well of him, Jeremy thought. Again a smile fought to surface. This time Jeremy allowed it. *His trust won't come cheap.*

Jeremy worked the spring secured lid free. Then he removed half a fruit, and stuffed the whole of it into his mouth. Juice drooled over his lips and down his chin. Mimicking the boy's fireside manners, Jeremy wiped the juice away with his shirt sleeve as his new companion looked on with approving eyes.

"I don't know what these are called here, but we call them peaches where I come from," Jeremy said.

The boy's eyes lit with greed. He took the jar and plucked half fruit from it. Without hesitation, he stuffed the fruit into his mouth and chewed. He smiled, and juice washed down his chin.

"Peaches," he said.

The boy finished the last peach half, settled from his squat to his haunches, and leaned back on his elbows. "Are you going to kill me now?" he asked.

Jeremy felt stung by the boy's words. He raised an eyebrow, and appraised this young man once more. "Would I have fed you if I was going to kill you?"

"I saw what you did in New Aralsk. I thought you might want to kill me too."

The fright Jeremy had seen in the boy's eyes was gone. Now the boy was testing him. "What's your name?" he asked.

"Mark Scott. What's yours?"

"Jeremy Wheeler," Jeremy said. He turned his gaze to the fire, picked up a short stick, and poked the kindling causing the fire to rise. "Are you from New Aralsk, Mark?"

"No. I was there a week when you arrived."

"Where are you from?"

Mark frowned. "I—I don't think I'll say. You wouldn't believe me."

"Why do you say that?"

"The people of New Aralsk didn't."

With his stick, Jeremy shoved hard on one of the burning logs. Bright cinders broke loose and spiraled skyward as the log burst into flame. "You might find me different."

"Doesn't matter. I'm not telling."

Jeremy grunted acknowledgment of the boy's answer. He tossed the stick into the fire. "What about new Aralsk? What did you see there?" Jeremy asked.

"I was on the street when you walked into town. Is that what you mean?"

"Yes. But before that too. How did you come to be there?"

"I didn't have any choice. Apep's Guard brought me. The

town's people kept me there. Later, the Guard was supposed to take me to Apep. They said I was to serve him. They said it was a great honor. I didn't think it was so great an honor, but I was chained." He held his right arm out to Jeremy. The wrist was circled with bruises and scabbed-over abrasions.

"Where were you before the Guard picked you up?"

"That's the part you wouldn't believe," Mark said.

"Then tell me what happened in New Aralsk and after." He wanted to keep the boy talking, to luxuriate in the sound of another voice. It seemed a long time since he had talked to someone without having to be on his guard.

The boy looked at the fire for a few seconds, then started to talk.

"The Guard caught me in the grasslands. They're huge, ugly, catlike creatures." His gaze came up to meet Jeremy's, reading his eyes. Jeremy allowed this, then he nodded for the boy to continue.

"I was afraid, and I fought them. They . . . beat me. When they stopped, I couldn't stand." A tear formed in the corner of Mark's eye and rolled down his nose.

"They chained me with other people and marched us to New Aralsk. The people carried me part way. I would've died if they hadn't."

Jeremy continued to watch the boy's face. His eyes shined with wetness, but they had gone dull inside.

"When we got to New Aralsk, there was another Guard unit, and a . . . a caravan." He wagged his head in a show of uncertainty. "I'm not sure if that's the right word, but it was a group of people with pack animals.

"I was still pretty messed up, so they left me for the next caravan.

"The people of New Aralsk didn't hurt me. They fed me and treated my scrapes and cuts, but they kept me chained."

Mark's gaze flicked to him, and once again, Jeremy nodded.

---

231

"One of those sailing wagons came into town every other day. The town's people unloaded them. In the evenings, everyone would sit on the sidewalks and stare at those weird lights and chant. You hear them?"

"I heard."

"It didn't make any sense, I mean, that thing about the lights serving the people. And they acted like they were hearing the lights."

"Did you ever hear the lights?"

"One night when the lights were bright, I heard something like mumbling. The night you came, I heard something again. It was like the buzz of a million mad bees."

He paused and squinted at Jeremy. "Are you sure you want to hear this?"

"Yes." Jeremy didn't think he would learn much, if anything, from the boy's story, but the smallest tidbit of knowledge might be of use, and he still felt the need for the sound of another voice, the feeling of communication.

Mark picked up a handful of pea-sized pebbles and began tossing them, one by one, into the fire. Each pebble caused the fire to give up a fiery spiral of sparks. "All the time I was there I tried to tell people this was a mistake, that they should let me go. They didn't listen. They didn't believe me. Sometimes, I wonder if I do. Maybe I'm crazy."

Jeremy chuckled, and Mark's head jerked up, fire and question in his eyes.

Realizing his error, Jeremy said. "It's just . . . I know the feeling. That's all."

Mark nodded, sighed, then continued. "They kept me chained. Everyone and no one was in charge, so the key to my chains was kept near. When you came into town, I was chained to a hitching rail. The key was on a post a few feet away.

"I knew you were walking into a trap when you came down the street. They were chanting, but the people were different from the other nights. I don't know how to explain it. Their eyes were glassy like always but different . . . knowing . . . evil."

Jeremy remembered the eyes of Syr while Apep possessed him. He wondered why he hadn't recognized *that* look in the eyes of the people in New Aralsk. Had that look been there? Had Apep been there?

"I don't know what happened in the warehouse, but you don't need me to tell you that. When the whole town crowded in there, I thought you were dead for sure. None of those buildings had back doors.

"While they were busy with you, I worked the rail loose from the hitching post. It took me longer than I thought. Still, I was free before the fire burned down the post with the key."

"How did the fire cross the street?" Jeremy said.

"Just before the flames boiled out of the windows and doors, several barrels rolled through the door. They weren't on fire. But they soaked the street in oil. Some rolled across the street, and stopped against the sidewalk. When the flames came out of the windows and door, the oil caught fire. It burned across the street to the barrels.

"I collected the stuff in my kit and some food before everything went up in flames. Then I headed for the forest."

"Why here?"

"The people of New Aralsk talked about the people of a town called Parabellum, in the forest. They said that the people of Parabellum don't follow Apep. I thought it might be the right place to go."

Mark fell silent. His eyes avoided Jeremy's. His face went grim.

"What is it?" Jeremy said.

"I . . . "

"Say it."

"I heard them . . . I heard their screams. I heard them

—

233

sizzle as they burned . . . , smelled it." Tears were in his eyes, and his face was scarlet.

Flatly: "And?"

"I know I shouldn't care. They were holding me for God only knows what, but . . . They didn't deserve that. No one deserves to die like that. What you did was wrong."

There was a long silence. They stared at each other in the flickering light of the campfire.

He had hoped the boy would understand what happened in New Aralsk, understand he had no choice, that it wasn't his fault. But he had allowed the child to wound him with his own guilt, and *that* was his fault.

"You're still a boy. I don't expect you to understand, but . . . I have obligations. I didn't choose what I have to do. More lives than those of New Aralsk are at stake if I fail."

He moved his face closer to the boy, and stared into his eyes, trying to see into his soul. "I don't intend to fail. If that means killing a town, I'll kill a town. If it means killing a hundred towns, I'll do my best to kill a hundred towns. If it means that I die, then I'll die. But, I *will* fulfill *my* obligations *first.*"

"And if it means *my* life?" Mark asked.

"I wouldn't like that. And I would pray you understood why you had to die."

## OF ALL POSSIBILITIES

### Prattville, Ohio, 1992

*"Marion Brand is scheduled for a community pass this week,"* Hank Davison said.

*"Only a year? It took them longer than that to catch him,"* Jeremy Wheeler said.

*"It's the system,"* Hank said grimly. *"There shouldn't be an insanity plea. He should have been executed."*

"*Will you help me?*"

Hank looked at him with hard eyes. "*It's not easy to kill a man. . . . Even when you have good cause.*"

"*He killed Cindy and Sam and—*" There were tears in Jeremy's eyes. His hand fisted, relaxed and fisted again.

"*And you're still not a murderer at heart. And you're not crazy. You might freeze up. He won't.*"

Jeremy shook his head slowly. "*I've been dead inside since the day you came to our . . . my house to tell me what he'd done. The only emotion I've had is* hate, *wanting to see him* dead. *I won't freeze.*"

"*You might get caught. Did you think of that?*"

"*I don't care about that. I'll be careful, but I don't care.*"

Hank nodded. His face was grim, concerned, but his eyes showed resignation. "*There's a rusted out '82 Toyota Cellica parked on the corner of Oak and Route 57 in Orrville. Keys are under the mat. There's a hunting rifle in the trunk. The car's registered stolen. The rifle was sold mail order in the early '60s. Can't be traced. Use them, then dump them.*"

"*How will I find Marion Brand?*"

"*He'll be using a brown, '90 Ford Fiesta. The community pass is from one P. M. to six.*

"*Don't leave anything behind. No shell casings, no finger prints, no hair. Wear gloves, a hat and a hair net or stocking. Don't hang around either before or after. Arrive at one. Do it and leave, immediately. Burn the clothes you wear.*"

"*You're a good friend,*" Jeremy said.

Hank's head snapped up, and his gaze zeroed in on Jeremy's eyes as if he had been slapped. "*I've given you everything you need to ruin your life. What kind of friend is that?*"

"*If you feel that way, then why are you helping?*"

"*Because I don't want to tell anyone else what I had to tell you. Because I don't want to see the face you wore that day ever again. Not even in a dream.*"

---

235

Jeremy Wheeler watched the soot-blackened, stone castle writhe in the heat-waves rising from the asphalt, parking lot. He had arrived only five minutes earlier, but the Toyota Hank Davison had provided already felt like an oven, even with the driver's door ajar. A bead of sweat broke free of his temple and rolled down his cheek.

The small steel door through which Marion Brand would pass was only twenty yards to Jeremy's right. The Ford Fiesta was three parking slots to his left.

Five minutes passed, then ten. The door swung open, and Marion Brand stepped through. He looked around briefly, then strode toward Jeremy and the Ford Fiesta.

Jeremy watched him pass, then slid from behind the wheel. The rifle was still in the trunk. Brand didn't deserve an easy death.

Brand walked to the Fiesta, not looking back. He seemed comfortable with his freedom. He didn't expect problems.

Jeremy approached from behind. Brand's concentration appeared to be on the car and the single key that dangled from the simple round key ring he held.

He slid the key into the lock, turned it, then turned to face Jeremy, a strange look of expectancy on his face.

Jeremy slipped the hooked gutting blade from his pocket, and paused long enough for the man to notice the sun's glint off the blade.

Marion looked down at the blade. His pupils dilated. Jeremy brought the blade forward in a smooth punching stroke. It lodged in Marion's crotch. He screamed. Jeremy drew the blade upward, and unzipped him to his sternum in one, smooth movement.

Again Marion screamed, but Jeremy imagined he heard Cindy's scream instead. He tossed the blade aside, and brought his knee up, sharply, between Marion's legs. Marion fell back over the Fiesta's hood, trying to hold himself together. Blood gushed from the opening. Too little.

"I'll see you dead. I'll drink your blood," Marion Brand screamed. He threw a hard right and connected solidly with Jeremy's chin. *The blow spun Jeremy to the side, and he staggered back, yet, he didn't feel the blow.*

*He turned to look at Marion again. Marion was trying to roll off the hood to his feet. Jeremy stepped forward, and manhandled him onto his back again. Then he sank his hands into the slit he had created. Marion's guts writhed around his hands. He grabbed slick handfuls and dumped them onto the hot hood. Marion's scream turned to a gurgle, but he still raised a foot and kicked at Jeremy.*

*Jeremy stepped back and looked at the blood on his hands. He felt something akin to pleasure surge inside him. He reached into his pocket, removed handcuffs, and snapped one cuff onto Marion's left wrist, then dumped him onto the asphalt.*

*Marion's guts trailed after him, from the car's hood down the fender to his lap.*

*Jeremy snapped the other cuff to one of the Ford's towing rings.*

*Marion Brand yanked at the restraint. His breathing was beginning to sound labored.*

*"Now you know how they felt," Jeremy said.*

*Marion yanked at the cuff again. His eyes seemed to flame. Then he smiled. Marion's pants tented over an erection. "They screamed for you. You weren't there. They blamed you for their pain. I enjoyed every moment of it."*

*Jeremy stepped back and stared at the man for several seconds. He could see cold hate and sexual excitement mix and swim up in this monster's eyes. Marion shuddered, and the hate in his eyes formed into a black worm, and flew from him.*

*A cold force struck Jeremy, and his mind went black. Unknown seconds later, he looked down to find his erection waning. A small stain slowly spread on the front of Jeremy's pants. He shuddered, then he turned and walked to his car.*

### DAY 16

The boy had stood over him, knife in hand, eyes glued to his still figure for half an hour now. His footfalls were stealthy,

---

237

but Jeremy's nightmare had awakened him hours earlier. Since then he had been afraid to sleep.

He forced his chest to rise and fall gently as the sun made the new day. Mark had to make the decision to trust him, or not. Five minutes passed, then five more, before Mark slid the knife back into its sheath, walked to the edge of the clearing and relieved himself.

Jeremy sat up and cleared his throat, trying to sound as if he had just awakened. Mark returned to the fire.

"It's a new day. Where do we stand?" Jeremy said.

Mark stood with his hand gripping his knife's haft. "I stood over you with my knife while you slept. I thought about cutting your throat and leaving you here before you did the same to me. I could've done that."

Jeremy rubbed the sleep from one eye and yawned. "What was your decision?"

Mark shrugged. "You're still alive."

"And the next time?"

"I don't know."

Jeremy smiled. It was an honest answer. "You going with me?" Jeremy asked.

"I'd like to. These woods are weird. They scare me."

Jeremy set his gaze on the forest and turned a slow circle. "Kid, this whole world scares the shit out of me," he said, agreeably.

Under a gray-blue sky marked with sparse islands of blue-white clouds, Jeremy Wheeler and Mark Scott followed the meandering animal trail that day and the next. They saw no signs of human life, and the journey was arduous. The trail rambled to such an extent that twenty, backbreaking miles resulted in an eastward gain of ten miles or less. Still, following the animals was faster and easier than cutting their own path through the tangle of vegetation covering the land. And it kept them out of the woods at night.

—

Jeremy measured Mark as they traveled. The boy was strong, full of juice, and he fought exhaustion without complaint. Soon, Jeremy began to wonder what part the boy might play in this nightmarish adventure.

As the sun reached its apex on the seventeenth day, Jeremy noticed the forest was beginning to thin. They would reach the mountains by nightfall of the next day. If they did not find someone by then, he would have to decide whether to double back to search for the woman who had returned from Apep's palace or to continue to rely on instinct to guide him. Neither choice made him very comfortable.

Jeremy didn't like this forest. He felt it was a threat even with the wide trail to separate them from the trees at night. Yet, this was where he would find a guide, and looking for Apep without a guide would be futile. And although he did not know how much time he had left, he was sure his time was almost gone.

On the second day of their journey together, Jeremy pushed until his muscles screamed. Then he began clearing a circle for the campfire.

Mark sagged to a sitting position on the stony earth and moaned. "How do you do it?"

Jeremy looked up from his work. "Do what?"

"How can an old man like you continue each day until you turn gray with the strain, spend the evening clearing a camp and building a fire, then start again at first light?"

Jeremy tossed an armful of kindling into the center of the circle he was clearing, peered at the boy through tired, scratchy eyes for a moment, then shrugged. "I come from a place where people take their comfort seriously, true enough. But there are things more important than comfort."

"What, for instance?"

"Commitment. Do you have anyone you care about? Someone to die for?"

Mark's face sagged. His gaze moved to his hands, which hung limply between his knees. "My mother."

"That's commitment," Jeremy said. "Where I came from, I worked fourteen years at a job I hated. I had a commitment to my family. The money I made fulfilled part of that commitment. Hell Mark, compared to that, this is a stroll in the woods!"

Mark nodded. He stood and helped clear the campsite.

Jeremy wondered if he had erred in weakening the wall between them.

They finished clearing the circle. Mark Scott was stacking kindling. Hunting had been fruitless today. There would be no fresh meat for the evening meal. The fire would serve only to keep them warm in the night and to ward off whatever demons the forest held.

"I'm not from here either," Mark said.

Jeremy looked up but said nothing.

"I don't even know how I got here. I remember the before, and I remember the after, but getting here just happened. It was as simple as stepping through a doorway. Then, everything in my life changed."

Mark finished the story of how he and his mother had gone through the portal in New Orleans and were captured in the grasslands. Now he was seated facing their small fire, knees up, arms wrapped around them.

"The rest is like I told you before. I was in such bad shape they left me in New Aralsk. The rest of the slaves went on to Apep's palace. My mom was one of them.

"After you burned New Aralsk, I headed for the mountains. I hope I can find someone who can tell me how to find Apep's palace."

"What then?"

"I don't know! I don't know what I'll do then. Okay? I

just know, I don't have the stomach for what happened in New Aralsk."

Jeremy grunted, then nodded, but deep down he thought the boy would do what was needed when the time came, even if it meant killing.

Later that evening, as Mark Scott sat with his back against a small bolder, hugging his knees, he asked, "Do you believe me?"

Jeremy had disassembled the small Detonics pistol, and was now wiping it clean with a cloth moistened with machine oil. He looked up from his work and the boy's gaze met his. Jeremy knew that if he had a need to lie to this boy, he would have been at a loss to do so.

As the boy's story had progressed, Jeremy had found his liking for Mark growing. He believed this could be danger-ous. Jeremy had a long way to go in this world, and he didn't know what awaited him. There might come a time when he would have to make a choice of the boy's life or his. And if there was a choice, his head had to be clear. He had to choose himself, because the lives of his family and for that matter all of those on his and Mark's world depended on his completing the mission Conrad LuPone's master, Dougal, had set for him.

Jeremy returned his attention to the gun, and without looking up he asked, "What do you want from me?"

"I want to know where we stand. If you don't believe me, you won't trust me."

"I believe you," Jeremy said.

"Just like that?"

"Just like that," he said, raising his gaze to meet the boy's.

Mark's eyes slitted. "Why?"

Jeremy didn't want to answer the boy's question. He was sure to do so would bring them closer in the boy's eyes, and if the boy started looking at him as a father, Jeremy didn't know

—

241

how he could maintain the distance between them. "Do I have to have a reason?" he asked.

"The people in New Aralsk didn't believe me. I'm not sure I would. Why do you?"

Jeremy gave the boy a shrug. "What the hell? Let's just say I believe you and leave it at that."

Mark sighed, released his hold on his knees and lowered them to the ground.

"Do you dream?" Jeremy asked.

"Of course I dream. What kind of question is that?"

"Have your dreams changed since you came here or . . . or just before?"

Mark's eyes widened. "How did you know?"

Jeremy's stomach tightened. He wondered if the boy had some connection to Apep, some unknown purpose. "What are your dreams about?"

"Strange stuff. I dreamed of the catmen, of wars with them. Things I've never done. Things that never happened. Yet it *seems* like they happened. You know?"

Jeremy nodded. He had suspected his dreams were not precognition, but history. But how could that be? He and Hank Davison had left the world of his dreams behind. And in his dreams, Hank and he had been strangers until the deaths . . . the murders of Cindy, Sam, and Linda. And that was an event which the dreams showed would not happen until December of 1990. It had only been September when he and Hank had stepped through the portal. Therefore, nothing he dreamed had happened before they had stepped through the portal, and with him here, none of it could.

Mark picked up a small branch and poked at the campfire with it. "Do you have strange dreams, too?"

Jeremy didn't answer.

"What do they mean?" Mark said.

Jeremy laid aside the oil wetted cloth, and started to reassemble the Detonics handgun. "Nothing. Don't worry about it."

"But they frighten me."

Jeremy glanced up at Mark. Why couldn't the boy just let go of it? Why did he push to know what was unknowable? "I'm not your mother."

Mark's face went stony. "There isn't much warmth in you, Jeremy. You fed me when you could have sent me back into the forest. But you haven't really taken me in."

Jeremy winced. Mark was right. He didn't want to be close to this boy, and he was transparent in that purpose. Mark reminded him of his failure as a parent. And failure here, in this world, would mean death for one or the other or both. He nodded, slowly accepting this. "Like I said, I'm not your mother."

"Can't we be friends?"

Now Jeremy sighed. "It's better if we're not. We're after the same thing but not for the same purpose. We both want to find Apep. You want him because of your mother. I want him because his life means the death of everything and everyone I care for. If I find him, I'll kill him. I won't allow you to slow me or to distract me. If I care about you, we'll both expect me to protect you. I can't. There are things more important to me and to the world."

Suddenly changing gears, Mark used the stick he held to point to the handgun Jeremy was assembling. "You clean that every night. Sometimes, I think, you caress it more than you clean it. Maybe you have more love for your gun than you do for people."

Jeremy realized Mark meant to hurt him with this little barb, but felt no offense. He supposed from the boy's point of view this was true enough. He looked at the handgun, smiled, gave it a final buffing with the oiled cloth, and wrapped it in that cloth. "Many people think of guns as evil. They're not. Guns are tools, pieces of metal that, used justly, can make the weakest person as strong as the vilest bully. If this gun survives, perhaps I survive, perhaps you do, perhaps my world does," Jeremy finished.

Mark said nothing. He lay down and was quiet until sleep took him.

*KAZAKHSTAN*

## *2035 A. D.*

*"There's a military base in the mountains. We could take everyone and hole up there," Mark Scott said.*

*"With everyone in one place, Apep's Guard would overrun us for sure," his brother replied.*

*"Jared, you're a good brother but a bad strategist," Mark said. "Apep doesn't have good control over his Guard. They're clumsy and dumb. "Besides, he has the gun registration records. His Guard is going door to door taking our people while they're defenseless."*

*Jared Scott nodded. "What's this military base called?"*

*"It doesn't have a name. It was just finished when Apep disbanded the military. I thought we'd call it Parabellum. The word came to me in a dream I used to have as a kid. There was a strange man in the dream who told me it meant, 'If you want peace, prepare for war.'"*

### *DAY 18*

Jeremy Wheeler awoke at dawn. He was surprised to find Mark Scott awake.

Breakfast consisted of a strip of jerky and water. They had used the last of the canned goods the night before. Jeremy judged the water would be gone before sunset.

Before noon Jeremy spotted a thin line of white smoke.

It curled a few feet above the tree tops, then was whisked away by the westerly breezes.

"We'll have to leave the trail now," Jeremy said.

"Whoa! I've been in there. I don't want to be in *that* forest at night!"

Jeremy stepped off the trail, and entered the brush without responding. Mark followed to the edge of the trail, stopped for short seconds, then moved forward a few yards and stopped again.

"The branches *move*. They *grab* at you. You can feel the roots crawl through the ground. Do you *hear* me? Can't we talk about this?"

Jeremy continued through the tight brush. The boy would follow, or he would stay. If he didn't follow, perhaps that would be better for him.


A quarter mile into the forest Jeremy stopped. Mark, close on his heels, bumped into him and fell into a prickly bush.

"Damn! Why the hell did—"

Jeremy ignored the boy. He stood stiff-legged, looking over the Ruger at the man who had formed in front of him, from a mist.

The man was blond, tall, thin—almost gaunt. His face was clean shaven, and he had close-set, hard, blue eyes separated by a narrow, hooked nose. A harsh, four-inch scar ran from the inner corner of his left eye, down his cheek to the corner of a thin, lipped mouth. He held a pump shotgun and wore green camouflage fatigues. Glossy-white, flexible plates dotted his chest, upper arms, and thighs. A helmet of the same material covered his head. Conrad LuPone, as the little man appeared in early morning mist on a day which now seemed so long ago, flashed in Jeremy's mind. Conrad had worn the white plates, also, he remembered. Yet, Jeremy's mind still questioned, *White over camouflage?*

Without preamble, a man simply appeared on Jeremy's

—

left and another on his right side. Both dressed the same as the man with the shotgun. Each pointed a small caliber, automatic weapon at his head. Jeremy allowed tight muscles to go slack in surrender.

He glanced over his shoulder at Mark. A fourth man held a knife at the wide-eyed boy's throat.

Jeremy lowered the Ruger's hammer and holstered the gun. The men seemed to take no notice of the handgun, once holstered. No one moved to confiscate it.

The man with the shotgun appeared to be in charge. He signaled to the other three with hand gestures too quick for Jeremy to decipher. Then he turned to Jeremy and Mark, each in turn. He placed a finger at his lips, then waved them to the north.

In silence, the group moved off into the forest. The man with the shotgun—Jeremy decided he would think of this man as Old-Blue-Eyes until he had a real name for him—took the point. Except for the sounds of Mark's and Jeremy's footfalls, the forest was silent. The four new travelers made no sound. They walked over debris without breaking a twig or crushing a leaf.

An hour later Old-Blue-Eyes signaled a stop by raising his hand.

They were now on a bluff, which overlooked a small village in the midst of the forest. The village was much larger than New Aralsk. There was a main street with perhaps thirty businesses, and there were several side streets lined with wooden frame houses with slate shingled roofs.

Jeremy felt a twinge of nostalgia. The town looked like Prattville or any small, Midwestern, U. S. town with the exception that no roads or trails led from the village. The forest isolated it.

Old-Blue-Eyes knelt at the edge of the bluff, maintaining his grasp on the shotgun, and signaled Jeremy to join him.

Jeremy crept forward and lowered himself beside the man. Old-Blue-Eyes touched his index finger to the corner of his right eye, and then pointed to a spot east of the village.

The trees were in their fall display. A patchwork of brown, red, green, and gold blanketed the country side. At first Jeremy saw nothing. Then a patch moved, then another, and he realized the forest was alive, a moving patchwork of color.

Jeremy turned his gaze back to the man, questioning. He didn't speak. Old-Blue-Eyes clearly preferred silence, and Jeremy could see this man was no stranger to the forest. He had good reason for his preference.

Old-Blue-Eyes smiled, and as Jeremy watched, he covered his face with a hemispherical black mask. It looked to be made of a dull, black plastic. The man's right index finger pressed a red button on the mask, at his right temple. He turned to face the village and surrounding forest for almost a minute. Then he pressed several typewriter-style keys which protruded from the side of the mask. The mask hummed. Old-Blue-Eyes appeared to speak, but the mask muffled all but a whispered buzz.

Several minutes passed before the man removed the mask. He was smiling. He handed it to Jeremy, and motioned for him to don the mask.

Jeremy examined the device. There was a single translucent band across the area that would cover his eyes. The rest was smooth and black. Tentatively, he placed it over his face. It was dark and silent inside.

Remembering Old-Blue-Eyes' actions, he found the button at his right temple and pressed it. There was a low buzzing sound, like the sound of a bee in a mason jar. The band covering his eyes flashed once, then, like a TV screen, came to life. The sounds of the forest filled his ears.

Old-Blue-Eyes appeared in front of Jeremy, and for sev-

—

eral seconds the device seemed to function as a simple pair of glasses. However, as Jeremy continued to look, his vision zoomed in, and he felt as if he had moved closer, *very* close to Old-Blue-Eyes. He saw the pores in the man's face. He heard the strong lub-dub beat of Old-Blue-Eyes' heart.

He removed the mask, and found the man no nearer than before he had donned the mask.

Old-Blue-Eyes smiled. His scar pulled at the corner of his eye, making it droop. Jeremy believed the man might have been handsome if it wasn't for the scar.

Jeremy returned the mask to his face, and pressed the button again.

The mask worked seamlessly with his vision and hearing. It seemed to propel him forward to where he looked, yet, within seconds of placing it on his face, he forgot it was there. Still, the difference was amazing.

He stared at the village. It grew closer until he felt he was standing in the main street. Then he turned his gaze to a sign on one of the buildings, and the sign moved closer until he could read it. He moved down the street and into an open doorway. He could see the people moving inside the building; hear their conversations. Everything was observable, even those things he *shouldn't be able to see* from his vantage on the bluff.

Jeremy gazed left, and his gaze continued turning left until he was able to look up at the bluff. He saw himself standing there in the black mask. He took a step backward, and removed the device. Suddenly, Jeremy felt as if he had been spun half a turn and hurled back to the bluff. His breath came harshly, and he felt disoriented. It had been harder to remover the mask this time. It had been difficult to remember it was there. And he had expected to find himself in the village rather than on the bluff with Old-Blue-Eyes. His mind fought the adjustment, then accepted.

He cleared his head with a shake, then looked at the man.

The man smiled back at him. Jeremy placed the mask on his face once more.

He moved toward the forest floor, and as he gazed left and then right he seemed to glide like a large bird coming in for a landing. He reminded himself he was on the bluff, not in the sky.

It took a few seconds to discover he was able to stop his descent, or move back, by adjusting his visual focus.

He soared over the forest, dropped to within one-hundred feet of the tree tops, and searched the patchwork until he found movement. Then he circled and descended to the tree tops, searching the forest floor for the source.

At first he thought the motion must have been an illusion, that there had been nothing there, then the patchwork changed. He descended, moving closer, gliding with the silence of a bird to the leaf-covered floor.

Suddenly, he realized what he was seeing. It was one of the catmen. Multicolored-mesh-camouflage covered and concealed the massive form of the beast, blending with the forest's foliage. Even at this apparently close vantage point, Jeremy had trouble recognizing the creature.

Something moved to Jeremy's left and again at his right, and he realized there was an army of the catmen among the trees!

Although his mind continued to repeat the message: "I am not here. I am on the bluff." Jeremy felt his muscles tighten, and his stomach clenched into a squirming knot, like the tangle of worms found at the bottom of a fish bait container.

His hands moved toward the mask, and then dropped to his sides again. *No. There's something down there Old-Blue-Eyes wants me to see, and I don't think I've seen it yet.*

The forest erupted with blasts of gunfire. The Ruger was in his hand. He swung around seeking his target before the

—

249

message at the back of his mind could stop him. Then he did stop.

Blasts of gunfire cut catmen apart all around him. They reeled and fell, victims of invisible assailants. He watched until the last creature vomited its blood and crashed to the forest floor. Then, he lowered his gun into the holster, and removed the mask.

# PARABELLUM

Jeremy Wheeler found the trip from the bluff to the village, long, uneventful, and silent. The sun was a bloated, red ball perched on the tree tops when the group reached the village's brick streets. It was then that the transformation in their traveling companions occurred. The men began to laugh, embrace, and slap one another on the back, giving congratulations for a job well done.

Eyes widening in surprise, Mark said, "They can talk!"

Jeremy understood the boy's confusion. He thought he would believe the village's inhabitants mute too, if he had not heard them speak when he had first visited the village, through the mask.

"Talk? You bet your ass we can talk, boy," Old-Blue-Eyes said. He clapped Mark on the back and chuckled.

Mark rolled his eyes.

"My name's Jeremy . . . Jeremy Wheeler," he extended his hand.

—

Old-Blue-Eyes grasped the offered hand, and shook it with enthusiasm.

"My friend here is Mark Scott," Jeremy continued.

Old-Blue-Eyes turned to Mark. The man's eyes were wide now, and his smile broadened. He took Mark's hand, which the boy didn't offer, and shook it vigorously. "A name to be proud of," he exclaimed. "Might you be a descendant of our great leader, General Mark Scott?"

Mark smiled shyly, "I don't think that's possible," he said.

Old-Blue-Eyes frowned. The face was a marked contrast to the one Jeremy had seen in the forest. The eyes were softer, and his facial contours seemed gentle now, save for the scar.

"That is too bad, he was a great man and deserves more descendants than we have found," he said. "My name's Kirk, Kirk Scott."

Jeremy's brow furrowed involuntarily. "Scott?"

Again Kirk's smile broadened. "Yes. I *am* a descendant of General Mark Scott."

Jeremy nodded, still somewhat confused. Was this Mark's connection to Apep, or was the name just a coincidence? And if it was a connection, was it better to leave Mark here or take him along. He couldn't decide, and he didn't know how he could dig further into this conundrum. Instead of trying, he asked, "Are we in Parabellum?"

Kirk Scott's grin was an ear-to-ear slit now. "You know of us then," Kirk said. "I'm the mayor of Parabellum, and the men you see here are members of the town's militia, as you will be if you stay. But, I'm getting ahead of myself. I'm afraid you'll have to excuse my babbling. I'm excited. Parabellum's militia has just encountered a full complement of Apep's Guard without one casualty on our side." Kirk danced a little jig. The other men clapped and hurrahed as they looked on, and for an flash in time Kirk reminded Jeremy of the movie star Richard Harris, in his younger days.

Kirk finished his dance and swaggered to where Jeremy and Mark stood.

"You must have many questions. This evening, Parabellum will celebrate our victory. You will come to the celebration. Tonight you will stay in my home. Tomorrow, we talk. Yes?"

"Yes!" Jeremy said, eagerly.

That evening, necklaces of bare, incandescent bulbs lighted the small town's park like a Christmas tree, blotting out the now anemic night-lights in the sky.

The celebration was a *fête champêtre*. A small band played in an ornate, whitewashed gazebo which occupied the center of the park. The village people attended in their finery. There was dancing and an abundance of food and spirits. And although the spirits weren't comparable with the Black-Jack in his pack, glad to be at his ease among friendly people, Jeremy drank his share of the brew.

To start the celebration, Kirk gave a speech from the gazebo. He extolled the militia, and congratulated the scientists for the improvements in their concealment devices and in the mask Jeremy had used to view the battle from the bluff.

Then he introduced Jeremy and Mark as potential citizens of Parabellum, and offered each a chance to speak.

Jeremy congratulated the village for its successful mission, and thanked the people for their hospitality and their offer of friendship.

Mark—his eyes fixed on an attentive, bright-eyed, young woman dressed in blue gingham dress with a tight bodice—said he was glad to have new friends, who he hoped would soon be close friends.

Jeremy listened to Mark's voice as he spoke, but he watched the young woman's face. He concluded, there could be more trouble here for Mark than the boy might suspect.

—

The fête was a tonic for Jeremy. The village with its familiar buildings, its brick streets lined with milk-glass, covered, street lamps, and its small park with its gazebo bandstand, reminded him of better times, of Prattville, of Cindy. And he tried to picture her face, but the image was muddled, weak, as if she were from a time, decades past, and this made him feel sad and *alone*, in the most intimate sense of aloneness.

Later in the evening, gaily dressed young women smiled at Jeremy and made challenging eye contact. He danced with some of these women, smelling their hair, their body scents and reveling in the sensual warmth of their bodies against his.

Then as the night grew old and the brandy had its way with him, he had fleeting, eye contact with a petite, blue-eyed blond with an inconsequential scar on her chin: The woman, his wife, from his dreams.

### *DAY 19*

It was early morning before Parabellum's celebration broke up.

Kirk's wife, Tara Scott, had left the party early with their two small children. Her parting words were that she would, "leave the celebration to the *heros.*" Jeremy was not certain, but he thought he heard a small amount of wifely venom in those words. Still, it was only a small amount.

Jeremy had lost track of Mark before the evening was half old. Yet, he thought that Mark was not alone. It was a happy thought. The boy would spend the evening and morning rediscovering the joys and trials of young adulthood, and tomorrow or the next day Jeremy could, with a clear conscious, leave Mark here with these people who seemed to have some strange, yet tangible, connection to the boy.

Kirk Scott lingered to shamble away from the celebration

---

with the last. Jeremy stayed with his host. It had been a good party.

As they staggered down the village's brick streets to home and rest, Jeremy noted that his muscles responded with stunned laxity, and he thought, although it could not take the place of Black-Jack, there was definitely something to be said for Parabellum's brew.

As they crossed one of the small, brick lanes lined with modest, Victorian homes, Kirk said, "Parabellum is a very old settlement. Before our ancestors came here, it was a long abandoned military base. That was some three-hundred years ago, or more."

Jeremy considered this for a moment, took another swig from his bottle, offered it to Kirk who shook his head, then asked, "Why did the Parabellum come here?"

"Apep. He was fast taking control." Kirk lowered his head and shook it, sadly. "Apep discovered a way to extend life, at his pleasure. That made him a powerful man. People in high places were greedy for his secrets. They traded their power and our freedom for his promises."

Jeremy nodded. Though not part of his dreams, he was beginning to remember the betrayals by government leaders, the cave-in of the media either through fear or greed. It was a time when no one knew much of what was happening outside their own community, and those who knew more wouldn't tell.

Patting the handgun he had donned once the dancing had ceased, Kirk said, "First the governments took the guns. It was intolerable for a life—which might otherwise last forever—to be so easily ended by a bullet or knife, the leaders said. So no one could have guns.

Kirk paused to remove a small, leather packet of hand rolled cigarettes from his shirt pocket. He pulled the drawstring, and offered Jeremy one of the thin reeds which Jeremy refused. Kirk shrugged, removed one of the smokes from

255

the packet and returned it to his pocket before striking a match to light the tobacco. He took one long drag from the cigarette and blew a thin column of blue smoke into the night sky. He said, "Then, when there was no danger of a successful revolt, Apep's troops came for the people who opposed him. There were rumors Apep used them in experiments." Their gazes met and Kirk shook his head. "No one knew for sure."

"And no one fought?!"

Kirk's look turned to one of incredulity. "Of course they fought. Some had hidden weapons from the time before registration. Pockets of resistance formed. A rebellion broke out. It was a decade of gorilla warfare before General Scott brought our people to hole up at Parabellum," Kirk said, spreading his arms wide in a gesture to the small town.

"How did they survive?"

The tip of the small cigarette flared red as Kirk took another drag from the smoke. He tapped the ash from the end of the little reed, which Jeremy could see was half consumed. "They fought," he said.

Jeremy stopped dead in his tracks. It was his turn to be incredulous. "Against all the armed forces?! With small arms?!" he said.

Kirk smiled. "Apep had disbanded the armed forces. He didn't trust them. He maintained control with his Guard, and he used his Guard to attack Parabellum. He was called Dougal then."

Apep was once called Dougal, and Conrad had been sent to bring him here by a Dougal. For some reason this didn't surprise Jeremy. He took a long swig from the brandy bottle, and once more, offered it to Kirk who, again, shook his head.

Jeremy asked, "What is his control over the Guard? Where did they come from?"

Kirk's blue eyes when blank for several seconds, as if he was gathering his answer from deep within, then his gaze met Jeremy's. "He is a sorcerer, a wizard, or a spirit of possession. No one is sure which. He *made* them. They answer to him, and they are fierce and fearless in battle.

"History says we lost many of our people early in Parabellum's struggle. Most of the arms found here were out of commission, but the original Parabellum were intelligent and inventive people. They learned to reactivate the arms they found and to build others. They taught their children the ways."

Kirk took one last drag from his cigarette then with a flick of his thumb it disappeared like a miniature comet, into the night. Kirk said, "By then Apep had ordered the centers of learning closed. There was no need for schools, because Apep picked the educated people he wanted, and those people lived forever.

"In two generations there was an elite government of immortal, educated people living in a central city over the mountain, and an enslaved population of mortal, uneducated people spread over the rest of the world. Apep ran the government, and the educated people did as he wished. Apep used the uneducated as an inexhaustible pool of slaves."

"Didn't others fight?"

"There were occasional uprisings. Then Apep blocked the moon's light with the night-lights. After that, the people in other parts of the world seemed to lose their will.

"Only Parabellum fights now," he added with quiet pride.

By the time Kirk finished his story, he and Jeremy were sitting in rockers on the wide L-shaped porch of his home. The story brought a note of gloom to what was otherwise an enjoyable evening.

In the dawn sun, dew sparkled on the tranquil lawns and gardens of Parabellum with the brilliance of diamonds. Birds twittered, and unflagging bees flitted from flower to flower to fulfill their birth-to-death commitment to the hive.

—

257

Jeremy awoke from a black, dreamless sleep to find himself seated in a cane rocker on the porch of a white, two-story, Victorian home. A wool blanket covered him against the cool, morning air. An empty, brandy bottle lay in his lap. His head ached, but it was an ache that reminded him of innocent times, times when his every move didn't involve the fate of everyone and everything he knew, times when he could, and often did, fuck up with impunity. And although this was not one of those innocent times, he welcomed the resemblance.

The clank of metal on metal, the rattle of porcelain, and the tinkle of glass came to him from the kitchen. The house was awake. It was time to join his hosts, to learn more, and to ask after "the-one-what-come-back." He wished now that he had broached the subject while the brandy had lubricated Kirk Scott's tongue. His talk might not be so free today.

Inside, he found Tara and Kirk sweating over a large, black, wood-burning stove.

"Breakfast in fifteen minutes," Kirk said, greeting him with a big smile. "You can clean up in the up-stairs bathroom. Kids should be out by now. Don't know where Mark got off to last night, but I'm sure someone took him in."

Jeremy nodded. "Mark knows how to take care of himself."

Breakfast was country style, a family affair with children and adults circling the large kitchen table with its checkered tablecloth and mounds of steaming foods.

The children dominated the conversation, changing subjects in mid-breath, and dropping names as if even a stranger should know them.

Kirk and Tara looked on, their faces lit with smiles, commenting here and there.

Later, over coffee—or what passed for it in this world—

—

and with the children off to school, Jeremy found the opportunity to ask his questions.

"Kirk, why is it that you haven't asked why I'm here?"

Kirk took a sip of his coffee, appeared puzzled, added a spoonful of dirty-brown sugar, and while stirring replied, "A person has a right to privacy. I figured you would tell us what was ours to know."

"And that's enough for you?"

Kirk sipped his coffee thoughtfully, then shrugged. "We know you are not of Apep's forces: He doesn't allow his people to have weapons."

Tara Scott daubed daintily at her mouth with a checkered napkin then, shifting to the edge of her chair, said, "There was some discussion at the celebration, a curiosity, on whether there was another village that resisted Apep?"

Shaking his head Jeremy said, "I'd like to say yes, but I don't know."

Disappointment washed across Tara's face, but only for a breath in time, then she brightened again. "Will you be staying in Parabellum?"

Kirk was pouring his third cup of coffee. He lowered the coffee pot to the stove, looked at Jeremy, and said, "If you stay, the people will raise a house for you."

"I can only stay a day or two," Jeremy replied. Jeremy was almost positive that upon entering the portal he had given up the option of returning to his world, his time, and if he survived, this place and these people would probably be as close as he would ever come to home again. "I hope to find some answers. I'll return after I finish my work, if I'm still welcome."

Kirk had spooned three large spoonfuls of the dirty-brown sugar into this cup of coffee, and was now stirring vigorously in an attempt to dissolve it all. "We will help you, if we can. What information do you seek?"

---

"I need to find Apep's palace or the place of his power: The place he does his experiments."

Kirk's brow raised, and he shifted his gaze to meet Jeremy's. Jeremy expected him to say something, to protest this foolhardy venture, but he maintained his silence.

"I need to know as much as I can about that place and about him before I continue, and I don't have time to waste," Jeremy said. "I've heard of a woman who returned from there. Rumor has it she lives in Parabellum."

Tara shifted uneasily in her seat. "There is such a person," she said. "She is a recent citizen. You had congress with her last night."

Kirk did a spit-take, spraying the coffee he sipped, then burst into laughter. Jeremy looked at Tara, confused and embarrassed.

"With your eyes," Tara clarified. She smiled, mischievously. "You had congress with your eyes. Everyone saw it. Only you and she were too busy to see how obvious you were."

Jeremy felt heat rise in his face. He felt like a young boy having his first crush discussed at the kitchen table. Yet this wasn't a first crush. This woman and he had had a long relationship, perhaps in another life, definitely in his dreams and in the memories that had gradually come to him since his arrival on this world.

"Leave it to Tara to get to the marrow," Kirk said. He used his napkin to wipe up the coffee he had sprayed, then to wipe his tears of laughter.

"Oh, now I've embarrassed you." Tara appeared surprised. "I didn't mean to. I *do* apologize."

Jeremy sipped his coffee, trying, despite his red face, to appear unruffled. He knew that he was doing a bad job of it. "Apology accepted," he said.

"I'm sure Lori will give you the information you seek,"

Kirk said. "We also have a teaching computer that can provide information."

"Oh?!" Jeremy said. He felt his heart quicken. This had possibilities.

"That is, it will give you everything that was in storage before Apep closed this base three-hundred years ago. People were distrustful of others in that time. Computers tracked everything and everyone then. They even recorded the swirls on the ends of a person's fingers, though I can not guess why. They are all different," he said, holding his hands out, fingers splayed for Jeremy's inspection.

Jeremy nodded. What could he say? Kirk was describing his world.

Kirk removed a large brier pipe from his shirt pocket and a small poke of tobacco from a pant pocket. He began to load the pipe's bowl with his fingers. "The original Parabellum citizens used the computers to learn. That is how they were able to repair the weapons. We teach our children with the computers.

"Parabellum has two hard and fast rules. One is, that everyone must take part in our education program. It is the one way to resist the night-lights. In fact, we don't allow children out at night, unless we have the streets lighted as they were last night. Children do not have enough education to resist the voice of the night-lights," Kirk said.

"Mark does," Jeremy said.

Kirk finished loading the pipe, stuck the stem between his teeth, and turned to the stove where he lit a small stick in the fire and touched it to the tobacco. He puffed and a fragrant, blue smoke rose from the bowl and stretched to the ceiling. "We consider Mark a man in Parabellum," Kirk said. "Many his age have died in defense of our homes."

Jeremy understood. Sometimes, growing up was a matter of necessity rather than time.

"What's your second rule?"

---

"Everyone who lives here must be a member of the militia," Tara said. "We all do our part to protect the village. Everyone thirteen years old or older is part of the militia. The children hold the second line. If Apep's Guard had broken through, yesterday, the children would have fought them.

"You will see much affection given to family and friends in Parabellum. Especially to the children," Kirk said. "We do not know if our children will grow up or how long we or they will live. But we are certain that no one from Parabellum will die in Apep's camps."

"Is that enough?" Jeremy said.

Kirk paused thoughtfully, took two more puffs from the pipe and said, "It is more than the rest of this world has, and it is more than *you* will have if you leave Parabellum." He raised a hand as if to halt any objection Jeremy might have to his statement. "I'll not attempt to dissuade you, but we have sent forces against Apep in the past. None have returned."

Jeremy placed his empty coffee cup in its saucer. "I thank you for the warning. When do I see Lori?"

# JEREMY WHEELER
# MEETS LORI
# HELLMAN

She smelled of spring flowers, or was that only Jeremy Wheeler's imagination? The woman was petite, dressed in a blue dress which attracted attention to her ample bosom while saying "stay away." Her golden hair bounced when she moved. Her face was finely sculptured, except for her lips. They were full, luscious, inviting. And her sky-blue eyes were the kind that made a man forget what was on his mind for as long as he gazed into them. . . . Or that was the way Jeremy Wheeler would always remember Lori Hellman on their first meeting in this world.

But it was the large, sun-bleached pup (of varied ancestry) standing at her side that jarred Jeremy.

"Rudy!" Jeremy exclaimed, recognizing Hank Davison's dog at once.

The pup tilted his head, growled, and wagged his tail at the same time before advancing to take Jeremy's scent. Finally, appearing to recognize him, Rudy sat and allowed Jeremy to stroke his head and scratch behind his ears.

"Where did you get the dog?" Jeremy said.

"The dog means something to you?" Kirk Scott said, glancing from Jeremy to Lori and back.

"He belongs to a friend," Jeremy replied. His gaze moved from the pup to Lori Hellman's drowning-pool eyes.

"Hank isn't here," Lori said, her gaze shifting down in what appeared an unconscious act of shyness, and then back up again to lock with Jeremy Wheeler's.

"This is Lori," Kirk said. He shifted uneasily from foot to foot, and looked from Jeremy to Lori and back again, seeming confused by the questions and the common ground shared between these two strangers. "Lori, this is Jeremy."

"We were introduced very long ago," Jeremy said, and immediately, he felt foolish at having expressed as fact, what could have only been a dream.

Jeremy's gaze flitted to Kirk. Kirk's forehead wrinkled, and there were questions in his eyes. Then Jeremy returned his gaze to Lori, and it locked there with her gaze. He saw wonder in her eyes.

"Yes. We met very many years ago," she said. And immediately, Jeremy knew, just knew, Lori Hellman had experienced the dreams and found memories. He wondered if the dreams and the memories she had found were the same as those he had found. *If the dreams were the same*—And at once, he didn't want to know. He crowded the thought out.

He asked, "How did the dog—?"

"We found him after we attacked one of Apep's Guard

Units last week," Kirk said. "No one knew whether he was with the Unit, or following. He took to Lori right off. She keeps him for the town."

Kirk sighed, and his voice took on a wistful note. "We used dogs to patrol the perimeter of the town until Apep's Guard killed them. We hoped that we might find a female for him. We would like to have dogs again."

Jeremy felt Kirk's gaze flick back and forth between them, yet he lacked the will to break eye contact with Lori.

"Is there something I'm missing?" Kirk said.

"May I talk with Lori . . . alone?"

Kirk turned to Lori Hellman, and raised his eyebrows in question. She nodded, although her gaze never completely abandoned Jeremy Wheeler's.

"Jeremy, I'll meet you in the Scientific Laboratories Building at noon," Kirk said. He left.

Jeremy stooped and stroked the pup. Rudy allowed several strokes, then he stretched out on his stomach, placed his head between his paws, and cocked first one eyebrow and then the other at the remotely familiar stranger.

Lori watched Jeremy for an interminable moment, then asked, cautiously, "We *do* know each other, don't we? *You're* not from here."

"I think we're from the same place," Jeremy said.

"Prattville?" her voice squeaked, almost too soft to hear.

The hair on his neck stood attention at the word. Somehow he sensed, knew, the Prattville they would speak about would be not only the Prattville they had left, but also the Prattville which had not yet been. That knowledge frightened him. He nodded.

"Oh, say it, won't you?" Lori blurted. "I've been so all alone, so hopeless since I entered this world. Can't you just say it?"

Jeremy's heart went out to her. Though they had met only now, he knew that in some crazy mixed-up way they had a long history—marriage, a child, death—in a lost time. And he understood how alone and helpless she felt here, in this strange place, away from everything and everyone familiar. He felt that way himself.

"Yes, Prattville, the Ohio Prattville, the United States Prattville, the Earth Prattville," he said in a rush. He saw tears appear in her eyes. She wouldn't let them fall. She was as strong and as tender in this reality as she was in his slowly evolving memories.

Jeremy Wheeler told Lori Hellman (Wheeler?) how he had arrived in this world and what had happened to him since his arrival. He felt at ease in the telling.

She grimaced, then hid her eyes from him when he spoke of Hank's maiming by the giant beetle. Through the rest, she was silent, tight-lipped. Yet he still couldn't bring himself to speak of his dreams and of the life he remembered spending with her in their world.

When he finished, she rose from her chair. "Would you care for something to drink? I have some tea we liberated from one of Apep's caravans. There's coffee or brandy if you prefer."

"The tea is fine. If it's no trouble," he said. But tea wasn't what he wanted. His real thirst was for her story, and deeper, beyond that, for her.

Over tea Lori told her story. She spoke stone faced, stilling even the emotion in her voice.

"The people of Parabellum think I am from this world. I'd like to keep it that way," she said.

He nodded.

Her eyes met his. "With Conrad LuPone's help, I stumbled through the Prattville portal."

Jeremy's muscles drew taunt at the mention of the little man's name. Conrad LuPone had seeped into his life like an acid mist, and like acid, the message this man brought with him had eaten away Jeremy's foundations: family, friends, his whole world.

But amazingly, his edge softened as Lori told him how Conrad had rescued her from certain death by a catman, and of his sacrifice so she could escape in the mountains.

"Before I escaped, Conrad gave me a message for you, Jeremy. Somehow, he knew we would meet."

Jeremy watched her strangely familiar movements as she spoke. He tried to reconcile this reality with his dreams. And everything was splashed with the precognitions or memories that had started as daydreams but had become real as the days passed. They had known each other. They had shared more than was possible in a dream, and in some way, that life was the reason for their being here. He wondered if she was having the same thoughts. Then her eyes met his, and something hot, like a flint's spark, passed between them.

Her gaze grasped and held his for several seconds before she spoke. Her voice was gentle, meek. "Conrad LuPone claimed we are special. He said Apep won't kill us. His Guard is instructed to take care with us, even if it means giving up their lives."

She paused, and her brow screwed up, quizzically. "We know each other, don't we? You've had strange dreams since you came here?"

And finally, the shoe was dropped, and there was no way to avoid the thought, *If the dreams were true, then his reasons for being here—Cindy, Linda, Samantha, his parents, his world—were dead, gone to dust centuries before, and not only that—*

"I don't dream," he said, dropping his gaze from her face, hoping she wouldn't see the lie in his eyes. He didn't want to talk about the dreams. He didn't want to *know*.

"You're lying," she said. "I can hear it in your voice, and see it in your eyes. If the dreams are true—"

*—if the dreams were true, and deep inside he knew they were,*

*then Conrad LuPone's words were true, the desolation of this world and his loved ones was his fault.* His jaw muscles locked, gritting his teeth so tightly he had to force his next words out. "They're lies. They're Apep's tricks."

Lori shook her head vigorously. "Not his *trick*. His *bane*. He *wants* us to remain ignorant.

"Hank Davison," her face dissolved in pain for a second then came back to normal, "is in one of his vats now. And each in turn, there is room for everyone you knew on earth. And in spite of our advantage, in our time, there'll be room for us." Again there were tears in her eyes. "We have to kill him, Jeremy. He's our responsibility."

"Our responsibility? Our leaders sold out. The people followed like sheep. Was that our fault?" A fist gripped his heart, and his head began to throb as he realized he was, once again, remembering things he couldn't know, things Kirk had not told him. Things not yet learned in dreams or daydreams.

Rudy had been watching Jeremy and wagging his corkscrew tail. Now, he sprang to his feet and moved between them. He faced Jeremy, growling, showing his teeth.

Her voice deep, filled with a strength belying her size, Lori said, "Hush, Rudy."

Rudy cowered as if Lori had slapped him with a newspaper. He sat and fell silent. Yet, he continued to watch Jeremy with suspicious eyes.

Lori continued, "People in our world were conditioned to think they couldn't make decisions. How could people who didn't trust themselves or others with Lawn Darts, SUVs, all-terrain vehicles, guns or even finger-guns, for God's Sake, make important decisions? We listened to our leaders as if we were their children, and they took bits of our freedom, and made each bit sound as if it was just more finger-guns. It was for *our* own good, a *small* price to pay for safety, for immortality."

———

268

"Lawn Darts," Jeremy said, nodding, his eyes growing big. "But giving up Lawn Darts and all terrain vehicles and guns didn't make anyone safe. It just made us more dependent on the people who cozened those freedoms from us. Everyone began to believe that safety came from the politician's actions, not their own."

"It was a dream. Something to hope for," she said, joining his nod.

He smiled, remembering better times. "My father used to tell me, 'If you allow a politician to diminish you for your own good, you've failed, not the politician.' The people gave up their freedom for Apep's promise of immortality. That was not my responsibility, nor Dougal's for that matter."

Lori shook her head. "But the evil was," she said.

For an instant Jeremy felt warm blood on his hands, and he could see the evil, that which was Apep, swimming up at him from the eyes of Cindy's murderer, Marion Brand.

"If we succeed in what we've come here for, our world will never know it," Lori said. If we fail, the people of our world will be none the worse for it. Someone will act the vampire no matter what happens here. Whether that person is from here or there, isn't important. But this evil, Apep, is ours. He is our child."

"No!" Jeremy said. "Dougal Wheeler is our child. Apep . . . the evil . . . that was mine. I owned it. I earned it when I killed Marion Brand after he murdered Cindy, Sam and Linda. The infant, Dougal, inherited it innocently. The guilt isn't his.

"Don't you see? Dougal is fighting Apep now. Conrad said it was Dougal who wanted me to come here. Not Apep."

Lori's face roiled dark with anger. "Don't be a fool again, Jeremy. It doesn't matter where the evil came from. It's in him." Tears broke free and rolled down Lori's cheeks. "He's *ours*, Jeremy. *We* are responsible. And *so* is *he*."

Jeremy dissolved into confused silence for several sec-

———

onds, opposing emotions threatening to tear him apart inside, then he said, "But he's our son, part of us. Even the evil in him comes from my body. What can we do?"

Her drowning-pool, blue eyes locking with his. She looked delicate, but her eyes were bright now, and her face radiated confidence. "We will do what we failed to do in that other time. We'll kill him."

# HANK DAVISON
# MEETS APEP

Hank Davison woke with a lurch, making the straps binding him sound a flat tone against the cold, stainless steel table on which he was secured. He squinted against harsh laboratory lights.

A quick glance around told him, the room where he was tied was stainless steel, sterile, designed for dissection or vivisection. The walls were mirror-polished, reflecting the cheerless, greenish-white light from the banks of fluorescent tubes overhead. Several tables, similar to the one on which he lay, lined up to his left and right.

From the head of the restraining table, a voice as chilling as a snake's hiss said, "Ah! Awake at last."

Hank glanced up to find a tall man, with graying, brown hair and sallow skin. His lips were cracked, the face wrinkled beyond age, and his brown eyes—faded almost clear from

---

271

time—were ancient, cracking at the corners, tired beyond tired in the center.

The man smiled down at Hank. "I'm Apep," he said. "And I'm here to make your life as miserable as you made mine."

Hank Davison felt hate bubbling up inside him. So this ugly creature was the one responsible for Lori Hellman's death. Hank yanked at the straps holding him, was jerked back, and yanked again before realizing the futility of his action. "I've never seen you before, you miserable shit," Hank said. "But I've seen your work, and if I've done anything to make you miserable, then I'll die happy."

Apep laughed a laugh which, at first, rolled like water through a drain, then broke into a gasping, spewing wheeze. He brought a handkerchief to his mouth and blotted. "You'll die all right. You'll die with your face in the dirt alongside State highway 57, in Ohio. *But* you won't *die* happy."

"You're returning me to earth?" Hank said. He was confused by this interaction. To be killed, that was expected, but to be returned to Ohio. . . ? It made no sense.

Apep nodded. "You helped Jeremy Wheeler, and he killed my host, Marion Brand. That eventually put me here." Apep raised his hands, palms up, gesturing to the stainless steel room. Then he turned his gaze to Hank. "What you did must happen again for my plan to work, for me to be truly immortal.

"So, you must return to your place and carry out your part before you die."

Hank hacked up a gout of spittle and spat it at Apep. It hit him on the cheek and slid down to his jaw line. "I'll never help you," he said, voice deep, confident.

Apep wiped the spittle away with his handkerchief. He smiled and picked up a scalpel from a large stainless steel tray at the table's side. His gaze met Hank's then turned to the gleaming knife. A spark of light hit the blade, and ricocheted to Apep's eyes, then back at Hank. "You will," he said. "In the end, you will."

———

# THE SCIENTIFIC LABORATORIES BUILDING

*DAY 19*

Jeremy looked into the Fall sky. It was filled with sunshine that traveled to earth, ignoring the gossamer clouds painted across it. A gentle breeze tousled his hair and traveled on to rustle leaves and stir wind chimes into the random music of broken crystal and crockery. The fragrant scent of burning hickory floated to him from some cook stove as its fire burned low.

He walked along the main street of Parabellum for a block, then turned right at the white, Victorian house with the blue, slate roof. Three houses down the street, on the right, stood

---

273

a small, blue cottage. On either side of the cottage were two-story, New England style homes. Widow's walks perched high above the roof of each. Since, there were no sailors away from home in this village, he guessed the walks were for defense of the cottage.

He cranked the cottage's door bell and listened. Inside, chair legs scrubbed on a wooden floor. Footsteps approached the door. There was a pause, then a clacking noise from the throw of a substantial bolt.

The young woman who opened the door had long, auburn hair that fell around her shoulders in looping curls, which bobbed as she moved. Her smile was knowing, sly, her eyes witching, green. He remembered dancing with her at the fête. Even then he had felt a strange sense of intimacy, as if he had known her before, and well. He had the same feeling with Lori, but that was understandable and comfortable, although confusing. However, with this woman the feeling was not comfortable. Not comfortable at all.

"Please enter," she said, motioning with her hand.

Furnishings of a rugged country-style filled the room. There was colorful upholstery, paintings depicting farm life, and a multicolored, rag rug. A large fireplace dominated one wall. Small, ceramic figurines and bric-a-brac littered the mantle. Two, small, electric lamps warmed the room with their orange light.

The woman closed and bolted the door before speaking again. "Welcome to the Scientific Laboratories Building. My name is Cassandra."

He flashed her a smile. "Yes, I remember. We danced last night."

A knowing smile, sinister, almost evil in its effect, flitted across her face and was gone. "Oh? Did we? I can't seem to remember. There were so many men at the party last night." She looked into his eyes. The green of her eyes flashed with the lamp light.

---

Jeremy's muscles tightened. He had the feeling that Cassandra knew more about him than she should know, could know.

"I . . . I was to meet Kirk here. He said I could use the computer. . . ."

He tore his gaze from hers. "Is he here?"

"He's in the complex."

Jeremy scanned the cottage. It looked smaller inside than it had from the outside.

Cassandra tittered. "This is but an entrance. A foyer. The complex is below ground." She moved into the room, away from him. "The complex seems infinite. I haven't seen all of it. No one has."

"Oh?!" he said, questioning how this could be after three-hundred years.

She paused and peered at him as if he had said something incredibly stupid. He suddenly realized that he felt, for some reason he couldn't fathom, sheepish under the scrutiny of this woman.

"We use the smallest explored section. It was marked as A-1 Section when we found it. It's half the size of the town. The next larger section is twice that." Her voice was a tour-guide monotone.

"I see," he said.

Her eyebrows rose. "Do you?" She paused for a beat, then continued. "Others built the town and the underground complex before our ancestors arrived. The various sections of the underground complex had military uses in the past. We've attempted to find their secrets. Some of our explorers have never returned."

She shoved the painting above the mantle askew, snicked a recessed switch, then pressed down on one of the hearth-stones with her foot.

A low humming sound filled the room. She moved back toward the center of the room. The section of wall, on which

———

275

the fireplace stood, rose and folded into the ceiling, carrying the fireplace, mantle, and all that surrounded it. Moments later, a seven-foot cube of wire mesh filled the seemingly endless void in the floor. The cage was open on the front, and it seemed to float without support.

Cassandra walked onto the wire floor, and turned to face him. "You're coming?"

He walked to the cage, and looked past the wire into the void below. Bands of light spaced at intervals of fifty feet, circled the hollow. The intervals between the bands appeared to decrease until they blurred together into a single point.

A sharp clawed reluctance gripped his groin, then climbed his spine to squeeze his heart. He swallowed and darted his tongue to wet his lips.

"I don't suppose there is another way down?"

"You suppose right. There is no other way down. So if you're coming. . . ."

He thought he saw a smirk, hidden at the corners of Cassandra's eyes, and her lips tipped up at the corners oh so slightly. Something deep in the back of his mind was goosed but not jarred loose.

He glanced into the cavity, inhaled, tested the wire with one foot, then stepped into the cage. The floor dropped from beneath him. His heart went to his throat. His eyes darted to Cassandra's. Her eyes sparked green. She looked away. Again the buried memory was goosed. She was toying with him. *Why?*

The cage fell smoothly down the shaft. The bands of light surrounding the shaft flashed by with stroboscope fastness for what seemed minutes before the cage braked to a smooth stop.

Cassandra stepped off the lift into a wide corridor. He stayed close.

The corridor was twenty feet wide and ran as far as he could see in both directions. Harsh, white light spilled into the passageway from behind large, translucent panels lining the walls. It stung his eyes. The soft hiss of air, sprayed through many, louvered, air shafts, gave the corridor life, yet the smell of it was heavy with age.

"This is section A-1." Cassandra was using her tour-guide monotone again. "The Virtual Reality Laboratory is this way," she said, motioning to her right. She stepped onto one of two, black, rubberized strips that ran the length of the hallway.

"Step on, please."

Remembering the lift, he stepped onto the black rubber strip with his feet planted wide. He was prepared for the rubber strip to lurch into high speed travel. It didn't. It crept forward, picking up speed in almost imperceptible increments. Cassandra stood looking to her right, away from him, yet he was sure he could see the corner of her mouth curl.

The corridor widened to forty-feet a half mile from the lift. Kirk sat at a large desk positioned between the two moving walks. Jeremy guessed the area had been planned as an information center.

The walk came to a halt. Without a word, Cassandra crossed in front of the desk to the second walk. She did not look back until she was moving away from them, and then only from the corner of an eye.

The two men watched in silence until she was out of earshot.

"I hope you'll watch your step with that one," Kirk said, knowingly. "She can be trouble. Sometimes I wish we'd left her with Apep's Guard. She has caused dissension among the families here."

Jeremy continued to stare at the retreating figure. "I understand," he said.

This woman filled Jeremy with confusion, but more than that, she frightened him.

———

277

## THE VIRTUAL REALITY SYSTEMS 10,000

Jeremy Wheeler surveyed the room, feeling very small. Yet, all but a twenty-by-twenty foot area at the room's center was crowded with computers and vats of hissing, bubbling, gelatinous fluid.

Kirk Scott stood on a circular pad in the cleared area. He wore a tight, black mesh that covered him from neck to toe. A black helmet enclosed his head. A buzzing sound, like a sack full of angry bees, came from the helmet. Jeremy had heard the sound before, but it took him a moment to realize it was similar to the sound from the mask he had worn on the bluff, the day he had first met Kirk.

As Kirk moved, the pad beneath him writhed, forming an ever-changing surface, which tilted forward and back, or snaked up like steps, or sloped like a hill. Jeremy assumed the surface of the pad must flow in the opposite direction of Kirk's movement, because no matter what Kirk did, he always finished in the middle of it.

Kirk turned left, took several strides, turned right, then reached out. His arm sank with the weight of a virtual prize.

Kirk played out his silent drama for several more minutes. Then he touched electronic latches on either side of the helmet and removed it.

Jeremy gave the equipment a visual once-over. The sophistication of it made him feel hopelessly ancient.

"Our simulator is a VIRTUAL REALITY SYSTEMS 10,000." Kirk puffed his chest with pride. "The military used the 10,000 to train soldiers and those who designed weapons, three centuries ago."

With a sweep of his hand, Kirk gestured to the vats of gelatinous fluid. "Our ancestors added biochemical storage units and downloaded information from all the world's library computers. It is a very smart computer."

Jeremy nodded toward the pad on which Kirk still stood. "How does it work?" he asked.

—

Kirk tossed Jeremy the helmet. Jeremy caught it and found it to weigh only a couple of ounces.

"The suit is a computer-simulated world," Kirk said. "We learn by meeting the famous people or the teachers of the past, and taking part in a simulation of their world. The suit I'm wearing, tells the computer my movements, physical status, and emotional states. The computer defines the environment (kinesthetic, olfactory, gustatory, visual, auditory) through the suit, helmet and floor. In some limited situations the computer can even alter emotions."

Jeremy examined inside the helmet, and found it to be much more sophisticated than the one he had worn on the bluff. The viewing screen was larger, covering the whole front and wrapping to the sides far enough to cover even the greatest peripheral vision. He ran an index finger over the screen. It swallowed his finger giving only the faintest of sensations as if someone had softly exhaled over his fingertip. The screen and all the rest of the interior were obviously designed to mold to the head of the wearer without sensation. He wondered how the helmet worked to simulate a breeze, rain and the other perceptions necessary to make the virtual world real to the wearer.

"I want to know about Apep," Jeremy said. "What can I learn with the computers?"

Kirk smiled. "Everything and anything up to the point where he destroyed the world's data banks. Nothing past that.

"The computer can simulate any event from birth to death. You can take part in any event and pick your role."

A mischievous glint appeared in Kirk's eyes. "You can even change sex roles, although, many will not. I gave birth using the machine. . . ." He frowned, and shook his head. "I don't recommend it."

Jeremy thought he would follow this advice.

Kirk continued, "We use the simulator to learn our history and to train as chemists, farmers and technicians.

—

"The militia uses the simulator to sharpen fighting skills."

"Could I learn something about Apep that you don't already know?" Jeremy asked.

"Anything is possible. Our scientists have studied the data on Apep for many years. But what we learn, depends on the actions taken during the simulation. If you turn left in a simulation, you learn what is left, not what is right."

Jeremy nodded. He wished he had more time to study this computer.

Kirk stepped off the circular pad of the VIRTUAL RE-ALITY SYSTEMS 10,000 and gestured to it with a dramatic sweep of his right arm and hand. "Are you ready to try it?"

Jeremy did not know what he expected to discover. Lori could lead him to Apep. Yet, she would extract a price he was not sure he could pay. Accepting her help would cost him: He would have to take her with him. It would mean he might have to watch her die, *again*. He wasn't ready for that.

"The people of Parabellum had all but given up research on Apep's past. But, our laboratory has had a lot of use over the past month," Kirk said.

"May I ask who?"

Kirk smiled. "You can't guess?"

"Lori?"

"Yes. And . . . ?"

Jeremy's mouth dropped open. He stood silent for several seconds. "Mark?"

Kirk nodded. He appeared oblivious to Jeremy's reaction.

"Lori uses the computers every morning. Mark was in from early evening yesterday until almost noon today.

"I assume he heard of the computers from one or more of the young people at the dance. We are still analyzing the information he generated."

"Can I see that information?" Jeremy asked.

———

### DAY 20

The sun sat on the horizon like a puffy, orange pumpkin as Jeremy and Kirk left the complex the next afternoon.

Kirk could see the strain on his friend's face. He had spent twelve hours in virtual reality with a young Dougal *Wheeler*, the man now called Apep. He had spent another nine hours viewing the data from Lori's and Mark's trips into the computerized past of that same man.

Kirk saw nothing useful in the information generated. Yet, the grim face of this strange, gaunt man who limped beside him, told Kirk that Jeremy now had a more personal understanding of the evil he sought. And that understanding did not comfort him. It gnawed at him.

### DAY 21

Rays of Fall sunlight filtered through the dogwood outside Jeremy's bedroom window and made fireworks beneath his eyelids. He unstuck an eye and peered out. A loginess enveloped him. The clock on the night stand told him he had slept a full eight hours. He would like to sleep for years. He wanted to retreat, runaway from this world, its dreams which were not dreams, and its computers that told him things he wished he didn't believe.

Jeremy rolled out of bed and began to prepare for the final leg of his journey.

Breakfast was uncomfortable. First Kirk's and then Tara Scott's eyes focused on Jeremy's pack, then flitted away only to float back, an action repeated time and again without comment.

Jeremy felt grateful they respected his decision, and were not trying to change his mind. They were good people.

Kirk's conversation became more animated near the end

---

of the meal. His face was full of expression, and his hands flew in broad gestures. He gave advice through metaphor. He talked of battles with Apep's Guard, of the town, of his children and wife. Where he left gaps, Tara spoke of unrelated topics. No one attempted to coordinate the jumble of conversation. It was warm, human, loving.

At the door Tara hugged him. Tears slipped from her eyes, and rolled quietly down her cheek. Kirk, his rugged face strained with emotion, grasped Jeremy's hand and shook it. Then he embraced him, thumping his back energetically several times.

"God be with you in your search and your mission," he said. "You'll always be welcome in Parabellum."

"Yes, always!" Tara said.

"I'll return," Jeremy said. He tried to fill his voice with confidence. He forced a smile. But their gazes cast down as if they could sense it was all for show.

Jeremy paused. Mark would want to go with him. He had a right. He had obligations too. Yet, he would die quickly if they saw combat. And although he had meant it when he told Mark he would allow him to die to get to Apep, he wasn't sure that the boy, in his dying, would not cause him to pause, to make a fatal mistake, again. He was poor father material. He had proven that with Linda, Sam, Dougal. Yet, even a poor father could allow his heart to get in the way.

"Will you watch after Mark?"

Kirk nodded.

"Of Course we will," Tara said.

"Tell him I'll do my best to return his mother to him."

"He will be safe with us for as long as he wishes to stay," Kirk said.

Jeremy sighed, then nodded. He knew there was no need for thanks. He hugged Tara again and clasped Kirk's hand before turning away.

—

Lori Hellman pushed the shovel's blade deep into the loamy soil of her garden, lifted and dumped, bringing moist black soil to the top. She leaned on her shovel, wiped a trickle of sweat from her cheek and brushed back her hair. From around a corner at the end of the street, Jeremy appeared.

She studied his approach. His limp reminded her of his story about the *beast* of Aral's sea. This world had changed him. He was different from the man she had met, loved, married, given a son, and died with, in that time she remembered, but had never seen. He was harder. He had more purpose, more grit. She could see it in his stride. It was confident, if not smooth.

She concentrated on his face. The desert had left its mark on him there, also, but his doe-brown eyes still gave him away. He still had his soft heart, although he didn't wear it as close to the surface as he had in the past. And the changes in him were improvements. *I would follow him anywhere.*

Then she saw the pack, and confused panic filled her.

She was vaguely aware of the shovel striking the ground behind her. She ran toward him. Tears broke Jeremy into blurs of color, and made everything too bright.

"YOU'RE NOT GOING WITHOUT ME, JEREMY WHEELER! YOU'RE NOT GOING WITHOUT ME! YOU NEED ME!"

Jeremy stepped back as Lori rushed him. He offered a nervous smile, not sure what to expect.

Her eyes, her lips, the fragrance of her hair, the feel of her skin against his was strong in his memory. He reminded himself he had to be strong. He might have to watch this woman die. Yet, the obligation was theirs. *Mostly mine,* something in the back of his mind insisted.

"We have to leave today," he said. "Don't ask why, I just know,"

"I'll be ready in a few minutes." She straightened, wiped

———

the tears back from her eyes with the fingers of either hand, and sniffled. She shook her long, blond hair back from her face. The sun caught in it, reflecting gold. "You'll need me, whether you know it or not." Her voice was confident.

He knew she was right. Yet, he wished she was not, wished he could leave her here, safe.

Lori was ready to leave in thirty minutes. He realized she had anticipated a hasty departure. She had packed clothing, food and weapons the day before. Still, she would not leave without a shower.

She exited the bathroom dressed in tight denim jeans, a long sleeved, cotton-twill blouse and walking boots. She had towel-dried her hair and pinned it back beneath a blue bandanna. The outfit made her look young, defenseless, *sexy*. Jeremy felt heat rise to his cheeks at the thought. He had felt the same heat at the celebration, or perhaps in a life they had not lived, but this time the lust caught him unaware and with strength sapping power.

He took Lori in his arms, and kissed her roughly, deeply. Then he stepped back and holding her at arms length, he gazed deep into her eyes. Was he taking this woman to her death? Was he risking her life because of her need, or his? Would she add anything to his chances of success, or would she be there only to *stiffen his purpose?*

"I can read it in your eyes, Jeremy," Lori said. "What you are thinking is wrong."

"I can't take you with me," he said in a rush.

"The hell you can't!" Her voice was firm, calm. "Who said you were in charge? This is *our* problem, not just yours. So before you get on your macho high horse you better know, I am going, *with or without you*. And I know where to find Apep. I'll be there when you arrive. If you arrive."

Jeremy cast his gaze down. From his first understanding of their history, he had assumed this thing with Apep/Dougal

Wheeler to be his personal war. Father against son. Son against father. In his mind, it was a war where he and Apep made the decisions. Jeremy had made the decision to protect Lori. It was natural. It was human. He loved her, and he didn't want to see her die at their son's hands, again. But he was denying her right to absolve her guilt. He was wrong, and as usual Lori wouldn't allow him that luxury, that failure.

"You're right," he said. "I just wanted—"

"I know what you wanted," she said. "Your soft side could kill you, again. Put it behind you."

The muzzle flash of a gun, paralyzing pain, two, dark eyes so close he was lost in them, hot breath on his face, a ripping pain at his groin, flashed through his mind. He shuddered, and forced the images from his head.

Lori walked to the bed, hoisted her pack from the floor to the bed's neatly made center, and opened it. She removed a gun belt and strapped it around her waist so the holster perched high on her hip. She lifted a semiautomatic pistol and magazine from the pack. With the gun's barrel pointed at the ceiling, she inserted the magazine in the haft of the pistol, and shoved it home. She pulled the gun's slide back and released it. It made a stiff, metallic click as it moved forward, sliding a cartridge from the magazine into the cylinder. She flipped the safety on with her thumb, then lowered the gun and shoved it into the firm grip of the brown, leather holster. Her face turned to him and formed a knowing, determined, *pissed* expression.

*She knows how to protect herself. But will she hesitate when it's her son in her sights? Will I?*

Mark realized, he hadn't seen Jeremy since the night of the celebration. He had left with Soja. The beautiful Soja, the wonderful Soja. A girl, not the same, but much like the girl from his dreams.

Soja had introduced him to the VIRTUAL REALITY

—

285

10,000 computer. In the past two days, what time he had not spent with the 10,000, he had spent with her. He thought he must be in love, but he wasn't sure. He had never been in love before, except in his dreams, and he had never heard that love was painful. He wished he could talk with his mother about this, and his dreams.

Mark packed his kit, and accepted the loan of a handgun from Soja. He had practiced with a gun in the 10,000, just in case. He still did not hold with killing, but guns were not alien to him. His father had taught him to shoot a handgun when he was twelve, and he could remember much killing in a dead past that was becoming more alive in his memory as what might be his last days, burned at an incredible speed.

He strapped the gun onto his slim hips. It hung low, looking huge, deadly, as much a part of him as racing tires on a Yugo.

He didn't know why leaving felt right, but the feeling was compelling. And if he had learned one truth in this strange new world, it was that instincts were almost always right. He could accept this, yet he wondered if Jeremy could. Adults always seemed so crippled with doubts, fears, indecision.

A trickle of sweat rolled down Jeremy's cheek. He looked up at a glaring, white sun sitting high above irregular webs of diaphanous clouds, then glanced at the guards on the widow's walks, above and to either side of him. The guards seemed to ignore them. He looked back to the small, blue cottage.

There had been little conversation on the short walk from Lori's home. Instead, they had consumed the sights, smells, sounds, and feelings of the day as if this was their last chance. Rudy followed them, nose to the ground, tracing and retracing haphazard, ghost trails in the wind-jumbled, Fall leaves.

They paused outside the cottage door, and gazed about, hesitating to crank the bell. Jeremy's eyes strayed to Lori, and found her girlish face upturned, her eyes full of fear and trepidation, her jaw set in resolution. He bent and kissed her. And when he looked again, he found the fear had left her eyes.

His hand covered the bell's crank, and rested there ener-vated by the significance of the act. Then her hand covered his, and together they cranked the bell.

Several seconds passed before Cassandra swung the large door open.

"Are you here again?" she said. Her face imparted no particular expression, but there was something in the tone of her voice and the flash of her eyes that made Jeremy feel as if she had read his most intimate thoughts, and found them amusing.

Jeremy felt the calm serenity, which Lori had imparted, desert him. He hesitated.

Lori stepped past him coming nose to nose, eye to eye with Cassandra. Lori eyes were unblinking, cold, blue ice. Her hand rested on the semiautomatic at her hip.

"We want access to the last level of the complex," she said.

Cassandra backed away, pupils dilated almost to the point of obscuring the brilliant green of her eyes. Rudy growled.

There was a surprised and delighted laugh. "She told me no one can go to Z-26," Mark said. "I had almost given up on you two."

Jeremy turned to find Mark sitting in a rocker. "What are you—" He stopped himself. He wouldn't question Mark's right to be here. "Are you going with us? Or are you making this trip on your own?"

"I'll be going with you. If you'll let me," Mark said.

Jeremy glanced back to Lori and Cassandra. Lori was mov-ing faster than he had expected. She had backed Cassandra across the room to the fireplace. Cassandra's back was against the mantle.

Lori reached past her with her left hand, and shoved the

painting askew. She snicked the recessed switch, and pressed down on a hearthstone with her foot. Her hand remained on the gun at her side.

A low hum came from the fireplace. Lori backed away. Rudy raised his ears at the sound, whined, growled, then backed across the room to Mark. Cassandra remained with her back against the mantle, appearing stunned, until the section of wall with the fireplace began to rise. Then she seemed to regain her senses, if not her composure, and backed off to the side. The endless void, which Jeremy remembered so well, opened in the floor. In half a second the insubstantial-looking wire, mesh cage filled it.

Mark, who had appeared absorbed in the interaction between the two women, took his feet, and walked to the cage. Rudy followed the boy.

"What about her?" Mark said.

"Ya—You can't do this," Cassandra broke in, her voice cracking, halting, hissing. "Level Z-26 is re-restricted. Apep will—" She stopped. Her pupils dilated, face twisted.

At that moment Jeremy remembered where he had seen this woman before. And although it had been centuries ago and only in a dream, he knew she was Apep's doxy, once a governor's wife but in the end only payment for immortality.

Cassandra's left hand disappeared at her back. Metal flashed when it swung back into view.

The Ruger seemed to jump to Jeremy's hand.

An explosion stung his ears. A dime-sized hole appeared in the center of Cassandra's forehead. A star burst pattern of red splattered the wall behind her. She folded in upon herself, collapsing to the floor like a struck tent.

Jeremy felt his stomach roll. Behind him, Mark retched. Jeremy turned to Lori. She still stared over the barrel of her pistol. A thin line of smoke curled from its bore. His mouth worked soundlessly for a second. Then he had nothing to say. It was over. There was no changing it.

The Ruger in his hand was at half-cock. Not fired. He lowered the hammer and holstered the weapon.

"So *she's* what happened to Parabellum's missing explorers, *her.* One of Dougal's own," Lori said.

"Dougal's a victim too," Jeremy said. "It's Apep—"

"If you continue to think like that, he'll murder us again." She shook her head, and for a wink in time she looked overwhelmed.

Mark screamed. Jeremy turned to see the wide-eyed boy pointing to the dead woman. At first he though the boy was having a delayed reaction to the shooting. Then, he heard a frying sound, and followed the line sketched by the boy's finger to Cassandra's corpse.

The skin on her face and arms had gone leathery. The bones were collapsing beneath. Blood fried from her pores and flowed from openings, natural and unnatural, onto the floor.

*Apep's own.*

———

# TO THE DEPTHS OF PARABELLUM

The lights, surrounding the shaft, flashed by with increasing speed for several seconds, then blurred into a single pulsing glow as the speed of the descending elevator increased.

Jeremy clutched the cage's wire wall with one hand, and tried to force his muscles to relax. The wind rushed through the wire floor and slapped at him, and for some reason he couldn't quite grasp, the word *IMMORTAL* played through his head.

Mark did flips and twists, floating weightlessly above the floor. Lori looked on, amused. Cassandra's death seemed forgotten or unimportant to them. Jeremy didn't feel easy about this casualness with death. But he could feel it too, as if time had flowed away, and Cassandra had died years, if not decades, ago rather than minutes before.

The descent of the elevator seemed interminable, yet a moan of disappointment escaped Mark's lips as the cage

---

slowed, and gravity began to over take him, spoiling his craft-less aerobatics.

A computerized voice with female inflection announced the approaching level as Z-26, and Jeremy began to relax. Still, when the cage came to a bouncing halt, he scurried out, hoping his companions had not noticed his unease with their roller-coaster-quick dissent.

He found Z-26 to be an enormous vault that stretched away in all directions as far as he could see. Pillars of light and glass broke the openness like trees on a plane. The pillars seemed to support the vast ceiling, perhaps one hundred feet above. He heard the breathing of his companions, the faint hums of distant machinery, and the hiss of air-exchangers, that was all.

"What now?" Mark said.

Jeremy's gaze shifted to Lori. "I guess we walk," he said.

Mark drew a finger gun, and sited it across the seemingly infinite expanse before them. Then he spun a neat circle on the ball of his right foot. "Where?"

Jeremy smiled, shrugged, and looked to Lori again.

She smiled, and removed a small, black box from her belt. She flipped the cover open to reveal a circular green display, and pressed one of several colored buttons inside the cover. A green arrow appeared on the floor of the vault, four feet in front of her.

Mark's eyes grew wide, with both surprise and question floating on them. "Is that a compass?" he asked.

"No," Lori said. "It's more like an electronic guide. I used the computers to program it. It has directions to Apep's lair. He's been in the same place for two-hundred years. I think he's tied there, imprisoned by his own experiments.

"The arrow will continue to point the way and stay four feet in front of the device. All we have to do is follow."

"Amazing!" Jeremy said.

"Glad you brought me?"

"Don't know what I'd do without you." He smiled, but dead green eyes flashed though his mind, and his smile went sour.

Mark's gaze rose to the ceiling and rode one of the glass-and-light columns back to the floor. "What holds the ceiling up?" he asked.

Lori rapped one of the tubes with her knuckles, and it gave up a hollow ring. "Energy beams inside these glass tubes."

"I spent some time in the 10,000 studying the construction of the complex. It was the last, the most advanced of its kind, an amazing structure.

"It was built before Dougal disbanded the militaries. Armies didn't fit his needs. They were a danger. After all, armies are people with guns. And people with guns are a threat to anyone who would dictate to them.

"Lasers cut the elevator shaft. Engineers carved out individual floors with smaller lasers mounted on robots and directed by computers. They used power beams to support the rock above. Don't ask how they work. For all I know, it's *magic.*"

The power beams cast no light outside the glass pillars that encased them. Their essence, a pale, blue light seemed captured in a multitude of tubes that marched away from them in all directions.

With no horizon and no light for orientation, the glowing, green arrow of Lori's electronic guide seemed to swing with every step. It burned into Jeremy's retinas, bucking and swinging, doubling then rejoining to double again, in a sober man's nightmare. It confused his senses, making him feel as if he was falling or tumbling.

Lori and Mark seemed to be having problems too. Jeremy watched Mark's silhouette stagger like a drunken sailor as his feet tried to follow both the arrow and its after image. Twice he fell. Lori did better, but her stride often dissolved into a halting, jarring lope. Rudy was unaffected. He followed his nose, tracing ancient trails that seemed to end at Mark's heel, time and time again.

They halted every hour, and Lori lit their lantern, so they could regain their orientation. There was nothing to see, just floor, but seeing it still existed, soothed Jeremy's confused senses.

When Lori's watch told them it was night, they bedded down.

Mark laid his bed near a pillar, curled up, and was asleep in minutes. Rudy continued his incessant trace of ancient trails for an hour or more before curling up in Mark's fold.

Lori and Jeremy undressed in the dark, and laid their bedrolls side-by-side. It seemed the natural thing to do.

Jeremy lay looking at the pillars, which floated in the dark like elongated stars. He imagined the hiss of the air circulators was the wind and the squeaks of dry valves, the thrum of insects.

"Jeremy?"

Lori's voice jarred him from an unthinking preamble to sleep. "What?"

"Can we talk?"

"In the morning."

She went silent. He felt himself settling back to that calm place just before sleep where there is no thought, no images.

"Time is growing short for us," Lori said. "We may not get another chance."

The words brought him back to consciousness. Time was now *their* enemy. Since his earliest childhood memory it had been his. He rolled to his side, and threw the lantern's switch.

"We can talk." He curled his left arm over his shoulder and propped his head on the elbow. "What's bothering you?"

She chuckled. It was a low unhappy sound. "There's so much, I don't know where to start."

———

"Just start. It'll all sort out."

"How can this be happening? How do we remember a life that we never lived?"

"Does it matter? Do you distrust the memories, the dreams?"

"Sometimes. I don't want to believe them. The last memory I have of you, in that time, is you hesitating when you had Dougal in your sights."

"He was . . . is . . . our son."

Her eyes narrowed, and he felt she was staring into him. "He didn't hesitate," she said. "He murdered us."

His vision darkened, and he saw a black worm swimming up from a black eye. He shook off the image.

"It isn't Dougal's fault. I infected him. It's my evil that wears him like used clothes."

"That's right. Apep wears Dougal like clothes and clothes don't live. You hesitated because you think of Dougal as someone alive, separate from the evil. That can't be true. You had the evil in you." She reached out and clutched his arm. "*You* had *Apep* in *you*, and *you* rejected *him*. If the evil wasn't part of Dougal, he would reject it, too.

"In our time people used to say, 'I like you, but not your actions.' But if we're not our actions, what are we?" Her grip tightened on his arm until it hurt. "We have to *kill* Dougal. He *is* the enemy."

He looked down and said nothing. She was right, he had let his love for a myth—for a child who didn't exist—make them, and their world, victims. His belief in the myth had killed them as much as Apep had.

"I understand," he said.

Her gaze sought his and locked with it. "What do we do when we find him?" she asked.

"I don't know. It always seems so easy in novels and movies."

—

"I brought three stealth suits," Lori offered. "The militia wears them to make them invisible to Dougal's Guard."

Jeremy felt an electrical surge of hope. "Like in the woods that first day?" he asked.

"Yes," she said, nodding. "I wore one that day. They aren't perfect, but they'll be helpful."

"What do you mean, they're not perfect?"

"They work by bending light around you. The device creates some kind of energy field. It's effective in bending light, and as an extra added attraction, it kills any bacteria on your body so the Guard can't smell the wearer. The problem is in the computer chips that control everything. They're slow in speed-of-light terms. It works fine as long as you don't move. When you move, you can be seen as a shimmer, like heat rising off the desert."

"Great!"

Lori rolled to her side. The blanket fell away from her breasts. She didn't attempt to cover herself.

They were so close now that their bodies touched. He peered into the drowning-pool blue of her eyes.

"Make love to me like you use to do. I need it and you need it," she said.

He killed the lantern and drew her to him. Circling her with his arms, his hands caressed down her back as their tongues teased. The softness of her skin and the warmth of her body sent a shudder through him. His right leg pressed between her legs, and the moist heat of her vulva burned into his thigh as she moved against him, groaning a sigh into his mouth. He tasted her lustful breath, and felt her rigid nipples against his chest.

She rolled onto her back as he moved downward, kissing a trail down her neck and across her breasts. There he teased her with tongue and teeth while his hands caressed. And when he returned to kiss her lips, she moaned, "Now! I need you *now.*"

Her legs came up and surrounded his hips, tugging at him, as he moved to meet her. Breath hissed from between clenched teeth. Her back arched when he entered her, and they writhed together as long acquainted lovers. All other thoughts left him.

Later she lay in his arms, listening to the rhythmic sounds of his breathing. This is more than right. It has the feeling of well-worn jeans, she thought.

### DAY 22

Rudy gobbled down a large portion of bread and dried meat, drank eagerly from his water bowl, then once again, began his obsessive tracing of old trails.

Lori, Jeremy and Mark sat to breakfast in the glow of the electric lantern.

"Do either of you think it strange that we all decided it was time to leave Parabellum at the same time?" Jeremy said.

"It was coincidence," Mark said.

Lori nodded, her attention seeming to be torn between their conversation and the contents of her pack, which she was now sorting through.

"I'd think that too, except for something Mark said."

Mark had scooped a large spoonful of cold, baked beans, and had carried it halfway to his mouth. His forehead wrinkled in concentration, and he lowered the spoon to his plate. "What'd I say?"

"When we arrived at the cottage, you said that you had almost given up on us."

"But I don't see why that's important," Mark said.

"You expected us," Jeremy said, emphasizing each word with a quick jab of the air with his spoon.

Jeremy turned his gaze to Lori. She stopped her sorting of the pack's contents, and returned a blank stare.

"Okay. Let's see how I can explain this." He paused, then started again.

"We all used the VIRTUAL REALITY 10,000. We were each in contact with a computerized replica of Dougal at various points in his history. Later, we all started doing the same things at the same time."

Lori's pack now lay forgotten at her feet. She said, "Wait a minute, I came with you. I didn't just show up at the cottage. I didn't have the slightest idea you two would be leaving yesterday."

"No?" Jeremy said. "Then why were you packed? And why had you gone back to the computers to program the compass or the electronic guide or whatever you call it? Why did you pack *three* of the stealth suits? And if you didn't know anything about what was going to happen, how did you know about this underground route? You didn't mention it when we talked earlier. Come to think of it, you did a lot of preparation in the day following our conversation."

She shook her head. "I can't explain it. All of those things just *seemed* right. I didn't think about them. I just did them."

"And I don't know why I knew it was time to leave yesterday, either," Jeremy said. "I didn't think about it before bed. But it was in my head when I awoke, and it was something I *had* to do."

They sat, gazes shifting from one to the other for long seconds, without speaking.

Finally, Lori broke the silence, "So where does that leave us? I mean . . . , what does it all mean?"

"I have a hysterical guess I think you should hear," Jeremy said, setting his spoon down and laying his plate aside.

"Tell us," Lori said.

Jeremy licked his lips. His stomach was tight. How could he explain to them what he had taught Dougal Wheeler as a child? He wondered how much Lori remembered of Dougal's

———

297

childhood. He said, "Through Dougal, Apep was very much in control of all the governments of earth *before* he had obvious control of everything. What I mean is, although he had control, the armies still existed. There was the *appearance* of government, though the governments were puppets. And someone built this military complex during that time. The computers, the VIRTUAL REALITY 10,000, and the three-dimensional computers in this complex were under Apep's control for at least some of that time."

Mark and Lori each stared to the other, questioningly, then turned their gazes back to Jeremy.

"Don't you see?" he said. "Dougal had control of the data that represents him in the computer. He could have set a trap."

Mark placed his plate at his feet, his appetite apparently forgotten for the moment. Rudy eyed the forgotten food, and sidled closer to the boy, tail wagging, hopefully.

"Like what?" Mark asked.

"I don't know," Jeremy said, shaking his head, slowly. "It could have been anything. The computer could have hypnotized us, or Dougal could have had the computer do some kind of futuristic mind control with anyone investigating him. Remember, Parabellum's explorers never returned.

"Have you heard of a Trojan Horse?" Jeremy asked.

Mark raised his eyebrows, and his blue eyes seemed to brighten. "I've heard the story of Troy and the wooden horse used to smuggle soldiers into the city so they could attack from inside. Is that what you mean?"

Jeremy rose to his feet now, and began pacing back and forth in increasingly agitated steps. "It's the general principle, but I'm talking about something more modern, something from our time.

"I've worked with computers a lot. I'm what they call a hacker. But not all hackers are sterling characters like me." Jeremy halted his pacing, and flashed them a smile. But his

—

attempt at humor had fallen flat. They did not smile back. Jeremy canted his head, then wrinkled his brow in disbelief before continuing. "Some hackers like to mess with the minds and data of big business and military computers. They're called crackers."

Lori stood to face Jeremy, her brow wrinkled in question. "So what has that got to do with us and the 10,000?" Lori said.

"That's where the Trojan Horse comes in. One of the ways crackers mess with other peoples' computers is by planting some destructive program code in another program. The code has to be in a program that the operator would be sure to use, part of the operating system or something else that would run every time the system is started. Then, on some specified day—April Fool's Day or Friday-the-thirteenth say—the program will become active and do something to the computer's works.

"It might erase data or print a message or produce another Trojan Horse program. The point is, it could do almost anything the cracker wanted it to do."

Lori's eyes lit. Jeremy realized, she remembered and understood.

"I still don't understand," Mark said, hopelessly. "What has that got to do with us?"

"Don't you see? If Dougal had control of Parabellum's computers before the Parabellum got there, or if Dougal planted a Trojan Horse in data downloaded by the early people of Parabellum, he could have laid any kind of trap for people like us, people who sought too much information about him."

"No," Mark said, waving his hands as if attempting to stop a runaway truck. "I understand that part. I can see how a Trojan Horse program could mess up a computer, but how could it hurt us?"

Jeremy smiled. Mark was quick. "The mind is like a computer, though more complicated. Have you ever seen a stage hypnotist?"

"Huh uh," Mark said, shaking his head.

Jeremy sighed. "Well, they use to be popular acts. The hypnotist would bring people up from the audience and hypnotize them. Some would have what hypnotists call an auto-suggestion given to them. The hypnotist might say something like, 'When you hear a bell, you will have an irresistible urge to take off your shoe.' The act would continue, and the participant would go back to his or her place in the audience. Later someone would ring a bell, and the person would take off his or her shoe."

"The enemy is *inside*, like a Trojan Horse!" Mark said.

"Right," Jeremy said. "And Dougal could have programmed the 10,000 computer to do the same thing to anyone who examined his data. There may be an enemy inside one or more of us. That would explain why we had the same compulsions on the same day."

Lori's brow furrowed. She shook her head, slowly. "What good does it do us to know this?"

"We have to be careful, question every move, and watch each other," Jeremy said. "There's no limit to the suggestions Apep could have planted. We could be the enemy."

"We *were* the enemy, before. In that other time, we were the enemy, Jeremy," Lori said.

They looked at each other dumbly.

"Should we turn back?" Lori asked.

"I can't do that," Jeremy said.

"Neither can I," Mark said.

"Then we continue and take our chances?" she asked.

"There is nothing else we can do," Jeremy said.

"Rudy can help us," Mark said.

Their gazes darted to the dog (which still sat close to the boy, gazing expectantly at the plate of dried meat, beans, black bread) and then turned to Mark.

"He didn't use the computer. We can't trust us, but we can trust him. He can be our eyes and ears."

"Good idea," Jeremy said. But he was less enthusiastic about the idea than he hoped his companions could detect. Rudy was a pup, and pups often erred. He didn't like to rely on a pup to do a dog's job. Yet he had no better idea.

"Yeah! You're going to be our eyes and ears, Rude-Dog," Mark said. He patted the large pup, enthusiastically.

Rudy's head dipped toward Mark's plate, and the pup stole a whiff before drawing back, drooling in anticipation of a scrap of the food. Jeremy watched the two for a minute, then turned away. He held serious doubts for the group's future.

They checked their equipment before breaking camp. Each watched the others as they unloaded, dry fired, re-loaded, and worked the slides, cylinders, and hammers of their guns.

Lori gave instructions. They tested each switch and button on the stealth suits, and each was double checked by their companions.

Without discussion they left their bedrolls where they had laid them the night before. Jeremy wondered if the others knew, as he did, that they wouldn't need the bedrolls again, or if they were simply following his lead. He didn't ask; was afraid to know for sure.

Four hours into the new morning, a dim dot of light appeared high up in the chamber. The dot lengthened and spread as they approached. Within half an hour the dot was a horizontal line. Within an hour the line had thickened, and now it appeared to stretch from edge to edge on the distant horizon.

"What is it?" Mark asked.

"The lights at Dougal's end of the complex," Lori said.

A tickle ran down Jeremy's back and took up residence in a niche above his ass. He felt as if someone was watching him. He touched a finger to the glowing red switch on the

———

belt of his stealth suit. "Should we activate the stealth devices?"

"Not yet," Lori said. "The devices overheat easily. If we turn them on now, they may malfunction at a critical moment. Besides we'll be moving. Anyone would see us smear against the light. They won't be of much help."

"But what about our scents?" Jeremy said, his finger still touching the switch, lightly. "If there are any of those cat creatures down here, won't they smell us?"

"The air circulators should take care of that for a while," Lori said. "And remember to lend an ear to Rudy. He should react if their scents become strong. When he reacts, we'll have to use the devices and pray they last."

The line of light continued to broaden until it stood like a stage before them, covering half the distance between the floor and the ceiling. Rudy's black outline floated in random patterns across that stage as the pup traced and retraced the floor scents. Then he stopped, nose still to the floor, and his low growl echoed through the hollow of the vast vault.

Jeremy, who now brought up the rear, saw Lori's outline wink out. There was a pause, and the thin figure of the boy's silhouette disappeared from the stage of light.

Jeremy slipped the glowing red switch on his belt. It glowed green, and Jeremy felt, suddenly, as if he was inside a protective bubble. Light, sound, even the movement of air around him seemed changed, reduced. He pulled a small earphone from his pocket, and placed it in his right ear. He clipped a much smaller object, a microphone, over a front tooth and waited. Several minutes passed.

"I think we've reached some kind of outer boundary." Lori's voice came over the device in his ear.

"Are you sure they can't hear us when we use these devices?" Jeremy said.

"I'm sure. Trust me," Lori said.

Two miles above, Apep stood in the middle of a small

room, in the bowels of his palace. He was dressed in a black robe. The hood of the robe dangled down his back. A cable ran up his back, and attached to a glowing terminal at the base of his skull. In his mind, he watched the images, fed to him through the terminal, of Lori, Jeremy, Mark and Rudy as his Guard grouped around them for the attack.

Apep said, "Unit one, move in five yards to your left. You will be ten yards from the two in front when you are in position. Unit two, you're too far back. Move in ten yards. You will be five yards off their right flank when you're in position. Unit three, maintain your position. They will walk right into your circle. Remember if anyone harms a hair on the man or woman's head, you will die *slowly* and in *great* pain."

He paused and watched, for several seconds, as his Guard moved to their positions around Jeremy, Lori and Mark. Then he smiled. "Come, Mother. Come, Father. Come and renew me. Make me *reborn.*" He laughed a syrupy, liquid laugh reminiscent of water rushing through an overloaded drain. A drool of spittle rolled from the corner of his mouth. For a moment, its wetness drew his thoughts as it was channeled down a wrinkle to drip from his chin. Then he forgot the sensation, and his thoughts went back to Lori and Jeremy.

The heat of urgency in his voice was apparent even to Jeremy Wheeler as he said, "Move to the columns at the edge of the light. Check in when you're there."

Over his earphone, Jeremy heard Mark Scott say, "On my wa—Hey!"

"What's going on?" Jeremy said.

His voice squeaked with tension, Mark said, "I just saw something, up front, to my left, at the light's edge. Like heat rising off a hot sidewalk."

"Lori is to your left, Mark."

Now it was Lori Hellman's voice in the earphone, "I didn't move," she said.

Jeremy's throat tightened. He looked to the stage of light in front of them. It seemed to float there, detached from their world of blackness, deserted, flat, unfurnished, just rock, concrete, and support tubes as far as the eye could see.

"Lori, does Dougal have stealth devices?" Jeremy asked.

"The troops who disappeared wore them. It's possible."

"Okay. Everyone on your guard," Jeremy said.

"Yeah. Like we need you to tell—" Lori's voice broke off.

"Lori? You there?"

A drop of sweat rolled off Jeremy's forehead and down his nose. His hand—moist now, too moist—rested on the grips of the Ruger. "Lori?"

"We're not alone," Lori said.

Jeremy's grip tightened on the Ruger. "What? How do you know?" The sweat was flooding down him now. The hand on the Ruger was cramping from the tension. *We've walked into a trap!*

"Just hold your water. I'm checking something." As always, Lori's voice was too calm for the situation.

Jeremy clamped his mouth shut. Seconds passed. Again, he could feel someone's gaze slide over him, greasy, suffocating. The hair stood on the back of his neck.

"I was right," Lori said. "We're not alone."

"Where?" Jeremy said.

"I don't know. The stealth devices have a motion detector. It doesn't tell where or how many."

"Couldn't it be Rudy you're seeing?" Mark said.

"I adjusted the device to ignore anything Jeremy's size or smaller."

"What do we do?" Mark said.

No one answered.

Jeremy could still feel the eyes on him. The tickle at the base of his brain was just the right size to tell him it wasn't his imagination. The image of spittle drooling down a square chin lit behind his eyes and was gone. He shivered.

Mark's voice came over the earphone. "There's something wrong. We've got to get out of here." Rudy's ears raised, and his head oriented to the invisible boy. A low growl escaped him, his lips curling back to expose his teeth.

"What's happening, Mark?" Jeremy asked.

"I . . . I hear something—"

"What?" Lori said.

"It . . . It's like the night-lights talking. Like in New Aralsk. It's like millions of angry bees." His voice was tight, urgent. "We've got to get out of here."

"No! Don't move!" Lori said.

She was too late. Jeremy saw Mark's image painted as a smear on the stage of light. Behind him five larger smears appeared, and closed on the boy.

The Ruger jumped to Jeremy's hand and belched flame. To his left he heard the rapid fire of Lori's autoloader. One by one, the smears trailing the boy disappeared. One large catman appeared on the floor in front of them. Smoke curled from a hole in the command panel of the stealth device on his belt. Blood poured from a second hole in his head.

Jeremy felt a puff of wind near his head. He heard Lori's scream, followed by the clamor of rapid fire from a single gun. He squated low and slung the cylinders of the Ruger out to reload. A powerful force struck across the front of his body lifting him from the floor and tossing him like a rag doll.

He struck the stone floor with a jarring thud, and lost the Ruger. His vision blurred, doubling then tripling before settling into a single coherent frame. Something butted against his side. Before he could react, a large rough hand circled his neck, lifting him from the floor. Carrion breath warmed his face.

Jeremy swung blind. His fists smashed into fur-covered muscle. Nothing happened.

———

He couldn't breathe. Bright points of light swirled in front of him. His vision dimmed. Where was the Detonics? He couldn't think.

His hand dropped to the buck knife. With the flick of his thumb, the blade snapped open. He brought the knife up in a slashing arc. The blade sank into hard muscle and gristle. He wrenched the knife, tearing at the flesh. The grip on his throat loosened. He gasped for breath, and slashed out with the knife again. The grip on his throat released.

Pearlescent, yellow blood spread across the stone floor, and trailed a snaking path away from him.

"Lori?" Jeremy gasped. There was no reply. Yet, for a camera's flash in time, he saw her standing in front of him, smiling down at Dougal, his baby, in her arms. Then something hard struck his head, and black bled into his consciousness.

# APEP'S PALACE

Apep was caught off guard when Mark started his run. He thought he knew them all, the boy, who as a man had founded Parabellum, the man and woman who had conceived the body in which he now was trapped, even until death. In spite of the ancient protection schemes he had planted in Parabellum's computers, he had thought these three wouldn't run. But the boy was different from the man he had become. And the dog, with its knowing eyes and white fangs, was a complete mystery, a wild card in the mix.

Through the eyes of one of his creatures, Apep watched the action going on around him, while he barked orders from the secluded room in the palace, above ground. He found it extremely interesting to watch Jeremy who had once driven him from his own body, leaving him with no choice but to enter Dougal's fetus or Lori who, in her own way, was as strong as Jeremy.

"Leave the boy, you idiots! I want the man and woman."

———

307

An hour after he had run, leaving Jeremy and Lori, Mark Scott sat huddled with Rudy, neatly tucked away in an air exchange vent on level Z-26. The gunfire had stopped only minutes after he started to run. His stealth device had over heated and burned out half an hour later. There had been nothing since, except the growling, hissing, grunting conversation of the creatures Jeremy called catmen.

Several of those creatures had passed the vent since he had sought shelter there with Rudy. They were searching for him, and perhaps Rudy, but for him for sure. He realized, it was only a matter of time before one of those ugly, furry faces peered through the louvers. Could he kill? Tentatively, he fingered the grips of his gun. He had killed the catman that had taken his mother through the split of light. And his dreams, his memories of a past he was sure—defying all rational thought—he had lived, told him he had already killed, and quite often. And yet, deep in the core of him the question remained, could he kill, kill in cold as well as in hot blood?

Rudy sat silent, tensing only when one of the creatures drew near. The pup seemed to sense they were hiding. He did not growl or bark. Still, when one of the creatures passed, his lips pulled back to expose domesticated fangs.

Another creature dashed past the opening. Its claws screeched on the stone floor. The sound reminded Mark of those he had heard as he and his mother battled the creature in the New Orleans Civil Court building. It seemed many years had passed since that night. And now, his chances of finding and freeing his mother appeared impossibly small. A tear formed in the corner of his eye, broke loose, and rolled down his cheek. He brushed it away with his sleeve.

He had run when his friends needed him. Why had he done that? Was he a coward? No, he didn't think that was the reason. Yet, why else would he run?

He stroked the pup with his left hand. The right continued to rest on the pistol grips.

---

Rudy's muscles coiled under his hand.

Mark traced the pup's fixed gaze to the louvered entrance and beyond, into glowing, blue eyes. He heard the crisp rasp of metal on leather as his pistol cleared the holster.

Lori woke. Her muscles tingled with a lazy reluctance to movement, and her mind seemed equally resistant to thought.

Nondescript music played faintly in the background. The room was cool but comfortable.

She slipped a hand to her left, across the sheet, seeking the warm body of Jeremy. Her hand found empty space. *At work so early?*

And when she opened her eyes, she found her surroundings familiar, reassuring. She read Jeremy's face in every object of the room.

She lay there several moments longer, trying to dispel the blank, free floating fog in her head. A certain vagary convinced her there was something to do, but she could not think what or why.

Apep disconnected the bundle of wire leading from his head to Jeremy Wheeler's, and stepped back from Jeremy's unconscious form. In the last few hours, he had learned more about the man who had cast him out of his body than he had been able to intuit in the past three-hundred years. And although the understanding was not Jeremy's purpose here, the knowledge was ... *very interesting.*

He stared at the familiar face as he considered what he had learned. The face was younger, yet more worn than he had ever seen it, but no more grim and no less determined.

Reaching forward he clasped Jeremy's jaw, and turned his head to the side. A small translucent block, filled with a multicolored, crawling liquid appeared at the hair line. He examined the fixture with a clinical detachment. Pins, as from a computer chip, descended from the liquid into the base of Jeremy's skull.

There were no signs of infection. The small trickle of blood was probably the result of Jeremy's thrashing about. Apep wiped the blood away with a small swab. His hand trembled.

"Such a small discomfort for so much knowledge, Father."

Mark fired two shots. The first smashed the catman's muzzle, the second obliterated his left eye. Yellow-green blood exploded from the back of its skull.

A second catman crowded in, shoving the first aside. It clawed at Mark's foot. Rudy dove at the creature's hand and tore off its smallest finger. The gun roared twice. Spent shells caromed off the gray stone walls of the air shaft, and stung Mark's body. The creature's face exploded.

Mark scrambled further into the shaft. Rudy followed, backing away from the opening, fangs bared in a low growl. Still, he was blocking Mark's shots.

"Back here, Rude-Dog! Back here now!"

Mark ejected the gun's magazine, and started a reload. He regretted not seeking shelter deep in the shaft, earlier. But it was dark in here, and he didn't trust this world with its giant creatures.

"We've got to move back, Rude-Dog."

Rudy's growl stopped, and the pup's eyes cut up to him in a, "Anything you say partner," gesture, but his tail remained tucked. Then his eyes moved back to the shaft. The low growl started again.

Mark pulled a magazine from his belt. Suddenly, Rudy yelped, dodged something unseen, and scurried back to him. Mark dropped the magazine, raised the gun and fired. There was a loud cry. He squeezed the trigger again. Nothing happened. The gun's slide was locked back leaving an empty maw where the last shell had ejected. The open cylinder seemed to scream, "feed me!"

Mark dove for the dropped magazine. Something big and rough grabbed his neck and shook him like a doll.

Rudy lunged at the unseen assailant, snarling. He flew against the stone wall with a sickening thud, and fell in a bloody heap.

Apep stood over Jeremy's unconscious body, smiling down at the face he had both hated and feared since before the birth of this body in which he had been trapped for more than three-hundred years. The man on the table looked so small, so fragile, not at all like the unflinching, unyielding, bigger than life figure Apep remembered. He was so unlike the man who had banished him to this small niche of hell.

*What makes you tick, old man?*

Again he swabbed the blood trickling from underneath the biomedical, computer chip, and again his hand trembled. Yes, he feared this man. Other than the excitement of seeing the pain in an upturned tear streaked face, fear of this dogged man with his hot, knowing eyes, was the only feeling Apep had ever experienced. It had always been this way. When it had mattered, the man had been the only human who could look beneath his carefully managed exterior. He wasn't like the others. Jeremy had never succumbed to his charm.

Jeremy had known about the lies. He had known about the theft, the fires, the mutilated animals. He had always known, as if he could read something deep inside him, something no one else could see. And unlike the counselors and teachers, the old man would not back off. Jeremy had been the only person who had been able to make him feel mortality: grease slick, temporary, as unsettling as a lump of fatty meat in the stomach.

"But the knowing didn't do you any good in the end, did it old man? I won that one."

Apep continued to stare at the face for several minutes, unable to drag his eyes away, then he turned to a small tray of shiny stainless steel and glass instruments.

At noon a knock came at Lori's door. She ignored it. Her mind was clearing. Yet, although she knew her situation should frighten her, it was still impossible to stir emotion.

A second knock sounded, and after several seconds, the door opened. Jeremy stood in the doorway. Then it wasn't Jeremy but a man with Jeremy's hair and eyes. There the resemblance ended. His face was more rounded, his skin sallow, cracking around the eyes and at the corners of the lips.

"I'm Apep." He entered the room. "I came to care for you."

Her eyes focused on the tray he carried. Mirrored metal, it held a syringe of liquid (swirling with color) several gleaming instruments, and a petri dish of liquid with three, two-inch cylinders soaking in it.

Lori attempted to sit. The room rocked, and she settled back onto the bed again. "There's nothing wrong with me."

Apep crossed the room in three, long strides. "Oh yes. You need an injection. But everything will be okay then."

He placed the tray on the bedside table, and rolled the sleeve of her gown off her arm.

"Where's Jeremy?"

Apep smiled. The smile was at once charming and disturbing. She had seen it before, over the flash of a gun's muzzle. "Jeremy is fine. You'll see him tomorrow. Then he, you and Hank Davison will leave."

"Hank's alive?" Lori said.

Apep tied a rubber tube around her biceps and examined her inner elbow. He inserted the needle. She didn't feel the prick. He released the tubing, and pumped the crawling liquid into her arm.

"And Mark?" she heard herself asking.

"I have provided for the boy and his dog."

"The dog ... Rudy is Hank's dog." She heard her voice as if from within a tunnel: distant, foreign.

Her muscles, and then her thoughts began to jerk as she fought to hold onto consciousness. The spinning room gained speed. Something tugged from the back of her mind, and the force drew her back into the bed, into the blackness.

When Jeremy awoke, he was in a comfortable room. Muted lighting surrounded him. The room, dressed in a warm maroon, smelled of perfume. *Poison*, his mind said. His bed had spindle posts and a canopy. Lori's face flashed in his mind.

He sat up and examined the room. It was Lori's and his. He felt for the Ruger. His hip was bare.

He was dressed in jeans and a simple, blue, polo shirt. His feet were bare, but a new pair of Converse brand, walking shoes, socks tucked inside, sat at the foot of the bed where he had always left his.

A double-wide closet was to the left of the bed. His clothes hung on the right side with shirts to the left, trousers to the right, shoes lining the floor. Everything was right, exactly as it should be for this room from a time he had yet to see.

Suddenly, he was breathing hard, deep. His heart thudded, threatening to run away. He willed himself to take measured breaths.

*You worked hard for this chance to right things. What do you do now?*

### DAY 23

Apep's bedroom was unornamented, sterile with mirrored, stainless steel walls, floors and cabinets, and a massive bed (three times king-size) with a chromed-steel headboard, footboard, and huge balusters which supported the canopy,

---

also of steel. If he had a choice, the coverings and the mattress itself would be sterile steel—he took no pleasure from earthly comforts, and in fact, the only thing he did enjoy about humans was the way they died, all wide eyed and terrified. However, Apep had to make some concessions to this fragile body in which Jeremy Wheeler had trapped him. For the time being, anyway.

He sat in his bed, propped up by mounds of pillows piled against its gleaming headboard. He couldn't sleep. It was a nasty habit anyway, he had long ago decided. It was just another thing forced upon him by his unfortunate association with the mortal body of Dougal Wheeler. And now, Dougal was gaining his father's strength, fighting him for control, sometimes winning control of this rotting body.

For several minutes he considered what he had learned during the previous night. The night had been long, yet, it was a night of enlightenment, a night filled with memories stolen from Jeremy through the electronic link of the biomedical chip he had attached at the base of his *father's* skull. The memories had played, then replayed, like old movies, gray and flickering on the backdrop of his mind.

When Dougal had seen what he was doing, he had fought for control of their body. But this time Dougal's soul was too weak. His efforts had only served to weaken the body. Now it was drained, nearer death than it had ever been. But that, too, was of no consequence. The struggle had been worth the weariness. Questions which had lain like rotting garbage in the back of Apep's mind for hundreds of years, were no longer questions. He had seen and recognized himself as the shining, black worm of madness, which Jeremy had seen in the eyes of Marion Brand and the infant, Dougal. He had been so long concealed inside this rotting casing that his self image had become dim, and he felt gratified that seeing his real image had turned Jeremy's blood to ice.

Now Apep knew, the fear filling all those years had been

mutual. And although he had not learned how Jeremy had resisted him, he was still gratified Jeremy had, at the least, feared him. Jeremy Wheeler was no ordinary man.

"A party! A party! Today is show and tell day!" he called.

Guards appeared from the hallway, and a bleary-eyed valet stepped from a small closet near the head of his bed.

"Don't just stand there," he said. "Prepare me."

Lori lay staring at the intricate pattern of country life woven into the tapestry which served as a canopy above her bed. The frightening, yet, familiar man was no longer with her, but her heart lugged at the thought of him.

*Was it a dream?*

She startled, sitting bolt upright, then looked to the curve of her elbow. The needle mark was there, and above it, to the soft inside of her arm, three larger punctures with a stitch in each and above each stitch a columnar bulge. She touched each wiry stitch with questioning fingers, then, in wonder, her fingers moved up and down the bulges.

*He put something inside me! My son put something inside me!* A chill went through her, brought not by the knowledge of the implant, but because she had acknowledged Dougal as her son. That sentiment had cost her life the last time she had allowed it. It was true that Jeremy had had Dougal in his sights, but so had she, and she had also been unable to squeeze the trigger. If the opportunity arrived, would she do the same this time? She realized she didn't know. But whatever happened, what Dougal had put inside of her had to be removed.

She moved to the foot of the bed and opened a drawer in the vanity there. Her sewing kit was there, as she knew it would be. She searched for the sewing scissors but found none. Then she spied the seam ripper, and her hand closed over it as a rap came at the door.

Two women entered. Lori turned from the vanity, a hair brush in her hand.

"We are here to help you prepare," said a woman with large green eyes and a pudding face. She wore a dress of a green broadcloth that buttoned to her neck and hung unornamented to her ankles.

Lori looked from one woman to the other, then back again. The two women had the look of hard-working, Amish women. They were remarkably similar: broad through the chest and stomach, with unnaturally muscular arms and dull eyes. The only marked difference was the color of their dresses, one green, one blue.

"Help me prepare for what?"

"The party of course," the woman in green said.

"Apep sent us," said the one in blue.

Lori narrowed her eyes and furrowed her brow in a look of defiance. "What if I don't want to *prepare* for the party?"

"Apep sent us," the woman in blue repeated. She stared at Lori blankly, as if this was the only answer needed.

"We are here to help you prepare," the woman in green said.

Lori looked at the women's faces, and realized these women had no concept of refusal when it came to Apep's orders.

"I can bathe myself, and I can dress myself, but you may help me with my hair and makeup," she said.

The women looked at each other uneasily, as if between them they could not come to an answer without some external permission. They reminded Lori of government employees. If it didn't fit the mold of things gone before, the answer was invariably no. *No chances taken here.*

"Sit over there," Lori said. She nodded to the bed. "I will tell you when I need you."

The women looked relieved. They understood orders. They moved to the bed and sat.

The room was vast, perhaps one hundred and fifty yards

on a side. In the center stood a small, wooden chair, and spaced at twelve-feet intervals, spiraling about that central fixture, stood cylindrical, glass chambers. Each chamber contained a bubbling, green liquid in which a human body was suspended. Attached to the base of each entombed body's skull was a small, rectangular chip in which a multicolored fluid swirled. The bodies were human and alive, and they twisted, turned, and gestured as if characters in some macabre play.

Apep surveyed the cylinders and the contemptible creatures in them. He smiled, walked to the chair, and sat. This would be the last time he would need the renewal process, and his body tingled with that knowledge. No longer would his daily renewal tie him to this room. No longer would he be forced to take the poison from these many bodies in exchange for continued life. No longer would his skin crack, his joints ache. No longer would the brown spots spread across his skin and his nails thicken and yellow because of the frailties of these bodies.

Today he would be reborn, and with this old body would go the world it had created. And he owed it all to Jeremy and Lori. Together, those whom he had killed and would eventually kill again, would carry genetic perfection and immortality to his past. And in the process of his new birth, they would rid him of Dougal Wheeler's soul. He chuckled at the irony of this.

With Conrad LuPone's help, Dougal had brought Jeremy and Lori to him. Dougal's plan had been to lose them in this world or, perhaps, to kill them and wait until his history was fatally corrupted. If the plan had been successful, his fate, and that of Dougal, would have been that of Conrad LuPone: a colorful explosion into atoms and energy. And Dougal had come close to success. Lori and Jeremy were dangerously close to staying here too long. The night before their capture he had already begun to feel the tug of infinity, the rumblings in the molecules of this body he wore. And although he knew he still had two days, at minimum, before their history corrupted irreparably, he was becoming nervous.

*If not for Jeremy's doggedness. . . !* His skin tingled with the thought of it, a basic disassembly of all the people places and things which Lori and Jeremy's existence had caused, molecule by molecule and atom by atom, into nothing, into nonexistence.

He felt Dougal stir within him, fighting to surface. Apep buried him under an avalanche of thought. He thought of the first time he had witnessed the effects of corrupting one's history. One of his engineers, an inoffensive little man who he had known for centuries had brought his mother to this time. He had watched as the man had screamed himself into oblivion. The process had been beautiful in its cruelty. He had fallen in love with it, immediately. So, when he had discovered Dougal's plan and Conrad LuPone's betrayal, it was a simple thing to send one of his Guard to kill Judith LuPone, the little man's mother. "Motherless son," Apep whispered, and he smiled at the memory of Conrad's disassembly. This was a process that he wished he could witness more often, and he would. When his plan was finally complete, he would no longer be subject to the uncertainty of his history and that of the bodies which had sustained him. When that day arrived, he could witness this effect, this disassembly, an infinity of times.

"Crazy as a loon. Just as Apep said."

Jeremy Wheeler shoved a coil of wire, coat hanger into his belt and turned to the voice, pretending to lose interest in the broken wires that surrounded him.

Three muscular valets stood in the doorway of his room. The man who spoke was tall and hard. His lips turned up at their pointed, little corners in a smirk. Tired, red cracks surrounded his disdainful, black eyes.

———

The man's two companions held less spirit in their eyes and were slightly shorter than he, no taller than six-foot, but broader, thicker through the chest. They were Tweedle-Dumb and Tweedle-Dumber, Jeremy concluded.

"Do you need help?" Jeremy said. He fixed them with a hard stare.

Dumb and Dumber appeared uneasy. They shuffled from foot to foot and cast their gazes to the floor. But the first man (immediately Jeremy's mind named this man "Jackass") continued to glare.

"Put away your toys," Jackass said, nodding to the litter of wire surrounding Jeremy. "We are here to prepare you for a party."

"Do I look as if I need help from the likes of you?" Jeremy said. His gaze locked with that of the insolent man. He had lost his last battle, but he would not allow these men to push him.

"Apep sent three of us to encourage you. Although, I think he over estimated," Jackass said.

Jeremy continued to stare into the man's eyes. This was a man who commanded respect, but he was also a man who answered to Apep. He would know how, and when, to bow.

"I'll be sure to tell Apep your assessment of his orders," Jeremy said. "If Apep allows his servants to second-guess him, to boast at his expense, then he must be weaker than I thought."

Jackass's fists clenched, but his arms remained at his sides. His eyes shifted. Jeremy had exposed a nerve. And now he wanted to prod that nerve until the man gave under the pressure. He wanted to do this in part because he needed that mean feeling inside him, and in part because he didn't want this man to search him and find pieces of coat hanger, twisted into a push knife, beneath his belt and the stiff wire garrote taped to his leg.

"I'll prepare myself," Jeremy said, turning to the closet. "Wait outside."

———

"Apep said—" the tall man started.

"And I said, 'wait outside,'" Jeremy said, his voice low, measured. It showed no outrage, no weakness, no question. He turned back to face the three men, his eyes slitted to make them appear as hard and resolute as he felt. "Obey me or I'll see you stripped of your skin and rolled in salt, like so much pork."

Dumb and Dumber blanched at this statement. Their gazes flitted each to the other and then to the man in charge. Jackass's pupils widened, his gaze cast downward, no longer meeting Jeremy's. "We will wait outside," he said.

The dining room was furnished in cherry. A brass and lead crystal chandelier hung above the seven-foot-long, rectangular, dining table which was surrounded by six, cane-backed chairs. Jeremy Wheeler found Lori Hellman Wheeler across that table, and their gazes locked.

He remembered this room, a piece of the past that was filling his mind with greater speed as each second ticked by.

Two of Apep's valets had led him to this room through a maze of tall, glass cylinders filled with a gelatinous, green liquid in which bodies, not dead and not alive, were suspended. The route had been circuitous, too contrived. Jeremy knew he had been led by way of the cylinders for shock effect. And it had worked, but to Apep's detriment, he thought. Now he was even more determined to send this demon, Apep, back to hell.

At the head of the room, oak pocket-doors slid back, silently, but the movement drew both their gazes. Apep entered the room and strode to the head of the table. His face was expressionless. His dark, almost lifeless, eyes moved from Lori to Jeremy and back again.

"You will be leaving today. You have both served your purpose here."

"What was our purpose here?" Lori said.

Jeremy was surprised at the calm in her voice. Apep smiled what Jeremy thought of as a reptilian smile." His eyes told Jeremy nothing. They continued to be as expressionless as those of a dead man.

Apep's right hand dipped into a coat pocket and removed a small, gold, pocket watch. He snapped the watch open, looked at it, then placed it, open, on the table before turning his attention back to Lori.

"We have time. I see no reason you shouldn't know about the role you play. As Dougal's parents, you have, and will, play an important part in the earth's future. My birth and raising, I am sure you remember."

Jeremy's gaze darted to Lori's face. It was calm, strong.

Apep turned to him. "I have hated you for imprisoning me in this body. For centuries I had moved from body to body. When one died there was always another at hand with evil in its soul. One whom I could control. Most often it was my previous host's murderer. His murderous soul welcomed a link with me, and the one who had bested me, became me.

"But, not you, Jeremy." He raised his hand, and index finger extended, he shook it with uncharacteristic weakness at Jeremy. Apep's eyes were now showing expression, growing flinty, and his lips narrowed to a thin line before he continued. "Not you. You changed. You rejected murder, hate. You rejected *me*." His fist came up and pounded his chest with a loud thump. "*Me?!*"

Jeremy felt a smile curl the corners of his mouth, despite every instinct to the contrary. He felt pride that this creature found his soul distasteful.

"So when you were closest to death—did you know that an ejaculation is the closest man comes to death in life?—I jumped. I fled *you*. But, there was no room, no *hate* to cling to in Lori. Yet, as I jumped, the fetus was born, and though there was little there, there was enough. I linked with its budding soul.

———

"That was a mistake. Dougal has tormented me, always pushing for control. He would like nothing better than to drag me into the uncertainty of an afterlife, linked to his puny soul, waiting for Judgement. And for a while, that fate seemed inevitable."

Apep bent over the table, and grasped the opposite edges with both hands, staring first at Lori, then at Jeremy and finally back to Lori, hate filling his eyes.

"Here, I rule. I control life and death. People bow *to* me, pray *to* me, live *for* me, die *for* me. I like it this way." He released his grasp on the table, and pounded it a jarring blow with his fist. "And I don't intend to die."

Then, amazingly, his anger seemed to dissolve. A smile creased his cracked and wrinkled face, and a spark flashed in his eyes. "Until you came, the only way I could avoid death was to tie myself to the glass chambers you saw on your way here. The process I developed has succeeded in maintaining life, but it has fed me with the poisons of the bodies I have used. I borrowed their genetic problems, and I can't cure myself of them, because I have to feed on the poisoned source, daily.

"My skin is failing; my fingers have gnarled, and my body gives me excruciating pain in spite of the medications I take. Yet each day I have to take more of that which poisons me."

Apep's eyes were alive with fire now. He began to pace.

"Immortality through genetic manipulation is tricky. It has more to do with taking flaws out than . . . than putting in something that's missing, although it involves both.

"The problem is, I was forced into this body before I had reason and resources to develop the science. To cancel the poisons, to change my genes after birth, although possible, would kill this weak, old body. So I had no choice but to develop a way to change this body before it was born, even before conception."

He stopped pacing, abruptly, and turned to face Lori. "And

———

that is your purpose here." He smiled, again, and what Jeremy saw in this creature's eyes was not pleasant.

"I had thought to have you both here, in the tubes, where I could administer the chemicals necessary to alter my genes and orchestrate the conception of this prison body. But Dougal managed to spoil things. He took control of the body, and held it long enough to send Conrad LuPone to draw you here, to scatter you, to hide you, or to kill you. Dougal knew that you would not have the heart to kill him and thus kill me. You have failed before. But by bringing you here before our birth, and holding you here, he could alter our history."

"He wants to die?" Jeremy said.

"Not just to die. He wanted to have never existed. He had hoped to keep you here, to fry me and him into atoms by reason of having never been born. He wanted to destroy everything and everyone who existed because of our existence. And his little trick would have worked, but he failed to account for his parent's cleverness. You found me before our time ran out. And all of Dougal's attempts to kill you and to warn you away, to put you in fear for your soul, only drew you here faster. Or did you think it was I who sent the catman to kill you in Prattville, or that it was me in the portal, in Syr, in the people of New Aralsk?

"It was a foolish, risky plan. The fool wanted to save a world that was only a faint memory to him. I didn't think him capable of such idiocy, and I live in his guts." Apep laughed.

Jeremy felt a spring of anger break surface in him, and he pounded the table with his fist. "You don't think we'll cooperate in your birth again, knowing what we know?"

Apep turned to face Jeremy. He lifted his arms slightly, palms out. "What you want is not important. And if what I tell you here would be of any use to you, do you think I would tell it? No." He shook his head, slowly.

"I have taken the precaution of planting a few—How did you call them when you trained me in man's magic? Trojan

Horses?" He shrugged. "Anyway, I have planted a few thoughts in both you and Lori which will benefit me as I grow. You'll teach me the magic I'll need, the magic-of-man it took me centuries to learn.

"When you go back to your time, the memories of here will be as a dream in you minds and fade over a good night's sleep. You'll vaguely remember a nightmare. But when the time comes, you will teach me."

Jeremy looked to Lori. She was looking at her arm and stroking the inner biceps.

"And the genetic changes?" she said. "How will you change your genetic structure? How will you live forever?"

Jeremy looked back to Apep. A sly smile crossed cracked lips. "You always said, 'there is more than one way to ford a stream.'"

A greasy feeling filled Jeremy. He looked to the inside of his left biceps. The ends of three stitches stuck above the skin. A tubular bulge ran up his arm above each stitch.

"Implants!" His gaze shifted to Apep and then back to Lori. Her terrified face stared back at him.

"Very clever!" Apep chucked, and his chuckle made Jeremy think of mice scurrying inside a wall.

Then to Lori, "Don't look so terrified, Mother. You want a healthy baby don't you? The implants will assure that."

Lori shook her head violently, her hands formed tight fists, knuckles white with strain. "You're not my son. You're a vampire that sucks the good from his soul."

A flat smile sliced Apep's face. "Either way, when you meet Jeremy, two years in your future, the genes in each of you will hold half the coding necessary to give your baby immortality. And I will be the beneficiary."

A low growl broke the stunned silence of the room. Apep's eyes flicked to the doorway behind Jeremy, and Jeremy was sure he saw fear in those eyes.

Jeremy turned to find Hank, Mark and Rudy standing in

the doorway. Gore covered the ragged dog. His eyes burned with hate. He was muzzled and restrained by a leash, but even so, his claws dug into the carpet, and he growled and strained to reach the object of his hate, Apep. A well-muscled man drew the leash up tight. Although there was no question that Rudy was well restrained, Jeremy knew, as with the boy Apep once was, of all who faced him, it was the dog Apep feared most.

"Keep that dog away from me!" Apep said.

Neither Hank nor Mark was restrained, but they had also been bloodied, and appeared to be having much difficultly standing. The three, large valets who had visited Jeremy's room, Dumb, Dumber and Jackass, flanked them.

"Even the cur must go back." Fear and hate sat in Apep's eyes. "But I've planted some very specific Trojan Horses in Hank Davison's little mind. He will see to it the dog has a very short life."

"The boy will need some first aid and some careful programming before he returns. But, I have sent his mother ahead with some interesting suggestions for his upbringing.

"General Mark Scott will not found Parabellum this time around. On the contrary, he will see to it that the people who would become Parabellum, will fall into *my* hands."

Apep's gaze darted to the pocket watch. He reached for it, snapped it closed, and returned it to his coat pocket. "Lori, Jeremy, Hank and the dog will go back now. You've all been programmed; the portal is right to return you to Prattville, and our time is growing short."

Jeremy turned his gaze to Lori. Their gazes met, and he knew she shared the same thought: *They had to kill Apep or die before he could send them back.*

Apep seemed to understand their exchanged glances. When Jeremy peered back to him, Apep backed away from the table. "Bring them along," he said. He turned and exited

—

325

the room. Five valets moved in, and funneled them toward the door.

Apep led them down a long, narrow hallway. Behind him Rudy's claws skittered on the highly glossed stone floors. He continued to lunge against his leash.

Rudy's snarls made Jeremy's flesh pucker into coarse bumps. He brushed his hand across his abdomen to assure himself the wire push-knife he had made from the coat hangers was secure in its tape sheath. With each step, the wire garrote taped to his leg twisted and buckled against his skin, reminding him of its presence.

Jeremy glanced around at his companions. Hank and Mark were watching their feet. He caught Lori's eye. He read the doubt there and understood. He remembered their struggle with the plan to kill Dougal in that other time. In the end they had both hesitated, and Dougal had allowed the evil in him to kill them.

*Yet, this time we have an advantage,* Jeremy thought. Now they knew what had gone before. This time the evil in Dougal could not kill them without destroying itself. They had little to lose. If they failed, they would be in no worse plight. And death—Dougal's or theirs—would remove the worm-of-evil from earth forever.

Some fifty yards down the hall Apep turned to his right. A large panel slid back. He entered the opening with the group following.

The room behind the panel was unfurnished, sterile. Walls, floor, ceiling, all the room was stainless steel, broken only by the sucking maw of a portal, a doorway to their past.

# THE FINAL BATTLE?

*DAY 23*

As Apep entered the room, he moved to the left and the valet who restrained Rudy followed. The growling dog strained against his lease.

"Get that beast away from me!" Apep bellowed.

The valet pulled back on Rudy's leash, and crossed within an arm's length of Jeremy. Jeremy's hand dipped beneath his shirt, and his fingers closed over the handle that formed a cross with a coiled blade of black wire. He winced as the tape tore free of his skin and the valet's head turned to the ripping sound.

Jeremy punched with the makeshift weapon. There was an insignificant *pop* melded with a screech as the six-inch corkscrew of wire pierced the valet's right eye, then skidded along the bone to his brain.

———

61-DAVI

Gouts of blood splashed over Jeremy's hand. He drew back his arm. The ruined eye, trailing the gray optic nerve, came with it.

The valet's muscles twitched spasmodically, and his hand forgot Rudy's leash. Rudy slipped, then regained his feet. He pumped twice against the slippery, metal floor and launched himself at Apep.

Apep's hand dipped into his sleeve and surfaced with a brilliantly, polished blade. He swung it in a slashing arc at Rudy's throat.

Mark screamed, tore free of Dumb, who was restraining him, and lunged for Apep's hand.

The blade, meant for Rudy's throat, struck the heavy wire mesh of his muzzle, sparked and glanced off.

Then Mark was on Apep. He sank his teeth into the wrinkled, yellow-gray flesh of the disgusting creature's wrist. The gutting knife flew free and skittered across the floor. Apep bashed the boy's face with his free hand, tore free of Mark and backed toward the wall. Rudy snarled, and held his ground next to the savaged boy.

Mark struggled to his feet. He looked around, seeming dazed.

Dumber wrapped his arms around Lori, and drew her solidly against him. If he saw the sparkle of light on the slim metal sewing tool she slipped from beneath her belt, he did not react. Lori twisted to the side and plunged the seam ripper into the valet's testicles. His body stiffened, vibrated, and his eyes glazed over. He dropped to his knees, dragging Lori down with him.

Dumber stood frozen, the back of the Mark's shirt in his hand. He didn't have long to think. Hank Davison brought a high, arcing left across the muscular valet's nose. There was a crack like a chicken bone snapping. Blood spurted from the nose, and the valet staggered back two steps, then lunged at Hank.

Jeremy heard the sounds of claws on stone approaching in the hall as he faced off with the tall valet whom he had reflexively named Jackass. There was hatred in the man's eyes, but there was also fear. He was edging toward the door.

Then Jeremy saw the gutting knife on the floor. Quickly, he stooped to pick it up.

Five feet away, Lori struggled to break free of the frozen grip of Dumber, who had dragged her down. Then Hank stepped to the side, and kicked out viciously at that valet. The heel of his boot caught the shuddering man in the left temple, and Dumber went limp. His body rolled off Lori, and fell in a lifeless mound on the stainless steel floor.

Someone shrieked and Jeremy glanced to his left to see the first catman through the door tear Jackass in half, with a single blow.

Jeremy turned his gaze to Apep. Apep was pressed against the shiny, steel wall, drooling and screaming orders to no one in particular. No one listened. Carnage dictated now, not Apep.

"Through the portal, Lori. Through the portal!" Hank yelled.

Mark looked to Hank, then to Jeremy, then to Lori and realized that five minutes from now every living human in this room would be dead. "Come, Rude-Dog!" he shouted. He ran for Lori, and tackled her, carrying her into the portal. Rudy scampered after them.

Jeremy's gaze followed Lori, Mark and Rudy through the portal. He glanced back at Apep, then to the portal, again. He could leap through and leave Dougal to reject or accept the evil he had inherited. He could leave the people of his future to suffer their own choices, to keep their freedom or to see it traded for promises of paradise. Or he could fight and perhaps die, trying to right sins he had never lived, only dreamed.

———

His decision made, he nodded. His hand clenched the rubber grip of the gutting knife. Claws shrieked against the metal floor close behind him.

He lunged for Apep, elbows tucked to his sides, kicking hard for speed as he passed Hank.

Hank Davison threw a body block into Dumb, who although unsteady, would not go down. Arms pinwheeling, Dumb staggered into the path of the catman following Jeremy. The creature tore the man apart with a flurry of blows, then found its feet tangled in dead arms and legs and went down, hard.

A second catman slashed at Hank, catching him full in the chest. His body moved only slightly. There was no pain. Hank dropped his gaze to the gaping hole in his chest. In his last seconds he turned his gaze, longingly, to the portal. Lori, the boy and Rudy had made it through. This was good. For an instant, he wished he understood all that had passed here. Then everything went black.

"What did you *do?* It's too early for this to happen!" Apep screamed.

Jeremy watched as Apep's eyes opened wide in astonishment. Then he felt the vibrations and heard the crackling-hiss of molecules breaking apart, the hum of atoms dampening into silence.

His left hand clutched the throat of Apep's robe. Molecules and atoms fried under his fingers, stinging like a handful of electrified hornets.

The worm, Apep's essence, his soul, surfaced in Dougal's eyes, seeking escape. The eyes cleared and were bright, and Jeremy was sure he was seeing his son for the first time—it was joy he saw in Dougal's eyes!

Then the floor became oatmeal under his feet. The robe

burned its way free of his hand in a frenzy of tiny explosions, molecules going nova.

Dougal roared a primal scream, and exploded like fireworks into a summer's night. The mushy firmness of the floor evaporated.

### DAY 24

Jeremy struggled up from the ground. He was nude and alone, surrounded by wide, empty plains on three sides and mountains on the fourth. He looked around in bewilderment. Everything of Dougal and Apep's making was gone.

All that remained to remind him of the past weeks in his future was the equipment and clothing he and Hank Davison had brought with them, and near that, Hank and near Hank, his heart.

Jeremy shuddered and backed away. Something soft and slimy crushed beneath his bare foot, and for an instant, he thought he saw the eyes of Marion Brand and the black worm cycling up at him from them.

A laugh as sour as bile spilled from Jeremy's lips.

# EPILOGUE

*Prattville, Ohio, April 22, 1991*

Lori crossed the kitchen slowly, leaning back with her hand on her right kidney to balance the weight of the baby, Hank Davison's baby.

*It has to be Hank's baby.*

Hank had not known of the child. He had disappeared before she discovered she was pregnant.

Some said it was the murderer who got Hank and that psychologist's assistant, Jeremy Wheeler. Others believed Jeremy Wheeler had been the murderer. She didn't think that was so. But she had no real reason for that feeling, she knew. It was just a hunch.

The contractions had started earlier in the day and now marched through her at narrowing intervals. It was a problem pregnancy from the first. At least Charlie Hascomb had been there for her since Hank's disappearance.

She reached for the phone, pausing momentarily to look at the two names scrawled on the phone pad.

Dougal—Gaelic for "Dark Man."

Marion—Hebrew for "Bitter Sea."

Briefly, she wondered why the names seemed to draw her. And then for an instant the image of a tall gaunt man, wearing a leather hat, a large, shiny gun holstered low on his hip, passed through her mind. She didn't know where such images came from or what they meant, but they always soothed her.

### APRIL 23, 1991

It was midnight. The halls of the small hospital were deserted. Mark Scott entered the stairwell just off the small waiting room on the first-floor, and climbed the stairs to the third-floor in silence.

A large, buck knife made a telling outline against his thigh. The fingertips of his right hand played over the bulge it made. The knife seemed to grow heavier the nearer he approached the nursery, and his muscles seemed almost to weaken with the strain of the carry.

He often wondered if he was crazy when he recalled the world of his future, and the two men whom he'd left there, perhaps to die. He thought that he would probably always carry the guilt of that desertion.

He exited the stairwell, and turned toward the nursery. He walked quickly, decisively. He did not look about. If someone stopped him now, he would simply claim ignorance of the rules, come back later.

The nursery was fifty paces from the stairs. A glass wall stood between the infants and Mark. Today there was only one. It lay sleeping. Its face was puffy, red. The right eye

---

333

was swollen, slightly. The start of fine, light-brown hair covered its head.

He wondered how something so helpless could grow to become so evil as Apep. His hand fell to the knife once more, and this time, his fingers caressed the length to experience the cold reality of it.

*A knife is up close and personal,* the VIRTUAL 10,000 replica of Jeremy had said.

The knife was right for what he had to do, and not for what the infant was but for what he must become. He'd finish the nightmare he, Hank, Jeremy, Lori and so many others had lived because of the evil inside this small body.

Mark's thoughts flashed back to Soja and Parabellum. He wondered if the town and the girl still existed in his future and if what he meant to do here, tonight, would end their existence as surely as Apep would.

The nursery's door swung open, smoothly. Mark stepped in and closed the door, gently, trying not to let it thud against the seal or to let the latch snap. His hand, slick with sweat, slipped into the tight pocket of his jeans and fumbled the buck knife from it. The blade snicked open and locked with a snap.

He swallowed. His throat was tight.

On wooden legs, he approached the crib. His dreadful intention seemed to have drained his body of its humanity and left in its place an automaton.

The infant breathed softly in its sleep. Mark brought the cold blade to its throat in a single, swift motion. The infant slitted one swollen, brown eye to him.

Mark stared into the eye, and felt his resolve weaken.

*I have to. I* have *TO.* His hand froze, ignoring his knowledge, obeying only his emotions. Beads of perspiration formed on his brow.

The infant fidgeted, kicking at its coverlet. Mark recoiled.

———

A small fist had come up and wove haphazardly, now, before the infant's face. A small pink bracelet circled the wrist.

Mark took another step back. *Pink!* Pink! *The bracelet's pink!*

He scanned the room, swiftly, for a second infant. The room was empty. Folding the knife Mark stuffed it into his pocket, then he moved to the crib, and bent to read the bracelet.

An inscription panel on the bracelet read "Baby Girl, Marion Hellman."

Mark's head wagged from side to side in disbelief. Then, feeling weird as hell, he unfastened the infant's diaper and looked to be sure.

*A girl!*

Mark's memories of his future started to crumble, deserting him quickly after the birth of Marion. He started his long trip back to New Orleans that night. Rudy went with him.

Three weeks later, Lori, Jeremy and Hank were a vague, pleasant memory: brave characters from a book Mark Scott had read long ago.

In July of 1991, Lori disappeared from Prattville in the midst of what appeared to be almost a repeat of the kind of horrible murders committed in 1990.

Police Chief Charlie Hascomb, married by then, applied for and received custody of Marion Hellman.

Six months later Charlie shot serial-murderer Marion Brand through the head as that monster stood, a gutting knife in his hand, over Marion Hellman in her nursery.

Marion Hellman did not seem frightened by the incident. Charlie found her cooing in her crib.

Cindy Wheeler met an antique dealer. They married in December 1994.

---

Linda started college life the following year as a business major. She moved to the Kent State University campus and rarely returned home.

Samantha started dating a high school football player and gave up rap music for hard rock. Later she began college life as a psychology major. But she refused to go to the same campus as her sister, and graduated, instead, from Ohio State University.

*JEREMY WHEELER*

## Through the Portal Forever?

Jeremy awoke, cold and nude. He had slept the night sprawled on the rocky ground, without shelter. He didn't know how he had gotten here, or where "here" was. The last he could remember was a large breakfast with Cindy. She had cried, though he couldn't remember why.

He found clothing in one of two hiking packs that lay nearby, and dressed in it.

Minutes later he stumbled over a body that lay behind some rocks. At first he did not recognize the dead man. His heart was torn out. Flies were beginning to blow the chest wound. His skin was waxy and a translucent, pale gray, and his eyes were dull and sunken like those of a three-day-old fish. Finally, Jeremy fitted the damaged face with a picture he remembered seeing in the *Prattville Courier Crescent*. It was Prattville's Police Chief, Hank Davison.

Jeremy wrapped the body in a thermal blanket he found in one of the packs, then buried it. He marked the spot with rocks so he could lead authorities to it later. Then he set out through the rocky land in search of people. He wondered how long it would be before he found his way back to Prattville and to Cindy.

Three days later he found a camp of shepherds. He stayed

the night, paying for their hospitality with gold he found in one of his packs.

Over the campfire that night he heard stories of a "God come to earth" who lived in a city of lights to the west. According to the stories, she took children to feed the lights of the city.

"The people serve Marion and the lights serve the people," the shepherds told him. Their stories poked something cold inside him. He had been having dreams lately, dreams of a life he had not lived and of a blond woman with a scar and drowning-pool blue eyes.

He set out the next day, in search of the city of Marion, The Bitter One.

# AUTHOR'S NOTE

Inspired by THE TALISMAN, a Stephen King and Peter Struab collaboration, I began writing IMMORTAL: A Linking of Souls on 7/13/91. The first draft, a 115,000 word manuscript written in the author omniscient viewpoint, was finished on 11/16/91.

With the naive zeal of the new author, I immediately submitted the manuscript to six potential markets and two agents in early 1992. The submissions brought some personal notes. It was termed "intriguing," "fast paced," a "potential page turner." One editor said the story had a "cool idea/concept" and said it had "major potential." Another asked to see my next effort. Several encouraged me to rewrite. None wanted to publish the novel. I rewrote and the resulting book, then just 71,000 words, was immediately tossed into a desk drawer, not to see the light of day for more than five years. During that period I wrote a second novel and started a third, neither of which were submitted for publication and both of which now sit in the same drawer which held IMMORTAL. I also wrote a drawer full of short stories, most of which were pub-

---

lished. My work has appeared in a variety of forums from horror to literary magazines. In 1996 I started NIGHT TERRORS Magazine, an award-winning, print magazine of ongoing horror, and in 1999 I added the popular online magazine CRIMSON to his editing/publishing workload.

In 1996, through my job as editor/publisher of NIGHT TERRORS Magazine, I received a short story from J. N. Williamson, a talented and prolific writer of novels. I subsequently wrote him, mentioned my novel, which was then titled A LINKING OF SOULS, and asked if he knew someone I could hire to critique it. Jerry was between books at the time and offered to critique the book if I would send it immediately. I took him up on the offer.

I received Jerry's critique, eight, typed, single spaced pages with almost no margins and an extensively marked up manuscript, in February of 1997. Jerry's critique was well balanced: encouraging, cautionary and thorough. In part, he wrote, "If you wonder, I believe A LINKING OF SOULS can become a novel that sells, and that there is a lot to admire about this heartfelt effort. I think a huge amount of work awaits you, mostly in the first 100 pages or more, . . .

"And I'm concerned for you, Don, because even when all that's been done, the novel probably won't fit into the snug genre/category most publishers seek."

I stole three months of time from NIGHT TERRORS, between receiving Jerry's critique and September, 2000, to do a third rewrite of IMMORTAL: A Linking of Souls, and what you have just read is the result.

Well, Jerry, I hope I've done justice to the effort you put into that critique. I grew the novel by 20,000 words and as you can see, I avoided the "snug genre/category" issue by publishing the novel through XLIBRIS. As to the rest, time will tell.

D. E. Davidson, 9/10/2000

———

Printed in the United States
4149

9 780738 842585